Kennedy Stern
Christian Suspense
Series
(Books 4-6)

by Alana Terry

Straightened

a novel by Alana Terry

The views of the characters in this novel do not necessarily reflect the views of the author.

IMPORTANT NOTE

This is not a novel that attempts to answer the question *Is homosexuality right or wrong*. Whatever your moral beliefs about homosexuality, I fully expect you to hold those same beliefs once you reach the end of this novel. However, I do hope that what you read in *Straightened* will lead to more open discussions, deeper empathy, and greater unity — three things that seem too often to be lacking in the homosexuality debate.

Please note that just because somebody in my novel espouses a particular point of view, that doesn't mean it is what I personally believe. I refuse to write preachy fiction, and I'm convinced that if we all agreed on every single hot-button issue out there, the world would be a boring place, and this novel would be void of all suspense and danger.

As it is, this novel is filled with plenty of suspense as well as danger, and I hope you enjoy it for its storyline as much as anything else you may glean from it.

Alana Terry

CHAPTER 1

By the time her plane landed, Kennedy's left leg was asleep from the thigh down. Her throat was parched from all that waterless air being pumped into the cabin at 30,000 feet as she traveled across the globe.

What a way to start her sophomore year. Her pulse pounded its complaints between her temples. She didn't have the mental energy to calculate an exact number, but she guessed it had been longer than twenty-four hours ago that she said good-bye to her missionary parents in Yanji, China.

Another year at Harvard. Another grueling schedule.

She hoped she was ready.

"It was nice talking to you." The man who had pestered her the entire flight gave her a slight wave as he walked past her on the jetway. She wondered how much more reading she could have gotten in on that last flight if it weren't for his incessant questions about life in China.

He was nice enough, and intelligent by all appearances. If Kennedy hadn't been so sleep deprived and already on her third flight of the day, she might have enjoyed their conversation. Asked him questions of her own. Learned about his home in Paris.

Not tonight.

Actually, it was morning now.

Whatever.

She shifted the weight of her backpack and reminded herself that her burden would be significantly lighter if she could learn to read ebooks instead of always insisting on print. Oh, well. A clunky piece of electronics could never replace that dusty smell of a well-worn, familiar volume. She'd worked her way through several Shakespeare plays on the flight from Yanji, China to Seoul. Crossing the Pacific, she'd finally had mercy on her dry corneas, taken out her contacts, and tried to nap. On her last flight from Seattle to Boston, she could have finished an extra play or two if Mr. Charming French Accent hadn't tried to engage her in conversation so many times.

And why had she felt so put off by his interest? This was the start of a new year. A new chance at academics, at life. How many girls her age would love to spend a trans-continental flight flirting with a cute Frenchie who was obviously curious enough about her to ask that many open-ended questions? And what had she done? Kept her nose buried in her book so she wouldn't miss the chance to read *A Winter's Tale* for the sixth time. And what for? The queenly statue would still be ready to dazzle the repentant King Leontes after Kennedy landed at Logan Airport.

Too late now, she thought as she watched her well-dressed traveling companion disappear into an airport bookstore. She thought about browsing the titles there, but Sandy — her pastor's wife and maternal proxy while Kennedy was Stateside — was already waiting outside baggage claim. The dorms wouldn't open until the end of the week, so Kennedy would spend a few days with the Lindgrens to allow her body to recover from the ravaging effects of jetlag before she jumped into another twenty-two-credit semester. She glanced at the time. It was a few minutes past noon, even though her biological clock knew it was the middle of the night back home.

Home? She had been so sure going back to China would be that breath of fresh air, that reprieve her soul had longed for during her freshman year at Harvard. But things were so different when she returned to Yanji last spring.

Home. Wasn't that supposed to be where you felt the most comfortable? The most accepted? She hadn't realized how much she'd changed from nine short months of school.

"Kennedy!"

At the sound of the familiar voice, a warm surge of peace rushed over her, like the comforting whiff of homemade apple pie flooding out of an open oven. There was Sandy with her brown hair hanging in a loose French braid. A pouting little boy was scowling by her side, and he held himself back as Sandy wrapped her arms around Kennedy's neck, flooding her senses with the mingling smells of fabric softener and flowery shampoo. "I'm so happy you made it. You must be exhausted."

Kennedy wanted to express how good it felt to be home, but the words stuck in her throat. "This must be Woong," she said instead. All she had seen was a picture last spring when the Lindgrens decided to adopt him from a South Korean orphanage. He looked about as mischievous as his photo had intimated, except now there wasn't a trace of that cocky grin. She leaned toward him. "I'm really glad to meet you." She always felt so out of place around children, never knowing what to say, how exactly to talk to them at their level without using that stereotypical baby voice she remembered hating as a kid.

Woong crossed his arms against his chest with something that was a mix between a huff and a growl. "Miss Sandy said you were Korean, but I knew she was lying."

"That's not a very nice thing to say."

It wasn't until Kennedy caught Sandy's quizzical stare that she realized she and Woong had been speaking in Korean. She straightened up and explained, "I don't think he expected me to be white."

Sandy put her hand on the boy's head, and he immediately squirmed out of her reach. "We're still at the language-learning stage. It's been ..." She tucked a stray piece of hair, tinged with gray, behind her ear. "It's been a struggle for us both." A loud sigh, heavier than what Kennedy imagined could reside in a soul as peaceful and joyful as Sandy's. "Maybe you could tell him ..."

"Hey, how do you know Korean anyway?" he demanded.

"My parents had a lot of people from Korea living with them, so I learned it that way."

"Why do you sound so funny?" he asked, but before Kennedy could explain about foreign accents, he turned to Sandy. "I'm hungry."

"It's one of the only English words he'll use," Sandy muttered. She patted Woong on the back. "You can have a granola bar in the car." She made a motion like she was removing a wrapper and then took a big imaginary bite. "Granola bar," she repeated.

Woong rolled his eyes.

Kennedy was thankful she wouldn't have kids of her own any time soon. A decade at the very least. Three more years of undergrad, med school, residency ... It was a good thing too, because Kennedy didn't have a never-ending reservoir of patience or compassion like Sandy. She would probably make about as good of a parent as Hamlet's mother.

"Enjoy your year of school, Miss."

Kennedy turned around to see her French travel partner. "Thanks. And good luck with your meeting thing." What had he said he was in Boston for? Some consulting gig, she thought, or maybe more like an interview. She wasn't sure. His title was something about quality control, but even though she'd heard her dad use that phrase, all she knew was it had to do with business and captivated absolutely none of her interest.

"Who was that?" Sandy asked once he was out of earshot. Her face held a bemused, almost teasing grin.

"Just some guy from the plane."

"He looks very nice."

Kennedy didn't answer. Her mind was elsewhere. On hopes that could never be fulfilled.

She wouldn't think about it. This year was a new start for her. No use pining about the past.

While Woong whined and tugged on Sandy's arm, Kennedy adjusted her carry-ons. She hadn't brought much with her this year. She stored most of her belongings in the Lindgrens' garage over the summer, except for clothes and a few books she had purchased ahead of time for her fall classes.

She tried to guess how much longer she could stay awake until her body crashed. Her dad was adamant that whenever she travelled internationally, she had to wait for dark before she thought of sleeping. Well, Kennedy would try, but she doubted she'd make it another hour, let alone eight.

By the time they reached the airport exit, Woong was trying to hurl himself onto the floor. Kennedy was sure he was about to tug Sandy's arm out of its socket as he flung himself on the ground for a full-fledged fit. The Lindgrens could only guess his age based on the records from the South Korean orphanage, but he was old enough to look ridiculous throwing a tantrum like a spoiled toddler. Kennedy stepped back, wondering if she should help Sandy get him up.

"Ok, son," Sandy finally said, letting go of his hand. "No TV time."

Up until then, Kennedy wasn't sure how much English Woong really understood, but at the mention of TV, he slumped down on the floor. His bottom lip stuck out so far past his chin Kennedy could picture a bird landing on it like her dad used to joke about.

"Ready for your snack?" Sandy asked. There was a tired, defeated undercurrent in her tone that was totally foreign to her.

Woong stared ahead for another few seconds before getting to his feet. "Ok." He only protested slightly when Sandy took his hand. Kennedy wheeled her suitcase behind them and followed the pair out into the blinding midday sun.

The drive to Medford was quiet. Kennedy lost track of how many granola bars she passed back to Woong before he finally stopped pestering for more. Sandy's praise and worship music played softly in the background as they turned into the Lindgrens' neighborhood.

"Oh." Sandy frowned when she pulled past a glistening gray Lexus in her driveway. "Looks like Vivian Abernathy is here."

Kennedy didn't respond. She wasn't sure she wanted to interact with anybody or anything right now, unless it was the soft mattress in the Lindgrens' guest room. She hadn't seen any of the Abernathys since last fall when she'd been kidnapped with their daughter Jodie. She wasn't sure she could face them without any haunting flashbacks of her abduction. She didn't want her first PTSD flare-up of the school year to come within an hour of landing on American soil.

"I bet she's checking in with Carl about those homeschool dances she wants to host in the gym." She was talking more to herself than anyone else. Kennedy couldn't remember seeing Sandy so distracted before. Usually the two of them couldn't drive for more than five minutes without Kennedy unburdening her entire soul. And as tired as she was after three long flights, she could use a listening ear. It had been a strange summer. So many things to process ...

"Woong, pick up those wrappers. And your father has company, so I want you to go play nicely in your room."

"TV."

Kennedy wondered how anyone could live with that shrill, defiant voice in their ears every day and still maintain their sanity.

Sandy got out of her seat and opened Woong's door. "You lost your TV privilege, son." She leaned closer and shook her head. "No TV."

Kennedy could hear Woong working himself up into another tantrum, a tantrum she really didn't have the energy to deal with. Besides, she was a little embarrassed on Sandy's behalf. Kennedy had always assumed Sandy was the type of mom who could make any kid behave within twenty-four hours. Was Woong destined to be the Lindgrens' biggest failure as adoptive parents?

"TV time!"

She could hear his sneakered feet kicking the car seats. She was too tired for this. Her bags were still in the trunk, but she could get them later. She shut her door quietly, figuring Sandy wasn't even paying attention. It made sense. Sandy had so much on her mind right now. Kennedy didn't want to be a bother. She let herself in through the garage door that led to the kitchen.

Wayne Abernathy, the Massachusetts state senator, was towering over a teenage boy who sat crumpled over the Lindgrens' dining room table.

"I don't care what you have to do to fix him," Wayne blasted at Carl.

Kennedy froze. Nobody heard her enter. Carl sat with his back to her, but she could still read the exhaustion in his posture.

Wayne brought his finger inches from the boy's nose. "Do whatever you have to do, Pastor. Either straighten him up, or so help me, he's got to find some other place to live."

Kennedy bit her lip, trying to decide if it would be more awkward to leave, make her presence known, or stay absolutely still.

For lack of better options, she settled on the latter.

Wayne's forehead beaded with sweat, and his voice quivered with conviction. "It's impossible for any son of mine to turn out gay."

CHAPTER 2

It was at that moment Sandy burst through the door, carrying a thrashing boy in her arms. Woong was stronger than his skin-and-bones frame suggested, and Kennedy was afraid Sandy would drop him.

"I'm sorry," she breathed, oblivious to everything but her son's flailing limbs. She dodged to avoid a head butt. "I didn't mean to interrupt." She didn't look at the guests or appear to notice the palpable tension. "Carl, can you get him to his room? I swear, this boy ..." She didn't finish the thought but let out a very unfeminine *oomph* as Woong's sneaker kicked her in the thigh.

Carl stood, and Sandy plopped the boy into his arms. Straightening her hair, she glanced at the dining room table and smiled. "Oh, hello Wayne. Nice of you and Noah to stop by."

She walked past them toward the hall. Kennedy doubted she'd have noticed if they'd both been bleeding out their eye sockets.

"If you two will excuse me ..." Sandy disappeared around the corner, the rustle of her skirt drowned out by Woong's shrieks as Carl hefted him down the hall.

Both Wayne and his son took that moment to look up and realize Kennedy was standing in the middle of the kitchen, silent and unmoving. It took a second or two before recognition lit up Wayne's face. "Hello, Miss Stern." He grinned his winsome smile that had secured him several state elections and extended his hand. Based on the way his dazzling teeth flashed at her, Kennedy figured he hadn't realized she'd been in the kitchen a few seconds earlier.

She glanced at Noah Abernathy, a teen boy she only knew by sight. Nice-fitting designer jeans, brand new by all appearances. A button-up collared shirt, starched and pressed, that looked about as comfortable as a pair of Shakespearian tights. His dirty-blonde hair was impeccably cut, with a hint of gel in the top.

"Son, say hi to Kennedy Stern." Wayne spoke through a tight smile that reminded her of a plastic Ken doll. He put his hand on Noah's shoulder, making his son flinch. "You remember her from last fall, don't you?"

"Hey." He didn't quite meet her gaze, but he looked up long enough for Kennedy to read the discomfort in his eyes. "Glad to hear you haven't gotten kidnapped lately." His slight smile vanished so quickly she wondered if she'd imagined it.

She didn't reply. A few months ago, a remark like that might have started her whole respiratory system hyperventilating from panic, but she was different now. Older. More mature. Her parents couldn't find an English-speaking therapist in Yanji, so her dad ordered her at least two dozen self-help books about anxiety and post-traumatic stress disorder, forcing her to sit down with him twice a week to summarize what she'd read.

Maybe it had helped, but she doubted it. Being away from people who wanted her dead or injured — that's what really helped. And having a sorrow settled in the core of her heart that outweighed any pain her panic would have caused. What's a little anxiety disorder when your best friend ...

No. She wouldn't dwell on him right now. If her self-directed summer therapy had taught her anything, it was how to take control of her own thoughts. It was a Biblical model as well, her dad was always eager to inform her. *Take every thought captive.* So far, she had gotten quite adept at cutting off painful memories before they had the chance to resurface and take over her emotions. Like starving a virus. If you don't feed it, it can't grow.

Wayne hadn't stopped gazing at her. "So, how are your classes going? You're a senior now, right?" He talked as if he had a perpetual microphone taped to his cheek. If he hadn't gone into politics, his face and dramatic inflections could have cast him perfectly as a news anchor or soap opera star.

"I'm a sophomore," she told him, certain he must have known. When she and his daughter Jodie were kidnapped last fall, the media had a field day broadcasting the abduction of two local teens. It served as better clickbait than *homeschooled thirteen-year-old and college freshman.*

Kennedy tried to remember the last time she saw Jodie. Maybe once at St. Margaret's Church. It was so hard to know what to say to her when they got together. Sometimes she wondered if Jodie had PTSD, too, if her parents had to drive her in their Lexus to a shrink. If she had to practice cognitive behavioral therapy or mindfulness-based stress reduction techniques after everything she'd gone through.

Carl made his way back to the dining room table, and Kennedy was about to slip down the hall to the guest room when Sandy bustled in. "How about cookies, everyone? Woong and I made a fresh batch this morning."

With a flurry of her floral skirt and long braid, Sandy pulled some of this and that out from the cupboards until she had spread four plates and napkins around the table and set a platter of baked goods, a bowl of fruit, and pitcher of lemonade on the Lazy Susan in the middle of the table.

"Help yourself." She spun some brownies toward Noah first. "Take as many as you want."

Carl was staring at her in bewilderment, and Kennedy couldn't blame him. Didn't Sandy know? Hadn't she heard?

As if by some enchantment cast by Sandy's complete oblivion, Noah and his father both filled their plates in awkward silence. Sandy poured the drinks and passed the cups around, then slipped a brownie and two cookies onto a plate for Kennedy. "Don't you want to sit down, sweetie?"

Kennedy was about to excuse herself to take the nap she'd been pining for since Seattle, but Noah slipped his head up. His eyes met hers. Imploring eyes.

Fearful eyes.

Kennedy sat down. "Sure. I suppose a snack would be fine."

"Oh, dear." Sandy slapped her forehead. "I'm so sorry, honey. You probably haven't had a decent meal since China. Your mother would be so disappointed in me. What was I thinking? What time is it over there right now? Supper? You poor thing. Must be starving. Those airlines used to serve full meals. You remember that, don't you, babe?" she asked her husband, who still sat wide-eyed in front of an empty plate. "Here, darling." She patted Kennedy's head several times as if she were a kitten. "Let me see what I can heat up for you. Wayne, Noah, have you two had lunch yet? Woong's in time-out, so I have a free minute to ..."

"Actually, we'd better go." Wayne slid his chair back noisily. He wore the same smile, which made a single vein pop out of his tanned neck. "Noah, what do you tell Mrs. Lindgren for the cookies?"

The younger Abernathy slouched over his plate. "I'm not quite finished yet."

Wayne slipped his hand onto his son's shoulder. "I said we need to leave."

Noah winced and then shot that same imploring gaze at Kennedy.

Carl opened his mouth, but whatever he was about to say was cut off by Sandy, who was tying a rose-patterned apron over her skirt and blouse. "Noah is welcome to stay here for a spell, Wayne. We'll feed him lunch, and I'll call Vivian when he's ready to come home. Actually, Woong and I need to do some back-to-school shopping this afternoon. I can just drop him off at your place."

Noah's brooding eyes lit up for a moment. Hopeful?

Wayne's frown looked just as practiced as his smile. "Actually, Vivian has some work she needs him to do around the yard. I've got to take him home, and then I'm off to ..."

"I think I'd like to stay." Noah's voice was soft, but from his father's reaction, you would have thought he was standing on the Lindgrens' Lazy Susan shouting profanities. Wayne's eyes flashed. Kennedy spared a glance at Sandy. Did she see the open hostility, or was she too busy hunting around the kitchen for lunch?

Carl cleared his throat. "Actually, sweetie pie, the Abernathys and I were kind of in the middle of something when you all came home. I think maybe the three of us should head to the den and finish our conversation a little more privately."

"That's a great idea." Sandy pulled down a bag of pretzels from the cupboard. "I'll call you back out when lunch is ready."

Nobody answered as Wayne and his son rose from the table and followed Carl down the hall. Noah shuffled his feet, looking exactly like Claudio from *Much Ado About Nothing* as he's being led to the scaffold to face his executioner.

CHAPTER 3

Sandy stared over her cup of lemonade and offered Kennedy an apologetic smile. "I guess I should have realized they were in a meeting. I just can't seem to think clearly these days."

Kennedy wondered how much she was supposed to say about what she'd overheard. How did pastoral confidentiality work in a marriage? Would Carl tell her everything anyway? If Sandy hadn't been so focused on keeping Woong from flopping out of her arms when they came in, she would have heard Wayne and Noah's conversation herself.

Kennedy took a sip of the overly sweet lemonade and winced.

Sandy sighed. "I declare I left my brain in Seoul when we went to pick up Woong."

Kennedy stared at the uneaten brownie on her plate. She hadn't seen this side of Sandy before, this tired side. This side that could hardly hold up a conversation.

Sandy was shaking her head. "I don't know sometimes. I just don't know."

Kennedy offered what she hoped was an encouraging smile. "Things will get easier once he learns English better, don't you think?"

"Oh, he knows English tolerable by now. Just refuses to use it unless it's to tell me he's hungry or thirsty or my soup's not flavored like what he's used to back home. He still calls it home. And I don't mean the orphanage in Seoul. That boy was saved from a life on the streets, and that's what he misses most." Another shake of the head that sent her French braid withering down her back. "I just don't know what to do."

Kennedy wished she had something to say, but she didn't. What did she know about any of this? What did she know about kids like Woong, kids who grew up on the streets in Korea and now were trying to adjust to family life in an American suburb? She had pitifully little experience with children, adopted or not. No siblings. No cousins her age. She'd never even babysat.

The strange thing was how hard Sandy seemed to be taking their new situation. It wasn't as though the Lindgrens were new to parenting.

Kennedy couldn't keep track of how many adopted and foster kids Carl and Sandy had raised in addition to their three biological ones. It couldn't have been easy, could it? Yet Sandy beamed whenever she spoke about any of her grown children. What made Woong so much harder?

"Do you want me to talk to him?" Kennedy found herself asking. "It might be nice for him to have someone who speaks Korean."

Sandy sighed. "Some folks in the adoption business frown on that. They say the best way for language learning is to quit the old one cold turkey, and if the kid spends too much time with a native speaker, it might hurt the bonding process with the adoptive family. But I've never been sure I buy into that entirely. I mean, imagine being that little. You've seen how skinny he is. My grandson Tyson's only six and weighs more than him. So picture being that small, going through half of what Woong did growing up on the streets, and then imagine how you'd feel if on top of all the other changes you couldn't talk to a soul? I sometimes think it's more than his little heart can handle. Maybe that's why he's acting up so much." She sighed and took Kennedy's hand. "I'm sorry to unload on you like this. That's not how I intended for your first day back in the States to start off. Tell me all about your summer. Have you heard how your friend's doing, the one from ..."

"I can't accept that, Pastor. I just can't."

The door to Carl's study burst open, and Wayne's voice flooded down the hall.

"Now, listen here," Carl was saying, "I know your son. He's a good kid who loves you. And you're a good dad who loves him. We've got to find a way to ..."

"It's unnatural." Wayne shook his head. "And it's sinful. You said so yourself, right from the pulpit. The Bible calls it an abomination. There's no way to get around it. An abomination is an abomination."

Carl planted himself in the hall so Wayne couldn't pass. With his arms crossed and his feet spread out, Kennedy got a hint of what he might have looked like as a linebacker playing for the Saints before he went into full-time ministry. "I think we're talking about two different things here. The Bible's referring to very clear-cut cases of living outside of God's standards of purity. But your son just told you he ..."

Wayne let out a harsh noise from the back of his throat. "He just what? Fantasizes about men? And you're telling me that's not a sin, that just because he hasn't gone to bed with ..."

Sandy made a noisy show of stacking and rearranging the dishes on the table. Both men turned.

"Maybe we should talk about this again in the den," Carl suggested.

"I need to get out of here." It was Noah now, standing behind the two men but refusing to raise his eyes to either.

"Listen here, son." Carl put his hand on Noah's back, but he squirmed away.

"I'm done. I'm not doing this anymore. Now that you know that this is the way I am ..."

"But that's what I'm trying to tell you," his father interrupted. "This isn't who you are. You're confused. Something happened to you." There was pleading in his tone.

Kennedy kept her eyes down, certain she wasn't supposed to be listening in on this conversation. But where could she go?

"Someone did this to you." Wayne spoke with conviction. Compassion. There was a slight tremor in his voice. Was he about to cry? "Who was it? Who did this to you?" He reached toward his son, but Noah slapped his hand away.

"Who did this to me?" His whole body trembled along with his voice. His words were laden with emotion, as if Kennedy could wring them out and smell his tears and sweat and fear and pain. "Ask God. The same one who calls people like me an *abomination*."

Wayne sighed. "I didn't mean ..."

"Yes, you did." Noah shouldered his way past Carl and his dad. "I'm taking the T. I'll see you later."

"Where are you going?" Wayne demanded.

Noah didn't turn around or offer any answer. The door slammed shut behind him, its dull thud reverberating through the silence of the house.

Wayne deflated. Kennedy wondered if he would go after his son. Carl and he stood planted in their places for several seconds until the microwave timer beeped. Sandy got up absently. "That's for Woong. I'm going to tell him he can be out of time-out." She sighed heavily. "Have a seat, everyone.

I think we'll just do something easy like grilled cheese for lunch."

CHAPTER 4

"I'd like to apologize for my son's outburst." Wayne wiped his mouth with one of Sandy's floral-patterned cloth napkins.

Kennedy blinked her heavy eyelids. Somewhere in the back of her brain, her mind was shouting at her that she didn't belong. Not here. Not now.

"Don't worry about it." Sandy filled his glass with more lemonade. "This is a big deal, what God's doing in your family. It's not going to be easy. Carl and I just want you to know that if you and Vivian ever need ..."

"I don't know what went wrong." Wayne shook his head. "I mean, we did Boy Scouts every week until he was in tenth grade. He did sports. I coached his Little League team three summers in a row." He looked across the table at Carl, his eyes imploring. "Where did I go wrong?"

Carl hadn't touched his grilled cheese sandwich. "You know, brother, five years ago I'd probably be asking those same questions right there with you. I'd be asking you if there was any abuse in the past, any members of the family or babysitters or someone who might have introduced him to that lifestyle. But you know, I don't think it's as simple as that anymore. I was at the Christian bookstore the other day. Had a book there, something like *Raising Kids Straight*. The whole thing was about giving parents a formula where if they did this, that, and the other thing, they could rest assured that their girls would grow up to be attracted to men and their boys attracted to women. But you know what? Some people struggle differently than others." He took his wife's hand. "It's quite possible your son would have dealt with these feelings no matter how you brought him up."

Wayne clenched his jaw shut. Kennedy saw his forearm bulge as he held onto his dainty lemonade glass. "That's not helping any, Pastor. The Bible says that if you raise children up the way they should go that when they're old they won't depart from it. Proverbs 22:6. Had that one memorized since the day Noah was born. Made God a promise I was going to do right by my boy. And I did. I know I've been busy. Work stuff. Travels. But you know me. I've been there for my son. Elections and campaigns and extra sessions and shutdowns, and I've still been there for my son. Talked to him every day of his life, even if I wasn't there to tuck him in bed. Boy Scouts, Little League, I went to as many of his games as I could if I was in town. I've done everything I could for that kid."

"We know that," Carl said.

"Then how could he do this to us?" Wayne's voice broke, and Kennedy's soul screamed with questions of her own.

"More," Woong demanded from the other end of the table, and Sandy absently set another sandwich on his plate.

Carl rested his forearms on the table. "I'm not sure your son chose to be gay. You heard him in there just a few minutes ago telling us how often he's begged God to change him."

"So why didn't he?" Wayne nearly sobbed.

Kennedy could hardly lift her eyes, not only from the jetlag but the confidential nature of this entire conversation. She shouldn't be here. She should excuse herself to another room, but at this point would that make Wayne feel even more awkward?

As Kennedy did her best to act inconspicuous, she tried to figure out what she believed. Was Carl right? Would Noah have ended up like this no matter how he was raised? Was being gay a choice you made, like becoming a vegetarian? Or was it something different? Something more intrinsic?

Wayne hung his head in his hands. "I just wish ..."

"What's gay?" Woong asked the question loudly and clearly, without any hint of an accent.

Sandy stood up and reached across the table for the fruit salad. "All right, pumpkin. You've had enough grains and dairy. I think it's time for you to get another helping of ..."

"Does it mean sick?" he asked.

"Being gay," Carl explained, and Kennedy watched him adroitly avoid Sandy's well-aimed glare, "is when a person of one gender finds him or herself romantically and physically attracted to a member of the same gender. It's a complicated psychological and biological issue with all kinds of theological implications that has become very divisive in contemporary Christian circles. The more conservative scholars tend to agree that ..."

"What's he saying?" Woong asked Kennedy.

"Here, son." Sandy plopped a heaping spoonful of strawberries and bananas on his plate. "I want you to eat up plenty of fruit so you'll get lots of good, healthy vitamins."

Nobody mentioned Wayne or his son for the rest of the meal. Kennedy excused herself to the guest room as soon as lunch was over. Sandy was taking Woong out for an afternoon of clothes shopping, and Kennedy didn't exactly want to be a third wheel while Carl and Wayne worked through whatever personal matters they were going to discuss.

Kennedy wondered about Noah's past. She'd lived a fairly sheltered life in Yanji, where homosexuality was never discussed on any public level. Gay pride and gay rights were unheard of. Even her parents never discussed the subject with her, unless it was her dad complaining about the pervasive *gay agenda* he saw in the media or American public policy. She had pieced together most of her understanding of the homosexual lifestyle from lunchroom gossip at her high school or an occasional sitcom her dad played in the background. She'd heard it rumored that her aunt's ex-husband's son was living some flamboyant lifestyle in a penthouse in Greenwich Village, but she hadn't seen him in a decade and couldn't even remember his name.

Kennedy's body pulled her toward the bed, but she had resolved to stay awake until sunset. She was going to be taking biology and organic chemistry this term, with two afternoons of labs a week. She wasn't going to start her semester in a half-fog from jetlag.

For students on the pre-med track, the first year was something of a gateway. If you made it through two semesters of general chemistry and didn't flunk out of lab or get sidetracked by something else like sociology or gender studies, you knew you had it in you to complete your four years of undergrad and fulfill all the prerequisites for medical school. Since she was part of the early admissions program, Kennedy was guaranteed a spot in Harvard Med School after graduating, but she still had to keep up her GPA and complete the same pre-med courses as everyone else. She was looking forward to her Shakespeare class as a nice way to give her mind a break from all the science and lab work she'd be focusing on.

All things considered, she was on the right path for a promising academic career. Professor Adell from her chemistry lab had emailed her over the summer to tell her she was the first student she'd had in over ten years to get a hundred percent on her final exam. There was a hint that if Kennedy wanted, Adell could probably find her a position as a TA during her junior or senior year. Her parents had been proud, and her mom had sent out a mass email to all her friends and relatives bragging about Kennedy's grades. She should be happy. But part of her dreaded going back to campus in four days, dreaded a semester without her best friend at Harvard with her.

She and Reuben had stayed in touch all summer, sometimes video chatting, sometimes texting at all hours of the day or night. She could look forward to long emails from Nairobi just about every day, and they had even started their own informal book club where they took turns recommending their favorite classics to each other and talking by phone each week about what they'd read. All that time together, and it wasn't until last week that they broached the subject they'd both avoided.

Reuben wasn't coming back to Harvard. Money was tight. His dad had taken a significant pay cut when the government in Kenya turned over, and the news anchor who broke the story about Reuben's condition had embarrassed the family enough they probably wouldn't have sent him back even if they could afford it.

Three whole months Kennedy spent in denial. Three months wishing and praying God would work some miracle to bring Reuben back to Cambridge. Twice she had worked up the nerve to write Carl and Sandy to ask if he could board with them to cut down some of the costs of campus living, but the emails were still sitting in her drafts folder.

It was so weird to think of a semester without him by her side.

She pulled one of her Shakespeare volumes out of her backpack. She knew she'd have to go back and read some of the histories for her class, but right now she wasn't in the mood for kings and battles. She turned to *Othello*. Good, but pretty depressing. What about *Twelfth Night*? That would work out better for an evening like this.

No, not evening. It was the middle of the day. How long would it take for her body to adjust to East Coast time?

She propped the pillows up on her bed so she could lean against the headboard comfortably, and she felt her body relax into a pool of heaviness as she started the first act. *If music be the food of love, play on.* She could have recited the opening lines from memory if she wanted.

She hadn't gotten halfway through the second scene when a fog thicker than the storm that broke up Viola and Sebastian's boat overshadowed her mind, and she plummeted into sleep.

CHAPTER 5

Kennedy stared at the glowing red numbers on the guest room clock for four full minutes before she realized it was ten at night, not morning. Well, at least it wasn't morning in Medford, Massachusetts. Try telling that to her circadian rhythm, which still thought she was living on the opposite side of the world.

She stared out the window, making out vague outlines lit by distant streetlights. This was ridiculous. She had only come in here to read a little bit and give Carl and the senator a chance to talk in private. She hadn't meant to fall asleep. Now it would take that much longer to wrangle her sleep schedule back to East Coast time.

Who wakes up at 10:16 at night? She counted back. Eight hours of sleep, almost to the minute. Her body mocked her with its stubborn adherence to China time. No problem if she were still in Yanji. No problem if she didn't have three days now to adjust to life in the western hemisphere before jumping headfirst into her second year of undergrad studies.

She had enjoyed her summer so much. Enjoyed the break from school, enjoyed the chance to finally relax. Joking with her dad. Evenings spent watching those stupid cop shows or campy action movies together. Shopping sprees with her mom. Reading for hours in the hammock in her parents' garden. Three home-cooked meals a day. No papers to turn in, lab reports to write up. She emailed Reuben every morning and sometimes didn't log onto her computer for the rest of the day.

Summer had flown by. She wasn't ready for school to start again. Grueling hours in the lab. Midnight snacking on Cheerios and Craisins because she was too busy to eat a real dinner in the cafeteria. If you could call anything the student union served real.

Summer in Yanji had been so stress-free. So uncomplicated. Just Kennedy, her family, her books. Lots of Shakespeare. She had never developed much appreciation for his sonnets but knew she should study up on them for her upcoming class. She still couldn't say she was a fan, but she felt the sonnets somehow added to his plays, as if in some ways she had gotten to know the bard better through his poetry, which made his drama that much richer.

Now, she frowned at the starless sky. It was stupid to try to get back to sleep. As far as her hypothalamus knew, it was the start of a brand new day. Her stomach was ready for some of her mom's buttery biscuits, maybe a fresh egg or two. And some fruit. The produce in the Yanji markets would have made most Cambridge residents drool from envy. Dragon fruit, mangoes, passion fruit, it was all there. All fresh and relatively cheap. She had lost five pounds last spring semester but gained it all back with interest in a month thanks to her mom's cooking back home.

Home? Whatever that meant. She didn't even know what to tell that French businessman on the airplane when he asked her where she was from. Ten years in Manhattan as a child, but she spent huge chunks of time at her grandma's in upstate New York. Eight years in Yanji, China, where she grew conversational in Korean instead of Mandarin because of her parents' ministry to North Korean refugees. And then a year in Cambridge, where other than Reuben and the Lindgrens the only real friend she made was her roommate Willow, a free-living neo-hippy from Never-Heard-of-It, Alaska.

Where was Kennedy from? Little bits of here, little bits of there, but never truly at home anywhere. The Lindgrens' had felt like home the times she stayed here last year, except now she was obviously out of place. What kind of houseguest goes to sleep at two in the afternoon and wakes up perfectly alert at ten? Her body seemed convinced it was time to jump out of bed and help her dad weed out junk mail at his office or walk the markets with her mom, shopping for ingredients for a huge fresh salad for breakfast.

Breakfast? Yeah, her body was ready for that, too. She glanced at her cell phone. Reuben would probably be waking up right about now. It would be good to hear how he was doing. Let him know she'd arrived here safely. He'd be starting his classes at Nairobi University next week. They would both be busy. What would happen to their relationship then?

She heard a noise coming from the kitchen and figured that if the Lindgrens were still awake, she'd grab a quick snack now instead of bothering the entire house later as they were getting ready to fall asleep. She hadn't even changed out of her traveling clothes. That would be the next step after breakfast: shower and change. She didn't know what it was, but something about flying always made her feel grungy and gross. Of course, that could just as easily be explained by the fact that she'd worn the same clothes for the past day and a half, but she was pretty sure there was more to it. Something about sitting in the same seat that thousands of other international commuters had used over the years, next to so many strangers whose personal hygiene habits could only be guessed at. She wished she still had those homeopathic throat lozenges her roommate Willow gave her at the end of last semester. They were supposed to come packed with a plethora of insanely efficient immunity enhancers. Kennedy would be happy for any boost she could get right about now. Who knew how many contagions she had breathed in while she flew around the world?

She crept out of bed and opened the guest room door, making as little noise as possible in case Carl and Sandy really had fallen asleep. She wasn't sure how heavy of a dozer Woong was either and found herself wondering what it must have been like for Carl and Sandy while they all adjusted to jetlag after they brought him home from Seoul.

The small light in the kitchen pantry was on, and Kennedy recognized Noah Abernathy's frame bent over a drawer. She wondered what had transpired during her eight-hour beauty nap. So he was staying with the Lindgrens now. Had his dad kicked him out for good? There was something about his posture or maybe the slight heave of his shoulders that made Kennedy stop in the hall. Was he crying?

Maybe she'd wait for that snack. But then again, couldn't she try to do some good? The Lindgrens were so hospitable, had encouraged so many people. Shouldn't she try to do the same for a boy who'd just been kicked out of his house? Then again, what did she know about the Abernathys or their family drama? It really wasn't any of her business, was it? And what in the world did she have in common with a gay teenage boy? She didn't need to poke her nose around in the Abernathys' private affairs. She was sure they had enough members of the press and low-scale paparazzi doing that instead.

She had just resolved to go back to her room when something beeped. The sound in the otherwise silent home made her jump. Noah pulled a cell phone out of his pocket. The glow from his screen cast a greenish light throughout the room.

The heaving in his shoulders stopped. He slammed his fist on the counter and muttered, "I'm gonna kill him."

From somewhere outside, a car door slammed shut. Kennedy started. Noah turned around and stared right at her.

CHAPTER 6

Noah shoved the phone into his pocket.

Kennedy was trying to form the words to an apology when somebody stepped in through the front door.

"I'm sorry it's so late. Are Carl and Sandy already sleeping?" Nick, the youth pastor from Carl's church, slipped into the dining room, making as little noise as he could in his somewhat clunky leather sandals. If Kennedy had thought she was disoriented waking up to a pitch-black house, it was nothing compared to this. She kept checking out the window to make sure it really was nighttime.

Nick was wearing beige cargo shorts and a T-shirt with Jesus and three of his disciples walking down Abbey Road. A speech bubble showed them singing, "All you need is love," and included a Bible reference from 1 John.

He gave Noah a side hug. "How you doing, brother? I was thinking I could take you out for coffee if it's not too late."

Noah hesitated. His hand hovered over the pocket of his pants.

"Or we could chat here if you don't feel like going out. Whatever you want. I just want you to know I'm here for you."

He still didn't respond. Kennedy wondered if the next three days living at the Lindgrens' would feel this awkward. Why was she always getting in everybody's way? She should be asleep now, not hanging out in the hallway while a youth pastor stopped by to check on a teen who most likely had been kicked out of his own home when his dad found out he was gay.

Why did she have to be awake for this?

"Tell you what." Nick flipped off his sandals. "I'm gonna get myself a glass of water. Me and some of the other guys were playing ultimate after youth group, and I'm parched. Once I'm done with that, you can tell me what you want to do."

Nick had to pass Kennedy on his way to the kitchen, and it was the first time he indicated he'd noticed her. "Oh, hey. When did you fly in?"

"I landed right around noon."

"You must be tired."

Kennedy wished she was. "Actually, I've been asleep since lunchtime. I just woke up."

Nick shook his head, and his blond dreadlocks shook around his shoulders. "Man, that's rough."

Noah's cell phone beeped again. His profile looked sickly in its green glow.

Nick finished a noisy gulp of water from the Lindgrens' sink. "All right, man. Wanna grab a snack? I've got a chill album in the bus. My uncle and his friends just put out a new ..."

"I gotta go." Noah shoved the phone back in his pocket and put on his shoes.

"Where you headed?" Nick asked. "I'll give you a ride."

Noah walked right by him. "I need to go home."

Nick frowned. "You sure? Back when we were texting, you said your dad ..."

"I need to go home," he repeated.

Nick shrugged. "No prob. As long as you feel safe there."

Noah let out a little snort. Kennedy didn't like the sound of it.

Nick was slipping on his sandals again. "Well, I guess I'll drive you home then, all right?"

"What's going on out here?" Sandy's sleepy voice emerged from the doorway of the master bedroom. She was tying the sash of her pink bathrobe as she came down the hall. "Nick? Is that you?"

He gave her a hug when she opened her arms to him. "Sorry for bothering you. I'd been texting a little with Noah and thought I'd pop over to see if he wanted to spend some time together. I wasn't trying to wake you up."

"Don't worry about that." Sandy brushed some hair out of her eyes. Kennedy hardly ever saw it down out of its braid. It was thicker than she would have guessed, with almost as much gray as brown. "Kennedy, did you get some good sleep?"

"Yeah, just not at the right time."

Sandy gave her a pat on the back. "I'm sorry, hon. I told Carl he should wake you up, but then Woong and I had to run out to do some shopping, and Carl got called away for a hospital visit, and by the time we all got home and got dinner going it was so late already we weren't sure if maybe you'd just sleep straight through the night. I guess that didn't happen, did it?"

"No." Kennedy had to match Sandy's smile even though she didn't find the situation amusing at all. The dorms opened in three days. She had to be ready, which meant she had to be on East Coast time.

Like, yesterday.

"So you're awake for good, are you?"

"Probably until tomorrow night," Kennedy answered. If she could make it that long without some sort of a nap.

"Well, let me get dressed, and I'll keep you company while these boys go out and do their thing. You're probably ready for breakfast of some sort, aren't you?"

"That's ok," Kennedy assured her. "I really don't need ..."

Sandy waved her hand in the air. "Don't mention it. Lord knows I've lost enough sleep with Woong over the past few weeks. I probably couldn't sleep straight through the night if I ..."

"She can come with us," Nick interrupted, shooting Kennedy a glance from the other side of the room.

"No." Sandy tied her apron over her bathrobe and then stared down at herself as if she couldn't figure out what she'd just done. "You boys need some together time. It's been a long day for Noah, and ..."

"I'm just dropping him off at home, that's all," Nick replied. "You don't mind if Kennedy tags along, do you?"

Noah shrugged. "Whatever."

"So you're going home?" Sandy opened a cupboard and stared at its contents blankly before shutting it again. "What was I getting?" she mumbled to herself.

"You just go back to sleep." Nick prodded her out of the kitchen as if she were a lost child. "I'll take Noah home, and Kennedy can come with me so she has something to do."

"Aren't you tired?" Sandy was fidgeting with the strings of her apron, but Kennedy couldn't tell if she was trying to take the whole thing off or tighten her knot. "You need your sleep, too."

"Not as much as you do." Nick guided her down the hall, and Sandy kind of floated back to her room, still fussing with her apron asking herself, "Now what was I doing with this old thing again?"

Nick gave Kennedy a little smile. "Sorry. I wasn't trying to shanghai you or anything. I just wanted her to get some sleep."

"Yeah, she needs it." Kennedy had to admit she was a little jealous. She'd give up her Shakespeare sonnet book and quite a few of the tragedies for a chance to go to bed now and wake up in the morning like a normal East Coaster.

"All right, Noah, so if all we're doing is taking you home, you really don't mind if Kennedy tags along?" He turned back toward her. "If you feel like getting out for a bit, that is."

She was feeling a little cooped up, and she had no idea what she'd do all night while the Lindgrens slept. She had plenty of books to keep her company, but her eyes were sore from all that dry air blowing into her contacts on the plane. She glanced at Noah to try to gauge his reaction.

"Whatever she wants." He didn't look at her. Kennedy got the feeling he didn't care who took him home as long as he got there. What had changed? Why was he so eager to get back to his dad's all of a sudden?

Nick jingled his keys on their colorful lanyard. "Well, you both ready?"

"I guess so." Kennedy followed Nick to the youth group bus. "You painted a new Moses?" she asked when they got to the driveway.

Nick pointed at the passenger door. "Yeah, we pimped it up right before we drove out to the Awakening Festival. They do it every August out in New Hampshire. Christian bands from all over. We took twenty teens or so. Wanted to give the bus a fresher look before we hit the road."

Kennedy looked at the painting of Moses parting the Red Sea. Last year, the scene had been pretty typical, something you might have found in a children's Bible storybook if it weren't for all the colorful tropical fish that were twice the size of Moses' head swimming around the waves. But now, instead of an old man with a beard, Moses was a rock guitarist on roller skates, holding up a large microphone instead of a staff.

"Pretty cool, isn't it?" Nick sounded so proud, Kennedy didn't have the heart to reply.

"So my uncle got a new member for the Babylon Eunuchs," Nick was saying once the van was running and they were all buckled in their seats. "They added a saxophone. Hear him in the background?" He turned up the volume on the stereo, and Kennedy tried not to wince at the music. If you could even call it that. The saxophonist seemed to be the only band member with talent, but his impressive riffs and licks just made the other musicians sound even more like amateurs.

Not that it took much.

"So, crazy day, eh?" Nick asked.

Noah shrugged. "I guess so."

"You patch things up with your dad? I kind of thought you'd be at the Lindgrens' for a while."

Another shrug. In the background, the leader of the Babylon Eunuchs cawed on about peace flooding his soul, setting him free. *Free from what?* Kennedy wondered. The lyrics were so vague, the band could have been droning on about a junior-high romance if it weren't for an occasional reference to the Holy Spirit.

It wasn't any of her business what was going on with Noah, but still she was curious. Had his dad just found out he was gay? Is that what caused the big blow-up at Carl and Sandy's? Kennedy had been sheltered enough she didn't know much about the gay lifestyle until she got to Harvard, and there it was plastered all over the place. Her roommate Willow argued that everybody was bisexual, with some people on one end of the spectrum where they were mainly attracted to men, some on the other attracted to women, and everyone else in a happy sort of middle ground where they could swing either way. But there were so many questions. She knew her dad lamented about gay-friendly churches, but she had never actually known a gay Christian. What did that make Noah? Was he gay or was he Christian? Or could he be both?

There was something else even more puzzling. Noah said God had made him that way. He hadn't chosen to be like that. It went against everything she read about in her dad's conservative political magazines or those family-values blogs he sometimes sent her links to. The writers there all made it sound like homosexuals were some sort of deviant cultural subset that "traded in" the heterosexual lifestyle for an alternative one. But what did that mean for people like Noah? Had he somehow "traded in" his straightness to become gay? And what did he actually mean by gay? Did that mean Noah was in a relationship with another boy? How serious of a relationship did it have to be to be considered gay? Or did being gay come first? Were you gay as soon as you started experiencing same-sex attractions?

Kennedy had crushes before. She didn't remember choosing any of them. The fact that she was committed to a life of sexual purity before marriage didn't mean she didn't like the idea of being kissed. Of being held. It wasn't wrong for her to picture that happening to her one day, was it? Where was the line drawn between normal biology and sinful lust? And was that line different for people who were attracted to members of the same sex?

She didn't know which was giving her more of a headache: these weighty theological questions that never seemed to arrive at any logical conclusion, the disorientation she felt at being wide awake an hour before midnight, or the terrible music spewing out of Nick's stereo.

The Abernathys lived in a house in Weston that would have made Baptista's mansion in *The Taming of the Shrew* look like a makeshift shanty. By the time Nick got them into their gated community and then past the security gate surrounding the family estate, the Babylon Eunuchs' instrumentals mercifully faded away as the last song ended. Kennedy hoped Nick wouldn't notice and start the whole half an hour of drivel all over again.

"You sure everything's all right?" Nick asked, and Kennedy wondered why he would drop Noah off here if he wasn't sure he'd be safe. Was Wayne the kind of dad who'd beat his kid for coming out of the closet? Kennedy couldn't tell. Wayne was a mystery, always presenting whatever side the public would find most endearing, but somehow managing to come across as the most genuine and sincere politician you could expect to meet. He'd dropped out of the state governor race last fall after his daughter was kidnapped. He said his family needed him, and he had determined to make them his priority. He and his wife Vivian had adopted their young nephew, Charlie, and were raising him as their own. By all appearances, they were a caring, close-knit family. But of course appearances could deceive, especially when you were talking about someone who could manipulate public opinion as well as Wayne.

Noah thanked Nick for the ride. "I'll shut the gate once you're out." He hopped out of the bus after the last of the security checkpoints. Kennedy wondered if Julius Caesar had been any more protected than the Abernathys.

"You sure you're doing all right? Kennedy and I don't have anywhere else to be. We can just drive around and talk if you want to."

"I'm fine. It's ok." There was something soft in Noah's smile that reminded Kennedy of his little sister Jodie.

"You need something, you text me. Got that?"

He nodded. "Yeah. Thanks."

He shut the door to the bus, but Nick rolled the window down right away. "Hey."

Noah turned around. "Yeah?"

"You stay safe. Got it?" There was something heavy in Nick's tone. Something more serious than Kennedy was used to hearing from the youth pastor with his outlandish dreadlocks and crazy shirts.

Noah gave one more nod and a tired half-smile. "Yeah, ok. I will."

CHAPTER 7

Nick invited Kennedy up to the passenger seat once they pulled out of the Abernathys' fortress. She figured if she didn't get him talking soon, he'd be tempted to fill the silence with more from the Babylon Eunuchs, so she jumped up front and buckled quickly.

"You ever been in their house before?" he asked, giving the Abernathys' mansion one last glance in his rear-view mirror.

Kennedy shook her head.

"I went with the Lindgrens to a Christmas party there a couple years ago. Nice place."

Part of Kennedy wished he'd say more. Wished he'd tell her a little bit of Noah's story, even though she knew it was none of her business. Her dad would chide her if he knew what she was thinking. Her whole life she'd grown up hearing his adages. *Don't judge someone just because they sin differently than you. Don't judge someone who fails a test you yourself have yet to pass. Don't judge someone until you've crawled into his skin and walked around a little bit.* He stole that last one from the novelist Harper Lee, but it was probably Kennedy's favorite quote of them all.

"So." Nick drummed a little beat on the bus's steering wheel, while on the dashboard his Peter, James, and John bobble heads bounced around with enormous smiles painted on their caricatured faces. "You tired? You want me to take you back to the Lindgrens' to get some sleep?"

"It's not too bad." She couldn't sleep now even if the fairies from *A Midsummer Night's Dream* were singing her lullabies. She glanced at the Frisbees strewn across the floor of the bus, along with some crushed water bottles and empty Gatorade containers. "But you've had a long night. I don't want to keep you up."

Nick waved his hand. "Don't worry about me. I had two energy drinks before youth group started. I'm in the same boat as you. Won't be getting to sleep for another two or three hours at least."

Neither one spoke. Kennedy stared out the window at the ornate lamps lining the Newton streets. What would it be like to live out here? The Abernathys' home was modest compared to a few of the other estates they passed. She thought about Woong, wondered what his life had been like living on the streets before he ended up at that South Korean orphanage. How was it that some people could live in such superfluous luxury while half the world's children were starving or malnourished? How could they be so calloused? So cruel to shut their ears to the cries of the needy?

Then again, it wasn't as if her own family was living in a hovel in Yanji. They owned a big home in an upscale expat neighborhood and more often than not had at least a few live-in housekeepers, gardeners, and security workers. She didn't have to work a campus job to buy her textbooks. Thanks to an inheritance from her grandmother, she wouldn't even need to take out student loans until med school. When she went hungry at Harvard, it was because she hadn't taken the time to eat, not because she was too poor to buy food or because the rains had failed to produce a crop. Maybe she was more privileged than she cared to admit.

When they left the gated community, Nick turned on a new CD.

"Is this Potter's Clay?" Kennedy asked. "I haven't heard them since junior high."

"I'm impressed. I don't find many people around today who know Potter's Clay."

"I'm a little surprised anybody still listens to them anymore."

Nick chuckled. "Don't be dissing on Potter's now. Not unless you want me to turn this bus around and drive you straight home."

Kennedy smiled and tried to remember the last time she and Nick had done anything alone together. Probably that one night last winter when they'd gone out for clam chowder at the little walk-up restaurant stand in Harvard Square.

"You hungry?" Nick's dreadlocks whipped around slightly as he turned toward her for a quick glance. "We could stop somewhere if you want."

"That sounds nice." What else was she supposed to do when her body was already awake for the day? She'd have to try to make it another twenty hours before she went to sleep again. Then maybe she could get herself back on East Coast schedule before she started her classes.

"I know this neat little bakery in Harvard Square. It's a drive, but it's not like we'll be fighting traffic. What do you say?"

There was only one bakery Kennedy knew of near campus that stayed open this late. "Are you talking about L'Aroma? My roommate goes there all the time."

"No kidding? It's a great little shop. So you up for it?"

Kennedy had been hooked at the word *bakery*. Her mouth watered as readily as Pavlov's pack of lab dogs'. "Sure. That sounds great."

They drove along in comfortable silence. Kennedy wondered what Reuben was doing right about now. It was morning in Kenya.

Lucky him.

She had spent a lot of time over the summer talking to both God and her mom about her relationship with Reuben. Of course, as soon as her mom heard about his diagnosis, she was against anything that even hinted at romance developing between them. She tried to be sympathetic, but Kennedy knew she was relieved that he wasn't coming back to campus in the fall.

It didn't make sense. People could be together with HIV. It wasn't the death sentence it had been a decade or two ago. Reuben was getting good medical care at Nairobi Hospital, and there were ways for patients to keep their loved ones from getting the virus themselves.

It could have worked out. That's what made the whole situation so depressing. It wasn't as if it were a breakup, because they had never actually been dating, but that almost made it worse. When you broke up with somebody, you could at least tell yourself you'd tried and it hadn't worked out. Why would you want to be with someone who didn't want to be with you? But Kennedy didn't have any of those nice platitudes to fall back on. She hadn't chosen to say good-bye to Reuben at the end of last semester. Would she even see him again? She still couldn't pinpoint exactly where home was for her, but Kenya was a long way off no matter how you looked at it.

"I think I'm mostly a night owl. What about you?" Sometimes Nick's thoughts materialized out of a vacuum. She didn't know if it was some sort of social awkwardness or just the result of him being so comfortable with his own personal musings.

"I stay up late when I'm studying," she replied, "but if there's nothing else going on I guess I'm more of a morning person. Except when I'm jetlagged."

"What time is it over at your parents'?"

"Right around noon."

Nick let out a low whistle. "That's got to be crazy to adjust to."

"Yeah, it's actually easier going from here to there for some reason. Coming back to the States has always felt harder."

"So what exactly is it your parents do in China?" Nick asked.

Kennedy was glad to have some trivial chitchat to offer. It beat moping in the bus, pining away for Reuben, while the apostles' heads bobbled up and down with their mocking grins. "They work along the North Korean border. Take in refugees. A year ago they had a whole group of them. Gave them training and then sent them back to North Korea as underground missionaries."

"Sounds dangerous."

"Yeah. One of the girls came back home. Back to my parents', I mean. She'd been captured. Tortured pretty bad, I think."

"That's intense. What about your parents? Do they ever get in trouble or anything?"

"The police stop by. They're at least under suspicion at this point. That's why they haven't taken in any new refugees lately. They've started to move more toward brothel rescues there in Yanji, which is less likely to get them in trouble with the law. Except now it's the pimps and stuff they've got to worry about."

"Sound like they're amazing believers."

Kennedy had never really thought about her parents in those terms. Amazing? Maybe. If you were to look at their ministry, at least. But she had the feeling that if Nick saw her parents' day-to-day lives, he might not be so impressed. Her dad spent fifty or sixty hours a week at his printing business, his legal front for living in China. Her mom had gotten so addicted to this TV medical drama she'd made Kennedy buy her a fourteen-disc DVD set in the States to bring to Yanji over the summer. Her parents argued and bickered all the time, and her mom was now menopausal and let everyone and everything within a mile radius know about it.

Probably not the picture Nick had when he called them such *amazing believers.*

He pulled the bus into the L'Aroma Bakery parking lot. There were a few other customers there, but it was quiet inside. They ordered at the counter and took their food and drinks to a table in the back.

"I wonder how Noah's doing." Nick took out his cell phone. "No messages yet. I guess that's a good sign."

"Are you two pretty close?"

Nick took a bite of his egg and veggie burrito. "Sort of," he said with his mouth full. "We got to talking a lot over the summer. That's when all this stuff started coming out."

Kennedy tried to guess if he was making a pun as she took a sip from her hot chocolate, careful to keep her nose out of the whipped cream.

"Today was the first time he told his dad. We had talked about it before then, but he never felt quite ready. I told him I'd go with him, and as far as I knew, that's what the plan was. I don't know why it all happened today. I wonder how Mr. Abernathy took it."

"I was there when he and Noah were talking with Carl. He was pretty upset."

Nick wiped his mouth on a napkin. "I'm not surprised. Senator Abernathy's been the most conservative member of the state house when it comes to gay rights and these so-called *family values*."

There was something mocking in the way he said the phrase. She wasn't sure how to read him.

He laughed mirthlessly. "Not gonna look too good to all his constituents when it comes out that Mr. Homophobe himself has a son who's gay." He shook his head, and the tip of one dreadlock nearly landed in his salsa.

Kennedy figured she'd probably come across sounding like a child, but Nick dealt with kids for a living. Maybe he wouldn't mind. "I have a question." She paused, wondering how to best word it. "When you say Noah's *gay*, what exactly do you mean?"

Nick's eyes widened, and Kennedy imagined him trying to figure out how to explain the intricacies of male homosexual intimacy to a nineteen-year-old college virgin.

She hurried on to explain better. "I mean, I wasn't trying to overhear, but they were talking all over the place, and it was getting pretty loud, and Noah said he hadn't ever ... He told his dad he wasn't ... He's never ..."

"Actually had sex with a man?" Nick finished for her, and Kennedy's face warmed to the temperature of her cocoa.

She nodded, keeping her eyes on the shavings of nutmeg on top of her whipped cream.

"That's a really good question."

She let out her breath. Why did these talks always have to be so awkward? Her dad forced her into conversations about so many weird, random topics, like how to file a sexual harassment complaint or how to react if she thought a date spiked her drink. But then there were other subjects they never broached at all.

Like whether or not a Christian boy who's never slept with anybody could be gay.

Nick took a noisy gulp of his herbal tea. "So, there's some people who say that you're not gay until you've actually had gay sex. That's probably where the confusion comes in."

Kennedy was glad L'Aroma wasn't very crowded. She didn't think this was the kind of conversation she'd like to have with a dozen other diners listening in.

"But then again, if you were to ask me if I'm gay or straight, it's not like I need to have slept with a woman to know that I'm straight, right?"

"I guess so." In the back of Kennedy's mind, she was wondering if listening to the Babylon Eunuchs would be more pleasant than this.

"So it all boils down to identity. And that's kind of a loaded word, because the way we've been throwing it around makes it sound kind of like it's this big choice, right? Like *today I identify as a white male.* Well, there's more to it than that, and that's where we get someone like Noah Abernathy. It's not like he woke up one day and said to himself, *Gee, I could use some extra attention. Guess I'll say that I'm gay.* In fact, he went years hiding it from everyone. You just look at his father, and you'll know why. This is the same guy who championed that photographer who refused to shoot photos at a lesbian wedding. The family-values set made her into this huge martyr when she got sued, said it's her right to refuse to participate in a supposedly sinful ceremony, but did you see her boycotting weddings of adulterers? Did she boycott weddings where the bride and groom had been living together years before they finally made their commitment legal?

No. So you get all these people like Senator Abernathy talking about family values and lamenting this so-called gay agenda, and so of course his son's gonna try to hide the fact that he's attracted to other boys."

Nick paused long enough to meet Kennedy's eyes.

"What was your question? Oh, right. What does it mean to be gay. In Noah's case, it means feeling so ashamed of who you are that you beg God every day to change you. You go to sleep just hoping and praying you'll wake up and find yourself attracted to girls. It means sneaking Playboys into the bathroom, hoping it'll do something for you, only it doesn't. It means finally getting the nerve to tell your dad about what's going on and have him kick you out of the house because you're an abomination. That's what being gay means. In fact, it has very little to do with who's sleeping with who."

Kennedy thought she understood, but that only led to even more complicated questions. She wasn't sure where to start. She knew there were Christians who argued that gay relationships could be just as godly and righteous as a marriage between a husband and wife, but she had always seen them as some sort of "other," entities she read about in her dad's pro-family publications who were trying to undermine traditional marriage across the entire United States. Where did Nick stand? He worked for Pastor Carl, who had no problem teaching from the pulpit that homosexuality was a sin. Kennedy had just assumed that's what every Christian believed, at least every mainstream evangelical.

Was she wrong?

Nick scooped up a big bite of egg that had fallen out of his burrito. "So, back when I was in high school ..."

Kennedy didn't know if he was changing the subject or continuing on with the original conversation. She didn't have the chance to find out. Nick's phone rang, that same one-line chorus she had heard in the car on his uncle's album.

"Hey, Pastor Carl."

His face turned serious. Worried.

"No, we dropped him off nearly an hour ago ... Yeah, Kennedy's still with me ... Are you serious? You've got to be joking."

Nick stared at the phone, and Kennedy felt the base of her abdominal wall plummet toward the ground.

"Yeah, we'll be there as soon as we can. Ok, bye."

He turned off his phone and took a deep breath.

"The Abernathys' home burned down. They say Noah's missing and his dad's dead."

CHAPTER 8

Kennedy and Nick didn't talk or listen to any music as they raced back to the Lindgrens'. Kennedy was certain she had dreamed up this whole night. She was probably still so jetlagged she was in Carl and Sandy's guest room coming up with some elaborately bizarre daydream. Or maybe she hadn't even arrived in Massachusetts yet. Maybe she was dozing off on the plane from Seattle, sitting next to the cute French businessman who would ask her a dozen questions about China when she woke up.

The bus jolted and hopped with every minor bump in the road. Kennedy was afraid she'd get carsick. She clung to the door handle as if she could ground herself that way. That's what she needed. Some kind of grounding stability.

Nick parked the bus lopsided along the curb since there were two police cars taking up the Lindgrens' driveway. He raced out without saying anything, and Kennedy sprinted behind him. She didn't know what she expected to see when she burst after him through the front door. A dozen police officers, maybe a few members of the press, men and women in suits holding notebooks and pens. Instead, there were two men in uniform sitting around the Lindgrens' dining room table, with a plate of cookies and muffins on the Lazy Susan in front of them.

Kennedy froze in the hall beside Nick, and the two officers looked up. She recognized them both.

"Just in time." Carl stood up and pointed at the man with reddish stubble spreading out across his chin. "I think you both already know Dominic, chaplain for the BPD."

He nodded and offered Kennedy the slightest trace of a smile.

"And this is Detective Drisklay."

Kennedy's lungs constricted once at the sight of the middle-aged man sipping coffee from a stained disposable cup.

"Miss Stern." He gave a courtly nod that felt almost mocking in nature.

"What's going on?" Nick asked. "Does anyone know how Noah's doing? Have you been able to find him yet?"

"That's what we were hoping you could tell us," said Drisklay in his characteristic monotone.

"Well ..." Nick pulled out his phone and glanced at the time. "It was a little over an hour ago when I dropped him off at his mom and dad's. Right after eleven."

"Did you go in the house? Did you see either of his parents?"

Kennedy's mind wandered slightly until she decided that if Detective Drisklay and her chem professor Adell ever created a love child, he would be a modern-day version of Hercule Poirot. She tried imagining his famous mustaches on a face like Drisklay's. If this weren't such a tense situation, she might have allowed herself a giggle.

"We didn't see anybody," Nick answered. "We just drove up and dropped him off at the point where the driveway turns around."

"Did either of you watch to see if he actually went in the house?" Drisklay fired off questions without showing any interest in Nick's answers.

Kennedy's stomach tightened. Were they in trouble?

"No."

"What about before you dropped him off? Did he act unusual in any way? Say anything that might give us a clue where he could be now?"

Sandy pulled out two chairs. As soon as Kennedy and Nick sat down, she passed them the cookies and muffins even though no one at the table was eating.

"We need to know where Noah might be." Drisklay took a noisy gulp of coffee.

Kennedy looked at Nick as if studying his face might jog her memory. It didn't help.

"He didn't really say anything in the car, at least nothing I remember. He was pretty quiet."

"Mrs. Lindgren, you said you saw him a few minutes before he left here?"

"That's right." Sandy was out of her bathrobe now and dressed in the same clothes she had worn that day. "Nick said that Noah was ready to go home, so I assumed that he must have patched things up with his dad. I was glad for the news. It's not right for a family to be torn apart by a ..."

"Would you say that he was particularly sullen or quiet when you saw him?" Drisklay interrupted.

Sandy frowned. "I'm sorry, Detective, but come to think of it, I was only half awake. We've just adopted our little boy from South Korea. Only been three weeks since we brought him home, and I'll be pickled if I've ever gotten a full night of sleep since he ..."

"So he didn't act any differently tonight when you saw him?" Drisklay's voice was even more drone-like than normal. Kennedy wondered if that was the way he showed frustration. Sandy twirled a long strand of hair around her finger. "No, he didn't act any different at all tonight. Kicked and screamed like usual until his father ..."

"He's asking about Noah, woman." Carl's voice still held its usually good-natured tone, but there was no sign of patience or humor in his expression. "He wants to know if you noticed anything different about Noah before he left."

Sandy frowned and stared at some of her split ends. "No. That boy's always pretty quiet, far as I remember. I recall one time we'd been invited over for dinner at the Abernathys', and he refused to ..."

"And you two?" Drisklay snapped, except his volume never rose. "Was the kid acting unusual in your opinion?"

Kennedy didn't know Noah well enough so she let Nick answer the question.

"Well, I did think it was a little strange he changed his mind about going home. We'd been texting for a while about how mad he was at his dad and how hurt he was. His dad kicked him out of the house. You probably heard all the details of that."

For the first time since the beginning of this impromptu interrogation, Kennedy turned her attention toward Dominic. The chaplain hadn't said a single word, but he leaned forward with his hands folded on the table in front of him and seemed twice as engaged as the detective.

Drisklay scowled. "So nobody can say that this kid acted any different than normal, and nobody has any clue where he went, is that it?"

Everyone stared at the other faces around the table, and Kennedy got the same sinking feeling she had as a third-grader when her teacher yelled at the entire class.

"I'll try calling him." Nick pulled out his phone. "We have a pretty good relationship. I guess if he has to hear about his dad from anybody, it may as well be me."

Drisklay set down his cup, splashing a few drops of black coffee onto Sandy's lacy table runner. "I'm not sure you're getting the full picture, here. We don't need to find the kid to tell him his dad's dead. We need to find the kid because as of right now, he's our primary suspect."

CHAPTER 9

Kennedy was certain she had heard wrong. Noah was just a boy. A boy from a good family. He wouldn't have done something like burn his house down. Sure, he'd been angry at his dad, but still ... Noah Abernathy, a murderer?

The police had to have the wrong information.

"He just got in a fight with his dad." Kennedy heard the tremor in her own voice. Her face flushed with every pair of eyes staring at her, but she had to convince them they were wrong. "They were upset at each other. That shouldn't mean he's a suspect."

Dominic pursed his lips together. "How well do you know Noah Abernathy?"

Kennedy ignored her burning cheeks and tried to remember if she ever had a single conversation with him. So maybe she couldn't tell the chaplain about his life goals and ambitions. But still ... a murderer?

"What about the senator?" she tried. "You can't be as outspoken as he is without making people angry at you. What if he said something ... What if there was some bill ...?" She didn't pay attention to politics unless her dad was railing on about some controversy or other. She didn't have a clue what she was talking about.

"This is clearly a sensitive topic," Dominic began, "not just because it involves a teenager that you all want to protect, but because of the nature of Noah's fight with his dad."

So this was how it would go. Now that his father had died, Noah would be dragged out of the closet and paraded through the streets for everyone in the Boston area to gawk at. If she thought the press made a field day out of her kidnapping with Noah's little sister last fall, it would be nothing compared to this oncoming media frenzy.

No wonder Noah was hiding.

Or was he? Maybe he didn't even know about his dad yet. Maybe he went out with some friends and had no idea what storm had rolled in on him and his family, a storm that was determined to strip him of all privacy and dignity.

"So Noah's dad got mad when he found out his son is gay." Nick was up out of his chair now and pacing around the dining room table. "That night his dad dies in a fire. It still doesn't mean the two events are connected."

"That's why we're here." Dominic spoke with the patience of a preschool VBS school teacher. "Well, that's why the detective is here. We need to get to the bottom of this, and we need to do it ASAP before the media blows it all out of the water. So if there's anything else you can think of that you haven't mentioned yet ..."

"He was texting someone." Everyone turned to stare at Kennedy again. "I came out here a few minutes before Nick came. Noah was in the kitchen when he got a text."

"Did he say anything?" Drisklay asked. "Did you see his reaction?"

"Yeah." Kennedy could visualize the exact way the light from Noah's screen had cast that eerie green glow all around him. "He was out here in the dark. His phone beeped, and when he read it ..."

Drisklay leaned toward her. So did Carl and Sandy. Nick stopped his pacing.

Kennedy licked her lips. Maybe she shouldn't have mentioned the text.

Dominic held her gaze from across the table. "What happened when he saw the message?"

Kennedy let out her air. Felt her lungs deflate. Her dad always told her that honesty wasn't just the best policy. It was the only policy. Try telling that to Noah Abernathy right about now.

Everyone was waiting for her response. There was no way to take back what she'd already said. Nothing to do but proceed forward and hope for the best. Hope she wasn't getting Noah into even more trouble.

"He looked at the message and said something like, 'I'm gonna kill him.'"

Nick and the Lindgrens stared at her. Drisklay actually wrote something down in that tiny pad of paper he always carried around. Dominic gazed at his folded hands on the table. Kennedy didn't meet anyone's eyes. Had she just condemned an innocent boy?

It was possible the text wasn't about his dad. Why would Noah ask to go home if he was still mad at his father? Besides, being mad and *saying* you're going to kill someone is a lot different than actually committing murder. What had he been doing out in the kitchen in the dark anyway?

She couldn't remember. Her body was still wide awake, but her brain was exhausted, covered by a thick, heavy mental mist as powerful as Prospero's magic in *The Tempest*.

Drisklay scraped his chair against the floor as he stood from the table. "Thank you folks for your time. I'll be sure to keep in touch, and you have my number if you think of anything else." He leveled his gaze. "Of course, you'll call if you see or hear from the kid." It wasn't a question.

Nobody said anything as he passed down the hall and let himself out.

"Well then," Sandy said, "what happens next?"

All eyes turned to Dominic, who still sat serenely at his place. Kennedy wondered how the chaplain stayed so stately and composed. Didn't he know what was going on? Didn't he care that an innocent boy had been accused of starting the fire that killed his own father?

Carl let out his breath. "I guess we should all try to get some sleep."

Sandy sighed. "I supposed that's all we can do right about now."

"Not to step on any toes, ma'am," Dominic interjected, "but I think there's one more thing that we can do first. The most important thing of all."

"That's exactly right." Carl grabbed Sandy's hand on one side and Kennedy's on the other. Nick sat back down, and everyone around the table joined hands.

"Now then." Carl's booming voice reverberated through the house, a harmonious sound that wrapped Kennedy's soul up in peace. "Let's pray."

CHAPTER 10

Carl and Sandy went back to bed as soon as Dominic left. It was past midnight, but as much as Kennedy's brain wanted to sleep, there was no way she could force her body to comply. The Lindgrens had offered Nick the attic loft since Noah wasn't using it. He didn't go up immediately, but lingered awkwardly in the hallway after everyone else parted ways.

"You're not going to get any sleep, are you?" He gave Kennedy a sympathetic half-smile.

"It's all right. The best thing I could do is force myself to stay awake until tomorrow night."

"I'm still kind of buzzed from those energy drinks. Have you seen the Lindgrens' game closet? They have just about everything. Do you play Scrabble?"

Kennedy loved board games. Over the summer, she and her dad had played a round of Scrabble or a game of chess at least once a day. "That sounds really fun, but my brain's turned to mush."

Nick was already rummaging through a large closet in the living room. "Well, what if we find something that involves absolutely no thought whatsoever?" He pulled out a colorful box. "Candyland?"

Kennedy laughed. "Sure. Why not?" It beat sitting alone in her room worrying about Noah.

Her mind still hadn't fully registered that Wayne Abernathy was dead. This felt more like a live drama, where everything was staged, no matter how realistic it felt at the time. Suspension of disbelief. That was the literary word for it. It's what allowed theatergoers to look past the audience members in front of them. What allowed sci-fi fans to ignore clear-cut rules of physics in order to enjoy a far-fetched story. It was the same thing now, only in reverse. Wayne Abernathy couldn't really be dead. She had seen him just a few hours ago. She wondered if his death had made the news yet and was glad for Nick — strange company as he was — and his preschool board game to keep her preoccupied.

As it turned out, if the goal was distracting herself, Kennedy should have picked a game that required more skill than simple color recognition.

She lost herself several times in her musings until Nick had to remind her to take her turn on more than one occasion. Neither of them talked about Noah. Neither of them mentioned the dead senator, but Kennedy could tell Nick was about as distracted as she was. When he won the game, neither bothered to suggest a rematch.

"I think Sandy's got some chamomile tea in her cupboards." Nick went to the kitchen and filled the kettle with water. "Care to share a cup with me?"

Kennedy couldn't pinpoint what was so strange about a single bachelor with dreadlocks taking chamomile tea as his nighttime beverage of choice, but she declined. "I think I'll just head to my room and read some." Who would have thought a game of Candyland could be so draining?

Nick looked like he had something else he wanted to say, but when he stayed quiet, Kennedy wished him goodnight and headed to the Lindgrens' guest room. She knew she wouldn't sleep, but her eyes could use a short rest. She'd slept the day away like King Duncan's drugged bodyguards in *Macbeth*, but she hadn't taken her contacts out. The lenses were dry and scratchy against her corneas. She rummaged through her backpack for some eye drops when she came across the book Reuben gave her last spring.

The Last Battle by C. S. Lewis. He had known back then. Had known he wouldn't be coming back to campus. Had known it was time to tell Kennedy good-bye. Part of her had known then, too. Known that as great as a friend as he was, it could never turn into anything deeper. She'd prayed about it over the summer. Prayed a lot. And the more her heart wanted to beg God to bring Reuben back in her life, the more she suspected he was asking her to let go.

It didn't make the sacrifice any easier.

Kennedy had dated a few boys in high school, but her dad had been right when he told her they weren't interested in her. Reuben was the first guy who'd really loved her. She was sure of it. He wasn't like those boys in high school who just wanted to flirt or make out. She couldn't understand it entirely, but she knew in some way his decision to stay in Nairobi was a sacrifice he was making for her. For Kennedy. So she could move on instead of falling in love with an HIV-positive exchange student who would only distract her from her academic goals.

The irony was she had no idea how she'd pass two lab courses this year without him by her side.

She thumbed through the pages of the Narnia book and reread the inscription Reuben had written for her on the front cover.

To my dearest friend Kennedy. Thank you for giving me the best year of my life. All my love, Reuben.

She shut the book and hugged it. Her mom told her it was best to move on. Stay friends with Reuben, keep emailing and Skyping if she wanted, but let him go as far as romance was concerned. The only problem was her mom never told her how. How to rip someone out of your heart who had never hurt you, who only wanted to do what was best for you. How to turn away from your biggest encourager, your biggest support. Everyone said sophomore year was the most grueling for pre-med students. And she was about to walk into it jetlagged and completely alone.

God has a plan. She was sick of hearing that from so many well-meaning Christians. *God has a plan.* Well, Kennedy had a plan too. What was wrong with hers?

She tucked the book into her backpack and checked her phone for emails. Maybe Reuben had written her. She had an entire folder of deleted drafts, letters she'd started to write to him, telling him she didn't care about the HIV, didn't care about the differences in culture. She wanted to be with him and would do anything she could to make it work out. But something always stopped her. Maybe it was the Holy Spirit. She didn't know. Some Christians were great at "hearing from God," at knowing just what he wanted them to do at any given time. But Kennedy was never like that. She had the Bible, and she had wisdom gleaned from her parents and the Lindgrens and other teachers from her growing-up years. And that was it.

Then again, even if she heard from God, even if a voice called down from heaven and told her it was time to give up her love for Reuben, she knew it would be just as difficult. Just as impossible. Maybe time was the answer. Maybe in a month, a year, she'd look back and thank God he hadn't allowed things to progress any farther between them. When she graduated from Harvard, she didn't want to have that nagging *what if* still stuck in the back of her head. What if Reuben hadn't been sick? What if he hadn't dropped out of school? What if the two of them hadn't been scared to share their emotions before it was too late?

Eventually, Kennedy would have to let him go. The only question was how.

She heard the teakettle whistling in the kitchen and lay down on the bed. Maybe she could convince her body to take a little nap. It couldn't hurt to try.

The second she shut her eyes, visions of Wayne Abernathy flashed through her mind. Had he burned to death in his sleep? What if the whole thing was a terrible accident, nothing more? What was going on with the investigation? She hoped they found Noah soon so at least he could clear his name. There had to be a good reason why he wasn't at his house during the fire. There had to be a good reason why he hadn't checked in with anybody.

Snippets from Dominic's prayer around the Lindgrens' dinner table played in her mind. Prayers for comfort for Vivian and the rest of the family. Prayers for Noah's safety, wherever he was. Kennedy noticed that Dominic never specifically prayed for Noah to be found. He just asked for the truth to be disclosed.

God knew where Noah was. Maybe that's what Kennedy should be praying about. Praying for Noah, the boy suspected of setting the fire that killed his own father. What did a little broken heart compare to something like that? And then the whole homosexuality thing. Kennedy could only imagine what Channel 2 would have to say about it when the story broke.

Poor Noah ...

A high-pitched beeping grated against Kennedy's ears. At first she thought it was the teakettle. What was Nick doing out there? Why was he making so much noise?

"Kennedy?" Sandy was yelling from down the hallway. "Kennedy!" There was fear in her voice. Fear and something else. Panic.

Anxiety swelled up in Kennedy's chest cavity, sitting heavy on her sternum and compressing her lungs.

"Kennedy!" Sandy threw the door open. "Come on, sweetie. We all have to get out. The house is on fire."

CHAPTER 11

Sirens wailed, and strobing lights pierced the darkness in flashing shades of red and blue. Carl held Woong against his chest as they huddled in the driveway across the street.

"What's that?" For once, Woong wasn't kicking or screaming.

"Those are the firefighters, hon." Sandy ran her fingers through her son's hair. "They're making sure everyone's safe."

Kennedy couldn't believe it. By the time Carl and Sandy got everyone out of the house, the entire back bedroom was engulfed in flames that now leaped and danced from the rooftop. So many firefighters scurried around that Kennedy couldn't guess how many of them there were. A few other neighbors were out of their homes as well in various stages of undress. At least it wasn't a cold night.

"How did this happen?" There was a tremor in Sandy's voice. Kennedy wanted to hug her but felt shy for some reason. Usually, Sandy was the one to comfort her, not the other way around. "Why would anyone do this to us?"

Carl slipped his arm around his wife's waist. "It might have been an accident. We won't know until they check everything out."

"Senseless," Sandy was muttering. "What were they thinking? That was Woong's room." Her voice cracked, and she wiped tears from her cheeks. "A little boy. A helpless little boy."

Carl held his son closer and cleared his throat. Then, as the firefighters doused the last of the roaring flames, he lifted up his booming voice in prayer. "Lord, great God and heavenly Father, we give you thanks. We give you thanks and praise, Lord, because there ain't nothing in that house that can't be replaced. We give you thanks and praise, Jesus, because you kept us all safe. The enemy came tonight. He came to steal, kill, and destroy, but you said no. No, you weren't going to let our family suffer harm. Our house could have burned to the ground, and you would have just provided us with another. But you knew, Lord, you knew how important we were to each other. You knew how precious each life here is, and you saved us. God, we love you. You didn't have to do it, Lord. You didn't have to get us all out of there in time. I'm sure there'll be mourning, Father. Mourning for the things we lost, the things we're sure we can't live without. But remind us, Jesus. Remind us of what we do have. Remind us of the way you stepped down and intervened and told the devil he couldn't destroy our family. He couldn't destroy our faith. The house can burn, but we'll go on praising your name. Yes, Lord Jesus, because you're our Savior, and there is nothing in this world more precious or valuable than you."

There was no amen, no loud announcements or proclamations, just a peace that settled in the air around them and lingered as they nestled together on the sidewalk.

"I'm hungry." Woong started to squirm, but Carl didn't put him down.

"Not now, son. We can't go home yet."

Kennedy stared at the house. The men had extinguished the flames, but a black, smoldering smoke still hissed from the rooftop. A firefighter in his bright yellow suit lumbered toward them, taking off his mask as he neared. "It got that back room pretty bad. Not sure how much you'll be able to save from there, but the rest of the house looks all right."

"Thank the Lord," Sandy whispered.

The firefighter frowned. "It's not safe for you to enter right now, and I heard the police are on their way. Want to rule out arson."

Sandy glared at her husband. "I told you it was ..."

"The thing is, we can't have you staying here tonight," he interrupted. "We have some numbers if you need help finding shelter. There's a social worker on call who'll help with all those arrangements unless you ..."

"You all can crash at my place tonight." Nick had been so quiet Kennedy almost forgot he was there. "It'll be a tight squeeze, but we'll manage."

"I don't know." Carl frowned. "What time is it? Almost two? Maybe we'd be better off just springing for a hotel. No use storing money in an emergency fund if you don't ..."

"Let me take care of you. Please." Nick pointed at the bus parked sloppily on the sidewalk. "I've got my keys right here. Woong and Kennedy can sleep on the couches. You two can take my bed. It might be crowded, but it won't be any inconvenience at all."

Crowded wasn't the first word that popped into Kennedy's mind when she entered Nick's apartment. The couch where Woong was supposed to sleep was covered in so many X-box games and discarded snack wrappers Kennedy couldn't tell what color the cushions were until Nick dumped everything into a big Ramen box. Woong had fallen asleep on the ride over, so Carl tucked him in as carefully as he could.

The other couch wasn't quite as big of a mess, but it still took Nick several minutes to sweep off all the Cheetos crumbs and popcorn kernels. "Sorry. We had an X-box tournament a couple nights ago, and I didn't get the chance to tidy up yet."

"Everything is just fine," Sandy lied pleasantly. Kennedy wondered if there was a polite way to ask for a sheet to place over the couch before she actually stretched out on it. She'd probably be too squeamish to rest here anyway. Who knew what kinds of bugs or rodents fed off all those crumbs?

"You better let me check on the bedroom before you get too comfortable," he told the Lindgrens apologetically.

Sandy smiled as she glanced at the music posters stapled up on Nick's walls. "Nice place, isn't it?"

Carl didn't answer. Neither did Kennedy.

"Doesn't she have a pretty face?" Sandy fingered a photo of a blonde girl, the only picture in the room that actually had a frame. She picked it up off the coffee table and passed it to Kennedy. "Looks like she belongs on the cover of a magazine, doesn't she?"

Kennedy squinted at the girl in her bright green and yellow sundress. There was something familiar about her smile.

Nick came out of the room and tossed two full trash bags by his front door. "It's not perfect, but I figured after all you'd been through, you'd rather get to sleep sooner than later. I'd change the sheets for you, but it's been a little while since I've made it to the laundromat, and ..."

"Don't you say another word, young man." Sandy came over and gave him a little side hug. "You've been more than hospitable taking us in like this. We sure are thankful."

Nick wiped his forehead. "Thanks. I just wish I ..."

Sandy cut him off. "Not another word. You have a good night, and don't forget that you and Kennedy need your sleep just as much as the rest of us. I don't want to come out here in the morning to hear you've blabbed the night away." She was smiling, but her words were stern so it was hard to tell if she was teasing or giving them an ultimatum.

"We'll behave," Nick promised.

Carl clasped Nick on the back. "You're a good man, son. You don't know what it means to me to have you taking in my family like this."

Family. Something in the way he said the word twisted Kennedy's heart between her ribs. Less than twenty-four hours on American soil, and she was already homesick? What she wanted more than anything was to call her mom and dad, but her phone was back at the Lindgrens'. So was her backpack, her Shakespeare books, her copy of *The Last Battle* from Reuben. Had the firemen saved it? It could have been so much worse. But it still happened. Was she supposed to be thankful? Sure, God had kept her and the Lindgrens safe, but couldn't he have stopped those flames before they even began?

Carl wasn't convinced it was arson, but what else could it be? Houses don't just burn themselves down. Especially not two in the same night. No, this was definitely not a coincidence. Someone had targeted Carl and Sandy. The same person who had targeted the Abernathys. Who could be that vindictive? That murderous?

And why should the Lindgrens think they were out of danger now?

The fire had started in Woong's room. She stared at his curled up form tucked under a ratty blanket on Nick's couch. Sure, he could be loud and he threw fits whenever he didn't get his way, but who would wish harm on someone so young? So helpless? Was the perpetrator really so cruel he'd resort to killing an innocent boy to get his point across?

And what point was he trying to make, exactly? If it had just been the senator's home that had burned down, there could have been a dozen different suspects with a dozen different motives, each one just as plausible as the others. But now that the Lindgrens were involved, too ... Who would want to harm both families? Who would want to burn both their houses down?

It seemed even more important to reach Noah soon. Could they get any real answers without him?

Kennedy watched Nick pull some camping gear out of an overstuffed closet. "Can I help you with anything?" she asked.

"Nah." He tugged a sleeping bag free. "I think I'll just set this up in the hall and try to get some sleep." He shuffled his feet and stared at the couch. "I'm really sorry the place isn't any cleaner. It's not always ..." He looked around. "Ok, well, it's sometimes this bad, but if I'd known you'd all be coming, I would have put in a little extra effort."

"I don't think anyone minds." Kennedy pointed at Woong, who had just rolled over with a contented sigh. He looked so much sweeter, so much more peaceful now that he was asleep.

"Well, can you think of anything you need before I set up camp for the night?"

She glanced at his microwave clock. Two thirty-six. It was going to be a long stretch until morning. "Got any books?"

A grin broke across his face. "I thought you'd never ask."

Nick had converted half the storage areas in his kitchen into little mini-libraries. "This is where I keep my theology stuff." He opened the cupboard above his stove. Kennedy was surprised by how orderly everything was. Either he cared a lot more about his books than he did the rest of his belongings, or he'd set them up the day he moved in here and hadn't touched them since. Based on how worn some of the covers looked, she guessed it was the former reason.

Kennedy skimmed the titles. There was a lot about youth ministry there, as well as two books on homosexuality and the church that caught her eye.

"I keep my politics stuff here," he said, opening another cupboard by the sink. His selection looked quite a bit like her dad's, except the titles were probably newer. Her dad liked to joke that all his reading money was now funneled into Kennedy's college textbook fund.

"Over here is my favorite." He opened up his pantry, where he kept a whole section of sci-fi and fantasy. If Kennedy got desperate she could flip through the poems in *Lord of the Rings*. Her dad had forced her to read the entire trilogy when she was a high school sophomore, but she had skipped the songs and poetry to make the story move along faster. Maybe she'd appreciate those parts if she could read them at her leisure.

"It's probably not the kinds of books you usually pick out." Nick frowned.

"No, don't worry about that. It's actually really cool how you made space for all them. I'm sure I'll find enough to keep me going."

"You want heavy reading, find Grudem's *Systematic Theology*. It's in the cupboard by the microwave. Big thick one. Probably changed my life more than anything else besides the Bible."

Kennedy tried to determine if there was a single book she could say the same thing about. There were books she loved, books that encouraged or inspired her, books that she could read and reread and always find something new. But change her life?

Maybe she'd check it out.

After spending a little time with Tolkien.

She pulled out *The Fellowship of the Ring*. "Thanks again."

"Any time." Nick lingered in the kitchen. Swept a dread out of his eye. Drummed his fingers on the counter and let out a nervous laugh. "Oh, speaking of Harvard ..."

Kennedy tried to hide her confusion. When had they been speaking of Harvard?

"I know you're probably going to be really busy this semester, and I totally understand, but I wanted to ask you something. And you're welcome to say no, it's not like it's going to hurt my feelings or anything, but well, I've been thinking about it for a while now, and I've been wanting to find time to ask you all night if you'd ..."

He didn't get the chance to finish, because Woong sat up on the couch with a shriek. As Kennedy and Nick rushed over, he let out a second scream that could have scared all three of Macbeth's witches speechless.

CHAPTER 12

"*Bul! Bul!*" Woong thrashed his limbs around wildly.

"What's he saying?" Nick asked.

"Fire." Kennedy squatted down by the couch. "The fire's out," she told him. "You're safe now. Safe." She repeated the word in Korean, but it did nothing to calm him down or keep him from kicking her in the chin. "Ow!"

Nick knelt down beside her and grabbed Woong by the shoulders. "It's ok. You're at my house. Remember me, buddy? It's Nick. I work with your daddy."

Woong flung himself forward. Nick moved in time for Woong's forehead to hit him in the cheek instead of the nose.

"Calm down," Kennedy told him in Korean, using as authoritative a voice as she could. She positioned her face so she'd be in his field of vision, but she was ready to move out of his way if he decided to try for another head butt. "Calm down," she repeated. "You're ok. Your mom and dad are here, too. Everyone's safe."

He scratched at her face. She would never underestimate the amount of damage fingernails could cause again.

"Wait a minute." Nick reached over and flicked on a lamp. "I'm not sure he's awake."

"He's not." Sandy bustled down the hall toward them. "Woong, honey? Woong, you're having a bad dream now. It's not real." She stayed a full yard away from him until Carl came up beside her.

"*Bul!*" Woong shouted again. His eyes were wide open, but they were vacant. Empty. "*Bul!*"

"There's no fire," Sandy told him as Carl grabbed his arms in a bear hug. Woong flung his head, still shrieking, but Carl dodged it expertly.

"Nick, hon, do you have a bigger blanket we could use?" Sandy asked.

Nick hurried out of the room. Kennedy had never seen someone act like Woong and was trying to figure out how Carl and Sandy could remain so calm. "Is he ok?" she asked.

"It's just night terrors, sweetie." Sandy accepted a blue and white checkered blanket from Nick and helped Carl wrap Woong up in it until everything but his head was swaddled like a burrito. She gave his forehead a kiss. "Daddy's gonna pray for you now, and then you'll get that good rest your body needs to grow big and strong, ok?"

Woong kept on thrashing as Carl started to pray. At first, Kennedy thought the Lindgrens were crazy for not rushing Woong to the emergency room. She had never heard anyone — man, woman, or child — scream so loud, as if his soul was tormented by a legion of demons. Halfway through Carl's prayer, Woong let out a loud, choppy breath. A minute later, he was sleeping peacefully in his father's arms.

"I love you, son." Carl kissed him on the head. "You gonna do the honors tonight, my dear?" he asked.

"I think so." Sandy stroked Woong's hair and then explained, "We like to spend the next hour or two with him just in case the same thing happens again."

"Why don't you let me carry him to the bedroom?" Carl stood up with his bundle. "I'll sleep on the couch."

Sandy adjusted her skirt. "Thank you, babe."

Carl carried Woong down the hall, and Nick shifted his weight from one foot to the other. "I guess that fire got him pretty freaked out, eh?"

Sandy sighed. "Well, maybe. But truth be told, he's been screaming about fires before tonight. That's how Carl and I knew the Korean for it. Heard it so often in his night terrors we looked it up."

"Have you asked him about it when he's awake?" Nick asked.

"The night terrors he doesn't remember. And the fires, well, we talked with the psychologist about it, but she says not to ask too many questions straight off. When Woong's ready to talk, he'll let us know what he's so scared of."

Kennedy was amazed at how calm Sandy could be after listening to those ear-splitting shrieks. It would be a miracle if one of the neighbors in Nick's apartment complex hadn't called 911 and summoned a dozen police officers to rescue a torture victim.

"So do you think he'll sleep through the night?" she asked.

"Oh yeah. Now that he's calm again, not even the Tribulation would wake that boy up. We just stay with him as a precaution, really. Gives us more time to pray over him, too."

Sandy wrapped her arms around Carl when he came back into the living room. He kissed her on the cheek. "Your bed buddy awaits you, my dear."

"Thanks, babe." She pecked him back on the lips and wished everyone a good night.

Carl sat on the couch with a loud sigh. "Well, I guess this doesn't make for too bad of a bed. You both go right ahead and keep visiting or whatever it is the two of you were doing before you got interrupted. I can sleep with the lights on and noise in the background." He stretched out his legs and rested them on the cluttered coffee table. "Been doing it straight for the last three weeks," he added under his breath. "And I'm a hard sleeper, so I won't even tell Sandy what you two yacked about all night."

Nick blushed slightly. Kennedy tried to guess what he was about to ask her before Woong broke out with his inconsolable screaming.

Carl groaned slightly as he shifted his weight. "And Kennedy, I'm apologizing in advance if I snore too loud."

"It'll be a while before I can sleep. It's a good thing Nick has so many books here or else ..."

"So you've looked through Nick's library, have you?" Carl frowned even though his eyes still smiled. "You read the one that tells you how all Christians should trade in their work shoes for leather sandals and turn into a bunch of hippie socialists? Because we all know how well communism works out as a political system, don't we?"

Kennedy glanced at Nick. He didn't appear to notice her at all. "It was just one title I said had at least some merit for Christians to consider."

"Right." Carl nodded. "And let me guess. You have just one title about how God's people have gotten the homosexuality question wrong for six millennia, but conveniently for all the gays and lesbians out there, God decided to tell the real story to some twenty-year-old theologian-wannabe who's letting the world know that as long as you're happy, God's not gonna judge you since, after all, he's a God of love, right?"

Nick rolled his eyes. "Right. And kicking your gay son out of your home and threatening to disown him is a much more Christ-like way to live."

Kennedy wished there was a way to step in and make them stop bickering. She wouldn't be surprised if Sandy appeared in the hallway and ordered them both to bed.

Carl was leaning forward now as if he were ready to spring to his feet at a moment's notice. "Now, I'm not saying what Wayne Abernathy did to his son was justified. But in the public arena, he did a lot of good upholding the sanctity of marriage."

"Because life-long gay unions are such a direct threat to monogamous, heterosexual couples like you and Sandy. And applauding a professional photographer for dropping a lesbian wedding after she's already taken their two-thousand-dollar deposit is a powerful step forward for religious freedom."

Kennedy hoped neither of them would notice when she slipped onto the second couch and picked up the Tolkien book.

"I'm not saying I agree with what that photographer did," Carl argued. "I'm saying that the state has an obligation to uphold religious freedom. They can't make a private business owner go against her conscience ..."

"Just like in the fifties they couldn't make a private homeowner go against his conscience and rent his house to blacks. Don't you hear what you're saying?"

Kennedy was glad her first year at Harvard had taught her to read and stay focused with all manner of strange noises assaulting her from all corners of her dormitory.

"This isn't the Civil Rights Movement, son."

Nick dropped into a folding chair. "No, but it should be. Jesus told us to reach out to the oppressed. The weak. The marginalized. And what do our churches do today? Paint big, huge *No Gays Allowed* signs on their entryways and pat themselves on their backs for their pharisaical righteousness. But look at what Jesus did. He sat down and ate with hookers and extortionists. He didn't hate on them. Didn't ban them from his congregation. Didn't vote for legislation to remove them from the public eye."

"You're absolutely right. And he didn't call everyone who disagreed with their lifestyles bigots and homophobes, either."

"True. He called them broods of vipers and sons of the devil instead."

Carl smiled faintly. "The people Jesus called a brood of vipers in Matthew 12 were those who refused to believe that God can grant miraculous healing. He called another group children of the devil because they wouldn't admit they were slaves to sin. Unfortunately for your argument, I don't read a lot of bigotry or homophobia into those passages."

Nick let out his breath. Kennedy flipped through *The Fellowship of the Ring*, trying to find Tom Bombadil's song.

Carl stood and put his hand on Nick's shoulder. "I know we have our disagreements. And I know you've had some painful experiences that make this a very real and very personal issue for you, and I'm not downplaying that. Not in the least. These are good discussions for us to have, and I'm glad God's using us to sharpen each other like iron sharpens iron. Let's just make sure we're using that sharpness for healing and edification, not for stabbing each other, all right? I'm talking to both of us now, myself as much as you."

Nick sighed. "You're right. I know it can be hard for us to ..."

He was interrupted by a discordant, tinny refrain.

Peace washes over me. Peace washes over me.

It was the Babylon Eunuchs and their ridiculously drawn-out worship chorus. Nick pulled his phone out of his pocket.

"Hello?" A frown. He looked confused. "I'm having a hard time understanding you. Is this Jodie?"

Kennedy glanced up from her book and winced. All night she'd been worried about Noah. Why hadn't she stopped to pray for his little sister, too?

"No, I can hear you now. That's a lot better."

She had never seen Nick doing any actual youth ministry before tonight, but she could understand why Jodie would have reached out to call him on a night like this.

"That's ok. You just gotta try to slow down your breathing a little bit ... Uh-huh. Your body just doesn't know what to do with all the fear and grief, so it ..."

Kennedy tried to focus on her book. Why was she always getting stuck in the middle of these horrifically private conversations?

"Sure, I can come visit you. You said you're staying at your grandma's house? ... Yeah, I know that neighborhood pretty well. You can text me the address and I'll find it just fine. Is your mom there? ... She's with the police still? Ok, well you know I can't meet with you alone, right? So maybe what I'll do is ..."

He glanced at Kennedy, and she nodded without waiting for the question. He covered the mouthpiece with his hand. "You sure?"

"Yeah."

"Ok, Jodie? You know what? How would you feel if Kennedy comes with me? Kennedy Stern? ... Ok, we'll be there as soon as we can. We're leaving right now."

Kennedy slipped on her shoes. Tolkien and Tom Bombadil would have to wait.

CHAPTER 13

"Thanks for coming with me," Nick said as they drove. "It's just policy for me not to meet with any of the girls alone."

"No problem. Where does Jodie's grandma live?" Kennedy asked.

"We should be there in about ten minutes." Nick glanced at his phone.

Kennedy wished he'd keep his eyes on the road and let her navigate. "Did she say much when you talked to her?"

He shook his head. "No, she was pretty broken up. Makes sense after your house burns down and your dad dies."

Kennedy didn't know how to answer. She prayed she would have the right words for Jodie. Maybe her jetlag was a blessing, at least in this instance. She'd be staying up all night whether or not anybody else needed her to.

Nick strummed his fingers on the steering wheel to an inaudible beat. She wondered if he was the kind of person who always had a tune playing in his head. Wouldn't it feel intrusive? Disruptive, maybe?

"So what'd you think of everything Pastor Carl said back there?" Nick's question caught her off guard.

"I'm not really sure, to be honest." She figured if she wanted to contribute anything constructive to these kinds of conversations with Nick, she'd have to switch from reading classics to politics and theology. If she found some extra time over the next few days, maybe she'd borrow a few of Nick's books or check out some of those websites her dad followed and see what they had to say on the subject. "Right now, it seems like I have a lot more questions than answers," she admitted.

"Questions are good. What kind of questions?"

"I don't know." Kennedy stared out her window. "Like if people like Noah are born gay or not. If it's a sin to be attracted to the same gender. Stuff like that." She got the feeling she was digging herself into a pit deeper than Ophelia's grave, and once she jumped down in it, there'd be no avenging brother waiting there to pull her out.

Nick turned to look at her. "Those are all good questions."

Kennedy was glad he didn't laugh. "What about you? Sounds like you and Carl have some differing opinions on the subject."

"Carl's old school." Nick glanced at the map on his phone once more. "And believe me, I know he means well. But he's got his blind spots. Thinks legalizing gay marriage would be the worst thing that could happen to our country, when really the divorce rates are proof enough the typical American refuses to take marriage very seriously in the first place. It's not like the Lindgrens will attend a gay wedding and then all of a sudden they're going to be tempted to dissolve their marriage, know what I mean? But they make it out like it's this big freedom of religion issue when it's not. I mean, seriously, what could be so bad about giving two women a piece of paper that says they live together and can share joint assets?"

A snippet of a conversation Kennedy had with her dad flitted through her mind. "But what about adoption? If you allow these couples to get married, what's going to stop them from adopting children?" She tried to remember the details of her dad's argument. Hadn't there been some big congressional hearing about how detrimental it was for kids to be raised in same-sex homes?

Nick chuckled. "Do you have any idea how many kids there are in foster care waiting for permanent placements who couldn't care less if they've got two moms or two dads or a partridge in a pear tree as long as they're loved and cared for?"

"But a nuclear family ..." Kennedy tried to insert before Nick interrupted.

"Let me ask you a question. Do you think kids do best in homes raised by two parents, a mom and a dad?"

"Yes." Of course she did. Wasn't sociology on her side? Didn't every single research study ever done prove her right?

"Ok, and what if one of the parents dies? Can a single mom or a single dad still successfully raise their kids, or does the state need to take the children away and find a nice, heterosexual two-parent home for them?"

"No. That would be ridiculous." She got the sense that Nick was mocking her but couldn't follow his line of reasoning. Not yet, at least.

"You're right. So if a single parent can raise a kid well, why is it so far of a stretch to assume that two same-sex parents can also raise a kid well? In some ways, wouldn't it be even better, since theoretically one parent could stay home if they chose to and spend more time with the children? Not to mention the built-in benefits that come from sharing parenting responsibilities, right?"

"But I've seen the studies." For the first time in her life, Kennedy was glad for those stupid politics links her dad would randomly email her. "Kids with a mom and a dad in the home get better test scores, have better health and nutrition, grow up to earn more money ..."

"Ok, so let's assume those studies are completely objective and true. That's a big jump right there, but let's assume it for the sake of argument. So what you're saying is that in order to give adopted kids a better chance at life, they need to go to heterosexual, monogamous homes, right? Because your study shows that's where kids thrive the most. So what if I gave you studies that say kids who grow up in minority homes face more challenges than whites? Shouldn't it logically follow that we make legislation that prevents Blacks and Hispanics from adopting? Or what about a study that says that kids are more likely to get a college education if their parents have a degree? Should we tell the girl who took night classes for a year to get her GED, 'Sorry, but you're not qualified to be a mom?'"

"That's not what I'm saying." Kennedy didn't know how to argue. It wasn't fair for Nick to drag her into these kinds of debates when he knew she hadn't studied to the degree he had.

"I'm sorry." He swiped his screen and studied the map again. "I mean, I totally get that a lot of Christians can't get past the book of Leviticus and have to hold onto the notion that all homosexuality is wrong. But that's what gets good kids like Noah out on the streets. I work at this homeless shelter for teens every other Friday night. You know what? A lot of them are there just because their biology doesn't agree with their parents' standards of normal. Did I tell you I met a kid once whose dad actually paid for him to have sex with a prostitute to try to 'fix' him and make him straight? I mean it. I couldn't make this stuff up if I wanted. The boy was a virgin. Most he'd ever done was flirt with a boy or two in some internet chatroom. So what's his dad do? Risks STDs and subjects his own child to unthinkable sexual abuse to straighten him out. I'm sorry, but does that sound like the way Jesus would handle the situation?"

Of course it wasn't, but that didn't mean Nick had all the answers, did it? She was tired. Tired of the arguing. Debates that spun around in circles like a dog chasing its tail, except there was nothing cute or amusing about any of it.

Noah's dad was dead. Their house burned. Carl and Sandy's too. Woong could have been killed. How could there be a resolution to this entire convoluted debate if either side resorted to arson and murder? Where was the justice? The compassion? Kennedy's roommate Willow had sent her a petition last semester. Some group in Africa was gang-raping lesbians in order to "cure" them. Of course, Kennedy had signed the appeal. At the time, that sort of abuse had felt so foreign. So far from her little Harvard bubble. Did things like that truly happen in the US? Could they?

And those weren't the only questions vying for her mental focus. Who had set the fire that killed Wayne Abernathy? And where was his son? Why was he hiding?

Nick's phone beeped, and he slowed the bus to turn down a residential side street. He leaned over to read the addresses better before pulling into a modest-sized home with a small picket fence lining the walkway up to the porch.

"Here we are. Let's go see how Jodie's doing."

CHAPTER 14

Jodie looked tired and even more timid than normal when she opened the door for Kennedy and Nick. She put her finger to her lips. "My grandma is trying to get Charlie to sleep."

As far as she could remember, Kennedy had never met Charlie, the Abernathys' nephew they adopted last fall.

Kennedy slipped her shoes off while Nick gave Jodie a big hug. "I'm so sorry," he whispered.

And that's when Jodie started to cry. Huge drops that seemed to defy just about every law of gravity and physics slid slowly down her cheeks, dissolving into the yellow and brown shag carpet of her grandmother's house.

"I'm sorry," Nick repeated.

Kennedy was always at a loss in situations like these, always felt as clumsy as a court jester when she tried offering comfort to someone. She looked around. Maybe there was some Kleenex she could pass on to Jodie. It beat standing around staring while she cried.

"Want to sit down and talk?" Nick gestured to the couch.

Jodie followed him, her head bent low. She had always been a petite and demure little thing. Now, she looked as pathetic as a puppy caught out in a rainstorm. She couldn't catch her breath between her sobs. The sound of her gasping cries seized Kennedy's lungs up as well.

Take every thought captive.

She wasn't a slave to anxiety anymore. Her deliverance hadn't come through some miraculous, dramatic event. Some healings took longer than others, she had come to realize. Jesus healed the leper with a single touch. He was healing her PTSD, by contrast, in small steps at a time, so that she had to measure her progress in months instead of days or even weeks.

God has not given us a spirit that makes us a slave again to fear.

She had the power of the Holy Spirit in her. That didn't mean she could cast out her anxiety like an unruly demon, but it did mean she could turn her thoughts toward Jesus. Ask him to carry her through this trial. Show himself real and present to her in the midst of the difficult times.

Kennedy focused on her breathing but then stopped herself. What was she doing? It was Jodie's father who'd been murdered, not hers. It was Jodie who was hyperventilating on the couch. And Kennedy was standing there worrying only about herself. What was a little tightness in your chest compared to the grief of losing your father?

When had she grown to be so selfish?

She sat down on the other side of Jodie and took her hand. "I'm sorry." It sounded so much lamer coming out of her mouth than Nick's. What was it he had that made him so present, so accessible to these teens when they needed him? It was a good thing he was the youth pastor, not her.

"Have you heard anything from your mom?" Nick asked.

Jodie sniffed loudly, and Kennedy glanced around once more looking for tissue.

"No, she's been talking with this detective all night. They say that ..." Her voice caught. She wiped her nose with her sleeve and tried again. "They say that ..." She rolled her eyes up toward the ceiling as if the words might be written up there. "The detective thinks my dad was murdered."

"It can take a few days for them to find out if something like this is arson or just an accident." Kennedy was glad for all those crime scene novels she liked to read in high school. At least she could offer something more useful than an awkward apology. "It's probably too soon for them to know anything now. They must just be talking with your mom in case ..."

"It wasn't the fire that killed him."

Kennedy caught Nick's eye. He looked as surprised as she was.

"What do you mean?" she asked at the same time Nick said, "Maybe we don't need to talk about that right now."

Kennedy shut her mouth.

"I just can't believe any of this is real." Jodie was leaning her head against Nick's chest. Kennedy understood why he hadn't wanted to come here alone.

He rested his cheek on the top of her head. "I know, kiddo. These things always seem to take a lot of time to sink in."

Kennedy wondered if Nick knew that from firsthand experience, or if it was something he read in one of his many youth ministry books.

"I keep thinking it's a bad dream."

Kennedy had heard people say things like that in novels, and it had always sounded so cliché to her. Maybe the authors actually got it right.

"That's normal. Sometimes it won't feel real for days." Nick spoke slowly. Kennedy realized how relaxing his voice could be if he weren't fumbling over his words or getting so worked up about political controversies. "That's the thing about grief."

"That's right." Kennedy patted Jodie's hand, wondering why that was such a common physical response. It's not like Jodie was a kitten or a puppy in need of attention. "Scientists think that maybe it's the brain's defense mechanism so that you don't have to ..." She stopped herself. Why was she giving the poor girl a psychology lesson? Maybe she should have read some of Nick's books herself. Or gotten lessons in grief counseling. Some people were just so much better at this sort of situation. Like Sandy. She always knew what to say when people were hurting. It was as if the Holy Spirit just opened her mouth and out poured words of comfort and love, as if she knew the very message the listener needed to hear. Kennedy tried to imagine what Sandy would say if she were here, but all she could think about was how tired she had looked when she headed to Nick's bedroom to sleep with Woong. Kennedy just hoped Jodie and Nick were too distracted to realize how horribly she was botching this conversation.

Jodie shook her head. "I can't figure out who would do this to him. He's the nicest guy I know. The best ..." She stopped herself again. A little moan escaped.

Nick patted her on the back. "For now, try not to worry about the investigation or anything like that. It could have been a bad accident. We don't know ..."

"It was the golf club." Jodie wasn't making any sense. Kennedy wondered if maybe she was delirious. Grief could do that, couldn't it?

For once Nick didn't seem to know what to say, either. They both waited while Jodie caught her breath.

"The golf club," she repeated. "Someone hit him on the head. Cracked open his skull. The detective said he was dead before the fire even started."

CHAPTER 15

As much as Kennedy would have liked to get more information from Jodie about the fire, she knew better than to press for details. Nick seemed to be doing a perfectly fine job offering all the comfort and support he could, so Kennedy let him do his work without trying to force herself into a conversation she obviously wasn't qualified to handle. Give her a spectrophotometer and a cuvette full of solution, and she could calculate the absorbance of just about anything. Give her a crying girl and a murdered politician, and she was about as useful as Friar Laurence was in keeping Romeo and Juliet alive.

For lack of anything better to do, Kennedy spent her time observing Nick, making mental notes about the way he handled things. Maybe it would help her in the future. If it had been Kennedy leading the conversation, she would have tried to fill in every single silence with some kind of clichéd word of encouragement. Nick, by contrast, seemed perfectly content with long spells of quiet. That was lesson number one.

He listened while Jodie talked about the fire, how she'd heard the alarms and hurried to get Charlie out of his toddler bed. "He was crying. Like he already knew something was wrong."

Jodie talked about how she ran with him downstairs to the mailbox, which is where their family had agreed to meet in emergencies. Up until that point, Kennedy thought her dad was the only one who came up with fire escape plans. She wondered if Wayne had grilled his family about safety measures in the event of earthquakes, tornados, and tsunamis, too.

During a long pause, Nick stood and got Jodie a glass of water from the kitchen. Lesson number two. Why hadn't Kennedy thought of that? She hated feeling so useless. At least when she became a doctor, she'd have plenty of things to do to keep her hands busy so she wouldn't feel so awkward and superfluous in the midst of a crisis. Still, it was a long time before she got her MD.

Jodie took a sip of water. Her hand wasn't shaky. Kennedy was jealous. Nick was doing such a good job calming her down, they couldn't even hear Jodie's choppy breathing anymore.

"So how long did you and Charlie wait alone at the mailbox?" he asked.

"My mom got there a minute later. She was calling 911. She asked me where Dad was, so I said I hadn't seen him yet. I'd only thought to grab Charlie and ..."

Nick didn't say anything. Kennedy wondered how much practice it took to get yourself comfortable with such silence.

"My mom went back in, and I was really scared for her. I thought maybe she'd get stuck in there, you know? Like in the movies when the door's on fire or something so you can't go out. Then I thought I'm glad she's so brave because my dad's been real busy lately with this bill thing he's working on, and so maybe he slept through the alarm. But then I saw my mom was in her pajamas, so wouldn't she have known if dad was sleeping or not 'cause she would have seen him in bed? So that meant he must be awake, but if he was awake, he would have heard the alarm and gotten us all out. So it was real confusing."

Kennedy tried to remember if she'd ever heard Jodie use that many words in a single sitting before. There must be something she could say in reply. A Bible verse, maybe? Tell Jodie that God works all things together for good? How does that comfort a girl whose father's been murdered?

Jodie's grandmother stepped into the living room and cleared her throat.

Nick jumped to his feet. "Hi, Mrs. Olinstein. I hope we aren't bothering you. Jodie said we could stop by for a minute. We didn't mean to ..."

"It's fine." She cut him off with a curt nod. Jodie's grandmother was a frail, somewhat haggard-looking woman, about how Kennedy imagined Vivian Abernathy would appear in thirty years if she were to forgo hair dye, wrinkle cream, and Botox. "Did you get her to tell you where her brother is?"

Nick looked at Kennedy as if she might decipher the old woman's words.

"No, we just got here a few minutes ago. We ..." He didn't finish his sentence.

Jodie's grandmother offered no smile. "I told her she had to tell what she knew or the police would be after her next."

Kennedy tried to think of some protest. Mrs. Olinstein must not know what she was saying. Maybe she suffered from dementia. Maybe she was an Alzheimer's patient who lacked a filter between her brain's thought and language center.

"I told you I don't know where he is." Jodie crossed her arms. Kennedy couldn't imagine her taking that tone with her parents. Maybe there was more to Jodie than she'd seen before.

Mrs. Olinstein stared right at Nick with a smile that was anything but warm. "She's never been a good liar, that one. It's strange. You'd think her dad would have taught her. Heaven knows he's got the experience."

Nick fidgeted with the fringe on a brown and orange afghan thrown across the back of the couch. "Maybe now's not the best time to talk about the senator like that."

Mrs. Olinstein's long, beaded earrings dangled against each other as she cocked her head to the side. "Why not?" Her voice was grating. "Bad form to speak ill of the dead? I didn't realize. Well, you'll have to forgive me. Let's change the subject, shall we? We can talk about why Noah killed his father and burned his house to the ground."

"Noah didn't do any of that." Hot anger radiated from Jodie's small frame.

"How would you know?" her grandma asked. "You don't even know where he's been all night." She smiled haughtily.

"He was with Marcos, ok? I heard them on the phone before the fire started. He went over to see Marcos."

Jodie's grandmother straightened her back and gave Nick a sickeningly sweet smile. "There now. See? I told you she'd been lying."

CHAPTER 16

Nobody said anything. Kennedy kept waiting for Nick or Jodie to break the silence.

Nothing.

Finally, Jodie's grandmother spoke. "All right, then. I see that she doesn't want to say anything else in front of me. Probably thinks that if she talks to you, she'll be protected under whatever pastor confidentiality laws she's read about on the internet. Fine by me, little missy. You just remember that whatever you tell your so-called pastor here, the lawyers are going to ask you at your brother's trial when they prove he's the one who murdered your father. Now don't let me interrupt your little heart-to-heart anymore," she added before anybody could protest. "I'll just check on the kid. Make sure he's nice and comfy. Would have been thoughtful if your mother brought me a crib or something else he can sleep in before dumping him off here. He's probably going to leak right through his diaper and spoil my mattress. Oh, well. That's what happens when Vivian adopts someone else's needy orphan against her better judgment. No, don't bother getting up for me." She waved her hand in the air in a gesture of dismissal. "I'll put myself to bed when I'm done, and I'll trust you to lock up after yourselves when you're through in my home."

She went down the hall and disappeared, leaving nothing but an angry afterglow that settled around the room like a gray New England smog.

"All right," Nick said after another long silence. "Who's this Marcos? And how do you know that's where your brother is, or are you just guessing?"

Jodie looked at Kennedy as if she were asking for support, but Kennedy was more confused than a seventh grader picking up *Romeo and Juliet* for the first time without any footnotes.

"Who's Marcos?" Nick repeated in a softer tone. "Is he Noah's friend from school?"

"I don't know." Jodie's voice was small. Timid. It reminded Kennedy of the very first time they talked over the phone almost a full year ago.

"Well, how do you know that's where Noah is?"

"They talk. Late at night. Our rooms are right next to each other, so sometimes he thinks I'm asleep, but I can hear."

"Is it his boyfriend?"

"I don't think so. I'm not sure."

Kennedy decided if she ever had a daughter of her own, she'd teach her to speak up loud and clear. Life lesson number one: No demure mumbling. It wasn't feminine. It wasn't cute. It was annoying, and that was about all.

"What do they talk about?"

Kennedy wasn't sure she'd be pressing so hard if she were in Nick's position. Hadn't Noah been through enough? Didn't he deserve at least some small shred of privacy? Then again, if he was still a suspect in his father's murder ...

It couldn't really be. Could it?

"They talk about boys." Jodie's voice was even softer. Maybe she didn't want her grandma to overhear. Unfortunately, with as public a life as Wayne Abernathy led, there was no way any of these details would stay secret for long.

"So, you mean like boys at school?" Nick gave Kennedy a questioning look. Apparently, he was as lost as she was.

"No, they talk about Noah. About how he likes boys. And they pray."

"Pray?" Nick repeated.

Jodie nodded. "He asks God to fix him. You know. So he likes girls and stuff."

Anger flashed through Nick's eyes. Unfiltered, unmistakable anger. He composed himself after a few seconds. "So this Marcos, he's like a counselor or something?" His voice was soft, but his whole body remained completely rigid.

"Yeah, maybe something like that."

"Is he older, then? An adult, I mean?"

"Maybe." Jodie shrugged. "I never met him."

"So how do you know Nick was going to meet with this Marcos guy?"

"I heard them talking on the phone. Noah was mad. Said it was all Marcos's fault, and then he said something like, *Fine. You can show me when I get there.* I didn't pay all that much attention. It was late, and I was trying to sleep."

Nick adjusted one of his dreadlocks that had fallen in front of his face. "Ok, well, we should probably call the detective. They're looking for him, you know."

For the first time, Kennedy felt like she could add something useful to the conversation. "If they find Noah, and this Marcos person can prove he was at his house tonight, it could help show your brother's innocent."

Nick shot her a warning look. What did it mean? Nick didn't really think Noah could have ...

"He wouldn't want me to tell."

Kennedy had to lean forward to hear Jodie better.

"He'd be embarrassed," she explained. "You know. Because of what they say."

Nick patted her knee. "You know when the media gets wind of this, they'll probably all be gossiping about it soon enough. I just want you to be ready for that. It's probably not gonna be very nice things they have to say about it."

"I don't want Noah to be embarrassed." There was something endearing and sweet about her gentle insistence.

"Listen," Kennedy tried, "if we find Marcos fast and prove Noah's innocent, the media might not have time to learn about everything. Ok? Is there anything you can think of that will help us find out where Marcos lives?"

Jodie pouted. "I don't think so."

"No last name? Phone number? Anything?" Kennedy hoped she wasn't being too pushy. She couldn't tell from Nick's frown if he disapproved of her prodding or if he was just serious from the entire night's events.

An idea flitted into her head, and she sat up taller. "What about his phone? If he talks to Marcos so much, we could get his number off your brother's cell."

Nick shook his head. "Noah's cell is either with him or burned down at the Abernathys' place, remember?"

"Well, maybe ..." She tried to think. Could Detective Drisklay pull up Noah's phone records or something? It happened all the time in police novels, didn't it?

"Wait a minute." Jodie was always graceful and well-manicured, but it wasn't until her face lit up that Kennedy could say she was decidedly pretty in every sense of the word. A smile, shy but persistent, spread across her face. "I let Noah use my phone once. He'd left his in the youth group bus that night you all went to play paintball." She spoke quickly. Freely. For the first time, she sounded youthful.

Excited.

"He wanted to borrow my phone. He said he was calling you to ask about his cell." She nodded at Nick. "But then he talked for like an hour and a half. Wait, that wasn't you, was it?"

Nick shook his head. "No, he never called me. I didn't find his cell in the bus until the next day."

"I knew it!" Jodie's eyes were bright. "That means he was talking to Marcos." She turned a hopeful gaze to Kennedy, who felt like she had missed something important.

Jodie jumped up and grabbed a small handbag from a coat rack by her grandma's entryway. Kennedy wondered what other thirteen-year-old would carry around a Louis Vuitton purse, or any purse at all for that matter. Kennedy had tried a small handbag once a few years ago and then swore them off until she was at least out of school. She hated the way a single strap made her feel so lopsided and off balance, and none of the really cute purses were large enough to fit a book in, anyway. She'd stick with her backpacks for at least the next decade.

A car pulled into Mrs. Olinstein's driveway. The headlights shined through the window, beaming shadows across the wall.

Jodie was scrolling on her phone, her face still radiant. "Look! It's here. An hour and twenty-three minute call. This is it."

The sound of a car door shutting. Then another.

Nick leaned forward. Kennedy did too, ready to stand up. Jodie buried her face in her screen and didn't seem to notice anything else. "This is Marcos's number. We can call him!"

The front door opened. Detective Drisklay sauntered in, followed by Jodie's mom who looked nearly as frazzled and frail as Mrs. Olinstein had.

"Don't bother. Marcos Esperanza won't be answering his phone any time soon." Detective Drisklay slammed his coffee cup onto the yellow laminate counter. "He's in the ER right now being treated for multiple stab wounds. Doctors aren't sure he's going to make it."

CHAPTER 17

Vivian Abernathy all but collapsed onto the couch as she leaned down to hug her daughter. "How are you, sweetie? Are you ok?"

"Yeah, Mom. I'm fine." As quickly as it had come, the enthusiastic spark in Jodie's eyes clouded over again, replaced by a shy quietness. For a thirteen-year-old, she had already been through so much. Kennedy was glad at least something remained of the little girl Jodie should have been. Jodie put her arm around her mother's shoulders.

Detective Drisklay didn't waste any time with greetings or small talk. "So who wants to tell me why you were all talking about Marcos Esperanza when I got in?"

Kennedy and Nick exchanged a glance. "Jodie overheard Nick talking to some guy before the fire," she explained. "She thought maybe if we found him, it might give her brother an alibi to prove he wasn't there when his dad was murdered."

"Or else prove that he's the one that attacked Marcos in the first place," Drisklay stated in a monotone.

Right. She'd rushed into the night so sure she'd prove Noah's innocence, but he was getting more and more enmeshed with every new development. First Wayne's murder and the arson that burned down his house. Then the fire at the Lindgrens'. And now some mysterious guy named Marcos, a counselor who talked and prayed with Noah on a regular basis, who was dying of stab wounds in the ER. It was a good thing Kennedy had slept so long at the Lindgrens' earlier, because she knew this would turn into one of those nights that never ended. It was already after three.

Jodie and her mom were having a whispered conversation on the couch when Mrs. Olinstein shouted out from down the hall, "Is that you, Vivian? This nephew of yours hasn't stopped crying since ..."

"Mom," Vivian called back, "he's my son now, not my ... Oh, never mind." She stood up with a heavy sigh. Kennedy couldn't even begin to fathom the grief she must be experiencing. Her husband murdered. Her son the prime suspect. It sounded like the penultimate act in a

Shakespearean play. All they need now was a nurse for Jodie, a lady-in-waiting for Vivian, and a few soldier lackeys to follow Detective Drisklay around. Of course, since this was a tragedy, there'd be no jesters offering witty puns or household servants providing comic relief. There was only one way plays like this ever ended.

Death.

"He's still whining," Mrs. Olinstein called out. She had a cackling sort of voice.

"I'm coming."

Kennedy had never heard anyone sound as exhausted as Vivian.

Jodie took her mom's hand. "I'll go lie down with him. You don't have to worry about it."

"Are you sure, sweetie?" Gratitude shone in Vivian's eyes.

Jodie kissed her mom on the cheek. "Yeah. I'm tired anyway. I'll go curl up with him and take a nap."

Vivian took Jodie's hand and rubbed it against her cheek. "You're a sweet girl. Get some good rest now."

Jodie left without saying good night. Her footsteps made no noise as she moved down the hall. Kennedy could hear her grandma start to chide her, but she couldn't make out any of the words.

"So." Detective Drisklay took a noisy gulp of coffee. "Who can tell me about Marcos Esperanza?"

Nobody answered.

"Nobody knows anything?" Drisklay paced up and down in front of the couch where the rest of them were sitting. "I find that surprising. Well, let's start then with what I know. What I know is we've got a thirty-something-year-old Hispanic guy in surgery right now because someone decided to butcher him with a knife. That someone was an amateur who obviously didn't know what he was doing, and it was also someone Marcos knew and trusted enough to let into his house in the middle of the night. Based on the wounds, we're guessing the suspect is right-handed, five-foot-seven or five-foot-eight, no more than a hundred fifty pounds."

"You can really tell all that just from the wounds?"

Drisklay didn't pay any attention to Nick's question. He was staring at Vivian Abernathy, who had started to tremble so much that her gold bracelets jingled against one another.

"My son had nothing to do with this. We don't even know anyone named Marcos Aspare ... Espar ..."

"Marcos Esperanza." Drisklay frowned and smoothed out his salt-and-pepper mustache. "He's a local Christian counselor. A very specialized Christian counselor. Runs a website claiming to cure gay teens."

Nick's body tensed up beside Kennedy, but he didn't say anything.

"I've never heard of him before tonight." Vivian's voice was quieter now. Less certain.

Drisklay shrugged. "You didn't know your son was gay before tonight, either."

"He's not gay. He's confused." Vivian spoke like an actor doing the first read-through of a brand new play.

Drisklay ignored her.

"So we've got three crimes now." Nick shifted his weight on the couch as he spoke. "We have Senator Abernathy murdered and his house burned, we have a second fire at the Lindgrens' home, and we have this Marcos dude stabbed. Noah's just a kid. If he was distraught enough, maybe he could have done one of these things. But there's no logical way to connect him to all three of those incidents. No means."

Drisklay tossed his disposable cup into the trash. "Means is simple. You drop the kid off at his home at eleven. Fifteen minutes later he's killed his dad, set the house on fire, and heads over to the pastor's. Once he starts that fire, he drives himself over to Marcos's place in Cambridge, and within an hour, he's hit all three targets."

Nick shrugged. "Ok, but that's still doesn't explain why. Why would a good kid with absolutely no criminal record start two fires, kill his own dad, and stab someone else in his home? There's no motive."

Drisklay scratched his short beard. "How's this for motive? You got this kid, a kid from a fundamental Christian home, a kid who's been told from preschool age on that God hates fags. Ok, cue puberty, and all of a sudden this nice fundamental Christian boy isn't interested in peeking at his dad's porno mags or fantasizing about girls on the school cheerleading team. His hormones are all swinging the opposite way. But he knows he can't be gay, because the only people who are gay are people who turn their back on God and religion. So he waits. Waits for his body to do a one-eighty. Except that doesn't happen. So he goes online. And since he's a good, fundamental Christian kid, he doesn't go to Hot Teen Boys R Us. He searches *How do I stop being gay?* and he finds this website from Marcos Esperanza, a 'reformed homosexual' who promises that a little bit of prayer and a little bit of therapy will straighten up even the queerest homo out there. So our kid sends him an email. Maybe it starts anonymous. They build trust. Emails turn into phone calls. Phone calls where this so-called reformed homosexual assures this boy that God will make him straight because that's what God wants. Except the prayers don't work. Maybe our kid tries it for a month. Maybe it goes on for a whole year or longer. But at some point, he's smart enough to realize that Marcos's so-called therapy isn't changing a thing.

"So now, our kid's got some choices. He can keep praying, keep hoping for that miracle that's going to instantly turn him into a lusty stallion who'll chase anything, but only if it's in a skirt. Or he can quit the Christian life altogether and risk hellfire and brimstone in order to be true to his God-given identity. Or maybe he can find a way to be both gay and Christian, because by now he's spent enough time online to know that that's an actual thing. That there are churches out there who would welcome him, queer as a rainbow-colored unicorn and all. Except there's a problem. Folks like his dad say those churches aren't real churches at all, see. They're sellout churches that don't offer true salvation. And our kid's had enough fear of hell shoved down his throat since the time he could crawl that now he's just confused. So confused that he dares to go to Daddy and tell him the whole story. Who knows what he's thinking? Maybe he thinks Daddy will have an epiphany right then and there and decide he's been on the wrong side of the gay debate his whole life. Maybe they'll cry and hug it out. Except that's not what happens. Daddy doesn't hug it out. In fact, Daddy threatens to kick him onto the streets unless he stops being gay. Boy says he can't stop being gay. Maybe he tells his dad about Marcos. Maybe he tells his dad how much he's prayed and how nothing's changed. But his dad can't be known as the politician with a gay kid, so he drags him off to talk to Pastor. If anyone can straighten his wayward son out, Pastor can. So they go see Pastor, and Pastor says homosexuality is a sin just like Daddy does. So here's Pastor and here's Daddy both saying the same thing. It's a sin to be gay. God doesn't want him to be gay. But our kid's smart enough that he knows he is gay. And Pastor can't help him, and Daddy won't love him, and God hasn't changed him.

"So back at home, he gets in a fight with his dad. Gets too carried away, swings a golf club at him. He wasn't trying to kill him. He just wanted to hear Daddy say, 'It's ok, son. I'll still love you no matter what.' But Daddy couldn't say that, and oops. Now Daddy's dead. So to cover it up, kid's got this great idea that he'll start a fire. And bam, the house goes down in flames. It was so easy and felt so good, he thinks he'll go try it out now at Pastor's house. That'll teach Pastor a lesson for calling people like him sinners. So now he's killed his dad and set fire to Pastor's house, and then he goes to see his good buddy Marcos. Because if you look at it from the kid's perspective, Marcos is the guiltiest of them all since he promised to make our boy straight, but all that praying and all that therapy didn't do jack squat to change him. And our kid's bolder now. He's killed his dad. He set fire to two homes. He doesn't need a golf club this time. He just needs a regular old kitchen knife. And that's what he uses to hack his old counselor buddy to shreds."

Drisklay stopped and stared straight at Nick. "So tell me again how there's no motive?"

Kennedy had sat spellbound during the entire recitation. For a few minutes, she felt as if she were part of a crime novel, sitting in the drawing room hearing the hard-boiled detective soliloquize the solution to the seemingly impossible mystery. But then Vivian Abernathy adjusted her assortment of gold bracelets and sat up with her spine rigid, and Kennedy remembered this was a real-life discussion about a real-life child who had just been accused of committing three horrendous crimes.

Vivian shook her head so her earrings jingled against each other, just like her mother's had. "I hate to ruin your theory, detective." Her voice was resolved. Assured. Kennedy wondered if Jodie would grow up to be confident like that.

"There's a problem with your explanation," Vivian continued. "My son couldn't have killed his father. I'm sure of it."

The corner of Drisklay's mouth turned up. "And why is that?"

Vivian Abernathy tilted her chin until she looked as regal as Lady Capulet. "Because I killed him."

CHAPTER 18

Detective Drisklay was the only one who didn't appear at all surprised at Vivian's confession. Kennedy sucked in her breath. Nick whipped his head around to look at Drisklay so fast his dreads flew through the air.

"You?" Drisklay didn't raise his voice. He still wore that bemused smirk on his face. "And why would you kill your husband?"

Vivian was no longer trembling. "Because he was going to disown our son. And I don't care what Noah's done. He's our child, and nothing's going to change that."

Kennedy heard her throat muscles working.

"They had a fight," Vivian explained. "After Noah came home last night, he went to his dad's office. I listened in. Wayne said he was meeting with the lawyer first thing in the morning. He was going to take Noah out of the will, begin the emancipation process to completely disown Noah. What kind of father would do that to his own child? His own flesh and blood? And so when they were done talking, I went in. Told Wayne he would *not* write our firstborn out of his will. We fought. I realized my husband wasn't going to change his mind. His golf bag was there in the corner. I took out a club. And that was that."

Drisklay appeared unmoved. "And the fire?"

"You said it yourself. It was intended to cover up the body. But Noah didn't set it. I did."

Drisklay gave a little shrug. "All right, then. If that's your story, you know I'll have to take you in. Shall I put you in handcuffs? Make it look more convincing?"

"I'm telling the truth."

Another shrug. "That's the judge and jury's job to determine. My job is to get you booked. By the way, I guess I should tell you that you're under arrest for the murder of your husband. You have the right to remain silent."

Even after hearing Drisklay pull out of the driveway with Vivian Abernathy, Kennedy wasn't sure any of it had actually happened. She couldn't raise her eyes to Nick. Didn't know what to say. Didn't even know what to think. Vivian wasn't guilty, was she? Something was wrong.

Besides, even if Vivian did kill her husband, that wouldn't explain who set the Lindgrens' house on fire and who stabbed the Christian counselor. Vivian couldn't have done all that. She was with Jodie during the fire until the police came to ask her questions.

That still left Noah a suspect at two of tonight's crime scenes.

Where was he?

"Well that was strange, wasn't it?" Nick finally asked.

Kennedy let out her breath. "Strangest night of my life, I think."

"Yeah. Mine, too."

She wanted to ask him questions. Ask him what he really thought about Drisklay's explanation. Kennedy had spent all night trying to think of ways to prove Noah's innocence. What if she'd been mistaken? If Noah hadn't done anything wrong, he wouldn't be hiding right now, would he? Unless he thought his dad really had kicked him out of the house. Was it possible he didn't have a clue about any of this? Didn't have a clue how thin a line existed between him and a prison sentence for murder?

Nick stood up. "So, do we tell Vivian's mom?"

"I suppose we have to." Kennedy hoped Nick would volunteer to be the one to break news like that. She'd be more comfortable sitting in the bus listening to the Babylon Eunuchs. "I guess we need to let Jodie know, too."

"You'll do no such thing." The crackling voice from around the corner sent cold goosebumps racing up Kennedy's neck.

Mrs. Olinstein emerged from whatever crevice she'd been hiding behind. "My daughter's a fool. A fool to have married an Abernathy in the first place. You two get yourselves home."

"What will you tell Jodie when she ..."

"I'll tell her what I decide is important and relevant for her to know." Mrs. Olinstein stretched out a bony finger. "Now leave, and I expect you'll be so kind as to lock my door on your way out."

"So, do you really think Vivian's guilty?" They were halfway back to Nick's apartment when Kennedy finally found the courage to broach the subject.

Nick shrugged. "I guess it's possible. A mother's love can be a pretty strong motivation in something like this."

She knew that sort of thing happened in books. But still, that didn't mean regular people like Vivian Abernathy could up and kill their husbands, did it? Kennedy had experienced so many things in the past twelve months. Surviving a kidnapping. Running away from a vindictive criminal. Confronting police brutality head on.

Still, everything in the past was a far cry from pre-meditated murder.

There had to be some other explanation, a logical scenario that wouldn't condemn Vivian or her son. "What about that Marcos guy?" Kennedy asked. "The counselor?"

Nick scoffed. "You don't even want to hear my opinion on the likes of him."

Kennedy hadn't been prepared for such a vehement response. She stared at his radio dial. Maybe he'd opt for some folksy grunge worship music.

"I wish he'd told me he'd been talking to that quack job." Nope. He wasn't reaching for the dial at all.

Nick shook his head. "If you ask me, that's when everything started to go wrong. When Noah thought he had to go so far as to change his orientation. I hate it when families do that to their kids." He slammed his hand on the steering wheel.

Kennedy tensed in her seat but didn't respond.

"I hate it," he repeated, more softly this time.

Kennedy glanced out the window. It was strange to see the midnight sky even though her body and brain were telling her it should be the middle of the day. She felt like Kate in *Taming of the Shrew*, riding in a cart with her new husband who forced her to admit the sun was really the moon. She couldn't believe how long of a day it had been already.

How long of a night, that is.

Nick strummed the steering wheel, but the upbeat rhythm was gone, replaced by a heavy, dour pulse.

He looked over at her. He couldn't be out of his twenties yet, but there were long furrows etched across his brow she'd never noticed before.

"I get pretty worked up about the whole ex-gay movement." His fingers held still. "That's because it was charlatans like this Marcos deadbeat who killed my sister."

CHAPTER 19

"We grew up in Oregon."

Kennedy wasn't sure that Nick was talking to her as much as he was releasing a story that he'd been trying too hard to hold in.

"Our childhood was perfect, really. Our parents owned this Christian campground. Most beautiful, anointed spot of land on the continent, I swear. People would come there and meet God. I'm not just using church lingo, either. I mean they seriously and literally met God there. And really, it was impossible not to, what with the mountains and this gorgeous lake. We're talking water so clear you can see the color of the individual grains of sand twenty feet deep. No pollution, no traffic. Just perfect."

He shook his head. "Man, I miss that place. They turned it into some ritzy resort once my parents sold it. Made the owner his millions by now, I'm sure, and he thinks it was good business practice, but really it was the land itself. That spot. If I didn't know my geography better, I'd have to say that must have been where Moses talked to God in the burning bush or something, because there's never been a piece of land that I could truly call hallowed ground like that place. Grace Harbor, we called it."

The night was still and calm. No traffic. No noise but the loud rumble of the youth group bus.

"So my sister," Nick continued, "her name was Lessa. Lessa Grace. We're only eighteen months apart. My mom says I was a real fussy baby, stomachaches and cholic and just a pretty grumpy disposition, but she says all that changed the day Lessa was born. Even the midwife, she knew there was something between us, a special bond. She actually handed Lessa to me first before she gave her to my dad. I'm probably loony, but I actually think I remember that day. There's this little yellow ducky blanket that I remember the midwife wrapped her up in. Even my mom forgot about it. It wasn't in any of the baby photos or anything like that, but when Lessa... After everything that happened, I was helping Mom clean out her things, and I saw it. That same blanket. Had this cute ducky in rain boots holding an umbrella."

Nick scratched his temple. "I wonder if my mom still has it."

Kennedy listened quietly. There wasn't anything to add. She could tell Nick was speaking more to himself than to her by now.

"So anyway, Lessa and I were close. It sounds so trite to say we were best friends because it went deeper than that."

Kennedy's thoughts drifted off toward Reuben, studying hard at Nairobi University and getting his health monitored at the hospital there.

"We shared a room from the beginning," Nick went on. "Mom says she wasn't planning on it happening that way, but I threw such a big fit the night she was born, and Lessa had been fussing so much my mom thought if she put her crib in the room with me, I'd change my mind in a minute or two. But as soon as she put us in together, we both slept sound as rocks. That's just how it was. We were so close in age we invented our own language. Mom's got it on video still. My sister's not even big enough to walk yet, and she and I are having these back-and-forth conversations just babbling, and I understand exactly what she's saying because I can tell Mom what it is that Lessa wants.

"My parents were great, loving folks. The kind to give a stranger the shirt off their backs and take him out to lunch if he needed it. But I think as Lessa and I got a little older, they started to wonder if it was wrong for the two of us to be together all the time. Not necessarily in a bad way, it's just that Mom homeschooled us since the campground was pretty remote, and even though there were kids and families camping literally in our backyard all year, Lessa and I were perfectly content playing together, just the two of us. We didn't ever seek out any other friends. I never played with little boys, she never played with little girls."

As she was listening, Kennedy thought back to her own childhood. She'd never had a sibling, could only imagine what it would have been like to have another kid to play with all day long.

Nick's dreadlocks swayed from side to side almost in time with his apostle bobble heads. "My parents were open-minded about a lot of things. At least that's how they started out. Then Mom got more and more involved in her homeschool niche. It wasn't like today where you have secular and agnostic and atheist homeschoolers all mixed up. In general, the homeschool community back in those days was very Christian and very conservative. They had this magazine my mom would get, tell her how to be a proper homemaker, junk like that. Made her feel bad because she didn't walk around all day in a long denim skirt with a scarf tied around her hair. That's the kind of conservative we're talking about. And it really emphasized what they called the *Biblical model* of femininity, which to them meant headscarves and homemade bread and submitting to your husband even if he's an abusive alcoholic. I'm not making this up. I remember I was about ten and I didn't have anything better to read, so I took her magazine in the outhouse with me, and it was this nineteen-year-old girl married to this middle-aged drunk who'd already broken her arm, and she's writing an article telling other women how freeing it was when she learned that God just wants her to pray for her husband and leave the changing up to him. I mean, come on. That's the drivel my mom was filling her head with.

"It was right around then that Mom started worrying about Lessa. I mean, my sister was the stereotypical tomboy. Climbing trees, hunting frogs, collecting bugs, dissecting them ... When she was littler, Mom was happy just to have the two of us outside so she could worry about maintaining the campground and scheduling retreats and running the business side of things without us constantly badgering her. But then as Lessa got older, and as Mom got more and more into her *housewife theology* as I call it, she started worrying about Lessa. Worrying she wasn't on track to grow up to be this model Proverbs 31 woman Mom read about in her magazines.

"The irony is Mom wasn't even that kind of wife. She was spirited. That's what Dad loved about her. She could hold her own in an argument. And she did. I never grew up thinking my parents hated each other, but I knew they fought. It never bothered me. It was just a part of life. Mom had a master's degree, but Dad only made it halfway through his bachelor's. The funny thing is these women she was learning from in the magazines, they were out to make her feel bad for having an education, for running a company. And when I say running a company, that's because Mom did all the behind-the-scenes stuff. The scheduling, planning, hiring summer staff, all that. Dad was the face of the camp. He did the welcome sessions and DJed the family dance nights and went around from table to table cracking jokes in the cafeteria, but Mom was the real CEO, CFO ... all that fell on

her. And she did it well. But she read about these model little housewives
who only cooked from scratch and dusted all day, and that made her feel
guilty. Guilty for having a master's degree, guilty for spending time away
from us kids even though Lessa and I couldn't have been happier. We had
the whole campground as our backyard. Life was perfect as far as we were
concerned.

"Anyway, Mom decided it was too late for her to become the model
of a docile, submissive wife, but she was going to train up Lessa the 'right'
way. By the time she was eight, Lessa was in charge of all the cleaning, all
the laundry for the whole family. If she complained, she was copying Bible
verses about cheerful attitudes or junk like that. In fourth grade, Mom
made Lessa start cooking breakfast and lunch for the family. We always ate
dinner in the cafeteria with the campers or I'm sure Mom would have had
her doing that, too."

Kennedy thought back on herself at that age. Her mom made her do
chores, and Kennedy complained about them. What kid didn't? But it
wasn't as if Kenendy had been forced to do anything simply because she was
a girl. It was more like she was the only kid around, so she had to pitch in
to help. Even so, the amount of work she grumbled about probably totaled
less than an hour a week, nothing like Nick's sister having to run an entire
household at such a young age.

"It was in fourth grade that Mom made her start wearing dresses.
Which is stupid if you ask me, because not even Mom wore them, not all
the time at least. She got Lessa a sewing machine and said by the time she
turned twelve, she'd have to make all her own clothes, so she may as well
start learning. Had to ask a church lady to come by and teach her, because
Mom didn't even know how to sew herself.

"It was around that time Mom finally put her foot down. She said Lessa
and I were too old to share a room anymore. She'd tried to separate us a
dozen times by then, but whenever she moved one of the beds into another
room, we'd end up together on the same mattress before either of us could
sleep. But Lessa was something of an early bloomer, and when she was
ten Mom said absolutely no more sharing a room, and especially no more
sharing a bed. I was still very much a kid. I had no idea what the big deal
was, and my parents weren't the type to talk about that sort of thing out in

the open. I didn't know about puberty or anything like that, and it hit Lessa first and I didn't even realize what was going on. All I knew was Mom was treating us like we were nasty for still spending so much time together, for wanting to sleep in the same bed or go skinny dipping down at the lake on weekends when none of the campers were around to see us anyway.

"It sounds like it shouldn't have been quite that big of a deal, but when Mom finally kicked Lessa out of our room, things started to deteriorate fast. I mean, it was probably a whole lot of causes at once, but back then I remember thinking it was the room issue that started it all. Lessa stopped doing things with me. Stopped climbing trees or racing outside or swimming in the lake in the evenings. We went a couple years where she hardly talked to me at all. Just focused on her sewing and her cooking and her cleaning. She was thirteen when I came to this crazy realization. I realized, *Hey, my sister's a girl*. Sounds pretty dumb when you put it like that, but up until then, she'd just been my sister. Someone to play with. Someone to force me to swim faster than I ever thought I could, racing from the far side of the lake to the other. It didn't matter that she was a girl and I was a boy. At least not until Mom started making such a big deal about it. So Lessa was thirteen, and she was wearing this sundress that she'd made, and she was leaning down to pick some weeds in the garden, and I said to myself, *Hey, my sister's a girl*. And that realization right there seemed to explain everything that'd been happening for the past couple years that I couldn't quite put my finger on. All those extra chores. How Mom would ride her if she didn't have what she called a 'cheerful disposition' about everything. Those hours of Bible verses Mom made her copy out if Lessa even hinted at talking back. Why we couldn't share a room anymore or go swimming anymore unless someone else was out there watching us, and even then Lessa had to cover up her swimsuit with one of Dad's extra-large T-shirts. I could go around the whole camp all day in just my swim trunks and no one would think twice about it, but even to walk from our cabin to the lake, Lessa had to have one towel wrapped around her waist to cover her legs and one more draped over her shoulders to hide everything else.

"There were rules for everything. Rules about who she could or couldn't be alone with, rules about who she could or couldn't talk to without getting dad's permission first. Rules about how long her skirts had to be, how much of her shoulders had to be covered even in the hottest summer days when no one else was around."

Nick was quiet for a while. Kennedy wondered if he had lost his train of thought or if he was absorbed in his own musings.

"She ran away when she was sixteen. Left me a note — nothing for my parents, but a long letter to me. I still have it. She asked me not to show it to Mom and Dad, and I never did. All she wanted them to know was that she was safe and she didn't ever plan to come home. And she never did."

The apostle heads bobbled stupidly. Kennedy would have given up her entire Shakespeare collection for the chance to throw them out the bus window, them and their annoying grins.

"I'm sure psychologists and theologians could have a field day dissecting my sister's story, arguing about whether it was that rigid upbringing that made her feel so ashamed of who she was as a girl that turned her into a lesbian or if she would've headed down that route no matter what. She didn't talk about it in that letter she left me. It's not like she was even in the closet at that point. I just think she was so confused she didn't know what to think about herself or her body or her sexuality or anything. Her whole life, from about the age of eight or nine on, it had all been a list of rules. Rules she had to follow because God had made her a girl. Rules that made her feel ashamed of her body, rules that focused so much on keeping men from lusting after her that she grew to hate everything about who she was. She was a binge eater by the time she left home. Still skinny as a rail — you've seen her picture — even if she packed away six or seven thousand calories a day, but I think either consciously or subconsciously she was trying to sabotage herself. Turn herself into the kind of person men would be less likely to notice so she wouldn't feel so guilty for drawing the wrong kind of attention."

They were back in Nick's neighborhood now. The van slowed down as its headlights lit up the apartment building ahead of them. "Anyway, sorry for blabbing your ear off. I don't even remember how we got started on this topic."

Kennedy didn't remember, either. All she knew was she was tired. Physically tired from her grueling day of travel yesterday, and emotionally tired from everything that had happened since she landed in the States. If this was any indication of what her sophomore year would be like, it was going to be a long nine months.

Nick parked, and she dragged herself out of the bus. His apartment was on the third story. *Thank God for elevators*, she thought as she forced her legs to uphold her weight.

Rest. That's all she wanted. Even if she couldn't fall asleep. Just the chance to shut her eyes. Turn off her brain, which had been reeling ever since she learned about Wayne Abernathy's death.

Nick unlocked the main door to his apartment building as quietly as he could. It was almost five in the morning. Kennedy hoped everyone would still be asleep when they got upstairs. She wondered if Woong would remember anything of his night terrors when he woke up.

She followed Nick into the elevator. Neither said anything. Kennedy could almost feel the gravity from his couch pulling her toward it as the elevator let them off on the third-floor hallway.

A figure in a hooded sweatshirt sat huddled in front of Nick's door. He glanced up, his eyes swollen and puffy and full of so much pain Kennedy was momentarily paralyzed.

"Noah?"

The boy sniffed loudly and wiped his nose on his sleeve. "I'm sorry I came here. I didn't know where else to go. Please. You have to help me. I made a huge mistake."

CHAPTER 20

Kennedy was glad Nick was there. Nick was the one Noah was looking at with those terrified, pleading eyes.

"I need help."

She could tell Noah was trying to keep his voice calm, but it wasn't working. A few hours earlier, Kennedy had been impressed with the way Nick could plant himself in the middle of stress, tragedy, and chaos and stay so quiet and serene. Now, she'd wish he'd hurry up and say something.

Anything.

What was he waiting for? Either he needed to call the cops and let them know he'd found Noah, or he needed to barrage Noah with questions so they could figure out exactly what had happened to his father.

Instead, he stood there, assessing the scene with his head cocked to one side, frowning sympathetically while Noah sat curled up in a little ball.

"We better find some place more private to talk."

That was it. All Nick could offer. Kennedy wanted to scream and pull out her hair. Or pull out Nick's hair, maybe. One dread at a time. *We better find some place more private to talk?* That was the best he could do? Even after he spoke the words, Nick stood there with his arms crossed as if he had all the time in the world. As if Noah's father hadn't been murdered. As if his mother hadn't confessed to the crime. As if Noah weren't the prime suspect in several other cases of arson and assault committed throughout the night.

Nick frowned. Had he forgotten how to speak? Had his sad trip down memory lane during the drive here slowed down his brain functioning? Had he forgotten how serious of a situation they were in?

How deadly?

"It's not too chilly out," Nick finally said, as if Noah had simply stopped by one afternoon to pay a social call. "Let's all go up to the balcony. We can talk there."

Another silent elevator ride, five more floors up. Nick spun his lanyard keychain around his finger one way and then the other. Kennedy felt dizzy. She didn't bother calculating what meal it would be time for if she were still in Yanji. All she knew was that she was hungry for something. But she wasn't about to miss getting answers from Noah in order to chase down a vending machine or scour Nick's apartment for something at least partially edible.

Once the three of them were seated around a big patio table on the roof, Nick clasped his hands behind his head and stretched his legs onto the chair across from him. "So, what can you tell me about tonight?"

Kennedy tried not to lean in. Tried not to show how eager she was to hear what Noah would have to say. Tried to act as inconspicuous as possible so the other two wouldn't realize how unfitting it was for her to be there right now.

"I made a huge mistake," Noah began, and Kennedy clenched her jaw shut. Had Drisklay been right, then? Was Noah really the one who had killed his father? Was she about to hear the entire confession?

"That's the amazing thing about grace," Nick answered. "There's nothing we can do to make God love us any less. Nothing we can do to make him take away the forgiveness Jesus bought with his own blood."

Kennedy bit her lip so she wouldn't start screaming. Didn't he realize he was talking to a murder suspect?

Noah's fingers fidgeted with the tops of his pants legs. "I'm not talking about cheating on a test or sneaking out and going partying. I'm talking about the really bad stuff. The stuff that gets you sent to jail."

See? Kennedy wanted to yell. *He doesn't need church platitudes.* What he needed was a good lawyer.

Nick looked just as relaxed as if he were watching half a dozen youth group kids playing X-box and trashing his living room. "First of all, God doesn't dump sins into categories. There's no such thing as a big sin and a tiny sin. All sin is equally horrendous in his sight. Whether you tell a little white lie or set off a bomb that kills a hundred people, neither one of those is too small for God to overlook or too horrendous for him to forgive. Second of all ..." He reached above his head and let out a noisy yawn. "Sorry. I guess we're all pretty tired here. Second of all," he repeated, "I'm really touched that you came to me. I'm glad you feel comfortable enough that you ..."

"I got in a fight." Noah looked like a caged lion about to attack the bars that confined him.

Nick shut his mouth. A confused, questioning look darkened his face. The same kind of confusion that was sloshing around in Kennedy's gut.

"You got in a fight?" Nick repeated. "Like a yelling fight or a fistfight?"

"A fistfight. A pretty bad one. I didn't mean to hurt him." Noah glanced over both shoulders as if he expected a helicopter to shine its blinding searchlights on him at any moment. "I think they're after me. I just can't bring myself to go home and tell my parents what happened. They'd be so ..."

Noah stopped. He stared at Nick.

"What?" The lilt in his voice matched the sinking feeling in Kennedy's stomach. "What?" Noah repeated. "What's going on?" He looked to Kennedy.

Nick sighed. "Listen, brother. I'm going to ask you something, and I need you to promise to give me a truthful answer. No matter what. Got that?"

Noah swallowed. Fear and uncertainty were etched into his features. He gave a small nod.

Nick leaned forward in his chair. "I need to know exactly where you've been all night."

CHAPTER 21

Noah stared into his lap. Was he trying to conjure up some sort of lie? He couldn't meet Nick's gaze, but his eyes settled somewhere around his shoulder. "I was at the Lucky Star."

Kennedy had never heard of the place but could tell how painful it was for Noah to admit. She tried to gauge Nick's reaction.

"I wasn't going there to get picked up or anything," Noah added hastily. "I was looking for somebody, and I ..." He cut himself off. "Maybe I should start from the beginning."

Kennedy wished he would.

Nick remained silent.

Noah took a deep breath. "Ok, so earlier tonight, I got a text from my friend, Dayton. He was at the Lucky Star and someone was making him uncomfortable, and he asked me to go get him."

Kennedy remembered Noah's reaction when he got a text in the Lindgrens' kitchen. Was it this Dayton guy he'd been talking to?

"So I headed to the Lucky Star, and I didn't see Dayton where he said he'd meet me outside, so I had to park and go in. I hadn't ever been there before, I swear it." He stared at Nick with earnest eyes. "And I went in, and ..." He swallowed loudly. Kennedy thought back to how good Nick had been comforting Jodie earlier and wished there was a sink up here so she could offer Noah a glass of water.

"So I went in," he began again, "and Dayton was backed into this corner getting harassed by this guy. That's why I don't go to those places, you know? And I thought they must have bouncers or security guards or something to take care of things like that, but nobody was doing anything. I mean, this punk was all over him, and everyone was just dancing and drinking like it didn't matter.

"And so I went up and tried to act natural and just told Dayton something like, 'Hey, we need to get going, it's late,' but at first the guy wouldn't let him go. Said something about how Dayton owed him a favor since he'd risked getting in trouble buying drinks for someone underage, you know? And he was really pushing it, so finally I kind of flagged down this bartender guy. I'd seen him watching us. I think he was catching on that something wasn't right, so I made eye contact and sort of gave him this *get us out of here* signal, so he came over and said something to Dayton like, 'All right, now, you've had too much to drink already, and if you don't want me to take a closer look at that fake ID you came in with, I'd get out of here if I were you.' So he was kind of pretending to kick Dayton and me out of the club, but the whole time he was sizing up this other dude, so that's how we finally got out of there."

Kennedy had heard her roommate Willow complain from time to time about jerks who harassed her when she went clubbing with her theater friends. Kennedy's dad drilled her about the dangers of date rape at least twice a month. She'd never thought of a boy like Noah having to worry about predators as well.

"Anyway, so Dayton and I finally get out of the club, and all I'm thinking is my dad's gonna kill me if I don't get the car home by midnight, and we're making our way to where I parked when this skinhead-looking dude just jumps us. I mean, no warning, nothing. Starts whaling on Dayton, calling him a flaming fag and a homo, and we're far enough from the Lucky Star now that there's no way the bartender or anyone else's gonna be able to hear us over the music and stuff.

"So he's beating on Dayton, and Dayton's too startled I think to fight back, but I get this skinhead off my friend and then I don't know what happened." Noah stared at his hands. "I really don't. I sort of blacked out. I remember throwing him off Dayton, and he landed on the sidewalk on his back, and I was leaning over him, and I seriously don't know what happened. Next thing I know, Dayton's pulling me off him shouting about cops, and the guy's lying there bleeding, and I ..."

Noah clutched his stomach. Kennedy worried he was about to throw up all over the patio furniture.

"I don't know what came over me. Dayton started running, so I started running, and I honestly don't even know if the guy's ok. What if I ... I mean, I might have ..."

He leaned down. Kennedy had just enough time to move her shoes out of the way.

An offensively rancid moment later, he straightened up, never raising his eyes past the level of the patio table. "I'm sorry."

"It's ok." Nick stood. "I'll just run and grab some paper towels. It's not a problem. Really." He seemed a little too eager to go. "I'll be right back," he called, already halfway to the stairwell.

Noah blinked. Kennedy strummed her fingers on her knee. That stupid chorus from the Babylon Eunuchs was stuck in her head.

Peace washes over me. Peace washes over me.

Who could expect peace at a time like this? When had the world turned so violent? Why did everyone hate each other so much?

Peace washes over me. Peace washes over me.

Had she ever felt that peace? That rush of comfort from the Holy Spirit that Christians were always talking about? What about Noah? Where was that peace when he and his friend were being harassed in that bar? Where was that peace when some skinhead jumped them without any provocation? She could see how upset Noah was about what he'd done, but he'd been defending his friend. Wasn't that a valid reason to ...

She frowned. "What happened to Dayton? Is he ok?"

Noah gave a little start. Had he forgotten she was there?

"Was he hurt?" she asked.

He squirmed in his chair. Maybe she shouldn't have brought it up. Maybe it was all too distressing.

He shook his head. "No, he was all right. We umm, well, I dropped him off at his home. He got a black eye and some bruises, but he'll be ok."

Kennedy wished Nick would hurry up. Even if she read every single book he owned on youth ministry, she knew she'd feel just as awkward and unprepared as she did right now.

She wasn't about to make matters worse by trying to say anything else. She'd just wait for Nick to get back. Wait and pray. It was obvious now that Noah was innocent regarding his father. The bar they were at could vouch for him. The bartender who kicked him and Dayton out to rescue them from the aggressive predator would remember their faces. Give Noah an alibi. Besides, a boy that distraught over a fistfight in the street could never lift his hand to actually murder anybody.

Noah lowered his head. "I really screwed up. I shouldn't have gone to get Dayton in the first place."

"You were trying to help a friend," Kennedy offered. She was still trying to figure out who Dayton was and exactly how his relationship with Noah worked. Were they friends? Boyfriends? Was it really any of her business?

"I'd told my parents we didn't hang out anymore. I wasn't supposed to go anywhere with him." Noah groaned. "My dad's gonna kill me when he finds out."

Kennedy's heart lodged itself halfway up her throat. What was she supposed to do? What was she supposed to say?

Noah was staring at her now. Apparently her attempt to keep her expression neutral had failed.

"What is it?" he asked. "What's wrong?"

Kennedy glanced around. Where was Nick? It would be the perfect time for a director to yell *cut* so the actors could review their script again and get back into the right story.

"What's going on?" Fear laced his words.

Kennedy stared at the patio umbrella just behind him. Nick was on his way. He would be here any minute. There was a reason he was the youth pastor and she was just the college sophomore. She couldn't handle something like this. Not alone. Not even if she had ten years to prepare.

"Why are you looking at me like that? What happened?"

The door to the stairwell opened. Kennedy let out her breath. Nick was back. He would know how to handle Noah's questions. He would know what to say. How to say it. Kennedy didn't realize she'd been gripping the armrests of her patio chair until one of her finger muscles cramped.

The door banged shut. Kennedy turned around expectantly.

Gratefully.

It was Nick, but he wasn't alone. In front of him, Detective Drisklay held out a pair of handcuffs.

"Noah, I need you to come with me, son."

Noah jumped up from his seat. Glanced behind him as if he might find a magic escape route off the rooftop. "Wait, I didn't do it on purpose. I thought he was ..."

"I wouldn't say anything else if I were you." Drisklay's voice was even. Void of any emotion. Kennedy had the impression he could get his arm sawed off and wouldn't change his expression.

"Wait, am I under arrest?" Noah glanced from Nick to Kennedy and back to the detective. His eyes were pleading. Fearful. "I wasn't trying to hurt him, I swear. I just wanted to find out ..."

Nick came over to his side and put his arm on Noah's back. "This isn't about that," Kennedy heard him whisper.

Noah's face clouded over with confusion. She wished she could shut her ears. Look away so she didn't have to witness this next scene, the part in the drama where any doubts whether it's a tragedy or a comedy are put to rest.

For good.

Noah didn't resist as Drisklay cuffed his hands behind his back.

"Your father's been murdered, and we have some questions for you. I strongly suggest you don't say another word until your lawyer shows up."

CHAPTER 22

Kennedy had read about people turning white from surprise but had never witnessed it firsthand until now. The blood drained from Noah's face as quickly as her stomach fell in her abdominal cavity.

"Wait a minute." She jumped up. This was all some sort of mistake. It had to be. "Noah can't be the murderer. His mom already confessed."

"My mom?" Noah looked so frail, Kennedy was afraid he might fall over on top of the detective. Maybe she shouldn't have mentioned Vivian after all.

Detective Drisklay appeared unmoved. "You know as well as I do she only said that to buy her son a little more time. She had her fifteen minutes. Too bad the rest of Boston slept right through it."

"So how do you know it wasn't her?" Kennedy asked. She had never believed Vivian was the murderer either, not until now when the only other alternative was even more unsettling.

"Want the list?" Drisklay raised a single shoulder toward his ear in a sort of half shrug. "All right. First off, Vivian's left-handed. Whoever clobbered the senator led with their right. And she obviously hadn't seen the body. She couldn't tell us how many times she hit him, what part of his office he'd been in, none of that. Like I said, she got her fifteen minutes, and then we had no choice but to let her go."

"My dad's dead?" Noah asked. Kennedy wished this was something like Woong's night terrors, a horrific dream he wouldn't even remember when he woke up in the morning.

Nick had his hand on Noah's back. "I'm sorry, brother."

"Hold on." Kennedy wasn't willing to let the detective get away with this. It was one thing to take in an innocent woman who was confessing a crime she didn't commit in order to save her son. It was another thing altogether to take a boy who didn't even know his father was dead and all of a sudden accuse him of the murder. Besides, it couldn't have been Noah. He'd been out all night.

"He was at a bar." The words poured out like water erupting out of a geyser. "He has an alibi. Tell him." She nodded at Noah. "Tell him where you were."

Noah didn't say anything. Was he in shock? Grieved over the news of his dad?

Drisklay nudged him toward the elevator door. He was going to take him away without any proof, without any due process ...

"He was with his friend. Someone named Dayton." Kennedy clutched at her own words, trying to sound bold. Why wasn't Noah responding? "Tell him," she coaxed. "Tell him that's where you were all night."

Noah shook his head. The movement was so slight, Kennedy could hardly perceive it.

"Tell him," she urged again, but her words had lost their forcefulness. Their conviction.

She was met only by silence.

Drisklay prodded Noah forward. "He knows his rights. Come on, kid. The sooner I take you in, the sooner I can sleep off all this coffee."

So that was it. Drisklay had arrested Noah. Carted him off like a common criminal. And Noah hadn't said anything. Why not? Was he ashamed to name the Lucky Star as his alibi? Was he afraid his mom would be mad at him for hanging out with that Dayton guy, whoever he was? Was he worried he'd get in trouble for beating up that skinhead? How could that be worse than being arrested unjustly for killing your own dad?

The sun was already starting to rise over the sleepy apartment complexes. Drisklay had taken Noah away at least a quarter of an hour ago, and neither Kennedy nor Nick had budged.

"I can't believe it." Nick hung his head over his lap until his dreadlocks were just a few inches off the ground.

"Why didn't he tell Drisklay the truth?"

Nick only repeated, "I can't believe it."

So that was it. Next would come the news. The media heyday. The swarms of locusts so ready to glut themselves on the Abernathy scandal. Trash journalists wanting to make a name for themselves. Websites typing out their clickbait headlines in the pre-dawn hours. It was probably all over Channel 2 already.

Gay teen accused of murdering his homophobic father.

She thought about emailing Ian, the journalist she'd met last year during her own series of media spotlights. But what would be the point? The one time she'd tried to go on air to tell the public her side of a controversial story, her best friend's medical history had been exposed and dissected in the course of a three-minute live segment. No, the most she could hope for was to keep herself out of the limelight and hope the winds blew something even more scandalous across the Boston harbors, something that would make everyone forget Noah and the Abernathy ordeal before the weekend.

"Why don't you think Noah told the detective about that club?" she asked. "Why wouldn't he say anything?"

Nick frowned. "It could be he's too embarrassed to admit he was at a gay bar, no matter what the reason."

"But still, if it was that or get accused of killing your dad ..."

A shrug. "Maybe he was scared of getting in trouble for that fight."

"Same thing," Kennedy replied. "If the only other option is to go to jail for murder ..."

Nick sighed. "I suppose the other possibility is Noah wasn't telling us the truth. He may not have been at the Lucky Star at all."

"But why would he make that up? Why would he tell a story like that unless he ..." Kennedy stopped herself.

Nick held her gaze. "You know it's possible that Noah's guilty, don't you?"

No. She couldn't believe it. And how could Nick? Wasn't he supposed to be Noah's advocate? Wasn't he supposed to stand by him during hard times? Isn't that what being a youth pastor was all about?

"Trust me, I don't like that idea any more than you do, but we still have to consider ..." His voice trailed off.

He could consider all he wanted. Kennedy wouldn't. She knew Noah was innocent. He couldn't even stomach beating someone up in a clear-cut case of self-defense. There was no way he would have killed his dad. It was impossible.

Unthinkable.

Nick checked the time on his phone. "Wow, it's already six. Maybe we should head downstairs."

Six in the morning? It felt like ten at night.

"Come on. You must be exhausted. Let's find you something to eat, and then we can crash for a few hours." Nick placed his hand on the small of Kennedy's back as they headed to the elevator. She did her best to ignore his touch. She didn't want his sympathy right now. She didn't want his food or his hospitality, either.

The only thing she wanted was the chance to prove Noah's innocence.

CHAPTER 23

The Lindgrens were still sleeping when Nick and Kennedy entered his apartment. She headed straight for the couch. What a night.

Or morning.

Whatever.

She stretched out, feeling the exhaustion seep out of the pores of her legs. She shut her eyes, realizing for the first time what a tension headache she had developed.

Noah was innocent. She knew that as clearly as she knew the periodic table. He couldn't have killed his dad. He was out all night. She'd heard him say so herself. Sure, it'd be embarrassing to admit he'd been at a gay bar, and not everyone would swallow his side of the story. But wasn't that still better than having people think he'd murdered his own dad?

She kept replaying Detective Drisklay's recitation from earlier that day. Or night. Whichever it was. He made it out as if Noah were a petulant toddler, ready to lash out at his dad for not agreeing with him. Parents and children disagreed all the time. Kennedy couldn't begin to guess how many fights she and her dad had gotten in while she still was in high school. Fights over how short her skirts could be, fights about how much makeup was too much, fights about the so-called losers he didn't want hanging around his home or his daughter. That still didn't mean she would ever dream of murder.

Noah was a well brought-up, put-together boy. He had pleasant manners, a kind disposition. His biggest fault was probably that he was so broody, but that could be explained by the frustration of being attracted to guys in a home as staunch and strict as the Abernathys'.

And where had that attraction come from, exactly? She'd been led to believe that people who were gay chose that lifestyle. What did that mean for people like Noah, people who hated being attracted to the same gender, people who'd been told their whole lives those attractions were wicked and evil? Should Noah feel guilty for liking other guys, or was it nothing more than a temptation, the same kind of temptation Kennedy faced when her roommate ogled the pictures in her calendar full of shirtless firemen with their hard jawlines and chiseled abs?

If there was one thing she remembered from sitting in Sandy's Sunday school class as a little girl, it was that temptations themselves weren't a sin. How did that translate in the case of someone like Noah? And how could Christians hope to settle down enough to agree on anything in the homosexuality debate until they discovered unequivocally the core reasons people ended up having same-sex attractions in the first place? Was it genetic? Hormonal? The byproduct of upbringing? Sign of abuse?

She thought about Nick's sister Lessa. He'd never finished the story. Kennedy tried to guess what happened to her. If her mom hadn't thrown herself into that "housewife theology," as Nick called it, would Lessa have run away from home? Would she have grown to be completely comfortable as a heterosexual, completely comfortable with herself as a woman?

And what did it mean to be perfectly comfortable as a woman, anyway? Kennedy's dad talked to her all the time about modesty, warned her not to cause anyone to stumble by dressing too provocatively. Sometimes when she was walking around campus, she'd catch another student staring at her and feel immediately guilty. If she didn't spend so much time on her hair, if she didn't worry so much about her clothes, would people stop looking at her like that?

Was it her fault if she wanted to look good? Was that something she was supposed to be ashamed of? It's not like she could crawl out of her own body, not like she could stop being a woman. If people turned their heads or entertained impure thoughts, wasn't that their problem, not hers? She couldn't stop being a female, so why should she feel ashamed of that?

Kennedy was a virgin, but that didn't mean she wasn't curious. It didn't mean she didn't struggle with desires. There were times when she wished she could free herself from all that sexual baggage. Stop thinking about sex, stop worrying about sex, and just go on with her life without the constant fear of getting date raped or harassed. Without worrying about whether or not she was dressed too immodestly or if she was causing anyone to stumble. Without worrying about who she'd marry and what it would feel like to be with him on their wedding night. If she could turn herself into an asexual being, there was the very real chance that she and Reuben could be lab partners again their sophomore year instead of him hiding down in

Kenya to protect her from falling in love with someone who would one day die of AIDS.

Her whole body was heavy. Why did her mind keep racing? Why couldn't she slow her thoughts down? They crashed and tumbled together: images of Drisklay cuffing Noah and dragging him to the exit, of Vivian claiming responsibility for her husband's murder, of Jodie crying softly into Nick's chest at her grandma's home. Had all that really happened in a single night?

She needed to take a deep breath. Slow down those chaotic thoughts. Ignore those flashing mental images.

She couldn't do anything to help Noah right now. All she could do was pray.

Pray ...

Dear Father, Kennedy began, but she fell asleep before she could say another word.

CHAPTER 24

"It's burnt."

Kennedy woke up to the grating sound of a high-pitched whine.

Pots crashed and clanged against one another in Nick's kitchen. "Woong, I told you, Miss Kennedy and Mr. Nick are trying to get some sleep. They had a long night ..."

"Yucky!"

Kennedy opened her eyes in time to see a dark brown pancake flying through the dining room and landing beside Nick's trash can. She heard Sandy muttering under her breath but couldn't make out what she said.

She sat up on Nick's couch and stifled a groan. Every muscle in her body was stiff. She could only guess what time it was. Had she slept another day away? Sandy was cooking breakfast, so it couldn't be too late, could it?

"Good morning, sweetheart," Sandy called from the kitchen. "Sorry about the noise. We were trying to be quiet."

"Yucky!" Woong screeched.

Sandy's hair was falling out of her French braid in small, frizzy strands that made the gray stand out so much more than the brown. "I already told you. Mr. Nick didn't have the same ingredients we use at home. They're different pancakes. Different." She spoke the last word slowly and deliberately.

"It's burnt." Woong pouted.

Sandy sighed and pointed to the stove with a spatula. "Would you like a pancake or two, hon?"

Kennedy wasn't sure why she didn't feel hungrier. Something from the kitchen didn't smell quite right.

"I'm sorry." Sandy leaned over the stove to flip her pancakes over. "All I could find was flour and salt. It's, well, it's not how I'm used to ..."

"Yucky!" Woong screamed.

Sandy sighed and took a small bite from the pancake. "I know, son. Maybe when Dad wakes up we'll go out to Rusty's, or ..."

"I'm already awake." Carl sat up with a loud succession of groans. "I'm awake," he repeated, as if he needed to convince himself. He turned to

Kennedy. "How'd last night go? Did you and Nick get much sleep?"

Kennedy tried to remember the chronology of last night's events, starting at the time the Lindgrens went to bed.

"Carl, darling, she just woke up." Sandy stepped into the living room to give her husband a kiss on his cheek. "And Woong's starving. We better find someplace we can eat, and then Kennedy can tell us about her night. It was two by the time we got here. I'm sure not much more could have happened between now and then."

"You'd be surprised." Kennedy glanced down the hall, where a few straggling dreadlocks were all that could be seen sticking out from a camouflage sleeping bag.

Sandy was rubbing Carl's back. "Well, let's let Nick get some more sleep. We can find some place around here that serves breakfast, and you can tell us all about it."

Kennedy sipped her hot cocoa at Rusty's Diner and hoped she'd gotten all her facts straight. She'd started the story as soon as the waitress took their order, and their food arrived when she got to the part about Drisklay arresting Noah.

"So Vivian's not the suspect?" Sandy asked and tucked a napkin on Woong's lap.

"No. She never was, really. I think she was afraid they'd go after Noah, so she turned herself in."

Sandy stripped the paper off a straw and slipped it into Woong's orange juice. "So what made them decide it was really Noah?"

"I don't know." Kennedy strained, trying to read Carl's and Sandy's faces. Did they think he was guilty?

Carl dipped his biscuit into the gravy. "Drisklay doesn't have to tell everything he found in his investigation."

"I know that," Sandy said. "I just thought maybe he gave some sort of clue ..."

"I really don't know what made him come after Noah." Kennedy's mind was still spinning. "It doesn't make sense to me."

"Hate can make people do some unthinkable things," Sandy mused.

Carl frowned. "Nobody's saying Noah really did it."

"I know that. I'm just thinking ..." Sandy shook her head. "Poor Vivian.

First her husband gone. Now her son ..." She clucked her tongue.

"Now, what about that guy who was stabbed? What did you say his name was?"

When he wasn't looking, Woong tore off a big chunk of Carl's biscuit and shoved it in his mouth.

"Marcos Esperanza," Kennedy answered.

"Why does that name sound so familiar?" he asked.

"He's some kind of counselor," Kennedy answered. "Works with teens who are struggling with homosexuality, or something like that." She remembered how angry Nick got learning about Marcos's work and wondered if Carl held different opinions.

Sandy smothered strawberry jam on a piece of her toast and set it on Woong's plate. "Who does Drisklay think stabbed him?"

Carl didn't give Kennedy the chance to respond. "He's a detective, babe. He's not gonna share all his research and fact-finding with a college girl. No offense," he added with a nod toward Kennedy.

"I know that." Sandy pouted and stopped Woong from stuffing the jam packets into his pockets. "I just wondered if maybe he said something ..."

"No. Nothing." Kennedy wasn't the only one looking for answers.

"Marcos Esperanza," Carl repeated. "I'm sure I know that name." He pulled out his phone. "I think I'm supposed to be able to get internet on this new thing. Can I do that even if I'm not at home?"

Kennedy reached out her hand and took his cell. "What are you trying to look up?"

"That Marcos guy. I need to remember why he sounds so familiar."

Woong knocked over a water glass, and Sandy reached for a pile of napkins to wipe up the mess. "It seems to me like that counselor is the key to everything. Once the doctors wake him up, he can tell Detective Drisklay who attacked him, and that should take them to the real murderer. Sounds simple enough, don't you think?"

Kennedy's gut twisted and her heart dropped in her chest when she clicked on the Channel 2 link that her Google search brought up. She shook her head.

"It's not going to be that easy." She handed Carl back his phone. "Marcos died from his stab wounds sometime during the night."

CHAPTER 25

Nobody talked about Marcos or any of the Abernathys as they piled into Carl's maroon Honda. While Woong let out an occasional protest to tell his parents he was hungry, Carl and Sandy debated where they should go. The fire marshal hadn't cleared their home yet, and the arson investigation was still ongoing. Nick's place had worked on short notice, but Kennedy was glad that nobody was seriously talking about staying there long-term.

"I say we splurge and get a hotel room," Carl was saying. "I'll be at my office, but you and Woong can spend your days in the pool. I think he'd like swimming, don't you?"

"I'd have to buy him trunks," Sandy mused. "And we still haven't finished our back-to-school shopping. Did you know that checklist we got from the school has over thirty items on it? I swear, Target and Walmart must be giving the school district a share in the profits or something. I don't remember ever having to spend so much the last time we sent our kids off to school."

"The last time we sent our kids off to school, Reagan was running for president."

Sandy shook her head. "Well, the budget's tight. That's all I'm saying. Have you talked with the insurance agent yet about the fire?"

"No. I've only been awake for an hour, babe."

Sandy sighed. "Well, we need to figure that out. We have enough for groceries for the rest of the month, but Woong's supplies plus the clothes he'll need is gonna be another couple hundred. I just don't see how we'll pay for a hotel without dipping into our emergency fund."

"That's why they call it an emergency fund," Carl muttered.

Kennedy leaned her head against the neck rest. She hated sitting in the back seat of cars. She felt like an eight-year-old making the five-hour drive upstate to visit her grandma.

"I'm hungry."

Woong's parents ignored him.

"Well, I say we book a hotel for the night. That gives you and Woong a place to stay. And you've got Kennedy, too. Dorms don't open until Friday, right?"

"Yeah." Kennedy hated to think of Carl and Sandy going out of their way to accommodate her at a time like this. Maybe she'd call her dad and see if he could help deflect some of the costs of a hotel.

Sandy pulled a hard candy out of her purse and passed it back to Woong. "The other option is we could look for rentals. It's got to be cheaper than a hotel."

Carl turned on his talk radio show. "I think that's a little drastic right now. Nobody's condemned the house yet. Might just need to patch up Woong's room."

"And in the meantime, we need a place to sleep." Sandy turned the volume down to low.

Nobody spoke. Kennedy had seen Carl and Sandy disagree plenty of times before, but this felt different for some reason. She hated to think that her staying with the Lindgrens was causing them so much stress. Maybe she could email the dean of students, see if she could move into her dorm a couple days early.

The radio host mentioned Wayne Abernathy, and Carl scarcely beat Sandy to shut it off.

"What about some kind of motel?" Sandy crossed her arms and stared out her window. "They're furnished, aren't they? More like a home than a hotel room. Don't a lot of them rent by the week?"

"It's a good idea, but we still have to see what the insurance adjuster says. I haven't gone over that policy in a decade. I don't know what it covers and what it doesn't."

"Even if insurance doesn't cover it right away, it will give us something of a home for the time being. They have kitchens, so we can do our own cooking. Save money on food."

"Yeah." Carl sighed. "I'll look into it. What about for now? I've got work to do at the church. Do you all want to tag along with me, or do you want me to drop you off at Nick's place?"

"We'll drop you off at the office and take the car to do our shopping. Kennedy, you're welcome to ride along if you're not too tired. Do you need new school supplies, too?"

Kennedy smiled at the thought of Sandy buying her packets of erasers and black and white composition books for her college classes. "It's all right. I can get all that stuff at the campus bookstore."

"Yeah, but it's so expensive there, isn't it?" Sandy turned around in her seat.

"I guess so." Eventually she'd need to find a place to take a nap, but she'd had a cup of coffee at Rusty's and didn't expect to sleep anytime soon. And actually, Sandy was right. It would be cheaper to buy her school things off campus somewhere. She had her dad's debit card in her ...

"Oh, wait. Do you think we could swing by your house? My wallet's back there, and ..."

"No, don't you worry about that." Sandy twisted around once more. Kennedy wondered if she'd have a kink in her neck for the rest of the day. "I know how it is for you starving college students. You've got more important things to do with the little bit of money you have, so you just sit back and let Carl and me spoil you for the day, all right? What about clothes? You need new shoes or anything?"

From the front seat, Carl muttered something about budgets and emergency funds.

"That's ok." Kennedy made a mental note to call her dad and get him to find a subtle way to reimburse the Lindgrens for anything they got for her over the next couple days.

Carl turned the radio back on, but as soon as he did, Sandy switched it to the praise and worship station.

Jesus, you're my Healer, my Shepherd, my Shield.

Kennedy shut her eyes. Her soul drank in the words.

Jesus, you're the One who makes me whole.

It had been a grueling thirty-six hours. There was no way she'd be starting her fall semester as rested and relaxed as she'd hoped. Somewhere, a teen boy was sitting in a jail cell for a crime he couldn't have committed. A father was dead, as well as a counselor who'd done what he could to help others. Woong was working his way into another fit after Sandy told him it'd be another day of shopping centers and clothes stores. But somewhere deep within Kennedy's spirit, buried so far down she had to channel all her mental energy to focus on it, was a peace.

A certainty.

The world was dark. Full of hatred and violence. But somewhere in the midst of the chaos, somewhere above the darkness and confusion, was a God of love. A God of refuge.

A God gentle and compassionate enough to give her soul the rest it so desperately craved.

CHAPTER 26

Kennedy lost track of how many stores she'd been in by the time Sandy pulled up in front of a little sandwich shop in downtown Cambridge. "Now, I know Carl's worried about the budget, but I can't have you and Woong starve now." She waited for the song on her worship album to finish before she turned the Honda off.

"So tell me, sweetie, how was your summer? I feel like you landed here, and then everything happened all at once, and we never really got a chance to talk about anything."

Woong jumped out of the back seat, obviously in a better mood now that they had pulled up in front of a restaurant and not another clothes store. Medford Academy was a charter school with a dress code nearly as strict as the one at Kennedy's girls' school back in Yanji. The trunk of the Lindgrens' Honda was filled with bags of khaki pants, khaki shorts, brand new socks and underwear, and a dozen or more polo-style shirts in just about every shade of blue, green, and tan. Sandy had been right about one thing. Getting her son ready for school, even a publicly funded one, was ridiculously expensive. What Sandy had spent on Woong's school supplies and clothes was more than the amount Kennedy had to budget for a whole semester's worth of college textbooks.

"Shut that door a little harder, son." Sandy took Woong's hand when he joined her on the sidewalk, but he quickly snatched it away and shoved it in the pocket of his shorts.

Once they were seated at a table in front of their oversized sandwiches, Sandy took a sip of her sweetened tea. "I'm still waiting to hear about your summer."

Kennedy had to stretch her mind back to what felt like the distant past. Had it only been yesterday she landed in the States? "It was good. I got a lot of reading done. Lots of Shakespeare. I wanted to get ahead for the lit class I'm taking."

Sandy nudged Woong with her elbow. "Honey, you need to finish one bite before you take another." She gave Kennedy an apologetic smile. "I'm sorry, dear. Could you say that again?"

Kennedy told Sandy about her summer reading list, about the classes she'd be taking this semester, about how relaxing it had been to spend three and a half months away from deadlines, lab reports, and research papers.

"You work so hard, pumpkin. I still remember how tiny you used to be with your little pigtails sitting in my Sunday school class. I want you to know Carl and I sure are proud of the young woman you've become. Woong, darling, swallow your food and then drink your juice. Now look here. See how many floaties you got in it?" She glanced up at Kennedy again. "And your friend, the one from Kenya? How's he doing? How's his health?"

Kennedy stared at her veggie sub. "Fine. There's a good hospital right there in Nairobi."

"Well, it's a shame he won't be around this semester." Sandy wiped some mustard off of Woong's nose with a napkin. "He was a real nice boy. I bet you'll miss him."

"Yeah." What else was there to say? It was like splashing sulfuric acid in your eyes and having the doctor look at you and say, "I bet it hurts, doesn't it?"

"Well, the Lord brings people into our lives. Sometimes it's only for a season, but he always knows what he's doing."

Did he, though? It seemed like such a waste. Such a senseless injustice for someone like Ruben to end up with HIV. For what? What good could possibly come from it? Of course, Kennedy knew the verse about how all things work together for good for those who love God, and she had seen that principle played out in her own life a time or two. But then she looked around her, at the injustice in the world, at the senseless violence, the hatred. That couldn't all really be part of God's plan, could it? If God could make good come from something like Ruben's sickness, couldn't he have stopped him from contracting the virus in the first place? If God wanted to show his glory and goodness, couldn't he do it by allowing his children to stay healthy and safe?

She was too tired to think through any of this. It was past midnight now in Yanji, and Kennedy was growing less and less sure of her resolve to stay awake until the sun set over Massachusetts.

Woong pushed his empty plate away from him. "I'm still hungry."

Sandy started to pile all his trash into a heap. "I have some snack things in the car. Help me throw all this away, and then we'll go take Daddy his sandwich. Maybe we can all have a little picnic at the church."

"So how do you feel after everything that happened last night?" Sandy asked as they drove back toward St. Margaret's to see Carl.

"I don't know." Kennedy hadn't had time to process anything yet. She wondered how she'd find room in her brain to fit all the equations and nomenclature rules she'd have to memorize this semester in organic chemistry when her mind was reeling over murder and arson.

Sandy sighed and glanced at Woong in her rearview mirror. "You can take a little nap, son. We're just driving over to Daddy's work, and Miss Kennedy and I are talking."

Woong didn't answer.

"I wonder if there's any news about the murders." Sandy shook her head. "It's just so hard to believe that Wayne's dead. No matter who it was. People are just so set in their ways. We're raising up a whole generation of folks who believe it's ok to hate somebody just because they believe different from you." She glanced again at Woong in the mirror.

"We had this foster boy once," she began. "Saw him all the way through his high school graduation. The only reason we didn't adopt him was because he didn't become legally free until he was seventeen, and we wouldn't have had time to make it formal. Name is Guy. Charming boy. Big dimples. Never seen someone so popular with the girls. And he never gave us no trouble. He was a good help around the house. Always eager to please. Pitched in with the littler ones without ever having to be asked. He and Carl got real close. Once he moved out and got a place of his own, he and Carl still had regular lunch meetings every week. And then one night, Guy asked us over for dinner. Said he had something important to tell us. We thought maybe he'd proposed to one of those girls he was always hanging out with. Or maybe he'd finally launched this computer design business he'd been working on. Anyway, whatever the big announcement was, I baked a big pineapple cake to celebrate, and Carl brought out the sparkling cider, and we went over to see him. He had this nice little place in Jamaica Plain. A little townhouse he was renting. Cutest little rock garden, quiet part of town. We were just tickled Guy was doing so well for himself, because we'd seen enough foster kids age out of the system and end up with nothing.

"So we got to Guy's house, and he'd fixed this delicious pasta dish, seafood and Alfredo sauce and homemade rolls. And we could tell he was nervous and trying to make a good impression, and we just wanted him to know how proud we were of him no matter what news he had for us. So Carl asked straight out what the big announcement was, but Guy said we should eat first and he would tell us while we had dessert. So I was cutting up the pineapple cake, and I was wondering by now if maybe it wasn't just an exciting announcement, but something he didn't quite know how we'd react to. Like maybe he'd gone and eloped, or maybe his girlfriend was pregnant and he didn't know what we'd say to that, but anyway, he just finished putting some whipped cream on top of Carl's piece of cake and then he says, 'I'm gay. I've been gay for as long as I can remember, but I was too embarrassed to admit it.'

"Well, this was a good ten years ago. Things like that weren't as out there as they are now. You didn't read about it every day in the news or things like that. So Carl and me both, we were pretty surprised, but we wanted him to know we appreciated him being honest with us. And so we talked a little, and he told us how he always felt more comfortable around girls, and even the ones he dated in the past, he just did it to try to fit in. And I'll go ahead and admit it, it was an awkward discussion. We'd dealt with pregnant teens and drug addicts and runaways by then, but not something like this, so it felt like new territory. We muddled through it, though. Guy hadn't told many people yet either, so it was a learning curve for all three of us, but it went all right.

"Then time went on, and we still got together with Guy, and he and Carl had their lunches even though Guy was busier now with his new business, so it weren't quite so regular. And we didn't talk much about him being gay, because I think he sensed it was something Carl and I weren't a hundred percent comfortable with. Kind of like our daughter Blessing wouldn't come home and tell us all the details from when she was out partying all weekend. You know, some things you just don't tell your parents, and once our kids are grown, we don't ask.

"Anyway, Carl and I didn't want to make a big deal about his lifestyle, because he was an adult, and far as I knew he'd never professed to being a Christian, and we just didn't feel like it was our place to judge. Well then, must have been about a year after he came out to us, Guy did the same thing. Invited us to dinner, only it was fancy steaks this time and lobster tails too, so we knew right away whatever it was, it was going to be big, and we just hoped God would give us the grace to handle it well. We'd read a few books by then, wanted to understand more of what Guy was going through, and what we'd both decided was we just wanted to keep our relationship with Guy open. If God wanted to deal with him and his choices, God could do that in his own time and in his own terms. We got some flak for it, too, Carl and I did. One of the elders at St. Margaret's in particular was pretty incensed we were still having dinners with Guy and getting together with him regularly. And Carl told him even if we didn't agree with all his choices, that didn't change the fact we thought of him as our son. None of our kids are perfect, but that's no reason to shut them out of our lives. But that elder just couldn't handle it. Ended up leaving the church, but that was over another issue.

"So anyway, Guy's serving up this lobster and steak, and Carl and I are just looking at each other wondering what's about to happen next. And this time, Guy doesn't make us wait for dessert. He just comes out and says, 'I met someone. We've known each other for a little over half a year now. And I've just gotten back from visiting his family, and I really want you to meet him, too.' So Carl (you know how he can get so thoughtful sometimes), Carl sits back and gets this little frown on his face, and I didn't know what to expect, but he says, 'Well, son, of course we'd be delighted to spend some time with him. Any friend of yours is a friend of ours.' And I thought that was pretty decent of him to respond that way, 'cause I know some fine, upstanding Christians who wouldn't have stood for it.

"So the big day comes, and we invite Guy and this friend of his over to our home, and we're both real nervous, Carl and me, 'cause we've never done this sort of entertaining before. But what we figure is we're all just people. Strange as it might be, this is a chance to get to know someone. Who knows how God's gonna use our time together, right?

"So Guy and his friend come in, and he's this real intelligent, real smooth kind of character. Real intellectual. This is the Southern girl in me talking now, but he was what you'd think of as a typical rich Yankee kid, really. Nice guy, though. Very polite. And I could tell Guy was going head over heels trying to impress him and make him feel comfortable in our home. So we start eating. It was something real simple we made up, something Carl threw on the grill if I remember right, and then Guy explains to us how he and his friend are planning a union celebration. I don't know if you're familiar with that phrase, but it's basically a gay wedding before gay weddings started to become a thing. And what Guy wants is he wants Carl to be the one to say the prayer at the ceremony. And Carl gets thoughtful again but eventually says he's sorry but that's not something he thinks he can do. And that's when things got ugly, because Guy's friend jumped in and said something like, 'What's the big problem? You marry straight folks all the time.'

"So Carl explains real calmly how it wouldn't be fitting for him as a pastor to give a blessing for this union. And by now, our son Guy, he's just trying to keep peace, but Felipe, his boyfriend or fiancé or whatever you're supposed to call him at that point, he says if Carl really cared about Guy, he'd give his blessing at this union celebration no matter what. And then he started to press Carl, demanding Carl account for it on a moral level, so Carl says it's nothing against the two of them personally, but the Bible's clear that homosexual activity's a sin. He wasn't saying he didn't want to be involved in their lives at all. He made it clear no matter what that they'd both be welcome at our home, that we'd give them the love and support we'd give to any other of our adult kids, but that union ceremony just wasn't something that he as a pastor could give his official blessing to.

"So things kind of blew up from there, and Guy left with Felipe, just stormed out before we got to dessert. We didn't hear from him for another month, maybe longer, and by then they'd gone through with their ceremony, and he wrote us this letter. Said that if we wanted to have any relationship with him, we had to tell him that we agreed with his decision. And Carl wrote back. Said that we wanted the best for him and his partner, and we'd love to keep on spending time with both of them, keep up a relationship, but we couldn't in good conscience approve one-hundred percent with their choices.

"And that's the last we heard from Guy. It's a real pity, too, because I think we could have all stayed good friends, even that Felipe he lived with. We had them in our home, invited them into our family. We were willing to keep those lines of communication open, see? We were willing to keep Guy in our lives no matter who he'd married or unionized himself with or however you say it these days. But they needed more than that. They needed us to say we were ok with their behavior, and that just wasn't the way we felt. They called us close-minded, but Carl and I, we didn't ask Guy or his boyfriend to change a thing in order to be part of our lives. We didn't say they couldn't live together or get married or anything like that. But they wanted us to change our beliefs, and if we didn't do that, well it wasn't good enough for them."

She sighed. "Our kids have done things we know are against the Bible, but when they're adults, they've got to make those choices for themselves. They don't have to be perfect to have a relationship with us. That's not the way God works. But Guy needed more than we could give. It would be like if our daughter Blessing — she's the one that got married last February. It would be like if she came to us and said, 'Mom, Dad, I'm marrying Damion, and I'm six months pregnant with his child, and unless you tell us we haven't been sinning, you can't come to our wedding.' That's not how it works. Yes, they sinned, but it wasn't Carl's and my place to make a big deal out of it."

Sandy pulled the Honda into the St. Margaret's parking lot. She turned around in her seat. "Aw, look at that. Sweet little pumpkin fell right to sleep. Well, he's had a long day." She gazed at her son with more adoration than Kennedy had seen in any sculpture or any painting of the Madonna.

"Tell you what," Sandy said. "Why don't you tell Carl I'm out here and I have him a sandwich and a small picnic packed for whenever he's ready. I'll just stay in here so Woong can get a little more rest. And take your time. The longer Woong sleeps, the easier it's gonna be on my poor nerves today."

As Kennedy entered Carl's massive church, she thought about Sandy's foster son. She knew it was possible for two people to have a close relationship even if they didn't share the same moral values. Her friendship with her roommate was a perfect example. Willow knew that Kennedy didn't drink, didn't do drugs, and wasn't planning on having sex until her wedding day. And as much as she teased her about it in her good-natured way, Willow never tried to change Kennedy's mind about any of it. Likewise, Kennedy knew Willow partied hard and slept around with just about everyone in Harvard's theater department. That didn't stop the two of them from enjoying a peaceful co-existence that eventually morphed into friendship. They enjoyed each other's company and shared a mutual respect for one another, different as they were. Kennedy didn't try to change Willow's behavior, and Willow didn't try to change Kennedy's convictions.

She stepped down the carpeted hallway, glancing into the large St. Margaret's library. As she approached Carl's office, she heard him talking with someone. The door was open, so she took a peek inside.

"Kennedy!" Carl boomed. "You get tired of my wife dragging you around from one store to another?"

His visitor turned around, and she recognized the chaplain from the Boston Police Department.

"Have a seat." Carl pointed to an empty chair. "Dominic just stopped by to tell me who set fire to our house last night."

CHAPTER 27

Carl seemed in a good mood for someone discussing the fire that nearly destroyed his home. "Should you tell her, or should I?"

Even Dominic had a slightly bemused expression on his face. "Why don't you do the honors?"

Carl crossed his arms and leaned back in his chair. "Well, my home insurance adjuster won't like it one bit, but at least now we know who our arsonist is. He's about three and a half feet tall, ten years in age (give or take), and his two favorite words are *hungry* and *yucky*."

Kennedy looked for any traces of a jest in Carl's expression. "Woong did it?"

"Yup." Carl chuckled. "Boy's been obsessed with fire since the day we brought him home. *Bul! Bul!* Shouts it all the time. Social worker thinks probably that's how he kept warm in the winters when he was out on the streets. Maybe that's why it's so important to him. We don't know. What we do know is he got hold of Sandy's long-nosed kitchen lighter. Probably saw her using it to start that busted burner on the stove or whatnot, and he decided to try the magical fire maker out for himself."

"So it was just an accident?" Kennedy asked, finally beginning to understand the reason behind the general lightness of mood.

Carl nodded. "Best news we could have gotten. Well, except now I've got to beg our insurance policy to cover the damage. But I'd rather shell out a ten-grand deductible than know someone is out to hurt me or my family. It sure is a load off my shoulders."

"Do you want me to ask the fire chief to come have a talk with your son?" Dominic asked. "Scare a little bit of safety into his system?"

Kennedy thought he was joking, but Carl paused as if taking the question seriously. "Let me run that by Sandy. She's been reading up on all the new ins and outs of adoption. Got a whole list of do's and don'ts, what topics you can broach, what topics are taboo, how much time you need to spend doing what with your kid each day .... To me it's just a bunch of psychobabble. Back when we were adopting out of the foster system, we didn't have time or energy for any sophisticated set of rules. But everything's different now. All these new adoption bloggers. A whole lot of stuff and nonsense if you want my opinion, but my Sandy, she swears by it. So let me ask first and see what she thinks. Maybe one of her books has a chapter about children who set fires to their new homes. I wouldn't be surprised."

Kennedy couldn't help but smile at Carl's attitude toward everything. She'd been something of a pyromaniac when she was Woong's age, too. She couldn't count the times her dad sat her down and lectured her for half an hour or made her watch fire safety videos over and over again until she could recite all their dozens of precautions and rules from memory. He never thought to have the fire chief show up, though. Maybe that would have been more effective.

Carl reached out and shook Dominic's hand. "Thanks again for the good news, brother. Now, let's pray our adjuster will accept our claim. I'm just waiting for them to pull out some kind of exclusion clause when it comes to children playing with lighters in the middle of the night. Now, if we could only find out who set fire to the Abernathys' place."

Dominic frowned. "Well, I have a feeling that's not going to remain a mystery for too much longer."

"Does that mean they have their guy?" Carl asked.

"In a manner of speaking."

"Well, who was it?"

Dominic sighed. "The fire started in Wayne Abernathy's home office. We've known that since the beginning. At first, everyone assumed the suspect set the fire to hide the evidence. Now, it's looking more and more like the senator was trying to get rid of evidence at the time of his murder. The department's best guess right now was he was burning some papers or files at the time he was killed. Whoever the murderer was, she left the fire going and didn't lift a finger to put it out before splitting the scene."

Carl leaned forward in his seat. "I'm sorry. Did you just say *she*?"

Dominic nodded. "I did. Video surveillance from the Abernathys' residence shows a young twenty-something pulling up into the Abernathys' place just after the son drove off. Someone let her past security — Abernathy himself, we presume. She left about fifteen minutes later, and within another quarter of an hour, the senator was dead and the whole mansion was going down in flames."

CHAPTER 28

Kennedy held her breath.

"Any clues as to who this mystery lady is?" Carl asked. Kennedy didn't understand why he didn't sound more excited. Didn't he see what this meant for the case?

"Your guess is as good as mine at this point," Dominic answered. "And of course, I'm telling you this off the record. It's got to stay under wraps for now."

"Of course." Carl drew his fingers across his mouth as if he were zipping his lips shut. "I won't say a word. But it would be nice to know something about the suspect."

"It's all conjecture now. Last I heard, they were working on retrieving her plates from the surveillance. That's gonna give us a place to start. For all we know, she could be anything from a hit woman to a jilted mistress."

Carl bristled visibly. "Wayne Abernathy wasn't that kind of man. He may have had some skeletons in his closet, but they weren't the kind that went around wearing high heels and risqué undergarments."

Kennedy might have giggled in different circumstances.

Dominic stood up. "Anyway, I can let you know more as information is released to the public. I'm just glad that you and your family can rest easy tonight knowing nobody's holding a death wish against you."

Carl and Dominic said goodbye, and Kennedy remembered she was supposed to tell Carl about his picnic lunch out in the car.

"This whole case just gets stranger and stranger, doesn't it?" he asked once they were alone.

"At least you got some good news. I mean, now you know that the fire was just an accident."

Carl nodded. "Houses can be replaced. That's just what I'll have to keep telling myself as we dish out a small fortune to pay for the repairs. But at least it's not winter. It's not like we're going to freeze while we wait for the builders to take care of it. Lots to be thankful for."

"Like Noah being innocent."

He frowned. "What did you say?"

"I said it's good news that Noah's innocent. Since the video showed the killer was a woman."

She couldn't understand why he looked so serious again.

"I guess you missed that part of the conversation." He adjusted his glasses, which were starting to slip off his nose.

"What part of the conversation?" Kennedy didn't like the way he was looking at her. Didn't like the tone he was using.

"When Detective Drisklay arrested Noah, it wasn't for murdering his father. It was for the stabbing that killed Marcos Esperanza, the counselor."

Kennedy stared at him stupidly. "But wait, when the detective came, he ..." She stopped. Had Drisklay actually said he was under arrest for the murder of his father?

Or just for murder? Was that why Drisklay took Noah in?

But he was innocent.

Wasn't he?

"Wait a minute." Kennedy did her best to replay the details of the conversation on Nick's roof. "He had an alibi. A friend he was out with. I forget his name. Dawson? Something like that. The two of them were together. The bartender at this club could vouch for them. They were jumped ..." She stopped when she noted the resigned sadness that clouded Carl's dark complexion.

"That's the same story he told his mom when he called her from the police station. Vivian phoned me earlier. Asked me to track down this friend, get the exact name of the bar." He shook his head. "That woman would do just about anything to keep her son out of prison."

Kennedy remembered how regal Vivian Abernathy had appeared when she confessed to her husband's murder. She knew she'd be handcuffed and taken into the police station, but she had looked so stately. So calm.

"I know about this Dayton friend of Noah's," Carl continued. "His mom came to see me a few months back, wanted to know what she should do when she discovered her son was using a fake ID and sneaking into gay bars. After I talked with Vivian this morning, I called his mom. Explained that Noah was in trouble with the law so I needed Dayton to tell me where they were last night."

Carl leveled his gaze. He had that same look in his eyes as Kennedy's parents twelve years ago when they told her that her grandmother was dying. That blunt but painful honesty you find every so often in a nurse who has the decency to tell you when you're a kid that yes, your shot's going to hurt, but then you'll be just fine.

Carl let out a heavy sigh. "Dayton's spending the summer with his father. He's been in Florida since June."

Kennedy let the words sink in. "So that whole story was a lie? The gay bar, the bouncer, the skinhead? He made all that up?" Kennedy couldn't believe it. Up on the patio of Nick's apartment this morning, Noah had sounded so convincing. She remembered his weak stomach. That wasn't the kind of thing even a trained thespian like her roommate could conjure up at will.

"People do crazy things when they're scared."

"Stupid things, you mean." Kennedy didn't get it. If all Noah was trying to do was establish an alibi, why did he pick something that was so easy to shatter?

"Like I said, he was probably scared. Told you guys the first thing that popped into his head."

"But he's the one who sought us out," Kennedy protested. "He wouldn't run right to us if he'd really been guilty."

"No? He's a kid, remember? A kid who's accused of murdering his own counselor, whether or not he meant to. It's very possible he turned to Nick because he didn't have anywhere else to go."

"But he was so shaken up ..." Kennedy stopped. Maybe it made more sense than she was willing to admit. The upset stomach. The obvious guilt. The fear. Did he make up a story about beating someone up in self-defense in order to cover a more heinous crime?

She still didn't want to believe it.

But maybe she would have to.

She and Carl stared at each other across his cluttered desk. She was so tired. She wished she could be like Woong and take a nap in the back of the Lindgrens' Honda.

"Oh, I forgot to tell you. Sandy has a sandwich waiting for you in the car. Woong's dozing, so she said you could take your time."

"Pastor?" The timid voice at the doorway made Kennedy snap her head up in time to see Vivian Abernathy scurrying in. She looked something like a mouse scampering away from a cat. A mouse in high heels and a short skirt.

Vivian held a bundle of papers in her hand and set it on top of a pile of Carl's unopened mail. "I'm so sorry to bother you, but you need to see something. I found the papers that explain why my husband was murdered."

CHAPTER 29

Kennedy knew Carl must be as exhausted as she was, but he did a good job hiding it. His tired eyes had softened into pools of deep compassion as soon as Vivian entered his office. If anybody's appearance could incite so much sympathy, it was Wayne Abernathy's widow. One of her earrings was tangled in her hair. Smudged eyeliner circled both her eyes, reversing any effect she may have expected from the heavy concealer she'd layered on. Her blouse was tidy and unwrinkled, but she had forgotten to tuck it in in the back, and her tailored skirt was twisted a full forty-five degrees off center.

She sat down. Kennedy wondered if Vivian even noticed her there.

"The detective called and showed me the surveillance footage, that woman who came last night. He wanted to know if I'd ever seen her before. I hadn't." She turned as if startled and looked straight at Kennedy but didn't pause before continuing. "At that point, I didn't care how she killed my husband or why, I just had to know if he was being unfaithful." She tilted up her chin. "And before you go and tell me all about how jealousy is a sin, let me finish my story, because it gets a lot more complicated than a simple affair."

Carl was leaning forward in his chair but didn't interrupt.

"I had to know the truth, so I went and checked Wayne's emails. The detective took his personal computer, what was left of it after the fire, but I had his passwords on mine. We didn't keep secrets, you know." She wore a haughty look, as if she were daring Carl to suggest her husband had anything to hide.

"It took a little bit of digging, but I finally found these. I printed them all up. I was planning to drive them straight to the detective, but I just ... I don't know. I needed to come to you first."

Carl hadn't touched the papers yet, and Kennedy wanted to scream at him to hurry up. She didn't feel like she could find any real rest, any real peace, until she got some answers. Answers that were sitting six inches away from her in a bundle that Carl refused to handle.

"Go ahead." Vivian pushed the stack toward him. "It's all in there. This will explain everything."

Carl frowned. Why was he waiting? Didn't he want to know the truth? Was there something in the pile he was afraid of reading?

Vivian rummaged through the stack. She pulled out one of the middle papers and set it on the top. "Let me show you. Last week, my husband received an email from this unknown account. Look at these attachments." She fanned out a few more pages and pointed with a blood-red nail that was slightly chipped at the end. "These are emails that my son sent to Marcos Esperanza. And over here ..." She spread out another bundle. "These are his replies. Conversations from the past five months. Conversations where my son divulges some very personal, very private ... Well, you know all about that side of it."

Carl nodded. "Yes, I do."

Vivian pulled out a page from the bottom of the stack. "See here, all these download attachments, I clicked on one. It was a tape recording of Noah's phone call with this counselor. I didn't listen long, just enough to know it's something my son would never want exposed." She shook her head. "From the day my husband entered the public arena, I prayed to God our kids would be spared from the scandals that so often fall on families like ours. Last year we went through everything with Jodie ... I thought that was bad." She let out a discordant chuckle. "Anyway, three days ago the person writing from this email address demanded a hundred thousand dollars from my husband to keep these records private. I know it's a sin for me to say so, but anyone who would betray my son's confidence and try to extort my family like this is a villain who deserves worse than death. I'll ask God to forgive me tomorrow, but today, I'm not at all ashamed to say it. I'm glad Marcos Esperanza is dead. And I hope right now he's suffering every imaginable torment for the way he destroyed our family."

CHAPTER 30

The gentle rebuke Kennedy expected from Carl never came. He sat silent for a moment, watching Vivian before he finally took one of her hands from across the desk. "I'm so sorry for what your family's going through."

Vivian was dabbing her face with a tissue when Woong's screeching voice sounded at the door. "I'm hungry."

Kennedy glanced at Carl and then forced herself to her feet. She could watch Woong for a few minutes so Carl and Vivian could have a little privacy. She shut the office door behind her.

"What's your mom doing?" she asked Woong in Korean.

"Talking on the phone. That's all she's been doing the whole time we've been waiting."

"I thought you were asleep."

Woong kicked at the church carpet with his shoe. "Sometimes I just pretend so she leaves me alone. I didn't think I'd have to sit in the car and listen to her blab for two hours. I'm still hungry."

"It hasn't been two hours. It's only been about twenty minutes." Kennedy tried to remember where in St. Margaret's they kept the vending machine. By the youth room, probably. She led Woong down a side hall.

"But she just talks on and on and on." Woong dashed forward the second the vending machine came into view, which also happened to be the same second Kennedy remembered she didn't have any money with her. She was about to tell Woong they'd have to wait to eat, but he squatted down in front of the machine and flipped open the snack slot. Adroitly, he snaked his hand in and pulled out two bags of potato chips. "Here." He tossed one of them to Kennedy.

She was so impressed he'd thought to share with her she decided not to chide him for stealing. "Thank you," she said, making a mental note to give Carl the change she and Woong owed the machine as she popped a salty chip into her mouth.

"No, I just wanted you to open it for me." He snatched the bag out of her hands.

She wasn't all that hungry anyway. "Hey, does your mom know you came in here? I don't want her getting worried."

"She's too busy blabbering."

Kennedy thought back to the way her own mom used to hog the house phone for hours at a time. "Well, sometimes moms are like that. They're so busy taking care of you that sitting down and talking to a friend makes them happy."

"She didn't sound happy." Woong's mouth was stuffed with chips so Kennedy could hardly understand him. "She was crying when I left."

Crying? That wasn't a good sign. "Who she was talking to?"

He shrugged. "I don't know."

Kennedy looked around. Maybe it was good Sandy got a little privacy. But what were she and Woong supposed to do? She could take him to the youth room. He might like the pool table there, and if she remembered right there was an air hockey setup too. Or they could go to one of the children's church rooms. What kind of toys did a kid Woong's age like to play with? Did they even play with toys still? The nursery was out of the question. Too babyish. Nothing but stacking blocks and board books.

That was it.

"Hey, do you like books? Do you want to go to the library and I'll read to you?"

"Ok." There was no excitement in his voice, but at least he didn't argue.

At first, Kennedy thought she could translate some of the simpler kids books into Korean, but she'd been exaggerating her language skills and underestimating the jetlag-induced mental fog. She settled with a Bible story book and read it in English, answering Woong's questions in Korean when he posed them.

"Why's he got that knife?" Woong placed a grubby finger on the picture of Abraham.

"He thinks the knife is to sacrifice his son."

"What's *sacrifice*?"

"It's back in the Old Testament, when God asked people to kill animals for him. It was the way their sins were forgiven back then, back before Jesus came and died on the cross." She could tell by Woong's face she'd lost him.

"They're killing animals?" he asked.

"Well, Abraham didn't bring an animal. Remember? God told

Abraham to take his son up on the mountain and sacrifice him there."

"So what kind of animal are they going to use?"

"No animal." She was beginning to wish she'd chosen a less complicated story. "Just Isaac. God told Abraham to go kill Isaac."

"He said to *kill* him?" Woong's eyes widened.

"Well, that's not what ended up happening, see." In the back of her head, Kennedy was wondering if Sandy would be upset she'd read Woong such a disturbing story. Why couldn't she have stuck with something better suited for kids, like Noah's ark or the talking donkey? She knew she was doing a poor job explaining and would have to start from the beginning. "God wanted to test Abraham to see if he'd obey, so he ..."

"I never knew God let people kill each other! That's so cool!" Woong jumped off Kennedy's lap and started making pretend machine gun noises, holding his imaginary weapon. Well, at least once Sandy learned what Kennedy taught her son, she'd never call on her to babysit.

Woong ducked away from some sort of pretend explosive. "I wonder if God will let *me* kill somebody one day!"

Kennedy shut the children's Bible and promised herself never to volunteer for children's ministry at any church at any point in her life.

Woong had just emerged from behind a desk to launch a grenade toward Kennedy when Sandy walked in. "There you are. I was wondering where you were hiding."

Kennedy blushed and slipped the Bible onto the table behind her.

Sandy grabbed Woong's hand. "Come on now. Daddy's done with his meeting, and we're going to have a picnic out on the back lawn. Doesn't that sound fun?"

Woong's countenance brightened significantly at the word *picnic*.

"Don't run ahead now," Sandy chided as they made their way down the church hall. "Remember last time when you knocked over those communion trays."

Woong didn't seem to hear. Sandy grabbed his hand again and managed to hold onto it for a full five seconds before he yanked himself free and sprinted ahead to his dad's office.

"God's gonna let me kill you one day!" he was shouting. Kennedy was glad he was speaking Korean so his parents wouldn't hear his bizarre proclamation.

When they got to his office, Carl gave Sandy a small kiss and then frowned. He wiped her cheek with his thumb. "Have you been crying, princess?"

Sandy's eyes scrunched up into a radiant smile that spread crinkle lines across her entire face. "Yes, but it's good news. At least, I hope you'll think so. Come on. Let's get this picnic spread out, and I'll tell you all about it while we eat."

Carl slipped his arm around her waist. "Honestly, honey, I don't think I can handle one more surprise. Could you just tell me? Any other day ..." he began, but Sandy cut him short.

"Of course. I'm sorry. I should have thought of that." She looked over her shoulder as if she'd lost something. "Oh, dear. Maybe today isn't the best time for this at all. I really should have prayed about this first. Now I ..."

"Just tell me what it is, woman." Carl's tone was tired.

"All right." Sandy twisted up the handles of her floral canvas bag that held the snacks she'd bought for them. "Ok." She took a deep breath. "While Woong was napping, I made a phone call. It was to someone we haven't heard from in ten years."

"Skip the guessing game," Carl sighed. "Please?"

"Ok." Sandy braced herself. "I was talking with our foster son, Guy. He says he'd like to get together."

CHAPTER 31

"You're mad now, aren't you? I can tell you're mad." Sandy passed Carl his lunch from the restaurant and pulled out a few other snacks she had picked up during their shopping spree.

"I never said I was mad." Carl's voice was expressionless as he unwrapped his sandwich.

"Yeah, but I should have talked with you about it first. It's just that I was telling Kennedy about Guy in the car, and I was thinking about Wayne and Noah never having a chance to reconcile before ... But still, it wasn't right for me to jump in full-speed and start making ..."

"It's not that, hon." Carl reached out to stroke her cheek. "I'm just tired, that's all. Tired of the hatred, the hypocrisy, the broken relationships. And I just can't help feeling like somehow this is all my fault. Maybe if I'd talked about how we need to love each other more, accept one another where we're at, maybe Wayne wouldn't have been killed. If I'd preached more on the importance of grace in our lives, maybe this wouldn't have happened." He shook his head.

Sandy rubbed his back. "You preach the word of the Lord. That's all God's ever called you to do."

Carl hunched over his food. "I know that, sugar. At least my head knows that. But my heart ..."

Woong frowned. "Are you crying?"

Sandy gave him a shush and a bag of crackers. "Dad's just sad, sweetie. That's all."

Carl nodded. Tears glistened in the corners of his eyes. "Yes, son, I'm sad. Sad that we live in a world where people are so full of hate. So full of violence. I'm sad that my own kid is forced to grow up in a world where parents would dream of disowning their child, no matter what the reason. I'm sad that we as the body of Christ would rather excommunicate a struggling member, gawk at his pain instead of walking beside him, try to guess his sorrows, try to make it our own. I'm sad that we Christians take one or two sins, the ones we think of as the really bad ones, and we crucify anyone who isn't as righteous and upstanding as we are, while we ignore our own pride and arrogance and hypocrisy." He sniffed and wrapped his arm around Woong, who surprisingly didn't struggle free from his hold. "And I'm sad that my friend is dead." He buried his face into Woong's hair. Kennedy glanced away, certain this was a scene far too poignant, too intimate for anyone but family.

"Here." Woong held out his bag of chips as an offering to his dad.

Carl kissed the top of his head, and Woong made a disgusted grimace.

"I love you, son," Carl whispered. "And nothing you could ever do would make me even dream of shutting you out of my life."

Something beeped, and Sandy pulled her phone out of her pocket.

She took a deep breath. "That's Guy. He wants to know if we can get together for dinner on Thursday. He says he'd like to introduce us to our grandson."

CHAPTER 32

Kennedy was grateful Nick had let her crash at his place for an afternoon nap. When she woke up and emerged from his bedroom, Woong was sitting spellbound in front of the TV, moving his body side to side while playing a racecar game on the X-box. Carl was on the couch reading a book, and Sandy and Nick were in the kitchen.

"Do you have any cornmeal here?" she asked. "I'd love to make you all some sweet corn muffins."

Nick frowned. "No, sorry. Most of the stuff I've got here comes from the freezer-meal section."

"Well, you really shouldn't eat like that, hon. You know they pump that full of salt and all kinds of artificial ingredients."

Nick grinned. "Why do you think I show up at your place so often?"

She smiled back. "We're always happy to have you."

He pulled two cans of tomato sauce out of a shopping bag. "Well, now it's my time to treat you. I didn't cook much growing up, but when I worked at the boys' home, I learned how to make a mean pot of spaghetti sauce."

"That sounds fine. Don't you think that sounds good, darling?" she called out to Carl.

"What?" He looked up from his book. It was one of the titles on homosexuality and the church from Nick's cupboard.

"I said, doesn't spaghetti sound good tonight?"

Carl gave a non-committal response and went back to his reading.

"Whoa!" Woong shouted and nearly knocked himself to the ground trying to lean over as his car took a sharp turn.

"Fun game, isn't it?" Nick asked.

Woong didn't reply.

"It's awful nice of you to cook for us." Sandy opened one of Nick's cupboards and frowned when all she found was books.

Nick dumped the tomato sauce into a rusted pan. "My pleasure."

Half an hour later, after two false alarms with the smoke detector, everyone was seated on Nick's couches with plates of spaghetti in their laps, except for Woong, who was on the floor surrounded by towels ready to sop up his inevitable mess.

"Sorry I don't have a more comfortable place for us to eat."

Carl patted Nick on the shoulder. "You've been more than hospitable, my friend. Words can't thank you enough." He set his fork down. "And now, I want to hear all about your meeting today with Noah. How is he doing?"

Nick gave him a sly smile. "I'll tell you about my conversation with Noah once you tell me what you think of that book I recommended."

Carl paused thoughtfully. "Well, it's well written. He's got a clear, succinct way of presenting his arguments."

"But you still don't believe he's on the right side of the truth."

Carl shrugged. "I don't have to believe everything an author says to appreciate the points he's trying to make, do I? You and I both know this is an issue we'll never agree on. And that's ok. I'm not afraid to hear your views, because I know what the Bible says on the subject. There are some issues that might be worth going to battle over. And even though we both feel passionately about this particular topic, here I am eating dinner with you, and here you are taking care of me and my family."

There was a peace that settled around Nick's living room, as cluttered and crumb-laden as it was. It was a peace Kennedy hadn't experienced since last year when she'd spent time with the Lindgrens.

A peace that made Nick's germ-ridden apartment feel like home.

"All right." Carl set his plate down on the arm of the couch. "I've given you my thoughts on your book. Now it's your turn to tell us what happened when you went to see Noah this afternoon."

Kennedy leaned forward so she wouldn't miss a single word.

"He was having a hard time. Obviously, that goes without saying. He said he talked with the family lawyer, and they're going to push for trying him as a minor and stick with a manslaughter charge. It's the best he can hope for right now. He never set out to kill Marcos. He's completely devastated."

"So what's the story with the counselor?" Sandy asked. "I still don't get what happened."

Nick sighed. "Basically, Noah was getting the same emails his dad did, emails demanding money or else all his conversations with Marcos would be released. Not a whole lot at first, amounts someone like Noah could get his hands on without drawing too much attention to himself. But then the blackmailer got greedy. Started asking for more and more, and Noah just couldn't come up with that amount of cash fast enough. That's when they got Wayne involved.

"So Noah got a text from his dad about these emails, and of course, he assumed Marcos was the one behind all this. Goes without saying he felt completely betrayed, so he went over there. Marcos denied everything, but Noah didn't believe him, and he was so distraught that ... I mean, he's the first to admit that he carried it way too far. That's why he's not going to fight the manslaughter charges. And I guess his lawyer is pretty hopeful that it won't be too bad, especially if they're able to keep him in juvenile courts.

"So he got in this fight with Marcos, kind of blacked out is how he describes it, and next thing he knows Marcos is bleeding, so he calls 911, doesn't say anything, just lets them pick up the call and hopes they'll send someone over, and he gets out of there. Hides downtown all night trying to figure out what to do, and eventually comes here. That's when Kennedy and I talked with him."

Kennedy thought back to their conversation on Nick's balcony. "So he really didn't know his dad had been killed until Drisklay told him?" she asked.

"No. He'd been running for hours by the time we saw him. He didn't know a thing."

"That's terrible." She knew the expression on Noah's face when the detective told him the news would haunt her for years.

Carl was shaking his head. "I still can't believe Marcos would do something like that, though. I met him a time or two. His testimony itself is miraculous. God delivered him from a life of homosexuality, gave him a wife and kids. Poured out so much grace on him ... He seemed so genuine. I can't believe he was a blackmailer."

"He wasn't." Nick wiped spaghetti sauce off his chin. "That's the real tragedy behind everything. Marcos was completely innocent. It was his office assistant, some new worker who was behind it all. She's the one who went over to the Abernathys."

"So she's the one who murdered Wayne?" Sandy asked.

"Yup. They ran her plates. They have her name and everything. Traced the emails back to her. Seem real confident they'll find her, and she's gonna have quite a lot to answer for."

Carl pouted and shook his head.

"Noah must feel awful." Kennedy couldn't even imagine what it would be like to know that you'd murdered someone, especially someone who ended up being completely innocent.

"Oh, it's a tragedy," Nick replied. "And that's not the worst of it. Before he left to confront Marcos, Noah went to talk with his dad. I guess it was this real cathartic heart-to-heart they had. Noah told his dad about the blackmail and everything else. And he told me he sort of expected his dad would just pay the hundred grand and keep everything quiet, because of course someone like Wayne wouldn't want to be seen as the father of the gay kid, you know?

"But that wasn't Wayne's response. And I have to hand it to him, I sort of despised the senator for a long time for making such a big deal about that lesbian wedding photographer, and I still think he was in the wrong there, but when it came to loving his son, he really stepped up. Noah said that his dad looked at him and said something like, 'It's going to take me quite a long time to process all this, but you're my kid. I made a promise to God when I started my political career that my family would come first, and that's why we're not going to give in to their threats anymore. You're my son, and nothing can ever change that. We're gonna go to the police and tell them what's happened, and if the media gets wind of it, so be it. I'm sorry for the embarrassment it will cause you, but I'm not afraid to go on record telling the world that my son is my son, and if they want to make a big issue about who he does or doesn't find attractive as a seventeen-year-old boy, that just shows how weak and cowardly and petty these folks really are.'"

The room was silent except for the sound of Woong slurping his noodles into his mouth one forkful at a time.

"That's what he said?" Sandy finally asked.

Nick nodded. "And really, I think that's probably why Wayne's dead. We don't know what happened during his meeting with that assistant, but Noah said his dad wasn't planning on paying any blackmail. I assume that's why she got mad and killed him. And maybe why the fire started, too.

Sounds like he might have been trying to burn some of the evidence when she got to him." He sighed. "I guess if there's any good side to the story, it's that Wayne died at peace with his son. And at least now Noah knows his dad loved him fully and unconditionally. No strings attached."

More silence. Even Woong ate more quietly than normal.

Finally Carl reached over to pat Sandy on the shoulder. "I've made up my mind, hon. I want you to text Guy and tell him we'd love to have him over. No, better yet, you pass me your phone and I'll call him myself."

CHAPTER 33

Kennedy had been wrong. She had spent the past day fully convinced that once she got all the facts straight about the Abernathy murder, once all her questions were answered, she could finally rest. The case was solved, but that sense of relief she expected remained elusive.

The Lindgrens had gone to bed. Kennedy should be sleeping soundly now, too. She made it all the way to sunset with only a short afternoon nap, but for some reason her body still refused to relax.

She'd taken Nick's *Lord of the Rings* volume out to his balcony and sat beneath the dim security light, staring at the same page for a quarter of an hour.

She tried not to think about Noah and his family, but that proved impossible. Where was he now? Nick said the lawyer would push for a reasonable bail, but they wouldn't have any of those details until his arraignment in the morning. It was probably a good thing her phone was still at the Lindgrens' house, or she would have wasted hours by now on all the news outlets, trying to gauge how messy of a scandal the murders had caused.

She thought about Vivian, bereaved of her husband, probably spending the whole night worrying about her son. And Jodie. Such a shy little thing. Would this family drama force her to retreat even farther into herself?

Kennedy knew she should pray but lacked the spiritual stamina to do so. As a little girl, she'd once gone to a Christian summer camp where the speaker shared a story about what happened when he told his atheist friend, "I'll be praying for you."

"Why?" the atheist wanted to know.

"Because it's so easy," had been the speaker's glib response. And for a decade or more, Kennedy had lived under the assumption that prayer was supposed to be simple, that if you could spend hours daydreaming about Shakespeare or your best friend whom you might never see again, you could just as easily spend that idle time in communion with the Father. *Pray without ceasing.* Isn't that what the Bible said? And for years, she figured there must be something wrong with her. Since prayer was supposed to be so easy, she was even more pathetic as a Christian for not being able to do it right or do it well.

Well, since then she'd learned how wrong that camp speaker really was. Anyone who said praying was easy didn't understand the mental energy it took to stay focused and faithful in spite of all of life's distractions. In spite of the heaviness that could storm around your brain like a tempest.

No, prayer wasn't easy. Neither was running a marathon. But that didn't mean either was impossible. It just meant you had to start slow. Baby steps. Disciplined training. Kennedy couldn't go outside tonight and run ten miles straight. But she could manage a mile. Maybe a little more. And if she did that every single day, after a week or two she could run two miles. Then three. The fact that she couldn't spend a whole night in prayer didn't mean that she should get discouraged and never pray at all. A couple minutes here, a few minutes there, and eventually her mind would achieve the degree of focus she needed for more prolonged spurts of time. She just had to be content to start with small bursts of progress.

She shut her eyes. *Dear Father ...*

"I was wondering where you ran off to."

Nick. He had a Bible in one hand and a mug in the other.

"I just made myself some tea. I'm sorry. If I had known you were up here, I would have brought extra."

"It's ok."

He sat down next to her. "How are you?"

She stared off to the part of the sky where the sun had recently set. All that remained was a faint blue afterglow that lit up some low-lying clouds. "All right, I guess."

"Pretty intense day, wasn't it?" Nick asked.

"Yeah."

He glanced at the Tolkien book. "I'm sorry. If you want to be left alone ..."

"No, it's all right. I can't focus on reading now anyway."

"I know what you mean." He shook his head. "Such a tragedy."

Kennedy couldn't have agreed more.

"But I guess we can be thankful for the good that's come from it."

She looked over at him. "What kind of good?"

"Well, Carl and his foster son wanting to get together, for one thing. And Noah knowing his dad still accepted him before he died."

"I guess so." She sighed. "I feel worse for Noah right now. I mean, you can't excuse what he did, but if he thought his counselor had betrayed him like that ..."

Nick set down his mug. "It's pretty horrible. I never liked that whole ex-gay ministry movement in the first place, but still, I would never have wished something like this on Marcos. Or anyone else for that matter. I might not believe in his tactics, but I know he was trying to do good for those boys he was counseling."

Kennedy was quiet for a moment. She recalled the beautiful girl in the green sundress photographed downstairs. "Can I ask you a question?"

"Mm-hmm." Nick was staring at the same cloud streak so far off in the distance.

"What happened to your sister?"

His face was close to hers. His expression so raw, still so distant. "She died. Committed suicide the year after I graduated college."

Kennedy didn't know what to say.

He stared at his clasped hands. "She'd been going to see a counselor, someone like Marcos, someone who was trying to cure her of her homosexuality."

Kennedy shut her eyes and could only see Lessa's bright, dimpled smile from Nick's picture.

"I tried to tell her to stop. She'd already gotten so much guilt from our mom over being a girl. Now she was going to this counselor getting even more guilt for being a lesbian. I'd done a lot of research by then. Made up my mind that being gay and being a Christian weren't mutually exclusive like so many churches teach. But as much as she hated Mom's structures and rules, she still had it in her head that was the ideal she was supposed to achieve. In the end, it's what killed her."

Kennedy regretted asking. It wasn't worth making Nick rehash such horrible memories. Not tonight of all nights. "I'm sorry."

He reached out and rubbed her back. His touch felt strange. Foreign. A certain shyness invaded the space between them. He took his hand away again.

Neither one spoke. Kennedy was too busy reliving pivotal moments of the day. Her talk with Sandy about Guy and his partner denying any sort of relationship with the Lindgrens unless they changed their views. Nick's sister dying because she felt so much guilt over her sexuality. Carl and Nick who would never see eye to eye on the issue but refused to let that drive a wedge of bitterness between them.

A breeze picked up. Kennedy hugged her arms against her chest.

"Getting a little chilly, isn't it?" Something about Nick's expression made her feel nervous. Flustered.

"Yeah."

More silence.

"So, anyway ..."

She didn't turn to look at him. Could only guess what he was about to say.

"You remember earlier in my kitchen? I was going to ask you something?"

She nodded, certain she wasn't ready for any of this. Not tonight. Not when she was so tired and confused and still hopelessly jetlagged.

"Well, what I wanted to know is if you'd be free Monday afternoons to help me run the Good News Club at Medford Academy."

"Oh." She'd been expecting something much different.

"You wouldn't have to worry about prep work or anything like that. I just need someone to be there, help take attendance, keep the kids on task. Just two hours a week is all I'm asking."

"Monday afternoons, you said?"

He nodded, his eyes brimming over with eagerness. "I could even pick you up."

"I'm sorry. I've got organic chemistry lab that afternoon."

His whole being deflated.

"Otherwise I would have loved to." She hoped she wasn't being dishonest.

"Ok, then." He stared off at the clouds again. "Maybe next semester or something."

"Yeah, maybe."

He stood up. "I think I'm gonna go back down now. It's getting late."

"All right. I'll be there pretty soon." She hoped he wasn't disappointed. Why did she feel like she was always letting him down?

"Good night." His footsteps were clunky as he walked away in his slightly oversized sandals. Kennedy sat in the dim artificial light, listening to the slight sounds of traffic, heavy from the darkness and silence that surrounded her.

CHAPTER 34

There were only four people in the Lindgrens' temporary home, but Sandy was bustling around so much it seemed as if there were half a dozen extra bodies. Kennedy glanced at the motel room, which she'd helped Woong tidy, spray, dust, and vacuum that afternoon.

"How much time do we have left?" Sandy opened the oven, leaned forward, and thumped on her bread rolls.

"It's ten to six. Exactly three minutes since you asked the last time." Carl was straightening his tie, glancing at his reflection in the small hanging mirror.

"I want a X-box." Woong seemed to know his parents were busy and didn't put too much emphasis into his demand.

"Should I call them?" Sandy asked. "They might need directions."

"He's got a GPS, and he has our phone number," Carl answered back. "Everything's going to be fine. You need to stop worrying." He leaned closer toward the mirror and tried picking a nose hair with his fingers.

Kennedy finished chopping the vegetables for the salad and set the wooden bowl on the table. The motel room came with a few random utensils, but Sandy had insisted on transplanting her entire kitchen to get ready for tonight's big dinner. There was no way to cram everything into the cupboards, so pots and spatulas and even blenders and crockpots piled out of boxes strewn against the far wall.

"I just can't believe it's been ten years. I wonder if ..." A knock on the door made Sandy freeze. "Should I get that?" she asked. "Maybe Carl should get it. Maybe that would be more appropriate. Carl, you gonna get that, honey?" She wiped her hands on her apron, another item she had snatched from her home while the builders worked on repairing the fire damage.

"Well, look who's here!" Carl's booming voice held no hint of the general state of nerves and anxiety that had zipped around the Lindgrens' home all afternoon.

Kennedy and Woong held back as Carl welcomed in the young man. "It's good to see you, Guy." He shook his hand warmly. "And who's this?"

He leaned down toward a young boy who held onto Guy's leg.

"This is Alec." Guy pried his son's arms free. "Say hello to Grandpa Carl."

Alec muttered something and sneaked right back behind his dad.

Sandy rushed forward with her arms outstretched. "Hello, Guy. Hello, Alec. We're so glad you came. Where's Felipe?" She strained her neck to look behind them.

"He couldn't make it." Guy cleared his throat, and there was an awkward silence before he squatted down. "And you must be Woong. Your mom's told me a lot about you already." He glanced at Carl and Sandy. "You say he understands English pretty well by now?"

Woong made an annoyed face and plopped down in front of some Legos.

"Why don't you go join him?" Guy tried to push Alec forward, but Alec refused to budge.

"Well, don't just stand here in the entryway. Come in." Sandy swept her arms grandly like a queen displaying her entire kingdom. "It's not much, but it'll work out fine for a week or two. Now, sit down. Dinner's already on the table, so I don't see any reason why we don't jump right in. Carl will pour the drinks, and you can tell us all about your design work. I hear you've been quite successful."

Guy had a handsome smile and looked quite a bit younger than Kennedy expected. Alec shied up next to his father at the table, and Guy kept a protective arm around him.

"You're sure a quiet one, aren't you?" Sandy asked as she filled Alec's cup with milk.

Guy nudged his son twice before Alec responded with the expected, "Thank you."

Sandy had to pick Woong up and set him in his chair to get him to leave his Legos, but at least he didn't throw a fit.

"Now, let's see." She stared at the table. "Everything's out except the rolls, and they just need another minute or two in the oven. I think we're ready to pray and bless the meal." She turned to her husband.

"Sounds like a good plan." Carl adjusted the collar of his dress shirt. Kennedy wasn't used to seeing him in a tie outside of church on Sundays.

He bowed his head. "Let's pray, then."

Alec leaned over and whispered something in his dad's ear.

"Everything ok?" Carl asked.

Guy cleared his throat. Kennedy couldn't tell if it was the lighting in the dining room or if he was blushing. "We'll talk about that on the way home, all right, bud?"

Sandy leaned forward. "What's he need? Does he drink milk? I should have asked first. We have orange juice too if that's better."

Guy shook his head. "It's not that." He looked toward Carl. "Go ahead. Everything smells delicious."

Carl bowed his head once more. "Lord, great God and heavenly Father ..."

Another whispered interruption from Alec's end of the table. This time it was clear that Guy really was embarrassed. "I'm sorry. He ..." He glanced at his son. "I should have done a better job explaining it before we got here. I just ..." He sighed. "I forget sometimes how much they pick up, you know? Things you don't think they've caught onto yet."

He held his arm around his son's shoulder. "Alec was just asking me if you were the ones who got mad at me for marrying his papa. I'm sorry. Like I said, we should have talked about it on the way here ..."

Carl got out of his chair and knelt down beside Alec. "Listen, buddy, that's a really good question, and you know what it shows me? It shows me you're a really smart kid. So I'm gonna give you an honest answer, ok? Your daddy and I had some disagreements. And that's not always a bad thing, you know. Even grown-ups disagree. And we get hurt feelings, too, and sometimes those feelings hurt bad enough it takes a while before it can get better."

Alec stared at Carl with wide eyes and leaned closer to his dad.

"The important thing to remember is we love your dad very much. We love you, too. And your papa. And sometimes we might not agree, but that doesn't mean we're mad at each other. It certainly doesn't mean we stop loving each other. Does that make sense?"

Alec nodded. Carl stood back up with a groan and returned to his seat.

"Now where were we? Oh, yeah. I think we were about to pray." He bowed his head. "Great God and heavenly Father, we praise you for family.

We praise you for love. We praise you for the way you can take people from so many different backgrounds, so many different stories, and you can weave our lives together so intricately. So beautifully.

"Sometimes it hurts, Lord. I'm not gonna sugarcoat it. Sometimes it hurts real bad when we can't see eye to eye. But Lord, first and foremost, you're a God of love. And today we declare that if your love is strong enough you carried that cross up the hill to Golgotha, if your love is strong enough you died for us while we were still your enemies, if your love is strong enough you reached out to us in our filth and sin and squalor, well, Lord, we've just got to believe your love is strong enough to help us see past our differences. Help us see past our debates.

"Only you can do that, Lord. Only you can cover over these divisions that have plagued us for so long. Only you can heal the hurts that have been experienced on all sides. Only you can let your perfect truth be proclaimed with perfect grace. You alone are God, and we love you, and we praise you, and we lift this up in the powerful and precious name of Jesus Christ."

The *amen* that sounded around the table mingled with the inviting smells of bread rolls, fresh fruit, and savory soup. It settled somewhere around Kennedy's shoulders, wrapping her up in a blanket of love and warmth before floating upward toward heaven, a perfect offering and fragrant aroma she was certain was pleasing and acceptable in God's sight.

Turbulence

a novel by Alana Terry

To my very own "Grandma Lucy," a missionary, Bible smuggler, prayer warrior, and encourager. I can't wait to see you again in heaven. I love you so much.

1926-2016

"Keep me as the apple of your eye;
hide me in the shadow of your wings."

Psalm 17:8

www.alanaterry.com

CHAPTER 1

T minus 3 hours 57 minutes

"Thanks for the ride." Kennedy gave Dominic an awkward smile.

He stepped forward. It would be the perfect time for a hug, but she knew better than to expect something like that. He cleared his throat. "Merry Christmas." He glanced at Kennedy's roommate Willow, who ran her fingers through her dyed hair. "Nice to meet you," he said.

"Yup. Thanks." Willow picked up her two bags without looking back and walked into Logan Airport.

Kennedy hesitated before turning away. "I better go." She shuffled from one foot to another, hating herself for feeling as foolish as a seventh-grader at her first boy-girl dance. She glanced up.

Dominic smiled again. Over the past semester, she and the police chaplain had gone out for coffee twice, dinner once, and a picnic lunch on Boston Common, but they never used words like *dating* or *girlfriend*. Everything about Dominic was slow. Peaceful. Sometimes Kennedy wished she could be as relaxed as he was. Other times, she was certain the deceleration would drive her insane.

"Well, have a great Christmas." He shut the trunk, and with his car effectively shielding them from any hint of physical contact, he gave one last wave. "Enjoy Alaska."

Her roommate was already halfway to the electronic check-ins before Kennedy could catch up. Willow adjusted her braided fabric carry-on over her shoulder. "Say good-bye to lover boy?"

Kennedy unbuttoned her leather coat. "I'm kind of hungry. Let's find our gate and then grab something to eat."

Willow typed into her cell while she walked. "Whatever." Her phone played a short electric guitar run. She stared at her incoming text. "Oh, my dad's wondering if you're a carnivore or not."

Kennedy didn't know how to answer. She'd never met Willow's parents before, and as excited as she was for the chance to spend Christmas break with her roommate's family in rural Alaska, she wasn't sure how well she'd fit in. "How do the rest of your family eat?"

Willow scrolled down on her screen. "Dad's a carnivore. Mom's like me, basically vegan except we'll have dairy if it's from our herd. You can choose. Meat or not?"

Kennedy shrugged. "Sure. I guess."

"All right. He'll be glad to hear that."

They were halfway to their terminal when the Guns N' Roses riff sounded again. Willow stared at her screen. "Ok, now he's asking how you feel about moose."

Growing up, Kennedy had never paid much attention to the kind of protein on her plate. *Meat* meant any animal that wasn't poultry or fish, but she was pretty sure moose had never made it on her palate before.

"I guess that's fine."

Willow wrinkled her nose. "I should warn you, it's probably roadkill."

Kennedy wasn't sure she'd heard correctly. "Road what?"

"Roadkill. You know. Driver hits a moose, moose bites it, and nobody wants to waste that much meat." She pouted at Kennedy's raised eyebrows. "You've got a lot to learn about Alaska."

Even though Willow was still typing into her phone, Kennedy had to hurry to keep up. "Maybe it's best I don't know where it's coming from."

Willow shrugged, but Kennedy thought she detected a smile hidden under her roommate's rather bored expression. So far, she and Willow had enjoyed their second year together as Harvard roommates. Kennedy had gone into her sophomore year so terrified of falling behind that she actually ended up ahead. She'd finished her final paper for her Shakespeare class the week before Thanksgiving and handed in her fruit fly lab report to her biology professor a few days later. That freed up the last few weeks for her to spend extra time with Willow, who was never busy with anything unless it was memorizing lines for a play or attending theater rehearsals. The two of them had gone to the movies twice and even grabbed tickets to watch *Mama Mia* at the Boston Opera House as a fun way to kick off the Christmas season.

Or *holiday season*, as Willow and nearly everyone else on campus insisted on calling it.

The two girls found their gate and decided to kill time at a small coffee shop around the corner.

"Wait 'til you try Kaladi Brothers," Willow told her. "It makes all the coffee from the Lower 48 taste like melted snow."

Kennedy crinkled her nose at the comparison and breathed in the frothy steam wafting from her hot chocolate. She warmed her hands on the red and white cup, relishing the heat that coursed up her veins to her core, remembering how anxious she'd started out this semester. How terrified she'd been at the prospect of taking two lab classes at once. As it turned out, organic chemistry wasn't nearly the nightmare she'd come to expect. Sure, it was a lot of memorization, but you'd do all right as long as you didn't fall behind.

And if there was anything Kennedy learned at Harvard so far, it was how to stay on top of her work, no matter what was going on around her. Kidnappings, panic attacks, race riots, murder investigations — she had survived them all. And now she was about to embark on a brand new adventure in Alaska, land of ice and moose and glaciers. Willow had told her they might even get to see the aurora borealis. Kennedy had never witnessed the northern lights before and hoped they'd come out at least once on her trip.

While Willow texted, Kennedy stared around at all the people, the hustle and bustle of the crowded Logan terminal. So many people going home, visiting family, reuniting with loved ones. Last year, she'd spent Christmas break getting chased by a murderous stalker. Not the most festive way to get into the holiday spirit.

Now, her heart was as cheerful as Scrooge's magnanimous nephew Fred. She'd made it through another semester with only one or two minor panic attacks on her record. She had every reason to expect a good report card, with all As except for a possible B-plus in organic chem lab. She'd worked hard, and now she was on her way to Alaska, which felt even more foreign than far-east China where her parents lived as missionaries.

The hot chocolate nearly burned her tongue as she took another sip.

She deserved this vacation. And she was going to enjoy every single moment of it.

CHAPTER 2

T minus 2 hours 39 minutes

Kennedy and Willow boarded the plane early since they were seated in the very back row. As much as Kennedy hated the exhaustion and paranoia that came from flying in a pressurized cabin with hundreds of other germ-ridden strangers, she found planes to be some of the best places to people-watch. It was a good thing too, since for the next twelve hours, there wouldn't be much for her to do except read, sleep, and stare at her fellow travelers.

Her pastor's wife had given her a few books to take on her trip, missionary biographies Sandy thought she might enjoy. The Lindgrens were in the middle of a huge home remodel to give their adopted son more space and repair damages from a house fire last fall. Sandy was donating most of their books to the St. Margaret's library or else passing them on to others, which was how Kennedy ended up with a backpack full of biographies about people like Hudson Taylor and Amy Carmichael, pioneers in the modern missions movement. She doubted it was reading her agnostic roommate would approve of, but Willow was currently obsessed with some high-def shooter game on her smartphone, so Kennedy didn't think she'd care. Besides, Willow had spent twenty minutes flirting with a math teacher from Washington at the gate and was hoping to angle her way closer to him for at least some of the flight.

Kennedy was in the aisle, which gave her a clear view of the passengers as they boarded: A short, white-haired woman with spectacles that made her look like she should be in a tree baking cookies with the Keebler elves. Ray, the twenty-something teacher who flung a charming albeit somewhat awkward grin Willow's way when he spotted her on the plane. A fat, middle-aged man in an orange Hawaiian shirt gripping the arm of a sullen-looking teenager. Her shorts might have been appropriate on a sunny beach but certainly not in the chill of Boston in December, and her Bon Jovi T-shirt was so faded it might have been as old as the band itself.

Many of the travelers appeared to be flying solo, a miscellaneous group ranging from single men in flannels and jeans all the way up to business women in heels, hose, and mercilessly pressed skirt suits. A balding man in Carhartt pants sat across from a younger one with an SVSU sweatshirt. Kennedy tried to figure out what the initials stood for.

Interspersed amongst the single travelers were a few families. A couple with four kids, none of them older than Kennedy had been when her family first moved to China, made their way toward the back of the cabin.

"I wonder if they know what century we're in," Willow muttered, raising her eyebrow at the mom's head scarf and the long denim skirts the girls wore.

Kennedy tried not to stare. They certainly weren't the type of family she was used to seeing around Cambridge. The mother sat across from Kennedy with two preschool-aged kids, a boy and girl, while the older daughters sat in the row ahead with their father, whose jet black beard reached to his shoulders.

"I didn't think the Amish were allowed to fly," Willow mumbled.

Kennedy couldn't tell if her roommate was joking or not. All the information she knew about the Amish came from her mom's love affair with historical romance, a genre Kennedy avoided as a rule whenever possible. Once a month or so back home, she had to sit with her mom and watch a sappy historical movie, usually about swooning heroines and sensitive heroes that more often than not made Kennedy want to barf. Some of the films were set in Amish communities. Others were on homesteads in the 1800s. It was hard for Kennedy to keep them separate in her mind.

"Actually, they're probably Mennonite," Willow finally decided. "Oh, well. At least the kids won't be too bratty and scream the whole flight. *Spare the rod,* all that junk."

Kennedy pried her eyes away to give the family a small semblance of privacy. She wondered if the children were self-conscious looking so different than everyone else. Did they care? Or were they so used to things being the way they were it didn't matter?

A rustic-looking passenger in a Seattle Seahawks hoodie plopped into the row directly in front of Willow and Kennedy. The girls wrinkled their noses at each other at the overwhelming stink of body odor and cigarettes. Willow reached into the braided bag under her seat and pulled out two air purifier necklaces she'd purchased for their flight. She handed one to Kennedy, and they both slipped the small gadgets over their heads. If there was one thing Kennedy and Willow shared, it was their desire to breathe germless, stench-free air.

Kennedy unzipped her backpack. She was in the middle of a biography about Gladys Aylward, a London parlor maid who ended up traveling to China as a missionary. When war broke out with Japan, she led over a hundred orphan children to safety. The story was mesmerizing, exciting enough to turn into a major Blockbuster success. It would sure beat those farm romances her mom watched. Kennedy only had five or six chapters left. She could probably finish it by takeoff if she jumped right in, but she waited, relishing the fact that she had absolutely no reason to rush. The plane would touch down in Detroit in two and a half hours, let off a few passengers, take a few others on, and then it was a ten-hour ride to Anchorage. Besides calling her parents when she landed, she had absolutely nothing on her to-do list. She could read during the entire flight if she wanted to, or sleep, or try to figure out Willow's silly shooter game in two-player mode. For the first time in four months, she had no lab write-ups, no research papers, no book assignments, nothing at all to worry about. She'd even promised herself not to jump ahead for her literature classes next semester. The only classic she had with her was *A Christmas Carol*, which hardly counted since she read it every December anyway. This break was all about relaxing. She still didn't know what to expect from Willow's family way out in rural Alaska, but she was ready for an adventure — an adventure she couldn't enjoy if she burdened herself with tons of assignments and self-imposed deadlines.

The seats filled up as quickly as could be expected with a hundred or more passengers with bulky luggage and winter coats banging into the seatbacks and each other. Kennedy took in a deep breath, thankful for Willow's air purifier, which looked like some kind of strange techno-amulet. Even if the benefits were all placebos, she was happy for something to give her a small edge against the germs blowing rampant around the cabin.

The two older Mennonite children carried small backpacks, and as if on some unspoken cue, they each took out a book in nearly perfect unison.

Kennedy watched with curiosity. She didn't have any siblings, never knew what it was like to share a room or share her toys, what it was like to have someone to play with or pester as the mood struck. She hadn't considered herself lonely as a child, but at times like these she felt a certain heaviness in her chest as she wondered what life might have been like if her parents had decided to have more than one kid.

A row behind the older children, the mother began to read a Dr. Seuss book to the two youngest kids. Kennedy had a hard time pinpointing why she found that so strange. Was she so accustomed to picturing women in denim skirts and headscarves as strict and stoic that it was odd to think of them picking something as frivolous as *Horton Hatches an Egg*? The mother laughed, a clear, joyful sound that forced Kennedy to study her face more closely. She was young, much younger than Kennedy had guessed when the family boarded the plane. Clear skin, shining blue eyes. Kennedy couldn't help but thinking of Scrooge's niece in *A Christmas Carol* with her little dimpled smile that Dickens lauded so eloquently.

A minute later, the wife frowned and stopped reading. What was wrong? Her daughter tugged on her sleeve, and she absently handed the girl the book before she adjusted her head covering and shifted in her seat. She stared at her two children, as if she were about to speak. She reached her hand out until she nearly brushed her husband's arm but withdrew it a second later.

Kennedy followed her gaze to the front of the plane, at two men with turbans and long beards who were boarding together. One was significantly older, but they both wore loose-fitting pants with long cotton robes instead of an American-style shirt. The noise in the cabin diminished, as two dozen whispered conversations stopped at once. Kennedy glanced around, trying to guess what was wrong. The Mennonite mother clenched her husband's shoulder. Willow must have noticed it, too. She nudged Kennedy.

"You'd think with those long beards they'd be instant friends, wouldn't you?" Mischief danced in her eyes.

The husband turned to look at his wife. Kennedy couldn't hear their words, but the worry on both their faces was unmistakable. Meanwhile, the younger man with the turban nearly dropped a heavy briefcase he tried to heft into the overhead compartment.

"Oh, great," mumbled the Seahawks fan in front of Kennedy. "Stinking Arabs." He looked around as if trying to find a sympathetic ear. "Why they gotta put them so close to the cockpit?"

Willow smacked him on the back of his head. He turned around with an expletive, which she answered with a mini lecture about the myriad pitfalls and injustices of racial profiling. Kennedy wasn't paying attention. She was still watching the Mennonite couple, studying the way the color had all but drained from the wife's face.

"I can't say what it is," she told her husband. "I just have this feeling something is about to go wrong."

He looked at the newly boarded passengers. "Because of them?"

She shook her head. "I don't know. I can't say. I just know that something is wrong here. It's not safe." She clenched his arm with white knuckles. "Please, I can't ... We have to ..." She bit her lip.

The husband frowned and let out a heavy sigh. "You're absolutely certain?"

She nodded faintly. "I think so."

"It's probably just nerves. It's been a hard week for all of us." There was a hopefulness in his voice but resignation in his eyes.

She sucked in her breath. "This is different. Please." She drew her son closer to her and lowered her voice. "For the children."

"All right." He unbuckled his seatbelt and signaled one of the flight attendants. "I'm so sorry to cause a problem," he told her when she arrived in the aisle, "but you need to get my family off this plane. Immediately."

CHAPTER 3

T minus 2 hours 12 minutes

Kennedy watched while the flight attendant escorted the family down the aisle toward the exit. She had never seen anything like that happen before and couldn't stop an uneasy feeling from sloshing around in her gut, the same foreboding Scrooge must have experienced at the London Stock Exchange when he listened to the businessmen joke about their colleague's lonesome death. She was glad her roommate was giving BO Dude an Academy Award-worthy lecture against racism, or else Willow probably would have shoved her sermon down Kennedy's throat instead.

Getting a family of six off the plane took a quarter of an hour at least before the captain made his first address to the passengers. It was the typical stuff Kennedy had learned to tune out after a decade of international travel, but he included a brief comment about the Mennonites.

"Of course, safety is our first priority on this flight. We had a family choose to deboard the plane a few minutes ago, and I'd like to thank our flight attendant Tracy in the back for making that transition as smooth as possible. I want you to know we have a commitment to each passenger's personal well-being, and if there's anything we can do to make your time with us more comfortable, please don't hesitate to ask your nearest flight attendant."

After that, it was more of the usual drivel about seat covers, floatation devices, and oxygen masks.

Willow leaned back in her seat with a huff. "Some people are stubborn jerks."

"Didn't go too well?" Kennedy wondered why Willow wasted her breath on the smelly Seahawks fan but didn't bother saying so.

"I just don't get it. Are we still living in the fifties or something?" Willow crossed her arms. "I assumed the human race would have evolved a little bit farther by now." She rolled her eyes. "Can't even get on an airplane wearing foreign clothes without having racist bigots assume you're a terrorist."

Kennedy didn't know what to say. Chances were the two men in turbans were polite, respectable travelers who passed the same security screens as everyone else. But wasn't there the slightest possibility ... She thought about how loosely their clothes fit. How many bombs or bomb pieces would fit strapped beneath ...

No, now she was the one racial profiling. There were ample security measures, the TSA, the no-fly list, enough safeguards in place that innocent citizens could travel in peace and safety.

Right?

Kennedy tried to recall the details from a news article her dad had sent her earlier that semester. Eleven men from Jordan boarded a plane and freaked the other passengers out by their bizarre behavior, passing items in bags throughout the flight, congregating in the aisles, spending five or ten minutes at a time in the bathroom one right after another. The journalist who broke the story, a woman who had been on board and witnessed the suspicious behavior firsthand, discovered that airlines were fined if they held more than two passengers of Middle Eastern decent for extra questioning on any particular flight. Even if the men had raised security flags in the pre-boarding process, the airlines couldn't have taken any extra precautions against a group that large. There were folks who believed that what the journalist encountered was a dry run, a dress-rehearsal of sorts for putting together a bomb mid-flight, while some postulated that the men planned to take over the plane but experienced some kind of glitch in the air. Of course, others claimed the journalist was a paranoid, racist bigot who needed to shut her mouth instead of accusing innocent, peaceful travelers on unsubstantiated and somewhat vague grounds.

Kennedy knew plenty of Muslim students from Harvard, knew they weren't the crazed extremists the media made them out to be. She would be incensed on their behalf if they were made to endure an onslaught of extra or humiliating security measures simply because of their race or religion. But common courtesy and political correctness had to end somewhere, didn't they? At least when it came to protecting an airplane full of innocent civilians. Or was that the kind of reasoning that allowed cops like the one that abused her and her best friend last year to keep on wreaking their own kind of havoc on justice?

"Bunch of bigots," Willow muttered, "holding up a full flight because a few of the passengers were born in the Middle East."

Kennedy opened up her Gladys Aylward book. Maybe Willow was right. Maybe the Mennonites were racist jerks, xenophobic Americans scared of any traveler who looked even remotely different.

But Willow hadn't heard their entire conversation, either. Hadn't heard the fear in the woman's voice. Not hatred. Not prejudice. Actual terror for her family's safety. Had the family done the right thing? Mennonites were supposedly a fairly religious group, right? Did the woman have that gift of discernment Christians sometimes talked about, that ability to hear the Holy Spirit's warnings more acutely than the average believer? If God told the woman the flight wasn't safe, did that mean Kennedy and Willow were about to head into trouble? But if that was the case, why wouldn't God have warned her, too? It didn't seem fair.

Then again, if God told Kennedy to get off the plane, if the Holy Spirit impressed on her soul that she needed to leave, would she? And risk Willow thinking she was a xenophobic racist bigot?

Or would she fasten her seatbelt, sit tight, and try to convince herself everything would be fine?

Everything would be fine, wouldn't it? Kennedy stared at the pages of her book, remembering the way God had protected Gladys Aylward and the orphans under her care so many years ago. He would take care of Kennedy that way, too.

Wouldn't he?

CHAPTER 4

T minus 1 hour 43 minutes

"Gladys Aylward? What a remarkable woman."

Kennedy was startled by the interruption to her reading.

A white-haired woman with thin-rimmed spectacles and a blouse that might have been ordered from a 1970s Sears catalog smiled at her. "I'm sorry, the restroom up front was occupied, so I came back here and couldn't help but notice your book. Are you enjoying the story?"

Kennedy didn't feel up to chatting, but since the back lavatory was occupied as well, she didn't think she had much choice. "Yeah. It's pretty interesting."

"They made a movie about her life. Did you know that?"

Kennedy shook her head.

"Well, it's quite an old one. The actress who starred in it — oh, I wish I could remember her name just now, but that's what happens when your brain gets as old as mine. Anyway, the story goes this woman became a Christian after playing the role. I assume then that you're a born-again believer?"

That phrase always struck Kennedy as strange. A *born-again believer*, as if there were any other kind. "Yeah. I am." No use getting into a theological debate on an airplane with an eighty-year-old grandmother.

A flight attendant tapped the woman on the shoulder. "Excuse me, can I squeeze past you, please?"

The old lady sat down in the Mennonite mother's empty spot and glanced at the bathroom. "Looks like I might be here a while." She smiled warmly. "My name is Lucy Jean, but I insist on being called Grandma Lucy."

"I'm Kennedy," she replied automatically, wondering how long the bathroom occupant would take.

"Kennedy. What a lovely name. You know, I still wish my parents had come up with something more creative than Lucy Jean. You don't get much plainer than that."

Kennedy was about to protest that it was an attractive name when Grandma Lucy asked, "Are you going to Detroit today?"

"No, I'm on my way to Seattle and then Anchorage to spend Christmas with my friend's family."

"How lovely. I have a granddaughter in Alaska."

"Is that where you're going?" Kennedy asked.

"No, I'm getting off in Seattle. Going home to Washington. I was just in Boston to see off my grandson. He's on his way to ..." She stopped herself to finger Kennedy's necklace from across the aisle. "What in the world is this? It looks New Age."

All Kennedy wanted to do was get back to her reading, but she gave her best impression of a smile. "It's an air purifier. You wear it around your neck, and it filters out germs and dust. My roommate got them for us for the flight." She nodded toward Willow, who was watching some violent movie on her portable screen.

Grandma Lucy frowned at the gruesome image. "And your roommate?" she asked. "Is she born-again, too?"

Kennedy was spared the chore of stammering an awkward reply when the math teacher Willow had been flirting with came up to their row.

"Bathroom full?" he asked.

Willow plucked out her earbuds and offered her most winsome grin. "Hey, Ray. I was hoping we'd bump into each other during the flight."

Kennedy unbuckled her safety belt. "It looks like there's a line, so why don't you take my seat and I'll come over here." She stepped across the aisle and sat in the window seat beside Grandma Lucy. Her contacts were getting dry anyway, so now was probably as good a time as any to take a break from reading.

Grandma Lucy took Kennedy's hand in hers. Her skin was surprisingly soft for someone with so many wrinkles. "That was sweet of you, dear. Now let me take a look at you." She stared for several seconds before she gave her hand a squeeze. "You don't have to tell me. Let me guess. You're studying to be a missionary, aren't you?"

Kennedy slipped her hand away, surprised at how warm it felt. "A doctor, actually."

Grandma Lucy nodded, as if she had known that all along. "Medical missions, then?"

Kennedy didn't know what to say. Did Grandma Lucy's version of a *born-again believer* require some sort of ministry focus to prove your devotion?

"I'm not sure. I'm still doing my undergrad studies, so I guess I have plenty of time to figure that out." She let out an uncomfortable laugh.

Grandma Lucy chuckled too, tentatively as if she weren't sure what was so funny. "It's just that when I first looked at you, something in my spirit said *missionary*. I'm sure that's what I heard." She frowned and looked around her, as if her train of thought had derailed and she had to visibly track it down.

Kennedy had an unsettled feeling in the base of her spine. Why did it seem as though every other Christian on this flight was getting direct messages from the Lord except for her? Had God ever spoken to her that way before? Or maybe he had tried, and Kennedy just didn't know what to listen for.

"You're sure you're not a missionary?" Grandma Lucy pressed.

"No, but my parents are."

Grandma Lucy's face lit up before Kennedy could continue. "That's what it was. I knew you had a missions call on your life the moment I saw you with that book. My family was good friends with Gladys, you know. She came to visit us on more than one occasion when we lived in Shanghai."

"Really?" Kennedy's interest was piqued, and since Willow was busy laughing with her new travel partner, Kennedy figured she may as well try to enjoy her conversation.

"My parents were missionaries in China. I was born over there, in fact, and my father had a little Christian store he ran for decades before the Communists shut it down. When war broke out with Japan, we ran into Gladys on more than one occasion. She was taking care of so many kids!"

Lost in thought, Grandma Lucy continued to speak of her time in Shanghai during the Sino-Japanese War. Stories of bombings, narrow escapes from death, heroic ventures her father undertook to help the injured, the selfless sacrifices her mother made to assist the war orphans.

"Of course, she never took in as many as Gladys," Grandma Lucy remarked with a smile that lit up her whole face and pushed her spectacles up on her cheeks. "But she did what God called her to, which is all he expects from each one of us, isn't it?"

Kennedy nodded, even though her mind was still back in war-torn Shanghai where Grandma Lucy had recounted stories of fires and destruction as readily as if she were talking about Sunday picnics in Central Park.

"And what about you?" she finally asked. "You say you're in medical school?"

"Pre-med," Kennedy corrected and spent the next few minutes answering questions about life as an undergrad student at Harvard.

"And are you part of a good church body over there?"

"Yeah." Kennedy didn't admit that she only made it to St. Margaret's once or twice a month, fearing it might make Grandma Lucy rethink Kennedy's previous claim of being a true *born-again* believer.

"That's good." Grandma Lucy nodded sagely. "I ask because that grandson of mine I just visited, he graduated from Harvard a few years ago, and it filled him with so many idolatrous, liberal views of God and religion and the world." She sighed. "He's a great boy, don't get me wrong. Has a heart bigger than most Christians who fill the churches across this country. Gets worked up over injustice and actually does something about it. Just to give you an example, before he left for work in Asia, he was in Detroit of all places, interviewing parents about this issue they're having in the education system there. The schools, they're falling apart. Not just the system, I mean the actual buildings are falling apart. One school's pipes were so bad, they were leaking lead into the drinking fountains. Had been going on for years before anyone fixed it. Just terrible. And then this whole big mess over the Brown Elementary School. You heard about that whole controversy, I'm sure."

"Actually, no." Kennedy tried not to sound embarrassed at the confession. She'd been so busy with her studies that if her dad didn't send her a link from one of his conservative news sites or Pastor Carl didn't say anything about it from the pulpit, she'd never hear about a particular current event. Especially not one from as far away as Detroit.

Grandma Lucy shook her head. "Terrible thing. I don't have all the facts. You'd have to talk to Ian about that. But it has something to do with them closing down one elementary school and merging it with another. Well, that was the plan. But the school they needed to shut down was mostly minorities, and the one they were going to merge with was more upper-class, and those parents got themselves all worked up. Made such a stink that the school district decided to build a new school for the poor kids instead, except the site they were planning to build on was in a bad part of town. I'm not talking crime. That's bad just about everywhere in Detroit from what I hear.

"But where they planned the new building, the land itself was no good. All kind of contaminants in the soil, toxic waste from chemical factories. Except the parents of these students, they weren't like the upper-class folks. They're working families, lots of single parents who are at their jobs during the day and can't attend meetings and forums. Even the ones who have time, a lot of them don't speak English well and they're too intimidated to stand up for themselves. So my grandson, he went and documented everything, got some statements from the families and a few other community members to show just how bad things had gotten.

"He sold it to one of the major networks, had it all lined up to air on national television, but then that night some big breaking story took its spot. Something about a murdered politician if I remember right, and that hogged the news for the next week or two until it was past back-to-school season and his network contact said nobody wanted to think about the education system anymore.

"He was pretty upset, obviously, not because of the money or anything, but because he believed in what these parents were going through. Really felt for them, I mean. He told me what he hated most was seeing how the school district gave in to intimidation when it came from the upper-class folks. The rich ones had the clout they needed to make the right kind of noise, but these minority families — the ones whose kids are going to suffer most in this new school they're building — they don't get a say at all. He thought he was giving them a voice with his camera, but it never even aired." She sighed. "He's got such a sensitive soul, I know God can use him for mighty things if he only gives his life to the Lord."

"It sounds like God's already using him," Kennedy suggested, but Grandma Lucy wasn't listening.

"I pray every day for that boy to come back to Christ. And now he's off travelling around Asia. Same thing. Human rights abuses, refugee crises.

Always ready to speak up for the downtrodden and oppressed. So he's off to China with his camera but without the Holy Spirit to guide him. I gave him a Bible, and I told him I'd be praying for him. You know, that's all any of us can do in these situations, right? What about that roommate of yours? Is she born again?"

Kennedy kept her voice low, glad that Willow was sufficiently distracted. "I don't think so."

Grandma Lucy stared over her spectacles. "I take it you've witnessed to her by now?"

Kennedy glanced at Willow, who was snuggled up by Ray so they could share the same screen. "Well, I ..."

"You can't ever be ashamed of the gospel," Grandma Lucy interrupted. "Your roommate ... I can tell by the way she carries herself, that blue hair, those long earrings, that she's looking for something."

Kennedy wasn't sure you could discern that much about the state of a stranger's soul at first glance, but she didn't say anything. Something in Grandma Lucy's words had snuck past Kennedy's conversational barriers and found its mark in a conscience already ridden with guilt.

A year and a half sharing the same three-hundred square feet, and what had she done with that time? How many opportunities had she lost, opportunities to share the gospel with Willow, who was hurting, longing for more out of life whether or not her hair color had anything to do with her spiritual condition?

On the one hand, Kennedy was certain that if she were to bring up God or salvation, Willow would go off on one of her tirades against religion. So what was the point? Willow said once that Kennedy was the only Christian she could stand to be around because she never tried to convert anyone. If Kennedy started preaching the gospel every minute of the day, telling Willow she was a sinner in danger of the fires of hell, that would only confirm her assumption that all Christians are judgmental jerks.

But even though her silence on the subject kept the peace between them, was that in Willow's best interest? Kennedy thought about the missionaries she'd been reading about in those biographies: Hudson Taylor, David Livingstone, Amy Carmichael. The Chinese called Gladys Aylward a foreign devil and threw mud at her the first day she stepped foot on foreign soil. But she had remained faithful to God's call and ended up leading hundreds to Christ.

Kennedy had never had mud thrown at her, had never been called horrid names, but maybe that was because she'd kept her faith so hidden. She thought about the refugees her parents trained to send back to North Korea as underground missionaries. How many of them would suffer imprisonment or death as a result of their witness? And here was Kennedy, scared of mentioning God because she didn't want to annoy her roommate.

Were her priorities that askew? Or was she just doing what God wanted her to do? What was it that Grandma Lucy had said earlier, something about nobody having to do more than God asked them to. Maybe Kennedy's job was to prove to Willow that not all Christians are out solely to win more converts or smugly judge sinful behavior. Maybe that's all God expected of her.

But how would Willow ever get saved if she never heard the gospel? Kennedy didn't like the guilt trip, Grandma Lucy's insinuation that if she really was a *born-again* believer she should have converted her roommate by now or else died trying like the martyrs of old.

Grandma Lucy laid her hand on Kennedy's forearm. "Now, you tell me your roommate's name, and I'm going to add her to my prayer list. Then I'll give you my phone number and you can let me know when she's been born again, all right?"

Kennedy sighed. "Her name's Willow."

Grandma Lucy pulled a tattered notebook out of her purse. "Willow," she repeated. "Oh, dear. She'll be one of the last ones, I'm afraid." She smiled and explained, "I keep my list alphabetized, so when I'm going to sleep I don't forget who's next on the list. I always start with my granddaughter Alayna and make my way down from there. The good news is by the time I get to the Ws, I'll be nice and warmed up. If I haven't fallen asleep, that is."

Grandma Lucy's eye twinkled, but Kennedy couldn't tell if she were making a joke or not. She didn't have time to wonder long before the bearded man in the turban jumped out of his chair with a startling shout.

"What's he think he's doing?" muttered the Seahawks fan with the BO. Several other passengers turned their heads as well.

The traveler pounded his fist into his seatback and yelled something frantic in Arabic.

The man in Carhartts stepped out of the bathroom and stood frozen in the aisle. BO Dude lowered his head onto his tray table and covered it with his hands as if he were a first-grader in an earthquake drill.

The man in the turban yelled aggressively, waving his hands in the air as if to emphasize a point.

"Get down," BO Dude hissed to Kennedy. "That maniac is about to take over the plane."

CHAPTER 5

Kennedy swallowed as the flight attendant behind her grabbed the phone from the wall. "Captain, this is Tracy," she whispered, and then her voice fell so Kennedy couldn't hear anymore. She glanced over at Willow, whose face had fallen ghastly white.

All sorts of horrific scenarios ran through Kennedy's mind. The man pulling a machine gun out from his billowing garments and raining lead on the entire cabin. Or revealing an armory of bombs and explosive taped across his chest and demanding entrance to the cockpit. That couldn't be it, though, could it? There were security measures. Metal detectors. TSA agents. He couldn't have boarded their plane if he was that dangerous, could he?

BO Dude turned in his seat, still covering his head and laying low. "We've got to take him down now," he hissed back to Willow's friend. "It's the only way. We take him down, or we don't get off this plane alive."

"Wait a minute," Ray protested.

The Seahawks fan had already unbuckled himself. "I'm telling you, it's either do something now, or we all end up blown to bits."

Kennedy thought back to the mother who had warned her family to get off the plane before takeoff. None of this could be happening, could it? Even her dad, as paranoid as he was, had never given her any hint of what to do in the event of a skyjacking.

"Stay in your seat, young man."

Kennedy was surprised at Grandma Lucy's authoritative voice.

"Turn up your hearing aid," BO Dude replied. "When a terrorist starts shouting in Arabic on a crowded plane, he's not asking for a bag of peanuts."

Grandma Lucy stood. She was short enough that she didn't have to stoop to keep from hitting her head on the fixture above. "No, he's not. And he's not speaking Arabic, either. It's Dari, which means he's from Afghanistan, and he's saying that there's something wrong with his father. It sounds like he might be having a heart attack."

She nodded at a male flight attendant who knelt down in front of the robed man and was checking his pulse with his fingers on the side of his throat. Kennedy let out her breath and felt sheepish for how quickly she had assumed the man must be a terrorist. So much for being against racial profiling.

Willow let out a forced laugh, and she and Ray went back to their movie.

The flight attendant Tracy who had been whispering on the phone now addressed the whole airplane over the PA system. "We have a medical situation on board and need everyone to remain seated. If you are a medical professional willing to offer assistance, please inform one of us on the flight crew."

Grandma Lucy reached out to stop the woman as she passed down the aisle. "I'm willing to help."

"Do you have medical training?" Tracy asked.

"No, but I speak a little Dari."

"Ok, come with me. We'll probably need to get him to the back of the cabin anyway. We have oxygen back here, and the AED if he needs it."

Grandma Lucy followed Tracy to the Afghani family in the front of the cabin. Kennedy wondered what it would be like in seven years when she had her medical degree and could offer assistance in an emergency like this. She still wasn't sure what field of medicine she wanted to go into. Pediatrics was out. She'd never felt comfortable around kids, and the thought of dealing with children with any disease more severe than the common cold was downright depressing. She figured surgery would be interesting, but she didn't love the idea of bending over cut-open bodies ten hours a stretch. She'd probably start off in internal medicine and decide to specialize from there once something caught her attention. She'd had her eye on immunology for some time now, but expecting her to choose a specialty now was like asking a seventh-grader to pick their college major. It just didn't work that way. How would she know what she enjoyed or what she was good at without a few more years of experience? Thankfully, nobody was in a rush except for Kennedy herself, who would be happy to have a more definitive ten-year plan than *graduate from medical school*.

At some point, of course, she wanted to marry. But when? If she was too busy to date anyone seriously as an undergrad, there was no way she'd find the time for a relationship in med school. Her residency would be even worse. Once she was ready to settle down with anyone, would there be any decent men still single?

Dominic was a good guy. She wished he enjoyed reading fiction so they had more to talk about. But even though she enjoyed her time with him and experienced a little girlish excitement when she'd get ready for one of their quasi-dates, she always felt like she had to prove something to him. Prove that she was spiritually fit enough to be in a relationship with a police chaplain. Prove that she was mature enough to go out with someone who had already been married and widowed before his thirtieth birthday. Prove to herself that she wasn't at least a tiny bit uncomfortable when they were together, struggling to find things to talk about that weren't God, the Bible, and Kennedy's life as a missionary kid.

She couldn't remember why she was thinking about Dominic by the time the Afghani son helped his ashen-faced father stumble to the snack station in the back of the cabin. Two flight attendants, Grandma Lucy, and a middle-aged man in a fancy suit hovered over him.

His son repeated the same word over and over.

"He says he can't breathe," Grandma Lucy translated.

"Sit him down here."

The well-dressed passenger knelt, checking the patient's pulse while Tracy strapped an oxygen mask across his face. Kennedy had a hard time focusing on their words as Grandma Lucy was standing over them holding a conversation of her own. With one hand lifted to the heavens and one aimed down toward the patient's head, Grandma Lucy raised her voice.

"God, you know this man's needs. You know his history. You know his body. You know exactly what's wrong and exactly how to fix it. And I believe in Jesus' name that you want to heal him. And so we pray for your healing. We pray for your ..."

"Here's the medical kit, doctor." A male flight attendant passed the case to the man in the suit, who flung it open and rummaged around. The patient's son gripped the doctor's hand and repeated the same phrase with an urgency in his voice that made Kennedy's lungs seize up in anxiety.

"No pulse-ox?" the doctor asked, pressing against the patient's fingertips and frowning at the results.

The patient signaled to his throat wildly.

"I know." The doctor spoke softly but couldn't keep a certain edge of tension out of his voice.

"This is all we have," Tracy explained apologetically, while Grandma Lucy lifted her head once more and continued her prayer.

"Lord, this doctor needs equipment. And you've promised that when we ask for anything in your name, you'll give it to us, and so we ask in the name of Jesus for whatever he needs to help his patient be healed. And we claim that healing, Lord. We claim it in the name of Jesus. We claim his ..."

"Ok, ma'am." Tracy set aside the phone she'd been talking into and gently pushed on Grandma Lucy's shoulder. "I think the professionals can take it from here."

"Actually," the doctor frowned, "I might need some kind of health history. Maybe she should stick around, only more quietly."

If Grandma Lucy was upset by his request, she didn't show it. She kept the same position but this time only moved her lips instead of giving free reign to her words. To judge by her facial expressions, however, the enforced silence only increased the fervency of her prayers.

The adult son continued to shoot rapid-fire questions at the doctor who tried assuring him in English that he was doing the best he could.

Tracy hung up the phone. "We're only twenty minutes from an airport with a hospital nearby."

"I don't know if he'll make it that long." The doctor yanked a stethoscope out of the medical kit.

"We do have an AED on board," Tracy told him.

Grandma Lucy opened her eyes and declared definitively, "He's not having a heart attack."

Tracy sighed. "Ma'am, I think maybe if you have a seat, we can ask for your help if we need it."

"It's not a heart attack," she repeated.

The doctor lowered the stethoscope. "No, it's not his heart. She's right. Sounds like pneumonia. Can you ask the son if his father has a history of lung disease?"

"I don't know the word." Grandma Lucy frowned. "But I'll try to come up with something." She asked a question in Dari and listened to the son's quick reply.

"I can't understand all of it," she admitted, "but he said something about medicine for a cough he's had."

"Medicine?" the doctor repeated. "Ask him if he has the medicine with him. Ask him if it's a new prescription."

Grandma Lucy nodded. It took a round or two of charades before the son understood what the doctor wanted. He hurried back toward his seat to find his father's carry-on.

"Should I tell the captain to land?" Tracy asked.

"Let's plan on it," the doctor answered. "But if we're dealing with an allergic reaction of some kind, we might be able to handle it here." He pulled a syringe out of the medical kit and checked the label.

The son hurried back up the aisle and thrust a pill bottle into the doctor's empty hand.

"This is what he's been taking?" he asked. Grandma Lucy didn't have to translate. The son pointed to the pills, then to his father and pantomimed dumping out a tablet and swallowing.

The doctor squinted at the label. "Penicillin. Probably for the pneumonia. Can you ask him if his father's ever had this drug before?"

Grandma Lucy didn't have time to ask before the patient shot out his hand and grabbed the doctor by the wrist. He motioned to his throat.

"His trachea's swollen shut." The doctor swept his arms to the sides to make more room. He uncapped the syringe. "Let's roll." He plunged the needle into the man's leg before anyone had time to look away.

Kennedy grimaced but still leaned toward them Waiting. Would the medicine work? How did the doctor know he'd given him the right amount?

The patient's eyes were wide with fear. His son knelt beside him, muttering what sounded like a prayer under his breath.

The doctor pulled the syringe away. More waiting.

"Shouldn't it be working by now?" Tracy asked.

The doctor frowned but didn't reply.

"Help him, Jesus," Grandma Lucy whispered.

The doctor listened to his heart once more. "Better get that AED ready."

Kennedy wanted to pry her eyes away but couldn't. She added a silent prayer on top of Grandma Lucy's. *Please, Jesus* ...

The man gasped in a wheezy breath. His son grasped his hand and let out an exultant proclamation.

"You're going to be ok," the doctor told him, and Grandma Lucy began loudly declaring her thanks to God.

The doctor listened to the man's lungs for a full minute before he put the stethoscope down again. "I think it's safe to say the worst is over. An allergic reaction." He looked at Grandma Lucy. "Tell the son his dad can't have these pills anymore. He'll have to take something else for his cough."

"So he's ok?" Tracy asked, reaching for the phone again.

"Let's keep him on oxygen for a little while longer, just to be safe. Make sure someone stays back here with him. When his shot wears off, he might go through the same set of symptoms again. I imagine if he feels better in half an hour or so, he can go back to his seat as long as his son keeps watch over him the whole time."

"So you don't think we need to divert the flight?" Tracy asked.

"As long as there's another EpiPen ready in that kit, we should be golden."

Tracy relayed the news to the captain on the phone, and the doctor returned to first class without another word. Grandma Lucy sat down next to the patient and struck up a conversation with his son. They had to repeat themselves several times, but they must have been communicating somewhat effectively because at one point they both laughed. A few minutes later, Grandma Lucy pulled a travel-size Bible from the pocket of her sweater and handed it to him. After a few more exchanges, she stood up with much more agility than Kennedy expected from someone her age.

"So he's all right?" Kennedy asked.

"Just fine," Grandma Lucy answered as she sat down by her with a subdued groan. "Hallelujah, praise the Lord. He's going to be just fine."

BO Dude leaned across the aisle and asked, "What's that mask they got on his face?"

"Some extra oxygen," Grandma Lucy explained, her eyes still lifted heavenward in rapture.

"Fabulous," he grumbled. "Who's great idea was it to put them both by a tank of explosive gas?" He turned around to shoot Ray an angry glare and muttered, "Told you we should have taken him down when we had the chance."

"You have nothing to fear from a nice gentleman like Mr. Wahidi." Grandma Lucy was probably two-hundred pounds lighter than the Seahawks fan, but she looked down at him as if he'd been half her size. "He's very polite and has just emigrated to the US."

"Stinking refugees," BO Dude hissed, tossing a few more colorful epithets into his salad mix of insults.

"Not a refugee," Grandma Lucy corrected, "an emigre, invited here by the United States government. I believe his son said he's a scientist."

The Seahawks fan let out a disgusted scoff but thankfully didn't say any more.

A few minutes later, Tracy walked back carrying a plate of cheesecake bites. "These are from first class, but the crew and I wanted to offer them to you to thank you for your help."

Grandma Lucy didn't take the pastries. "You better save these for that doctor. He's the one who did the real assisting, not me."

The flight attendant lowered her voice. "He's already in first class." She smiled and set the snacks on Grandma Lucy's tray table.

"Well, there's more than enough." Grandma Lucy handed out the desserts, one for Kennedy, two for Willow and Ray, and the last for BO Dude.

"Don't you want some?" Kennedy asked.

Grandma Lucy dipped her finger into Kennedy's strawberry swirl topping. "You don't mind if I share a little with you, right?"

Kennedy stared as Grandma Lucy licked her finger with a delighted smile. No longer hungry, she insisted Grandma Lucy finish the whole thing.

"How do you know that language they were speaking?" Kennedy asked when the desserts were gone.

Grandma Lucy reclined her chair and stretched her legs out beneath the empty seat in front of her.

"I did some mission work in Afghanistan in the seventies. I went over there to teach English, but God opened so many doors for me to share the gospel, too. All in all, I spent two years there, and I knew the language pretty well by the time I came back. I got more practice in Washington once Russia invaded Afghanistan, and I started a ministry assisting refugees, helping them get housing in the States, fill out job applications, learn English. It was a full-time job even though it was just volunteer work. And God kept opening doors to lead people to Christ. I had to quit after my daughter died. I moved in with my son-in-law to help raise the children."

"That's terrible. What happened?"

Grandma Lucy lowered her head into her oversized purse and dug around. "Killed by a drunk driver. Left behind two kids, a boy and a girl. Ian's the one I told you about, the one I just visited. Poor guy. Broke his little heart."

Kennedy tried to fathom the horror of losing a parent in such a terrible tragedy. "How old was he?"

"Just five. You know, I think that's part of the reason why he turned his back on God. It was a horrible thing to happen, and him being so young." She shook her head and started digging through her carry-on bag. "Oh. Here it is." She pulled out a handkerchief with cowboys printed on it in bright reds and blues. "Don't mind me," she said as she draped the cloth over her entire face. "It's time for my nap, and if I do say so myself, I think I deserve a good long one."

Kennedy didn't answer. She was tired as well. Grandma Lucy adjusted once or twice in her seat and then grew perfectly still. Kennedy glanced over at Willow and Ray, who were still absorbed in their movie. Oh, well. Kennedy would have plenty of time to spend with her roommate in Alaska. It wasn't as if she'd miss out on an hour of talk time on the plane.

She picked up her Gladys Aylward biography and by the time Grandma Lucy's slow, rhythmic snoring reached her ears, she had finished the book.

CHAPTER 6

T minus 36 minutes

Kennedy didn't know what to do to pass the time. Grandma Lucy was asleep. Willow and Ray were in the middle of their movie. She would have never guessed it, but traveling to Willow's home in Alaska was just as exhausting of an ordeal as getting to her parents' home in Yanji, China. After they reached Anchorage, they'd book a hotel for the night before Willow's dad picked them up for the four-hour drive to Glennallen. All in all, it would be more than twenty-four hours from the time they left campus until they arrived at Willow's home. She hoped she wouldn't be too tired.

Something Grandma Lucy said now sat like curdled milk in Kennedy's gut. Why hadn't she witnessed to Willow? Was she just waiting for the perfect time? Knowing her roommate, she doubted that would ever come. So what was she supposed to do — risk alienating her only real friend on campus to share a message she was certain Willow didn't want to hear, or stay quiet and do her best to ignore the fact that her roommate might die without ever learning the good news of salvation?

It was supposed to be easy. From the time she was seven or eight, Kennedy's dad taught her the four spiritual laws, the ABCs of salvation, the Romans Road of witnessing. And what good had it ever done her? She just wasn't the type to butt her way into random conversations and ask, "Do you know what it means to be saved?" She'd had the sinner's prayer memorized for a decade, but for what purpose? She'd never shared it with anyone, certainly never prayed it with anyone since that night when she was five and climbed up on her dad's lap and told him she wanted to become a Christian. She'd already said the prayer a dozen times or more in Sunday school by then, but she knew it was a way to get her dad to let her stay up late. He'd made such a big deal of her so-called conversion, giving her a brand new Bible with her spiritual birthday imprinted inside, taking her out for donuts to celebrate before church the next day, beaming proudly when he told Mrs. Lindgren about the choice she'd just made. Kennedy remembered wearing an itchy dress and squirming uncomfortably because she'd raised her hand to pray the prayer in Sunday school so many different times by then and didn't want her teacher to ruin her dad's enthusiasm by letting out their little secret.

And so Kennedy had been "converted," even though she couldn't remember a single moment in her childhood when she hadn't understood that Jesus died in order to forgive her sins. If she hadn't wanted to get out of an early bedtime that night fourteen years ago, she'd be just the same Christian she was today, right? So what was the big deal?

Well, maybe God was speaking to her heart about Willow. Isn't that how Hudson Taylor knew he was supposed to go to China, how David Livingstone knew he was called to Africa? When she read about the experiences of these missionaries, she always expected *The Call* to feel exciting. Invigorating. The conviction that God was right beside her, that he had a fabulous plan for her life, that he was going to do incredible things through her. She didn't think her mission assignment from the Lord would come in the form of nagging self-doubt and guilt.

She sighed. Well, if God wanted her to tell Willow about him, she'd do it, right? Isn't that what it meant to be obedient to Christ no matter what the cost? And if Willow threw a fit, well, God would just have to take care of the details, wouldn't he? What was the worst that could happen? It's not like Willow would uninvite her to her home and leave her stranded in Anchorage over Christmas.

Kennedy stared at the picture of Gladys Aylward on the back of her book. Such a quiet-looking, unassuming woman. Kind of like Grandma Lucy, who still snored comfortably next to her. Grandma Lucy certainly wouldn't be afraid of sharing the gospel with someone like Willow. But she also had less to lose. Grandma Lucy wouldn't have to see Willow every day for the rest of the semester, wouldn't have to live in the same dorm until summer break.

Maybe it was easier to share the gospel with people you didn't know. Maybe that's why those pamphlet pushers did what they did, why certain sects sent their congregants out ringing doorbells. If you get laughed at and have the door slammed in your face, are you that much worse off for it other than a little bit of a bruised ego?

Maybe Kennedy could bargain with God. If not Willow, what about the dozen students she knew by name or sight but didn't have to live with for the rest of her sophomore year? What about the girl in organic chem lab who was always burning herself on the Bunsen burner, or the leader of that campus singing group Willow auditioned for? The upperclassman had been ruder than Ebenezer Scrooge himself when he said her roommate didn't have the kind of stage presence they were looking for. If anyone at Harvard needed the gospel, it was him.

Yeah, God. Send me there instead.

She hoped the guilt would let up, but of course it didn't. She searched her memory for a Bible verse that would let her off the hook. *God loves a cheerful giver*? If Kennedy wasn't feeling very cheerful about giving herself a mouthful of humble pie, she shouldn't bother until her heart was in a better place, right? Or what about that verse where Jesus said he knew his sheep and his sheep knew him. If Willow was destined to be part of God's family, wouldn't God find a way to save her without any help?

Then again, isn't that exactly what the veteran pastor said to Hudson Taylor about his passion to carry the gospel to the Chinese interior? "When God pleases to convert the heathen, he'll do it without the help of people like you and me." Kennedy had been incensed when she read the minister's cavalier response, appalled that Christians in the 1800s could have resorted to such ugly, calloused excuses. But was Kennedy doing anything better? If God wanted Willow saved, he'd do it with or without Kennedy's help. Isn't that what she'd just told herself? Well, what if she was wrong?

She didn't know how it all worked out, didn't know what the Bible meant when it said that God *chose* some for salvation in some passages but in other passages talked about him *willing that none should perish*. Those were theological matters people like her dad or Dominic could discuss until they were hoarse with laryngitis, and it probably wouldn't make a hair's width of difference in Kennedy's day-to-day life.

But what if there weren't just people destined to salvation and people doomed to perish? What if there were regular, average individuals who would ask Jesus to forgive their sins if they had the right information, except nobody told them the actual path to heaven? She thought about a verse they read at a home-based Bible study Dominic invited her to a few weeks ago. After announcing woe on certain cities, Jesus declared if the miracles that had been performed there had been performed in Sodom and Gomorrah, they would have repented. It came from somewhere in Matthew, although Kennedy could only guess what chapter. But it was clear that there were some cities that would have repented if they'd been given a decent enough chance. And if that could be said of cities, couldn't that be said of individuals as well?

Something was changing in Kennedy as she read so many missionary stories. Apart from the inevitable guilt she experienced every time she thought about how many people she wasn't sharing the gospel with, she found a deeper conviction to try to pray better. She didn't quite know what that meant, and she was sure she was floundering just as poorly as she ever had, but at least she was more aware now of her own shortcomings and need for growth. She certainly wouldn't measure up to people like George Mueller, the orphanage director whose entire life was a story of God's inexhaustible providence coupled with man's boundless faith. She recalled how she kept a list of unsaved friends. He persevered for decades interceding for dozens, maybe hundreds of different people until they finally came to Christ. A few months after he died, the last person on George Mueller's prayer list became a Christian.

That's what Kennedy needed. To pray for Willow. Forget about alienating her roommate by forcing her into spiritual conversations. Pray for Willow and see what God did.

It sounded like a solid plan.

It also sounded like a pathetic cop-out.

Well, she was trying. God must be able to test her heart and see that much, at least.

She looked at her roommate. Willow was gorgeous, with a certain flamboyant style that attracted attention wherever she went. No wonder Ray had sought her out instead of someone like Kennedy, who felt herself about as dumpy as Bob Cratchit's wife in *A Christmas Carol*.

In general, Kennedy wasn't a fan of unnatural hair colors, but there was something so stunning about Willow's multilayered dye job. The highlights rippled in and out until her whole head was like a box of crayons in all shades of blue. There was an iridescent shine that made her hair glow with radiance.

Yes, Kennedy was definitely Emily Cratchit in comparison. Of course Willow would be the one getting the attention. Kennedy shouldn't be jealous. It was miraculous that Dominic took enough of an interest in her to invite her out a few times over the past semester. Even so, their few trips together hardly constituted a dating relationship, which she wouldn't have time for anyway, not with her studies and dual lab classes. Besides, there was something distant about Dominic. Maybe it was just a personality trait, but after a whole semester, she still didn't feel like she knew him more than she did the first night they met. She'd never seen him angry. Never seen him sad except for one weekend after he had to tell two frantic parents that the investigators had recovered their little girl's drowned body. Even then, he was mostly stoic as he related the horrible events.

Kennedy's mom was glad to hear that Kennedy had found someone, even though at first she'd been a little concerned about the age difference. More than anything, Kennedy got the sense her mom was just glad that Dominic didn't have HIV like other people who'd come into her life in the past.

Sometimes Kennedy wondered why she spent time with Dominic at all. It's not like she'd be ready to settle down and marry in another year or two. He'd be nearly forty by the time she graduated med school. There was no way she expected him to wait that long, even if he was the kind of guy she could picture one day settling down with.

She caught herself staring at Willow's new friend Ray, wondering how old he was, wondering what kind of women caught his eye, if he was the kind of teacher all the girls at his school giggled about at their lunch tables.

While she was lost in thought, he stood up and stretched his legs in the aisle. "It's been great visiting. I wish I could stay longer. I don't think I've seen a Freddie flick since I was a teenager."

Willow's smile was as dazzling as always. "Well then, you were long overdue. Come back in a little bit and we can watch the rest."

"Yeah, sure. If I finish grading these geometry tests before we land, I'd like that a lot." He turned to look at Kennedy, who hoped he hadn't noticed her staring. "You can have your seat back now. Sorry I stole your friend for so long."

Kennedy made some sort of awkward reply and just barely got out of her seat without tripping into him in the process.

"That was smooth," Willow teased when Kennedy sat down next to her.

Kennedy rolled her eyes. After a year and a half sharing the same tiny dorm, she was used to Willow's sarcastic sense of humor, but she didn't have the patience for it. Not right now.

"So what'd you and Granny yak about over there?" Willow asked. "For a while there, it looked like you'd found yourself a new best buddy."

Kennedy didn't know why she felt defensive of Grandma Lucy all of a sudden. She did what she could to change the subject. "Ray seems real nice."

Willow lifted one shoulder in a shrug. "He is." She brushed her blue bangs out of her eyes. "A little bit too nice for my taste, but it was fine."

Kennedy didn't know what to say next. She hoped Christmas vacation with Willow's family wouldn't be this awkward. On campus, they never had a hard time coming up with topics to talk about. That was because something was always going on. Willow had new plays to rehearse, new theater friends to gossip about. Kennedy was always reading a different classic, and since Willow wanted to be as cultured and literate as she could without actually having to sit down and read anything, she often asked Kennedy for the abridged versions. But now, with half the day left just to get to Seattle, Kennedy was afraid they'd already run out of conversation topics. It wasn't as if she could talk about people like Gladys Aylward and Hudson Taylor, missionaries who Willow would insist destroyed indigenous cultures with their colonialist zeal and ethnocentrism.

She sighed. How was she supposed to witness when she could barely hold a simple conversation? God must have other plans for Willow. If she was going to hear the gospel message, it would have to come from somebody else. Wasn't it Jesus himself who lamented that a prophet is never accepted in his hometown? That's what was going on here. The two girls were just too close. Willow had seen Kennedy at her worst, had walked with her through the most painful moments of her post-traumatic stress flare-ups, through losing her best friend and lab partner last year after making a complete idiot of herself on a live news segment ...

"What's going on in that brain of yours, genius?" Willow asked.

Kennedy was glad she didn't have to answer truthfully. "Nothing really.

I guess I'm just tired." She looked over at Willow, who didn't respond. Kennedy tried to figure out who she was staring at. "What are you ..."

"Shhh." Willow grabbed her arm and didn't let go. "Quiet," she hissed.

"What is it?" Kennedy whispered.

Willow leaned in until their heads touched. "That guy there. The one with that gaudy Hawaiian shirt."

Kennedy stared. "What about him?"

"Lean over this way."

Kennedy didn't see anything out of the ordinary besides the fact that he was so overweight. That and the way his teenage daughter sat so close to him. Still, Kennedy had flown internationally at that age and probably fell asleep on her dad's shoulder half a dozen times or more.

"That is so wrong." Willow reached up and turned on her alert light.

Tracy was stocking a snack tray behind them. "I'll be right there."

"What is it?" Kennedy asked as unease crept up her spine like a hairy tarantula.

The flight attendant bent over toward Willow and turned off the light. "What can I do for you?"

"That man in the Hawaiian shirt." Willow nodded with her head.

The woman frowned. "What about him?"

Willow's penciled eyebrows narrowed dramatically. "He was pulling her hair back. Like this." She snatched Kennedy's ponytail and gave it a half-hearted tug. "Like he was threatening her."

The woman paused and glanced at Kennedy. "You saw it, too?"

"No, but I ... Well, the angle's different here, and it ..."

Tracy let out her breath and donned a plastered smile that only slightly concealed her annoyance. Or maybe she was just tired. "Well, if you see anything else suspicious ..."

"Something's not right." Willow shook her head. "Something's definitely wrong over there."

Tracy gently touched Willow's shoulder. "I'll tell the other attendants to keep their eyes open, ok?"

Willow ran her fingers through her glossy hair. "There's got to be something ..."

The woman leaned a little closer. "Thanks for bringing it to our attention. You did the right thing."

Kennedy couldn't tell if she was saying what she needed to say to end the conversation or if there was genuine concern behind her voice. How many people did these flight attendants come across each day? She'd never thought about it before, but it seemed like it must be one of the grossest, most thankless jobs imaginable. Cleaning up used barf bags, listening to squealing babies, reacting during any number of medical emergencies ...

"Oh, before you go," Kennedy piped up.

"Yes?" Now the exhaustion in Tracy's voice was unmistakable even though she still tried a winning attempt at a smile.

"How's the patient doing? The one who needed the extra oxygen earlier? Is he ok?"

The smiled warmed for a brief moment. "I can't discuss that, but I can tell you that if we thought he was in any danger, the pilot would have diverted the flight a long time ago to get him to a hospital." She straightened her crisp uniform. "I'll be around in just a few minutes with drinks."

Neither girl answered. Willow continued to stare at the fat man and his teenage daughter. Kennedy tried but couldn't pinpoint anything abnormal or suspicious about either of them.

After a few more minutes, Willow pulled out her phone. "How about a game of Scrabble?" she asked.

Kennedy felt like she must be letting God down every minute of the day. She couldn't talk to her roommate about Jesus. She couldn't tell her about the way to salvation or the price he paid so her sins could be forgiven. But she could play a Scrabble knockoff on her roommate's smartphone and wrack up three or four hundred points by the time the score was settled.

Kennedy smiled even though she knew her expression would be even less convincing than the flight attendant's.

"Sure. You go first."

CHAPTER 7

T minus 11 minutes

"I don't even know why I bother to play you." Willow sulked dramatically.

Less than half an hour after they started their game, Kennedy was declared the winner by fifty-seven points. Her highest word, *quench*, had surged her score ahead. Willow never had the chance to recover.

Kennedy wadded up her pretzel bag and shoved it into her empty cup. Why hadn't she thought to pack a few snacks to take with her on the plane? They would touch down in Detroit soon, but they wouldn't get off until Seattle, where she hoped they'd have time to grab some real food.

"I'm going to use the bathroom." Kennedy unbuckled.

"You'll have to go up front," Willow told her. "That guy in the Carhartts locked himself in a few minutes ago."

"Again?" Kennedy asked, remembering how backed up the bathroom line had grown earlier in the flight. Oh, well. It would be a good idea to stretch her legs anyway. What was that her dad was always worried about? Embolisms midflight or something like that. Kennedy seriously doubted she was in any danger of developing blood clots at her age, but she'd end up with a whole body full of sore and achy muscles if she didn't move around a little bit.

She glanced across the aisle where Grandma Lucy still slept with the cowboy handkerchief covering her face. She hadn't joked when she said she'd earned herself a nap. In front of Willow, BO Dude was busy chewing his pencil and working on a crossword puzzle that only had four answers filled, with a glaring spelling mistake in the top row. Several seats ahead, Ray leaned over a stack of papers and was so busy with his quintessential red pen he didn't even notice her pass, or if he did, he didn't acknowledge her. The girl in the Bon Jovi shirt sat in front of him, and Kennedy slowed her pace so she could observe her longer without getting caught staring. Her father in his Hawaiian shirt had an arm around her, and the girl seemed a little squeamish, but that didn't mean a whole lot. How many teen girls did Kennedy know who wanted to be affectionate with their dads in public?

The girl twisted in her seat and looked back until her eyes locked with Kennedy's. There was something piercing in her expression that made Kennedy's breath catch in her trachea. Had Willow just made her paranoid, or was there something more to it? Something more sinister? There wasn't time to gawk in the aisle until she figured it out. She had to keep moving, but right as she was about to pass, the girl shot out her leg like a mischievous third grader trying to pull a prank on a friend.

Kennedy stumbled and grabbed the back of a seat for balance.

"Oh, I'm sorry." The girl leaned forward, grabbing Kennedy's hand. The haunting eyes never left hers. A flicker of resolve was replaced by fear as her father coughed up a loogie, which he noisily spat into his empty soda can.

"Are you ok?" the girl asked. Her eyes were wide.

Kennedy felt a sympathetic quivering in her core and shoved her fist into her pocket. She tried to sound confident and nodded. "I'm fine." She didn't dare dart her eyes to the father but added quickly for his benefit, "It was just an accident. I should have been paying better attention."

With that, she rushed past the last few rows, threw herself into the lavatory, and flung the lock down. Her hand was burning. The same hand the girl had grabbed after intentionally tripping Kennedy. The same hand the girl had thrust a crumpled napkin into. The same hand that trembled as Kennedy pulled it out of her pocket, unfolded the note, and read, *My name is Selena Weston. I'm being kidnapped.*

CHAPTER 8

T minus 7 minutes

Think. She had to think. Kennedy hadn't gotten into Harvard for her social graces or athletic skills. She had a brain somewhere beneath that skull and head of thick hair. She could figure this out. Come up with a plan.

The last thing she wanted to do was alert the fat man to anything suspicious. If he found out the girl had signaled for help, who knew what sort of trouble she'd be in? But how did the authorities handle situations like this in the middle of a flight? It wasn't as if Kennedy could simply call 911 and ask the dispatcher to send a few squad cars down to rescue an abducted teen. How had he gotten her on the plane in the first place? Weren't the TSA agents supposed to have an eye out for that sort of thing?

She had to let one of the flight attendants know, but she had to do it so the father — no, the abductor — wouldn't notice. Which meant that as soon as she was done in the bathroom, she'd have to walk down the aisle, right past Selena. She'd have to act so natural it would make Willow and all her theater friends applaud her performance if they knew what was going on. Then she'd give the note to Tracy in the back of the plane.

The plan would work. It would have to work.

Finding she no longer needed to pee, she exited the bathroom on unsteady legs. She'd already resolved not to look at Selena. Not to draw any further attention. She'd walk right by as if she didn't notice her there. If only her body would stop trembling.

She held onto the back of a seat for support and fixed her eyes on Ray, still bent fastidiously over his pile of math tests. Willow was most likely right. He was probably too much of a nice guy for her, if *nice guy* meant a respectable working man who had responsibilities that prevented him from partying hard seven nights a week.

He glanced up from his papers. "Hey there." He knitted his brows together. "Are you all right?"

Kennedy tilted her head up. "Just a little motion sick." It wasn't necessarily a lie.

He gave her a sympathetic frown. "Try some Ginger Ale."

She tried to keep focused on him, but her legs grew even more unsteady when she saw the man in the Hawaiian shirt leering at her.

"Is she the one?" he snarled at the teen.

Selena's eyes were wide with fear. Kennedy bit her lip. She tried to ignore his angry glare and focused on Selena, who winced as Hawaiian Shirt dug his fingers into the flesh of her arm. "That the one?" he demanded again.

Selena's eyes were sorrowful. Pleading. She gave a slight nod.

Kennedy's body sensed the danger before her gray matter could create a single coherent thought. The result was nearly complete paralysis. A surge of epinephrine raged throughout her system, begging Kennedy to flee, but there was nowhere to go. The aisle was too narrow. A step closer and she'd be within the abductor's reach.

She froze, while Ray the nice-guy math teacher cocked his head to the side like a curious puppy.

It was all the time Hawaiian Shirt needed to lunge out of his seat and grab Kennedy's arm. "Give me that paper, you piece of trash."

Tiny snippets of her self-defense lessons sped through her mind, reflexes that came about three seconds too late. She yanked her arm back. He only tightened his grip. She wrenched her hand down, trying to twist his forearm. He threw his body weight into her but didn't let go.

Kennedy knew she should call for help, but her breath had been startled out of her.

"Hey! Let go of her!" Ray bolted out of his seat and flung himself against Hawaiian Shirt, trying to grab his arms from behind.

A shrill screaming pierced Kennedy's ears. "Help!" Selena covered her head with her arms to shield herself from the scuffle. "Somebody, help."

Ray let out a loud *oof* as Hawaiian Shirt punched him in the gut. Kennedy realized she was free and tried to distance herself but ended up tripping on Selena's arm rest. She fell, clawing at the man who yanked her to her feet.

"Hold it!" An authoritative voice cracked through the cacophony.

More noise. More punches. She was so startled she couldn't even tell if she was hurt or not.

"Freeze."

Kennedy couldn't see who was talking. She could hardly even focus on who she was supposed to be fighting off. She found herself pounding her fists against someone significantly smaller than the fat man in the Hawaiian shirt. When her eyes finally focused, she saw she was beating Ray, who held her by both shoulders and was telling her she was safe.

Kennedy's whole body quivered uncontrollably. The stress, the trauma, the anxiety she'd ignored during the fight raged through her system with the energy of a nuclear explosion.

"It's ok," Ray repeated as humiliating tears slipped down Kennedy's cheeks.

He held her a little closer, as if trying to offer reassurance without making it an official hug. "You're safe," he whispered and nodded toward a mustached man in a dark business suit who was about to cuff Hawaiian Shirt's hands behind his back.

Kennedy had to steady herself on one of the seat backs.

"I don't even know that man," Selena was sobbing. "He told me he'd kill me if I didn't go with him."

Tracy wrapped her arm around the crying girl and ushered her to the front of the plane.

Kennedy reached out her arm for something to steady herself on.

"Easy," Ray said. "Here, let me walk you back to your seat."

"She was being kidnapped." Kennedy's brain refused to focus on more than one face at a time. She fought her way past the nauseating dizziness looking for Selena.

"It's ok," Ray assured her. "She's going to be fine. Everything's going to be just fine."

Kennedy sucked in a choppy breath and thought that maybe in a few minutes she could believe Ray's assessment of their situation.

Something buzzed, and the captain addressed the cabin. "Well, folks, it looks like we had a little excitement back there. The good news is we'll be landing in Detroit in about twenty minutes. Let's show the flight attendants and air marshal on board our appreciation for working well under pressure to keep everybody safe."

Subdued applause sounded throughout the cabin until Hawaiian Shirt guffawed. "Safe?" He let out a soul-haunting chuckle. "That's what you think, chump."

He swung his head back until his skull smacked into the air marshal's face. Kennedy instinctively clutched Ray's arm as the man in the SVSU sweatshirt jumped into the aisle. In one swift motion, he grabbed the pistol from the marshal's holster, raised it above his head, and brought it down on his skull. A grotesque thud sounded above the hum of muffled cries.

The man in the sweatshirt kept the gun held high in the air. "This is your captain speaking. I suggest you buckle up."

CHAPTER 9

Kennedy glanced back at Willow, but she couldn't focus on her roommate before Ray pulled her into an empty seat. "Get down," he hissed in her ear.

"He's got a gun," shrieked a woman from the front of the plane. "Everyone watch out. He's got a gun."

Kennedy stared at the marshal's crumpled form, as if she could wake him up by sheer will power.

"Here's how it's gonna go." The SVSU man had his back to the emergency exit. His voice carried throughout the whole cabin. "You will all address me as General. This here is my lieutenant." He nodded at the fat man in the Hawaiian shirt. "You are now under our care and protection, got that?"

"What do you want?" squeaked the hysterical woman.

Kennedy's breath wheezed into her lungs when General leveled the gun in the direction of the speaker.

"What I want is silence," he boomed and then let his volume drop. "Silence and a little cooperation. You give me my space, you give me some respect, and we're all gonna get through this just fine. Got that?"

Kennedy didn't realize at first how badly she was trembling. She curled her legs up against her chest and leaned a little closer toward Ray.

"Who here's got a cell phone?" General asked as Lieutenant Hawaiian Shirt busied himself binding the unconscious air marshal's ankles and wrists with a roll of thick metal wire. "I said who's got a cell phone?" General repeated in a roar.

A few passengers tentatively raised their hands, but most like Kennedy held perfectly still. She heard BO Dude's voice in her mind. *We take him down, or we don't get off this plane alive.* She knew logically a whole cabin full of travelers could subdue two men. But the gun ...

She looked to the back of the plane but all she could see of Willow was the top of her blue hair. Was she ok? Was she as terrified as Kennedy? What about Grandma Lucy? Was she asleep with the cowboy handkerchief draped over her eyes? Did she have any idea what was happening?

BO Dude sat with his arms crossed. "What're you gonna do? Pass around a pillowcase for us to dump our cells in like we're in some sort of action flick?"

Kennedy watched him, wished he'd get up and act. Take down the crazy man from SVSU, wherever that was.

A smile softened General's features momentarily. "I'm not gonna take your phones. In fact, I want you to pull them out. I've got something to say that some of you may want to record."

The PA system sounded. "This is the captain speaking. Yup, me again. And if you're a passenger who doesn't have a death wish, I suggest you buckle up."

High-pitched screams, including her own, drowned out Kennedy's other senses as the airplane tipped onto its side. Beside her, Ray fumbled with the safety belt to strap her in.

The plane dived forward. Kennedy squeezed her eyes shut, trying to calculate how long it would take a plane to freefall forty-thousand feet given a constant acceleration due to gravity. She couldn't keep any figures straight in her head.

The plane straightened again, and Kennedy opened her eyes. Apparently BO Dude had been the only passenger brave or senseless enough to get out of his seat and take advantage of the confusion to confront General. He landed one misplaced punch by General's ear before the plane lurched again and both men stumbled off balance. By then, General's fat lieutenant had joined the skirmish. He punched BO Dude in the jaw before the captain rolled the plane to the left.

Kennedy's shoulder was thrown against the window a moment before her head. She couldn't see anything, couldn't focus. A roar like the ocean howled in her ears. The plane's engines, or her own pulse?

When she opened her eyes, she saw General holding a gun up to BO Dude's head.

"Captain," he called out in a loud voice, "I'd say you better straighten this plane out right now." He glanced around the cabin with a cocky grin. "As for the rest of you here, I suggest you get out your phones." He spoke in a monotone that gave Kennedy more chills than Scrooge when he faced the Ghost of Christmas Yet to Come.

Once two or three dozen phone cameras were pointed at him, General started his monologue.

"My name is Bradley Strong. Until this morning, I resided at 324 Trenton Street in Detroit, Michigan. I have here as hostages one hundred and seventeen passengers and five crew members of Flight 219 ..."

The speech was interrupted by some kind of metal music screaming from the PA system. Kennedy threw her hands over her ears to dampen the sound.

"Turn that off!" General yelled. He stared at the cabin ceiling, as if the speakers themselves could understand him.

"Once more, this is your captain." He spoke over the sound of the death metal with a hint of amusement in his tone. "I'm sorry for the interruption, but we have a strict no-feeding-the-lunatics policy onboard, which means that we won't allow this cabin to become a soapbox. I'd ask all you sane, reasonable passengers to please put your phones away and ignore empty threats from ..."

"How's this for an empty threat?" General asked in a chilling monotone.

Kennedy had time to shut her eyes and scrunch her body into an even smaller ball before the shot cracked through the pressurized air. She didn't see BO Dude fall or hear the thud his body made when he dropped.

"I hope some of you were recording that." General spoke more quietly now that the horrific music had stopped streaming over the speakers.

She waited for the captain to speak.

Silence.

"What did I tell you earlier?" General shrugged. "All I want is a little respect and cooperation."

"Are you ok?" Ray whispered.

Kennedy tried to nod, but she wasn't sure if her muscles actually worked. For a brief second, she felt an uncontrollable urge to giggle. She imagined the captain flooding the cabin with nitrous oxide, pictured how General would look as he tried to fight it but finally gave into the irresistible urge, like Patrick Stewart playing Scrooge in *A Christmas Carol* and learning to laugh for the very first time when he woke up on Christmas morning.

Kennedy glanced around the cabin. So many people. She didn't know much about guns, but knew there couldn't be that many bullets, right? What if they all took their chances, all stormed General at once? There might be a few injuries, but nearly everyone was guaranteed to survive. If the plane were full of Vulcans, they would have made the logical decision by now.

She felt another almost irresistible urge to bust her gut laughing when she pictured Leonard Nemoy playing Spock and incapacitating their assailants with his Vulcan death grip. If this were *Star Trek*, the smelly man would have worn a red uniform instead of a Seahawks sweatshirt.

Thinking of the fallen passenger forced stark reality into Kennedy's cerebral cortex. This wasn't a sci-fi show. This wasn't a comedy or staged melodrama. There was no laughing gas. There was nothing humorous at all here.

She trembled even harder, certain now she was about to throw up. She saw a barf bag in Ray's seatback pocket and pointed. "Could you ..."

She didn't get the rest of the question out. Ray moved his foot out of the way, but some of the spray still landed on the leg of his pants. Kennedy wanted to apologize but was too scared to talk, scared that if she drew attention to herself, she'd be the next person General chose to turn into a sacrificial example.

General stepped over the crumpled man's body and addressed the cabin again. "Now that I've got your attention, let's try this one more time. I want you all to get your cell phones out. Now."

Ten seconds later, at least a hundred cell phones were pointed at General, who smiled for the cameras before he began his speech one more time.

CHAPTER 10

"My name is Bradley Strong. I reside at 324 Trenton Street in Detroit, Michigan. For all you law officers listening in, I wouldn't bother sweeping the place if I were you. Everything's scrubbed."

His voice was smooth, confident, as if he'd been born to speak into video cameras at forty thousand feet.

"You might be interested to know that I'm on Flight 219 and have here a hundred and seventeen passengers ..." He glanced down at his feet. "Actually, correct that. I have here a hundred and sixteen passengers and five crew members as my hostages. I'm with my lieutenant, who for the time being shall remain nameless."

He nodded at Hawaiian Shirt and smirked at the cameras. Kennedy wondered how many of the recordings were streaming to a live audience. How long until the news channels picked up the feed? How long until her parents learned where she was? She wished she had her phone with her, not so she could immortalize General's morbid oration but so she could call her mom and dad.

She had slumped down in her seat as far as she could go. She didn't want to see General. Didn't want to think about the dead man at his feet. Ray wasn't recording the video either. "Do you have a phone?" she asked him, trying to figure out how to call her parents without having their number memorized.

"I'm not going to raise publicity for terrorists."

Kennedy wanted to shut her ears. No. He couldn't use words like *terrorist*. Terrorists were men from the Middle East who strapped bombs to their chests and hoped to die with their victims. This was different. A skyjacker. A mentally deranged criminal, but one who wanted to stay alive. Which meant he wanted to keep the plane in the air.

Kennedy thought back to all her dad's stupid crisis training. He hadn't ever mention skyjackings, but he'd given her advice about other sorts of hostage situations. The first rule he always drilled into her head was that the typical abductor didn't want to harm his hostages. He needed as much leverage as possible. Well, her dad could spout off rules and generalizations all day long, but that wouldn't change the fact that a man had been shot in the head no less than twenty feet from where she now cowered in fear.

She shouldn't even be here. She should be in the back of the plane with Willow. *Willow.* What if this was it? What if General had a bomb and was planning to bring the whole plane down? What if he was going to shoot hostages one at a time, starting at the back of the plane? Kennedy might never get another chance to talk to Willow again. Never tell her anything about the Lord.

God, I'm so sorry.

What use did her apologies serve? *Man is destined to die once.* She knew that verse from Hebrews. *Destined to die once and after that face judgment.* If something happened to Willow, if she died without knowing Jesus because Kennedy had been too uncomfortable to ask the most important question ...

And after that face judgment. It was Kennedy, not Willow, who deserved to be judged.

Please, God. Help us survive. She'd never thought very highly of folks who made bargains with God when their lives were in danger. Men like Martin Luther who would have never joined the monastery if he hadn't uttered a rash promise seconds after lightning struck the ground beside him. But now here she was, begging God for one last chance. Like Jonah drowning in a storm-tossed ocean, pleading with God for mercy and another chance to preach repentance to the wicked city of Ninevah.

One more chance.

If for no other reason than that Kennedy would never forgive herself if Willow died today. She thought about Gladys Aylward, who was sent to stop a murderous prison uprising with nothing but the power of the Holy Spirit defending her, protecting her. For a moment, she pictured standing up with that same degree of faith and conviction, telling General to drop his weapon. It was possible, wasn't it? But her body refused to move, and her only hope was to stay as inconspicuous as possible.

That and pray for Willow's protection.

She's not ready to die yet, Lord. Kennedy had lived her entire Christian life believing in a literal hell. She knew there were some theologians who doubted the existence of an actual lake of fire, but Kennedy had never given their unorthodox hypotheses much credence. But as she looked back, she realized she'd spent the past nineteen years living as if hell weren't a real, physical place where people she knew and loved would spend eternity separated from God if they never learned about his grace and forgiveness. If she actually believed in hell as the Bible described it, was there any way she would have lived with Willow for the past year and a half without even attempting to broach the subject of God's love and mercy?

She's not ready to die yet, Lord, Kennedy repeated, and realized the same went for her. She hadn't seen her parents since last summer. She had so many plans for her life. College graduation. Med school. *Just think of all the things I can do for you if you let me live longer.* There she went again, bargaining with God. If she'd been so concerned about serving him with her life, maybe she should have made better use of the past nineteen years. Maybe she should have focused more on her own spiritual growth so she wasn't terrified to share the gospel with others. Was getting a 4.0 GPA worth seeing her roommate and those around her condemned for all eternity?

It couldn't happen. God loved Willow. Just as much as he loved everyone else on this plane. He couldn't let them all die, not without a chance to hear ...

A chance to hear ... Could it be that God was giving her that opportunity now? She remembered the story of John Harper, a Christian evangelist from Scotland who found himself crossing the Atlantic Ocean for a speaking engagement at Moody Church. Unfortunately, the ship he was travelling on was none but the Titanic, and when it started to sink, he gave up his own life vest to a passenger who wasn't a Christian, certain that the atheist needed it more than he did.

When the boat capsized, John Harper floundered in the freezing water, swimming from one frantic survivor to another, praying with all of those he met before he himself succumbed to the cold and surrendered his soul to eternity.

Was it possible God was calling Kennedy to be that bold? It couldn't be. John Harper had been an evangelist even before the Titanic's fatal voyage. He had practiced sharing the gospel his whole life. That wasn't Kennedy's spiritual gift, her area of expertise. And so, just like the reluctant prophet

Jonah, she begged God to send someone else. Someone like Grandma Lucy. She'd been a missionary and told people about Jesus all the time, including the son of the Afghani man with pneumonia. If God would call anyone to tell the passengers on this flight about the way to salvation, he'd assign the task to Grandma Lucy.

If she was even awake.

Kennedy thought about the man who'd been shot just moments earlier. Had he been a Christian? Would she ever know? And if he died unsaved, was there anything she could have done to change his fate? No. She couldn't handle that sort of liability. She didn't want it. Let her be the one to pray quietly in the background or offer moral support while others went out and shared the gospel. Kennedy couldn't live with the weight of someone's eternal destiny on her conscience. It wasn't her responsibility.

"I suppose some of you are wondering why I'm doing this." General's words snapped her back to reality. To the fact that a madman with a gun was addressing the world via a hundred different recording devices and was about to explain his rationale.

Kennedy silenced the protests of her guilty conscience. She wasn't about to miss General's words.

CHAPTER 11

"My children attend Brown Elementary School," General began.

Kennedy was surprised. She would never have pictured a heartless murderer as the type who would also be a father.

"Unless you're from Michigan, you probably haven't even heard about our little school. That's because the media doesn't care. They don't care that Charles Weston has failed our kids as the district superintendent. Traded in our children's health to save the state a few bucks by building their school on toxic land."

General paused and stared at the cameras. "The soil's got arsenic in it. And not just little bits. We've got numbers. Forty times higher than the safe amount. And that's the level advised for adults, not little five-year-olds eating dirt off the playground," he added. "Want an example of how bad it is? Three construction workers on the new school site got sick within one week on the job. One ended up in the ER. Breathing problems. Is that the kind of soil you'd want to send your kids to play in?"

The hand that held the gun was shaking. Kennedy wondered if one of the passengers close by him could tackle him while he was focused on his speech. Tackle him without getting killed in the process.

"The site of the new school building, they used to have a pharmacy company on it. Know what the workers dug up? Two underground storage tanks." He wiped his forehead with his fist. "Charles Weston dumped them in secret before anyone could test what was in them. He says it's old ground water, but why's water got to be buried ten feet under? And why'd he order the tanks moved in the middle of the night before anyone could test what was in them?" His voice was as impassioned as Kennedy imagined old-time evangelists like Charles Spurgeon's and Dwight Moody's must have been.

"Now, let me ask you something," General continued. Kennedy couldn't tell if he was talking more to the passengers or to their video cameras. "If you were told that your kids' school was going to be built onto a hazardous waste site, that they'd be exposed to contaminants from the air, the soil, and the water there, what would you do?"

He looked around, and Kennedy watched several passengers shift uncomfortably in their seats under his gaze. Did he really want an answer?

"What would you do?" he demanded again.

"Take it to the district office." Ray's voice beside Kennedy made her jump. She crouched down, hoping General wouldn't focus any of his attention on her.

"Take it to the district office," he repeated with a menacing grin. "And guess what? That's just what we did. We got a petition, demanded a public meeting. Well, Charles Weston and his stooges set up a meeting all right. At four in the flipping afternoon. Know why? 'Cause he knew the parents would still be at work and wouldn't be able to attend. Do you know how bad things have to be to get eighty parents to show up at four in the afternoon on a work day? And we handed Superintendent Weston our proposal. Merge Brown Elementary with Golden Heights just five miles over. Why not? The building's there. The teachers are there. They even have old trailer classrooms that nobody's used in a decade."

He cleared his throat loudly.

"You know what Weston said to our proposal?" He waited again for an answer before supplying one himself. "Absolutely nothing. Know why? Because he didn't show up. He sent his secretary to read a four-word speech Weston penned himself. *Shut up. Go home.* Of course, he put it more eloquently than that. I'm summarizing."

Kennedy's brain was in full-fledged cognitive dissonance mode. This man who cared about justice for his children couldn't be the same man who'd murdered a crabby Seahawks fan minutes earlier. This father who refused to risk his children's health couldn't be the same terrorist who helped Lieutenant kidnap a girl, disabled an air marshal, and hijacked their plane. A familiar constricting of her lungs. A suffocating, choking feeling she'd worked so hard to avoid all semester.

At least her body understood this was a perfect time to panic.

She bit the inside of her cheek, hoping the pressure might give her something to focus on other than her terror. Her mouth still tasted like vomit. She squeezed her eyes shut, trying to push back the darkness and paralyzing dread that threatened to envelop her. How many times could anxiety take control of you before you lost yourself completely in the fight? How many times could she try to overcome her PTSD only to find herself thrown into a new scenario more terrifying and dangerous than the last? How many times could she pray for healing and fail to find it before her spirit succumbed to depression and despair?

No. She couldn't give in to dark thoughts.

But where else was there to turn?

Her breathing came in shallow spurts. She felt each restrictive inhale like the stinging of killer bees swarming inside her lungs.

God help me, she whispered and wondered why she even bothered. How many times had she prayed before in a crisis? How many times had God left her to flounder, left her to fend for herself in a helpless, hopeless situation? How many injustices had she prayed against, only to find her prayers powerless to confront the degree of evil and devastation that swarmed unchecked around the globe?

Her soul begged God to help her, but her mind knew she was completely alone. God had no reason to listen to her. She was nothing. A college student. She'd never led a single soul to Christ, never gone on a single mission trip. Even as a teenager in China, she'd spent more time reading or shopping for clothes than praying and studying with the North Korean refugees her parents took in as part of their Secret Seminary training.

Her last year and a half at Harvard had been a huge waste of time. What did God care about her GPA? What did he care about her lab results? She'd made academic success her idol, couldn't even get into the habit of attending church every week, and refused to share the gospel with the one person on campus she talked to on a regular basis.

She was a failure as a Christian, especially when she compared herself to her parents' Secret Seminary students or the heroes of faith she'd been reading about in her biographies. God had no reason to save her, no reason to spare her life, no reason to listen to her prayers at all.

Please, God ...

She remembered what Pastor Carl had said during the last sermon of his she'd heard. He talked about God's love for everyone, his unconditional, limitless love. Where was that love when he allowed Hawaiian Shirt to kidnap a helpless girl? Where was that love when he stood by while BO Dude got shot? Where was that love now when every single breath

Kennedy took was shallower and more forced than the last?

Kennedy had grown up learning about God's love, but what good had it done her? It hadn't stopped her from getting kidnapped her freshman year. Hadn't shielded her from the horror of police brutality last spring. Hadn't kept her lab partner from contracting an incurable disease. It hadn't even healed her PTSD.

Maybe she should stop fearing the inevitable and be glad she ended up on a doomed plane. Maybe this was God's way of putting her out of her misery so she would stop embarrassing him as she stumbled through her so-called Christian existence.

Please, God. She wanted to barter. Wanted to beg. But she knew it was pointless. God's mind was already made up, wasn't it? Either she would die on this plane or she wouldn't. No degree of pleading or whining would change that. She just wished she could talk to her parents one last time ...

General was still lecturing about the toxic land Weston and the school district had purchased for the new elementary building. Funny. Kennedy thought she'd care more. If she was about to die, it made sense that she'd be curious about her murderer's intentions. But now that she was resigned to her fate, what did it matter? Was getting blown up by a Muslim extremist any different than getting shot point-blank by an angry father from Detroit?

You died either way, right?

A heaviness settled over her, not like the peace she'd sometimes experienced in the midst of a crisis where she knew God was ministering to her, but a joyless acceptance of whatever fate would throw her way. Maybe if she'd been a better believer, God would have more reason to save her. For now, she'd just have to sit tight and wonder if the end would come from a bullet, a bomb, or a forty-thousand-foot drop with a fiery finale. Which would be less painful? And if you ended up dead no matter what, did it matter?

"Before I sign out," General concluded, "I have a message for the district superintendent, good old Charles Weston. If I don't hear from you in five minutes, I'm taking out another hostage. You can find my phone number as well as a full description of the crimes you've committed against the children of Detroit on my personal webpage."

After a longer-than-necessary dramatic pause, General growled to the passengers, "Now turn those cameras off. Countdown's started."

CHAPTER 12

The only thing Kennedy could think about was getting back to her seat. Get to Willow no matter what was about to happen to them. Grab her phone and find a way to call her parents. Was it day or night now in Yanji? Adjusting from one time zone to another had become second-nature to her, but now she couldn't focus on anything.

Did her parents already know what was happening? Had the whole country watched General's tirade? What if none of the cell phones could stream from this altitude? What if he'd given the superintendent an ultimatum that nobody heard? What if this Weston guy never responded? Would General just keep shooting people until he ran out of ammunition?

"How many bullets do you think he has?" she asked Ray.

"Not enough for all of us." His answer was hardly comforting.

She glanced back and tried to spot Willow. General was pacing the aisle and seemed distracted, but his Hawaiian-shirted lieutenant who stood vigil over the dead body kept his eyes fixed on the passengers, scowling at each individual in turn.

It wasn't right. She should be with her roommate. With her backpack and her phone. Several of the other passengers were whispering into their cells, probably calling loved ones on the ground.

Kennedy looked at Ray. "At least everyone must know what's happening by now, right?"

Ray frowned. "That's just what he wants."

She didn't know what to say. She didn't know a thing about politics, about hostage negotiations. In her mind, it made sense that the more people who knew about the situation the better. It meant that many more people were working together to find a way to protect everybody on board.

She thought about the family that had gotten off the plane, and she was thankful those children didn't have to experience this kind of terror.

"So you don't think anybody's going to call?" Kennedy asked.

Ray sighed. "All I know is if everyone on this plane refused to play into his little act, he'd have no leverage. That's all these terrorists want. Sensationalism. His only goal's to drive media attention to this school issue, and he'll try anything to do it."

Kennedy didn't answer. She was thinking about Grandma Lucy's grandson and how his story had been replaced with something more noteworthy. Ray was probably right.

"Get a plane full of civilians," he went on, "and you're guaranteed media updates every minute. Everyone's talking about the passengers, the skyjacker, the issues involved, and bam. The story's viral."

He tapped onto his phone's newsfeed and showed her the screen. "See?" He read the headline out loud. "*Home-Grown Terrorism: Flight 219.*" He scrolled a little farther down. "Or here. *Detroit School District's Dirty Soil Secret*. All he had to do was take over one plane, and Brown Elementary School's a household name. If he hadn't already shot a man, half of these news outlets would be hailing him a hero right now."

Kennedy didn't care about the hijacker's cause. Callous as it sounded, she didn't even care about the school kids in Detroit as much as she cared about getting off this plane. Why hadn't the captain said anything in so long? Was he even with them anymore, or had the plane switched to autopilot? Had something horrible happened to him in the cockpit?

"I want to go back to my seat," she said. "I really should stay with Willow."

"I wouldn't do that if I were you." Ray shook his head. "You don't want to draw attention to yourself ..."

"But Willow ..."

"... would rather have a living friend than a dead one," he finished for her.

Kennedy bit her lip. Maybe he was right. What would happen if General didn't get his call by the time his five minutes ran out? He'd already proven how easily he could kill. There was absolutely nothing to stop him from doing it again.

A hundred and sixteen passengers. It wasn't terrible odds. Earlier on the flight, she'd been feeling sorry for herself that she wasn't the kind of girl to stand out in a crowd. Maybe that would work out in her favor. What threat did a nineteen-year-old college sophomore pose? As long as she crouched low in her seat, didn't try anything stupid, General would never notice her.

For a fleeting moment, she pictured herself standing up in the cabin, telling all the passengers, including General and Lieutenant, about Jesus. It was crazy. Maybe she was having dark thoughts, but she wasn't suicidal. No, she just had to get through these next couple of hours alive. That's all it would be. A couple hours max. They were already close to Detroit. The plane couldn't stay in the air indefinitely. It would have to come down one way or another. *This too shall pass ...*

And then she'd tell Willow about the Lord. That was the bargain she'd make with God. If he got both of them out of this alive, she'd spend the next year if necessary preaching the gospel to Willow every hour of the day.

If they survived.

General was walking up the aisle next to Kennedy when his timer beeped in his pocket. He raised his eyebrows and stared at his phone.

"That's five minutes," he declared. "Time's up."

CHAPTER 13

Nobody talked. Kennedy kept her eyes on the ground as General passed her by. He wore faded Nikes, with the sole of one shoe starting to peel away. She couldn't explain why it struck her as strange. Here he was, ready to kill over a hundred civilians while an entire nation watched, and he was wearing shabby shoes.

Maybe he wasn't so scary after all.

Or maybe that was the cognitive dissonance talking.

He strolled the aisle slowly, his gun swinging low in his hand. Why didn't someone grab it?

"Are you recording?" he asked the man in the Hawaiian shirt. Kennedy wondered what news source his camera fed. Were people watching this in real time? What if he had a bomb? What if the plane exploded? They wouldn't really air that live on network television, would they?

At least while General addressed the camera his focus was diverted from the rest of the passengers on the plane. Five minutes had come and gone, and nobody called. Kennedy would have never guessed a school zoning issue could lead to terrorism.

No, not terrorism. That was the wrong word. General wasn't a terrorist. He was psychotic. He didn't have any political connections to any other organizations. He was working on his own, just him and Lieutenant who jumped in to kidnap girls or take out air marshals as the need arose. That didn't make General a terrorist. To be a terrorist, he had to have some umbrella organization sending him out, pumping his brain full of propaganda and then sanctioning this suicide mission.

He wasn't a terrorist. He was just insane.

"Mr. Weston," General's voice boomed throughout the otherwise still cabin. "You've had five and a half minutes to respond to my request to talk. You've sat at the negotiating table with your teachers' union. You know how this goes. If I don't stand by my threat, my word means nothing anymore. I just want you to remember, Mr. Weston, that everything that happens from this moment on is your fault."

There was a malicious sort of coyness in his tone that sent pinpricks zinging up and down Kennedy's spine.

"Entirely your fault," he repeated. He marched the aisle slowly, staring at each passenger in turn. His eyes landed on Kennedy for a brief second, and her blood chilled the same way Scrooge's must have when his door knocker revealed the face of his long-dead partner.

He kept walking. Slowly. Deliberately. All the way to the back of the plane. Not to Willow ...

Kennedy's stomach flipped in her gut as he smiled gallantly at the flight attendant. "Come here, darling."

She hesitated for only a minute and then stepped toward him.

"What's your name?" he asked, his voice purring like a cat's.

"Tracy."

He held her by the arm, positioning her slightly in front of himself. "Tell me, Tracy, do you have children?"

She was shaking. She bit her lip and nodded once.

"How charming," General answered. "How many?"

"Two." Her voice was hardly above a whisper. She squeezed her eyes shut.

General pouted into the camera. "I assume you'd like to see them again, wouldn't you?" He raised the gun toward her temple.

She nodded once more. Her teeth chattered until she clamped down on her jaw. Kennedy saw the strain in the muscles of her neck.

General let out a dramatic sigh. "Mr. Weston, you have two new orphans on your conscience."

The shot deafened Kennedy's ears and reverberated throughout the cabin.

CHAPTER 14

Kennedy hid her face in her arms as General addressed the superintendent of the Detroit School District once more. "You have another five minutes, Mr. Weston. I'm sure you're getting the picture by now. The plane's fully loaded, and I've got all the time in the world. You know how to reach me."

Ray wrapped an arm around Kennedy's shoulder. "It's going to be ok," he whispered. It was a lie but a compassionate one.

She didn't bother replying.

Five minutes. And then the terror would begin anew. Who this time? And how could any of the passengers on board survive this horror? This uncertainty?

Kennedy's teeth chattered. Just like the flight attendant's had before ...

Would she ever get that image out of her brain? Could she ever erase the memory of the day? If she survived at all ...

A nice trip to Alaska. That's all this was supposed to be. Her chance to see the northern lights for the first time. Spend a few weeks with Willow, get to know her family, try her first taste of roadkill moose. Why did she have to be on this flight? Why did she have to be so far away from home?

She wanted to call her parents. Wanted to hear her dad's strong, comforting voice. She'd even take the inevitable ten-minute interrogation from her mom about everything from Kennedy's dating life to her personal hygiene habits. Why had she ever left home in the first place?

In the 1800s, missionaries would take months getting from one destination to another. Sometimes they died in the process. Shipwrecks, illnesses at sea were very real dangers these men and women knew about when they set out. For a long time, missionaries to China would pack their belongings in coffins since many of them expected to die on foreign soil.

But that wasn't the world Kennedy had been born into. People traveled across the world every day of the week. Kennedy had probably circumnavigated the globe half a dozen times by now, all without event. Flying was safe. You were more likely to get mauled by a bear than get killed in a plane crash.

What had gone so horrifically wrong?

General still paced the aisles, and Kennedy's body tensed every time he walked past. How many minutes had already gone by? When would his timer beep again?

She squeezed her eyes shut, hoping to open them and realize she was still in her dorm, waking up from a nightmare. She and Willow would laugh about it, and then they'd walk to the L'Aroma Bakery in Harvard Square and share a quiet breakfast together before Dominic drove them to the airport to enjoy a safe, quiet Christmas break.

When she opened her eyes, General had stopped just a foot or two away from her. She tried to keep her breathing as quiet as possible, which was hard to do on account of the panicked spasms in her lungs.

"That's five minutes," he told his lieutenant. "Let's roll."

Kennedy turned so the cameras wouldn't catch her face. Did her parents know what was happening by now? Were they as freaked out as she was?

General positioned himself in front of Lieutenant's camera. "Mr. Weston, you've had five more minutes to do something about the situation at Brown. I'm a little disappointed I haven't heard from you yet. I wasn't hoping to have to do this, but you've left me with very few options."

General walked toward the front of the plane, and Kennedy's body relaxed just a little the farther away from her he got.

"Mr. Weston, you're a family man. You have kids of your own. Kids you would hate to see hurt, so I know you can empathize with my situation here." He grabbed Selena, the girl who'd been kidnapped, and pulled her up from her first-class seat. "Say hello to Papa," he told her.

Selena's voice trembled. "Daddy?"

General grimaced. "Daddy?" he repeated in a grating falsetto and chuckled into the camera. "I expect I'll be hearing from you soon. As a show of good will, you've got two extra minutes."

His cell phone rang less than ten seconds later. He grinned and pulled it out of his pocket slowly and deliberately before tapping a button.

"Hello, you're on speaker phone."

"Great, that's great. You should know how much I appreciate ..."

"Who's this?" General's face darkened into an ugly scowl. "I want to talk to Charles Weston."

"I know. Believe me, I understand your concerns." The voice was smooth. Silky even in its digitized form.

"Who are you?" General demanded again.

"This is Franklin, but all my friends call me Frank. Come to think of it, you had a brother named Frank, didn't you, Bradley?"

"I don't care who you are," General snarled. "I didn't ask to talk to some negotiator shrink. If I don't get Charles Weston on the phone in five seconds, his daughter bites it."

Selena's eyes were wide, but she didn't tremble or make any noise.

"I can only guess how tense things are up there, Bradley," the buttery voice said. "Listen, I've got Mr. Weston on the way right now to chat with you about his daughter, and while we wait for him, how about you take me off speaker phone and we have a little man-to-man chat, just you and me in private?"

General was so tense, it looked as if his eyes might burst out of his skull without warning. "You're staying on speaker."

"Hey, that's cool," Frank went on, "but I want to ask you something. I know you've had some trouble up there. Is there anything you need? Are any of the passengers hurt? We've got a doctor down here. He can talk you through any first aid you might require."

"Just shut up and get me Weston," General snarled.

There was a long pause before the voice came back. "Ok, I just heard from your man. He says he's real concerned for his daughter and wants to patch up this little misunderstanding you two have as soon as possible."

"Great. Put him on the phone."

"Yeah, that's not feasible right at this moment, but I'll tell you what we can ..."

"No," General interrupted, "I'll tell you what. You get Weston on the phone with me in three more minutes, or I kill his daughter."

Selena didn't cringe. Kennedy wondered if she knew what was going on or if her brain had shut down completely because of all the trauma.

Frank's voice on the other line was just as even and calm. "Hmm, I don't think you want to do that. Sounds to me like Selena's your biggest bargaining chip right now, wouldn't you say? Let's think about another way to settle these differences you two men are experiencing or ..."

"Fine," General spat. "Three minutes to talk to Weston, or another hostage dies." He punched his phone off so hard Kennedy would have been surprised if his screen survived the ordeal.

"Set the timer," General snapped at Lieutenant. "Three more minutes."

The entire cabin was silent except for the droning of the engines. A numbness akin to Selena's psychological coma seemed to have settled into the collective psyche of the passengers. Nobody was crying. Nobody was carrying on whispered conversations. Most, like Kennedy, stared blankly ahead.

Waiting.

Three more minutes. Kennedy found herself thinking about Einstein's theory of relativity. Technically, since they were on an airplane, wouldn't three minutes up here pass more slowly than on the ground? Too bad the difference was miniscule. If this were a sci-fi book, maybe they could take advantage of the time distortion, but this wasn't speculative fiction, and the grating squeal from Lieutenant's timer pounded in Kennedy's brain like a siren when it went off.

"Time's up." General started his slow march to the back of the plane.

Past Kennedy and Ray. Past the rows of passengers who were too tired or shocked to even cringe.

All the way to the back of the cabin.

No. Kennedy's heart screamed the word. *No. No. No.* Was God listening? Could he hear?

General stopped when he reached the last aisle. Kennedy couldn't watch. Why didn't her body turn away? Why didn't her eyes close?

No.

It couldn't be happening. It wasn't happening. There was no way to wrap her mind around any of this. Her brain was begging her for answers, pleading with her to come up with some sort of mental contortion that could explain away this sort of terror, this sort of unfathomable reality. Every joule of energy was focused on that one word. That one thought. That one prayer.

No.

"Stand up."

This wasn't real. This wasn't true. But it was. She couldn't deny it.

Couldn't twist reality any other way as General yanked Willow to her feet by a clump of her striking blue hair.

CHAPTER 15

Kennedy was about to spring out from her seat, but Ray held her back.

"There's nothing you can do," he hissed in her ear.

That wasn't true either. He was lying. Her eyes were lying, too. That wasn't Willow who stood with her hands covering her face. That wasn't Willow lifting up one soft request for her life. That wasn't Willow cowering just a foot away from General's gun.

General waited while Lieutenant maneuvered himself to get the best camera angle. Willow had ceased her begging but was looking around the cabin wildly.

Looking for Kennedy?

Jesus saves! She should scream it now. Scream it as loudly as possible. Shout out the four steps to salvation, the sinner's prayer, anything. Give Willow some sort of hope that she could hold onto. Give her that chance to receive God's gift of salvation. How many opportunities had Kennedy already missed? How many times could she have broached the subject in their cramped dorm room? What kind of fellowship might they have shared together?

And now, she was too late.

"Mr. Weston, I'd like you to meet a young friend of mine." General smiled as Willow tried to shrink into the wall to get away from him.

Just tell her, something burning inside Kennedy's soul shouted. *Tell her now.* But the words wouldn't come. Ray was holding onto her shoulder, whether to offer some sort of protection or to keep her from joining her roommate in her death.

"She doesn't want to die, and if you must know the truth, I don't want to kill her. But a word is a man's bond, isn't that right, Mr. Weston?" General raised up the corner of his lip in a half smirk.

Take me instead. The thought came to her in an instant, and her brain flashed with an image John Harper, the preacher on the capsizing Titanic who gave away his own life jacket because he couldn't stand the thought of a man dying without having the chance to know Christ.

Take me instead. Why wouldn't her mouth work? Why wouldn't her body move? Why wouldn't Ray let her go?

"Anyway, for those of you watching this drama unfold, I want you to remember one name. Charles Weston. Detroit School District superintendent. If it weren't for Charles Weston, I wouldn't have to send my children to a schoolyard that's put grown men in the hospital. And if it weren't for Charles Weston, I wouldn't have to shoot this rather pretty passenger."

"You'll do no such thing, young man."

Kennedy gaped at the old woman who addressed General with so much boldness and conviction.

He let out a gruff laugh. "You, granny? What are you going to do?"

Grandma Lucy was out of her seat, the cowboy bandana still in her hand. "Do?" she asked. "I'm going to save this young woman's life."

Kennedy's heart was racing. She was going to throw up again. Any minute now. She couldn't hold it down much longer.

Grandma Lucy stepped next to Willow, who flung her arms around her like a preschooler clutching at her mother's skirt.

"I've given my word," General explained. "It's time for me to kill a hostage."

Grandma Lucy swept Willow behind her. "Then you'll kill a hostage whose soul is ready to enter paradise, and you'll leave this poor child out of it." She sucked in her breath, stuck out her chest, and waited.

The air in the cabin changed. Denser now. Was anybody on board still breathing?

General glanced once at Lieutenant and then shrugged. "A hostage is a hostage." He held out his gun until the barrel was only a foot away from Grandma Lucy's forehead.

She didn't flinch. "Before you kill me, there's something I'd like to tell you. Something your audience might be interested in hearing."

He raised an eyebrow impatiently. "Yeah? What's that?"

She tilted up her chin. "That Jesus Christ is the risen Savior of the world. He is my shepherd, my redeemer, my healer, and my coming king. If you kill me, my soul will leave this broken jar of clay and enter into the presence of God."

"Great," General muttered. "So I guess I'm doing you a favor."

"Yes, you are." Grandma Lucy took a step closer to him, pressing Willow several paces behind her with a protective sweep of her hand. "And since you're doing me such a great honor, I want to return the favor."

"How you expect to do that?"

Grandma Lucy's voice was perfectly steady. "I'd like to pray for you."

He scoffed.

"I'm volunteering to die for your cause. In a way, I'll be your first martyr, isn't that right? So you let me pray for you, and then I promise not to interfere when you pull that trigger. In fact, by killing me, you'll be winning yourself lots of added publicity. Know why? My grandson made a documentary about Brown Elementary School last fall. Put four months of his own time and his own money into it."

General shuffled from one foot to another. "I never heard about a documentary."

"It never aired," Grandma Lucy told him. "But I guarantee that if you kill me, everyone will be clamoring to watch my grandson's show. The public will be on your side. You'll be sure to get justice. Now, will you let me pray for you?"

He stared at Lieutenant once more before finally grumbling, "Fine. But keep it short."

Grandma Lucy had already closed her eyes and raised her hands toward heaven. "Father God, sweet Savior, my friend, this is a man who is hurting. This is a man who has a deep desire to see justice. This is a father who cares for his children, who hates the thought of seeing them come to harm due to man's ignorance and greed. Give rest to his soul, Father God. Comfort him. Strip him free of the burdens he carries, his anger, his rage, his insecurities. Settle his spirit, Lord, so that he can find true rest in you, the giver of life. The author of peace. The comfort of our souls. Teach him, Holy Spirit, that there is no other name under heaven by which he can be saved than the sweet name of Jesus Christ, the Lamb of God who takes away the sins of the world. Show him that his sins will be washed clean, whiter than snow, if he confesses his sins, if he believes that you died for him, that you took the penalty for his sins upon your bloody shoulders when you hung on that beautiful, glorious cross. Show him, Jesus, that you are the way, the truth, and the life, that no one can come to the Father except through you. Give him a burning desire to know you, Lord, so that he can say like the Apostle Paul that *Christ came into the world to save sinners, of whom I was the worst.* Without you, sweet and merciful Jesus, we are all wretched. Without you, we are sinful, unable to do anything good. But because of the blood that you shed ...”

“That’s enough!” General roared.

Kennedy cowered involuntarily in her seat.

General raised his gun once more. His whole body was shaking. “I said that’s enough,” he snarled again, even though Grandma Lucy stood calmly and hadn’t said a word.

Kennedy tensed her muscles. Braced herself for the upcoming explosion. Squinted her eyes so they’d be ready to close that much faster as soon as he pulled the trigger.

“Go ahead, young man,” Grandma Lucy urged. “I’ve been ready to meet my Jesus for over fifty years.”

Kennedy squeezed her eyes shut and covered her ears with her hands.

CHAPTER 16

Click.

Kennedy pried one eye half open. Had she heard right?

Click.

No louder than a retractable pen collapsing on itself. General stared at his gun in stunned rage.

Grandma Lucy opened her eyes and smiled at him sweetly. "I should have mentioned one more thing. God promised me in the book of Isaiah chapter 54 that no weapon forged against me would prevail."

General stared stupefied.

Ray sprung out of his seat. "His gun doesn't work!"

Three other men jumped up at the same time. Two tackled the fat lieutenant in his Hawaiian shirt from behind, sweeping his legs out from under him and letting his own body weight do the rest. Ray and someone in a dark suit confronted General head on, both working to twist the gun out of his hold. Ray finally succeeded and slid out the cartridge, tossing it up the aisle toward Kennedy. The second man doubled over when General punched him in the gut, but by then a few other passengers and the unbound air marshal had joined in the fray. Kennedy could only see a blur of colors, hear the cacophonous sounds of *oofs* and curses and flailing limbs. Breath whooshed back into her lungs, choppy and uncertain at first like a child just learning to toddle. Would it ever end?

She tried to focus on Ray to make sure he was ok, but she could never keep her eyes on him for long. Her brain couldn't follow the disjointed movements of the skirmish, didn't dare hope the passengers would succeed.

Were the cameras still rolling? Did the viewers see what was happening?

"We got them!" The male flight attendant shouted. "We have both men subdued."

The cabin filled with air again. Relief. Release. Kennedy pried her fingers loose from her seatbelt. So it was really over. Their salvation had come in by way of a grandmother with the boldness of an advancing army and the miracle of a misfired weapon.

"You're all dead!" General shouted as the air marshal dragged him to the back of the cabin. "Nobody's getting off this plane alive!"

The PA system came on. "Folks, this is your captain speaking, and I just want to say thank you to everyone back there who kicked some terrorist butt."

Nervous laughter and subdued applause began to melt away the fear that had frozen like armor around Kennedy's psyche. She allowed herself a smile, noted the strange sensation of her facial muscles as it spread across her face.

A woman with shocking blue hair, glossy as a marble, threw herself into the seat by Kennedy and wrapped her arms around her. "We're safe."

"You're all dead!" General shouted from the back of the plane.

A sob rose from Kennedy's chest and lodged itself in her throat.

Willow shook her gently by the shoulders. "It's ok now."

Terror, fear, guilt, and shock took over Kennedy's entire body. She hadn't realized how much energy it had taken just to keep them all contained. Now they came bursting out of her core with the explosive energy of a nuclear detonation.

Willow didn't seem surprised by the tears that coursed down Kennedy's cheeks. She didn't laugh at her. Didn't tease. Just gave her another hug, whispering those beautiful words over and over again like a prayer of thanksgiving.

"We're safe."

CHAPTER 17

The moments that followed General's failure felt more surreal than any dream Kennedy could remember. While General and his lieutenant sat bound in the back of the plane, the passengers slowly began to talk again. Move around again. Breathe again. The two dead bodies were covered with blankets and moved out of the aisles. Out of sight. Could Kennedy ever forget? What had she known about Tracy? A mother of two. Frazzled at times, perhaps, but she did her job well. What would her friends say about the kind of person she was off hours? Her husband or any other loved ones she'd left behind?

She squeezed her eyes shut. Thank God they were so close to Detroit. She had to wrangle her thoughts. Take them captive. Avoid thinking about Tracy and the other murdered passenger. At least not until she landed on solid ground. Not until she achieved the psychological security that would come from getting off this plane.

"You're all dead!" General shouted before the air marshal punched him in the face.

Kennedy, Willow, and Ray were scrunched up together in the row where his math tests had been strewn across the aisle. The three of them struggled together to make sense of his mess.

"Folks," the captain said, "I'm sure we're all ready to get off this aircraft. I'm happy to report that we're beginning our descent now to Detroit. I imagine the deboarding process will be a little bit unorthodox, and we've got a whole army of first responders ready to assist in any way they can. Please buckle up and prepare for a safe and uneventful landing."

Kennedy still had a hard time believing it was over. As if a nightmare that ghastly couldn't end so simply. Were they really about to touch down in Detroit? She didn't care if it took them a week to get to Anchorage. For now, she was just ready to have her feet connected to the solid earth.

Everything had happened so fast. The hijacking, the countdowns, the scrimmage that overcame their would-be killers. Kennedy had the feeling it would take her all of Christmas break and half of spring semester just to process everything that happened, and then another few years of prayer and counseling to actually move past it.

The skyjackers had been thwarted. That's what mattered. Willow laughed at something Ray said, but Kennedy could only hear their tentatively joyful conversation as though through a fog.

Her roommate had almost died. Everyone had been close to death, but Willow had been a foot away from a loaded gun. If it hadn't been for Grandma Lucy ...

"Where are you going?" Willow asked when Kennedy got up from her seat.

"I think the captain wants everyone to stay buckled," Ray told her.

Kennedy wasn't listening. She made her way to the back of the plane, where Grandma Lucy sat in the corner, hunched over her Bible. She looked up with a smile before Kennedy sat down.

"I was hoping for a chance to chat with you." She moved her purse so Kennedy could settle in beside her. "I've been reading. Here in Isaiah." She pointed to some verses in her large print Bible.

Lift up your eyes to the heavens, look at the earth beneath, Kennedy read to herself, nodding as if she fully understood whatever spiritual mysteries Grandma Lucy expected her to find.

"Keep going," she said. "Read it out loud."

Kennedy took in a breath. "*The heavens will vanish like smoke, the earth will wear out like a garment and its inhabitants die like flies. But my salvation will last forever, my righteousness will never fail.*" Well, she had certainly seen God's salvation today, seen it in a way she would never forget. But something had been bothering her ever since it happened. Something she had to know now.

She looked up from the book. "Were you sure the gun wouldn't fire?"

Grandma Lucy slipped her spectacles back up her nose. "No. I wasn't. But I had a peace." She stared at Kennedy pointedly. "Did you?"

"Know about the gun?" she asked.

Grandma Lucy shook her head. "No. Did you have that peace?"

Kennedy thought back to the darkness, the overwhelming despair, the guilt she'd experienced when Willow stood at the end of the barrel. She stared at her lap. "No. I didn't."

"That's nothing to be ashamed of." Grandma Lucy tilted up her chin.

"God works in each of us in different ways. For me, God used our little excitement today to teach me that I'm ready to go home. I've had my share of health issues lately. Twice now I've surprised the doctors by leaving the hospital in my own car and not in a hearse. And both of those times, I struggled. Told God he couldn't take me home yet. I still had to see my grandson saved. I still have to be here to pray for him through whatever trials God uses to bring him to salvation."

She stared past Kennedy's shoulder with a faraway look in her eye.

"When I stared at that gun, though, that's when I knew. The battle for Ian's soul, the battle I've been fighting restlessly for years now, that battle was never mine to begin with. That battle belongs to the Lord and no one else. If he wants me to stay put and pray for my grandson, love him, witness to him, then bless the Lord, oh my soul, because I'm longing to wrap my arms around him the day he finally gives his life over to Christ. But if God calls me to heaven first, then I figure I'll just go on praying for Ian there. I don't see why I can't. That was what God wanted to teach me today. I wonder what lesson he had in store for you."

Kennedy fixed her eyes on the open Bible before her. *Hear me, you who know what is right, you people who have taken my instruction to heart: Do not fear the reproach of mere mortals or be terrified by their insults.*

She took a breath and tried to collect her thoughts. "I think the worst part about today was knowing that if Willow died and went to hell, I'd have to live wondering if I could have done something. If it was my fault that she never learned about the gospel." She shook her head. "I can't believe all the excuses I made. How scared I was of looking dumb or being called judgmental."

Kennedy was ashamed to admit her shortcomings to someone so bold and obedient, but Grandma Lucy just smiled and took Kennedy's hand in hers. "Peter was scared too, remember? But then the Holy Spirit came down at Pentecost, came and settled on him, and the very first time he opened his mouth to preach, the Bible says three thousand new believers were added to their number that day. He wasn't anything more than a simple fisherman with a very good habit of saying the wrong thing at the wrong time, and that's how God used him. So just imagine what he can do with you."

Kennedy sighed. "I'm not sure I'll ever find that kind of power or boldness."

"That's because you're still relying on your own strength. Trust me. I lived my life that way for decades. It wasn't until I followed God's call to Afghanistan that I finally learned what it was to be filled with the Holy Spirit, to surrender not just my eternal life to him, but my day-to-day life as well. Every hour, every minute submitted to him. *What do you want me to do today, Jesus? Who do you want me to tell about you?* That's what I'd ask him. He gave me small assignments at first. Maybe he told me to share a little bit of my lunch with a woman on the streets. And I did that, and then the next time he told me something, it would be a little more out of my comfort zone, like maybe he wanted me to invite two prostitutes into my home and give them a place to sleep. And each time I obeyed, I found a deeper sense of peace. It wasn't that God needed me to reach out to these people. He could have used anybody. But he was inviting me to join him in his work. I stopped looking at it as the relationship between a master and a servant and started to think of it as the partnership between two good friends, both working together for the same goal. He stretched me so much overseas. Taught me what it means to live by the Spirit. I know you're born again, but have you surrendered your life to the Spirit?"

She gazed at Kennedy so pointedly Kennedy stared at her hands in her lap. "I'm not really sure. I think so. I mean, I'm doing my best to read the Bible each day. Remembering to pray."

Grandma Lucy smiled gently. "Let me tell you a story. I got married over fifty years ago. My husband isn't with me anymore, but when we were on our honeymoon, do you think we had to schedule time to spend together?"

Kennedy couldn't figure out what point she was trying to make. "No."

"Of course not. Now, I can tell you there were times in our marriage where we did have to make a conscious effort to connect with each other, but for the most part, we spent time together because we wanted to. Do you see the difference?" she asked and went on without waiting for an answer. "You probably grew up hearing your Sunday school teachers and pastors telling you that to grow in your walk with the Lord, you need to read your Bible and pray every day. Am I right?"

Kennedy nodded.

"And that's true. Without prayer and Scripture, we're not going to mature. But I think what happens is we think of the spiritual disciplines, things like prayer and Bible study, as the definition of spiritual maturity, not the means to grow closer to Jesus. Do you see the difference?"

"I guess so," Kennedy answered even though Grandma Lucy's words didn't seem to connect with her brain in any meaningful way.

Grandma Lucy smiled softly. "I just want you to know that God has so much to offer you. Peace and joy and the riches of his presence. But we get so distracted. We think that if we check morning devotions off our to-do list, we've done everything God expects us to do for the day. It's human nature. I'm not picking on you personally. That's just the way we're programmed. But the Christian walk isn't about a to-do list. Tell me something. If you set aside three hours every single day to study the Bible, do you think you would grow in your faith?"

"Yeah," Kennedy replied tentatively, "but I don't have time to ..."

"I didn't ask about time," Grandma Lucy interrupted. "I just asked if you think it would change your everyday life."

"I'm sure it would."

Grandma Lucy leveled her gaze. "Why?"

"Why?" Kennedy repeated. "Because it's ... Because when you ..."

A smile broke through Grandma Lucy's wrinkled face. "Because we all think that the more time we spend with God, the holier we become, right?"

Kennedy was confused. "Yeah, but isn't that the way it works?"

Another soft smile. "Let me tell you something else. When I first got married, my husband and I both had full-time jobs. I was in real estate at the time. My husband was a teacher. I was busy in the evenings. He left for school at six in the morning. Sometimes we'd go a full week without sitting down for a single meal together. Tell me something. Can you grow close to your spouse with a schedule like that?"

Kennedy frowned. "I guess not."

Grandma Lucy wagged her finger playfully. "You'd think so, right? But actually, that was one of the most intimate times in our relationship. We were so busy we knew we had to put in the extra effort to connect with each other. We'd write letters to each other back and forth in a diary. He'd come home from work and leave me a note while I was out showing houses. In the morning when I woke up, before I started my day's paperwork I'd fill page after page of ridiculous, sappy mush for him to read when he came home in the afternoon."

"Oh." Kennedy had no idea what any of this had to do with her own personal walk with Christ. Maybe Grandma Lucy was just rambling and had lost her original thought.

"Years later when the kids were grown, my husband lost his teaching job and decided to drive trucks. We sold the house, everything. For twelve months, we ate at rest stops, slept in little pullouts, and traveled the country together. Every waking minute, there he was. And want me to tell you something? It tore our marriage apart. By the end of the third month, we couldn't stand each other. The day he delivered his last load was the day I filed for divorce. I'm not saying it was the right thing for me to do. I'm not pretending to be proud of my decision, but that season is what ultimately destroyed us."

By now, Kennedy didn't know what point she was trying to make. Apparently, Grandma Lucy didn't either. She pouted and glanced around the cabin as if looking for some sort of cue card.

"It was when I left my husband that I realized just how terrible I was at being a Christian on my own. I was a disciplined believer, prayed out of a check list and read three or four chapters from the Bible every single night without fail. But that didn't mean I was surrendered to God the other twenty-three and a half hours of the day. Do you know what the Bible says Christian maturity looks like?" She raced ahead without letting Kennedy respond. "The Bible says they'll know we are Christians by our love. Plain and simple. Not how complicated our prayer list is. Not how many times we've read the Bible cover to cover or how long we spend studying it each day. I'll tell you what. There are some deplorable people who I'm sure have read the Bible more than I have and use it to destroy others."

She shook her head. "If we don't have love for each other, what good is all the Bible studying or all the devotional time in the world? What's all that learning doing for us if we're not allowing God's Word to change us? Transform us?"

"Not much, I guess." Kennedy still couldn't tell if she was being reprimanded like a naughty pupil or inspired like a boxer about to jump into the ring.

"And that's where the Holy Spirit comes in." Grandma Lucy's eyes lit, and she nodded sagely, apparently glad to have discovered her train of thought once more. "He's there, waiting for you to fully surrender, waiting for you to invite him to take full control of your life." She stared pointedly at Kennedy. "You strike me as a competent, capable young woman. You're smart, you got yourself into Harvard, you're doing well in your studies. But are you relying on God each and every day? Are you making him the focus of your life? Are you studying to be pleasing to him, or are you studying because you get a thrill from that sense of achievement? When you think about becoming a doctor, is it so you can fulfill the call God has on your life, or is it so you can prove to yourself that you can succeed?"

Kennedy bit her lip. Thankfully, she didn't have to wait long for Grandma Lucy to fill in the uncomfortable silence.

"God has amazing plans for you, but until you learn to surrender to him, until you fall on your knees and beg the Holy Spirit to guide you in every decision you make, you'll always feel like there's something missing." She patted Kennedy's hand. "It's a lot to think about. But when I look at you, I see someone who has so much potential, someone who could do so much to advance the kingdom of God. That's the call you have on your life. To shine his light in a way that everyone around you will recognize the truth of the gospel." She smiled. "And I think you and I both know that can start with your roommate whenever you're ready."

Kennedy had known those words were coming even before Grandma Lucy spoke them. "I'm not sure I'll ever be ready."

Grandma Lucy's eyes crinkled softly. "Here's what Paul says to the Corinthians. He says, *I tell you, now is the time of God's favor, now is the day of salvation.* That pressure you're experiencing, that prompting in your heart that you felt when you saw Willow about to get shot, that's the Holy Spirit. He saved your roommate from death. He didn't have to. He's given both of you a second chance. I suggest you don't waste this one."

Kennedy nodded. Grandma Lucy was right. She hadn't said anything Kennedy didn't already know, but somehow it felt different hearing it from her.

"I just wish I had that kind of boldness," she admitted.

"We can pray for that right now," Grandma Lucy offered and raised one hand heavenward. "Father God, precious Jesus ..."

Her prayer was interrupted by a high-pitched wail coming from the wall directly behind her seat. Kennedy crouched down and covered her ears.

From his confinement behind her, General let out a hair-raising laugh. "Didn't I say you were all about to die?"

CHAPTER 18

"What's going on?" Kennedy asked the flight attendant who rushed past her.

"Smoke alarm," he shouted and pulled a fire extinguisher out from a cabinet.

"Don't waste your time," General chuckled. "It's too late for any of you now."

The flight attendant gave him a half-hearted kick and then flung the bathroom door open. Thick, black smoke poured out from the lavatory. Kennedy's eyes stung, and her lungs were momentarily paralyzed.

"Get to the front of the cabin." The flight attendant waved them away. Kennedy reached across the aisle for her backpack.

"What about me?" General asked, fear lacing his words for the first time.

"You shut up."

Another low chuckle. "I deserved that, I suppose. Just remember, I did this for my kids."

The flight attendant didn't respond. Kennedy grabbed Grandma Lucy's hand, and the two stumbled down the aisle.

"Fire!" As soon as word got out in the cabin, half the passengers jumped out of their seats and lurched forward as one chaotic, undulating mass.

Thick, black smoke choked the air as everyone tried to scramble forward at once.

"Stay calm!" Grandma Lucy shouted behind Kennedy, but even her authoritative voice couldn't carry over the din of the panicked passengers.

"Folks," the captain announced over the PA, "I understand there's a situation in the back, and we're doing what we can to touch down as soon as possible. When we land, we've got to exit the aircraft in a calm and orderly manner. It's going to be a fast descent, so I need you all to come to the front of the cabin as far away from the smoke as you can and get yourselves buckled in."

He may as well have been speaking to himself. Even if Kennedy wanted to move, she was pressed on all sides by people struggling to surge ahead.

"He's trying to kill us!" a woman shouted.

"I can't see anything!"

Grandma Lucy put her hand on Kennedy's shoulder and used it for balance as she stood on one of the empty aisle seats. "Listen, all of you!" she hollered, and the din diminished slightly. "The captain is getting us on the ground. We'll land in just a few minutes and then we'll get off this plane. Right now, there will be more injuries if we all scramble ahead like this. So grab a seat, buckle up, and if you haven't made peace with God yet, I suggest you ask him to forgive your sins in the name of Jesus."

"We're going to die!" someone shrieked. Even if Kennedy could find an empty seat, there were too many bodies pushing against her. The smoke was so thick she couldn't see Grandma Lucy standing on the chair. Had she fallen? Would she see her alive again? She wanted to duck down, knew the air would be cleaner the lower she got, but with the crowd this frantic, if she ended up on the ground there was no way she'd get up again.

The smoke stung her eyes. Kennedy was completely blind now. Her sinuses burned, and she pictured black, sticky tar caking to the epithelial lining of her respiratory tract.

God, help me.

Someone elbowed her in the face. She stumbled back, but a mass of passengers pressed against her from behind. Grabbing her hair, trying to propel themselves forward.

A scream. Not of fear, but of pain. Someone was hurt. Kennedy shot her hands out, trying to regain her bearings. The sea of people had carried her so far she had no idea where she was or if the emergency exits were in front of her or behind. She pried her eyes open, but the smoke was too thick to see anything.

"Let go!"

"Get off!"

"Help!"

The screams were as haunting and terrifying as anything Dante could have dreamed up in his *Inferno*, and for a time Kennedy's mind could only focus on one coherent thought: *This is what hell must be like.*

"I can't breathe," gasped a woman next to her. Kennedy tried to reach out to find her, but as soon as she repositioned her arm someone elbowed her in the gut.

In the midst of the chaos, passengers shouted for one another, calling their loved ones by name.

"Where are you?"

"I can't see you."

"Are you ok?"

Kennedy had to conserve what air was left around her. She was already dizzy. Was that from the fear or the lack of oxygen? If she fainted, if she lost her footing for just a moment ...

Someone scratched at her face. "Let me through!" A passenger tried to climb up Kennedy's back. She struggled to shove him off.

God, don't let me fall.

Where was Willow? Was she safe? Would she make it? Would any of them survive?

General's voice ran unchecked through her brain. *You're all dead.* He had planned everything. This was his end game.

God, I don't want to die.

Where was Willow?

The passengers pressed ahead, like a legion of lemmings with only one collective thought. With the plane still in the air, Kennedy could only guess where they expected to end up.

Willow. She had to get to her. God had given them a second chance. Grandma Lucy had said the same thing. Would God save her roommate from the gunman only to have her perish in a fire?

"Willow?" She tried to call out, but she couldn't take in enough air to give her voice any volume. "Willow?"

She had to be somewhere, but where?

Dear Lord, show me where she is, and I'll do anything. I'll say anything. Just let her be ok and get us both out of this alive. Please.

Back. Somehow she knew she had to go back. But how could she with all the passengers pressing against her from behind? And why would she want to go where the smoke was the thickest?

God, are you sure?

The impression was there just the same. She had to find her way out of this maddening throng.

She didn't care about the bruises she'd sustain from being prodded and pushed from so many sides. She didn't worry about the germs she was contracting by pressing herself against so many strangers. *God, make a way for me.* She envisioned him parting the bodies around her like he did for Moses at the Red Sea, but that's not what happened. Still, she eventually managed to shove her way to the outskirts of the frantic throng. Safe from the crowd, she dropped to her hands and knees, as much from exhaustion as from a desire to find breathable air.

"Willow?" She was somewhere nearby. Kennedy knew it. Or was that wishful thinking coupled with smoke-induced delirium?

"Willow?"

"Yeah." The voice was frail. Faint. Accompanied by a small cough.

"Where are you?"

"Over here." It was like playing Marco Polo inside a cloud of tear gas.

Kennedy reached ahead with her hand until it clenched a warm, sweaty palm. She could hardly speak, from relief as well as smoke exhaustion. "Are you ok?"

"I can't move."

Colorful spirals fired through Kennedy's optical nerve. She would black out any minute if she didn't get more oxygen.

"My necklace," Willow explained. "I fell, and it's stuck against something. I can't get it loose."

Kennedy probed with her hands until she felt the leather string that held Willow's travel size air purifier. It was hooked to the bottom of the seat and twisted so there wasn't room to slip it over her head.

"It's going to be ok," Kennedy promised, wondering if her last words to Willow would prove to be a lie. She fumbled with blind, clumsy fingers, but every time she tried to free the string, it wound up tighter around Willow's throat.

"We need to cut it." Kennedy would have tried her teeth, but she couldn't pull on it without choking her friend. "God, we need to cut it." She sounded like Grandma Lucy praying out loud like that, but she was well past the point of caring what Willow thought of her faith. She swept her hands around on the floor until she felt a purse beneath one of the seats. Her fingers trembled as she unfastened the clasp. All she needed was a pair of scissors. A nail file. Anything. Why couldn't the passenger have carried a Swiss army knife in her purse? Stupid TSA regulations.

"I'll have to pull it," Kennedy told her, wincing when she thought about how hard she'd have to yank to get the necklace to break free.

"I don't care. Just get it off."

Kennedy's breaths came out in worried, choked sobs. She couldn't do this. She wasn't strong enough. What if the strap cut into Willow's skin before the necklace gave way? What if she choked her friend to death?

"Just get it off," Willow begged.

Kennedy could feel the heat from the back of the cabin. She didn't have the lung capacity to let out the cry that welled up from her throat. *God, please.* She whispered a silent prayer and yanked with all her might. Willow's head jerked forward and banged Kennedy's knee, but the strap itself held fast.

"I'm sorry," Kennedy squealed.

"Just get it off."

Kennedy braced herself and pressed one hand against Willow's head to keep it still this time. *Ok, God. You performed miracles in the Bible. You performed miracles in the lives of so many missionaries. It's time for a miracle now.* She thought about Grandma Lucy's boldness. Could she conjure up that degree of faith? "In the name of Jesus," she whispered to the necklace, "I command you to break free."

Another yank, so hard Kennedy grunted from exertion.

Nothing. The leather held fast just like the last time, except now Willow didn't respond at all. Had she blacked out? Was she ...

Kennedy leaned down, and her own purifier swung and hit Willow in the face. She grabbed the device to throw it over her shoulder when she felt it. The leather was tied in the back. She ran her hands along Willow's strap until she felt the bulky knot.

"I've got it now," she assured her, but Willow still didn't respond.

God, you can't let her die. You need to give me just one more chance. I won't chicken out again, I promise. Please?

Kennedy slid the leather out of its knot. Her friend was free, but Kennedy couldn't rejoice.

Willow's body lay perfectly limp.

CHAPTER 19

Kennedy planted her fingers against the small dent in Willow's neck. *Please let there be a pulse. Please let there be a pulse.*

There it was. Slow and weak, but at least Willow was still alive. Kennedy leaned down, throwing off her own necklace after the purifier hit Willow in the face again. "You're going to be ok." Tears streamed down her cheeks and dripped onto Willow's body as the plane lurched, flinging Kennedy to one side and then the other. Howling wind roared through her ears. The cabin floor jostled violently.

From the window Kennedy made out the vague flashing lights of an ambulance.

"We've landed!"

"Out of my way!"

"Watch it!"

Shouting from the front of the plane. Cries of triumph.

Kennedy held onto Willow. In a few minutes, this would all be over.

"Hang on," she pleaded.

"Step aside!"

"Let the paramedics on board."

Kennedy wrapped her arms around Willow and cradled her head in her lap. "Just hang on." It was silly of her, really. Willow couldn't hear a thing, could she?

God, you promised me a second chance. What if this was it? What if Willow was slipping into a coma, a coma she would never wake from? Hadn't Kennedy promised God to share the gospel with her roommate if he gave her one more opportunity?

"Over here!" someone yelled.

"Help!"

"Don't block the exits."

Flames now leapt and roared from the back of the aircraft. The heat stung her back like a scalding acid. She wouldn't leave Willow. Some might say she was being heroic, but in truth she didn't think she possessed the energy to move. She was too tired to feel scared. The firefighters would save the two of them, or they wouldn't. Either way, time was running out.

"If there's anything you need to know right now," she whispered into her friend's ear, "it's how much God loves you."

"We've got the exits clear."

"I see someone there toward the back."

Kennedy wasn't ready to leave. There was more she was supposed to say. About sin and repentance, about Jesus' death and resurrection. Why was her brain so fuzzy?

"We're here. You're going to be ok."

Strong hands pried her to her feet.

"No!" She tried to kick but her legs collapsed beneath her. "No!" She thought she was screaming, but she couldn't hear herself.

"We'll send someone back to get your friend. But you've got to come with me now."

No. This wasn't how it was supposed to happen. She stretched her neck to look behind her, screaming at the flames that danced and flickered just a few feet away from Willow's body. No, this wasn't what was supposed to happen.

"Save her, not me." Kennedy was sobbing, but she didn't have the breath to make herself heard. Didn't have the energy to fight anymore. The faceless form of her anonymous rescuer held her in a steady, iron grasp as strong as the chains that clung to Ebenezer Scrooge's macabre partner.

"I have to go back," she whispered softly before her vision deserted her and everything fell to black, infinite darkness.

CHAPTER 20

Kennedy blinked her eyes open. Why did they hurt so bad? What was wrong with her contacts?

"Ow."

She tried to sit up.

Ow.

A man set his hand on her shoulder. "Easy there. Don't move too fast."

"Where am I?" Had she swallowed boiling water? Why did it feel like her lungs were burning?

Burning.

She threw his hand aside and sat up. The entire room spiraled in front of her. "Where is she?"

"Shhh." He put his finger to his lips like an over-doting nursery nanny. "You're at the hospital. Everything's going to be just fine."

"Where is she?" Kennedy asked again.

"The girl who was kidnapped? She's fine. She's in another room waiting for her dad to fly in and pick her up. Everything's fine."

"No, it's not," Kennedy insisted. "Where's Willow?"

A nurse in Snoopy scrubs walked over. Whispered something to him. What were they saying? What was wrong with her roommate?

The nurse gave her a smile. As if she wanted to be on friendly terms. Kennedy wouldn't believe a word she said.

"You must have had an angel watching over you on that plane. You're a very lucky woman."

Kennedy didn't care about luck. Didn't care about who saved her or how or why.

The nurse lowered Kennedy onto her back. Why was she so weak? Why couldn't she stay seated on her own? She tried to swing her legs off the gurney. "I need to go."

"Not yet. You took in a lot of smoke back there."

She didn't care. She felt fine. If that's what you could call having your lungs covered in tiny pieces of ashy glass that cut you with every inhale.

"I need to find her."

242

The woman looked just as clinical when she was frowning as she had when she smiled. "I need you to stay still."

Kennedy pictured herself fighting her way out of bed. Exhaustion clung to each individual muscle fiber. Where was Willow? She turned her head. Why were the lights so bright? Patients were lined up on gurneys, and nurses scurried back and forth in front of a busy station. She didn't need to be here, wherever here was. She was fine. She didn't need all these gadgets and monitors. She turned the other way and looked out a small window but didn't recognize the parking lot outside.

Where was Willow?

Time passed with stubborn sluggishness. Nurses came in, went out. Hooked up an IV, smothered her face with an oxygen mask that made her feel like she'd suffocate from claustrophobia. She drifted to sleep. Woke up. Still no sign of Willow. Some of the other patients nearby were talking to official-looking businessmen with clipboards and recording devices. It would be Kennedy's turn any minute. If the other passengers were fine, so was she. If they were ready to give statements, so was she. Anything to get out of here.

Anything so she could find Willow.

"Excuse me, Miss. We found you with a backpack and an ID belonging to Kennedy Stern. Is that your name?"

Kennedy nodded at the professionally dressed woman with glossy black hair.

"I'm Michelle Boone with the Federal Air Marshall Service. Do you feel up to answering some questions about what happened on the flight? I've heard multiple reports now about a ..."

"Is everyone ok?" Kennedy interrupted.

The woman frowned.

"On the plane," Kennedy pressed. "Did everyone get off safely?"

Agent Boone flipped a few pages on her clipboard. "Did you have a relative on the flight?"

"My roommate. We were traveling together."

An even deeper frown. "What is your roommate's name?"

"Willow Winters."

Something passed through the woman's eyes. Recognition.

Compassion. Pity. She tapped her pen several times against the pages on her clipboard. "I'm afraid I'm not at liberty to discuss anyone's medical condition unless it's with immediate family. You don't ..." She paused. Studied Kennedy. "You don't have a way to contact your roommate's next of kin, do you?"

Kennedy ripped the oxygen mask off her face and yanked the blood pressure cuff from her arm. She sat up, ignoring the dizziness that threatened to send her careening back into darkness.

"What happened to her?" She reached a hand back to steady herself and stifled a cough that made a valiant effort to crush each one of her ribs.

Two medics scurried over, trying to coax Kennedy back onto her back.

"Where's Willow?" she demanded. "Why won't you tell me what happened?"

The government agent held a hushed conversation with one of the medical professionals and finally turned back to Kennedy. "You need to lie down again, and then we can talk about your friend."

"Just tell me," Kennedy pleaded, but she allowed the nurses to lay her down. Tears leaked from her stinging eyes. Hot tears. Scorching tears. "Just tell me," she repeated and noticed that one of the women was holding her hand. What did she think that would accomplish?

Boone cleared her throat. "Your roommate was unconscious when we found her. She wasn't ..."

Kennedy felt her throat muscles seizing shut. She wasn't hearing right. Something was wrong with her ears.

The agent swallowed once before continuing. "She wasn't breathing."

What was she saying? This was a government official. Why couldn't she answer one simple question?

"Where is she now?" Kennedy's voice was quiet. Uncertain. Was she ready to hear the truth? Could she accept whatever news she received?

The Snoopy nurse was rubbing her back as if Kennedy were five years old and scared of the dark.

Boone's expression didn't change. "I haven't gotten an update yet, but I think it's probably wise if you ..."

The door to the makeshift triage unit swung open, and two paramedics pushed in a young woman sitting in a wheelchair. She was covered with several layers of blankets and twirled her blue hair around her finger. "All I'm saying is that if I'm gonna need a blood transfusion or anything, you need to guarantee it's coming from another vegan or I'm not accepting it."

Kennedy's body responded before her conscious mind figured out what was happening. She lunged out of bed, coughing in between peals of laughter, immediately tangling herself in the myriad wires that connected her to so many monitors and machines. "You're here!"

Willow fashioned a half-crooked grin. "Yeah, I'm all right."

Kennedy laughed until she choked on her own cough. "Where have you been?"

"Hypobaric chamber," Willow answered. "It was wicked awesome. You should try it."

"All right." A blond paramedic put his hand on Willow's shoulder. "I think that's enough excitement for now." He turned to Kennedy. "As soon as her oxygen levels improved she insisted on finding you."

Willow gave him a playful nudge. "You weren't supposed to say anything."

The federal agent tapped her clipboard. "Miss Stern, now that you've seen your friend's safe and sound, I really do need you to answer some questions for me. I have you listed as sitting in the back row by the lavatory. What can you tell me about a male passenger wearing Carhartts pants?"

CHAPTER 21

By the time the sun set through Kennedy's hospital room window, she had already spent two hours on her cell, first with her mom, trying to convince her she was alive and at least physically unharmed. Next she cried with Sandy while her pastor's wife convinced her that the emotional trauma of the day could lead to wholeness and healing with time and help from the Holy Spirit.

Kennedy had also walked the entire triage unit three times looking for Grandma Lucy, but none of the emergency responders recognized her description. She was exhausted after all her interviews with various federal officials. She was ready to leave Detroit behind, but the airlines as well as the hospital staff wanted her and Willow both to spend the night for observation. At least half of the passengers on Flight 219 had sustained injuries, some from smoke inhalation and some from the chaos that ensued when everyone tried to stampede off the plane at once.

By evening, though, the busyness and chaos at the hospital died down, and Kennedy and Willow were wheeled on their gurneys into a room of their own. Kennedy's stomach flipped slightly when the nurses left and she was alone with Willow for the first time since their rescue. What was she supposed to do? What was she supposed to say? She'd made a promise with God, hadn't she? She couldn't just forget about it.

But how do you start a conversation like that?

"Wanna catch a flick?" Willow pointed the remote at the TV. "There's gotta be something interesting."

Kennedy didn't know what to say. Now more than ever she understood how quickly life can change. How quickly life can end. But she still couldn't bring herself to open her mouth and start a conversation she didn't think Willow was ready to have.

"Sure," she answered. "Just nothing too scary." She meant it, too. She was done with drama and terror. She'd even take one of her mom's cheesy farm romances if she had to. As Willow flipped through the channels, Kennedy shut her eyes, thankful when her body slipped off to sleep so her mind could finally enjoy some peace.

Her dad woke her up at six the next morning, ready to fire instructions over the phone in case any lawyers asked to talk to her. He was sure a suit against the airlines was inevitable and didn't want her to get taken advantage of by greedy attorneys. He also made her promise to call him before the airlines forced her to sign forms or waivers. Kennedy didn't care about any of that. She just wanted to forget the entire nightmare had ever happened. According to the most recent news reports, the only other passenger who died on the flight besides the murdered hostages was General himself. He was bound to a cabinet near the back lavatory and hadn't been able to free himself during the fire. His fat lieutenant in the Hawaiian shirt somehow escaped. At least they didn't recover any of his charred remains. Nobody knew what became of the passenger in Carhartts either, a man identified as an electrician with three kids who all attended Brown Elementary.

A nurse gave Kennedy discharge instructions right after her breakfast of stale English muffin and some sort of egg substitute, but she couldn't leave the hospital before passing another round of interviews with Michelle Boone and about half a dozen other Feds and airline workers. "They'll be here any time," the nurse told her cheerfully. By the time an orderly dropped off cold grilled-cheese sandwiches for lunch, the only person who had stopped in was the cleaning lady.

Kennedy and Willow passed the day playing Scrabble or watching corny sitcom reruns from their hospital beds. Every time Kennedy thought she could muster up the courage to steer the conversation in a spiritual direction, she remembered how frightened she'd been on the plane and wanted to run away as fast as the little boy unfortunate enough to sing carols in front of Mr. Scrooge's office. She wanted to nap, but her body couldn't relax.

A liaison from the airlines knocked and entered their room at three thirty. It was seven at night before all the interviews were done and another airline employee handed Kennedy and Willow a hotel voucher and tickets to continue their trip to Anchorage the following morning.

"I can't believe we're stuck in Detroit another night," Willow complained. "How in the world are we supposed to get to this hotel?"

Kennedy didn't care how they traveled as long as they arrived without any further run-ins with terrorists.

Willow pulled her pockets inside out. "Seriously, how are we supposed to do anything? I don't have my wallet, I don't have my ID. How am I even going to get on the plane tomorrow?"

Kennedy's head was throbbing. "Let's just worry about that in the morning. They'll have records we were on that flight. It's not like they're going to keep us in Detroit forever."

As they walked through the hospital lobby toward the exit, Julie Andrews crooned about bright copper kettles and warm woolen mittens. If Kennedy had the energy, she might have found the irony humorous.

"I'm dead serious, we need to go back and find that liaison lady. I can't do anything without my ID."

The last thing Kennedy wanted to do was backtrack. How could she explain how desperately she needed to get herself out of this hospital? She didn't care if they had to walk to the hotel as long as there was a bed waiting for her to collapse onto once she arrived. In the past twenty-four hours since she arrived in Detroit, she doubted she'd slept three hours at any given stretch.

"I was wondering if I'd bump into you two again." The voice was too jocular. Too full of that raindrops-on-roses type of cheer that was so grating on her ears.

Kennedy stumbled ahead even as Willow stopped to give Ray the math teacher a half-convincing smile. "Hey, good to see you. Are you ok?"

He nodded. "Yeah, they discharged me earlier but I'm just now finishing all the interviews. You two? You both all right?"

No, Kennedy wasn't all right, and she wouldn't be until she found a bed to sink into. Preferably a bed with fluffed pillows and warm, heavy blankets.

"The airline gave me a hotel voucher." He checked inside an envelope he was holding. "The Golden Lion. You heard of it?"

"That's where we're going, too," Willow answered, and Kennedy wondered if she was going to give him their room number and a spare key as well.

"I don't know the bus system in Detroit. I think I'll just take a cab. You two ladies want to join me and split the fare?"

Willow fingered her glossy hair. "Actually, our wallets are incinerated by now, I'm sure."

"Well, I've got ..." Kennedy began before Willow elbowed her in the ribs.

"Wow, that's rough. Then let me call a cab for all of us. It's the least I could do."

If Kennedy was lucky, it's all he would do.

Willow gave him a smile and positioned herself between him and Kennedy. "That would be fabulous." She linked her arm in his, and together they headed out into the freezing Detroit evening. By the time they arrived at the Golden Lion, Ray had invited both Kennedy and Willow to have dinner with him in the restaurant downstairs.

"My treat." He smiled at Willow, who had all but scrunched herself onto his lap on the cab drive over.

"I really need to get some rest." As soon as the words left Kennedy's mouth, she saw the grateful look on her roommate's face.

"Are you sure?" Ray asked. "You'll need to eat something eventually."

"I'm still feeling awful," she confessed. "I hardly slept at all last night. I just want to get to bed."

Before Willow followed Ray into the Golden Lion café, she leaned over and whispered in Kennedy's ear, "Don't worry about me if I'm late. I'll see you in the morning."

By the time her elevator took her to her room, Kennedy was too tired to care what Willow was doing or who she was doing it with. It was no different than life in their dorm room, really.

So much for telling her about the gospel, Kennedy mused as she plopped onto the bed. Her lungs still hurt whenever she tried to draw a deep breath. She thought maybe a hot, steamy shower would help clear out the last of the smoke and guck she'd inhaled, but she didn't think she had the stamina.

She shut the blinds to block out a dreary Detroit sunset, with more smog and clouds than actual sky. She thought about Alaska, about the northern lights she wouldn't be seeing. Not today, at least. She still wasn't even convinced she'd get on that plane and fly to Anchorage with Willow in the morning. Part of her was ready to swear off airplanes for good, take a bus back to Cambridge and spend Christmas with Pastor Carl and Sandy like she had last year.

As excited as she'd been for the big Alaska experience, she'd had enough adventure for one vacation already. She pulled out her phone and started searching Greyhound rates. If she caught a bus first thing in the morning, she could arrive in Boston by dinnertime. The Lindgrens wouldn't mind, and the Greyhound rates were reasonable. A hundred and five dollars for a one-way ticket. She could put it on her dad's debit card. Her parents were probably just as ready to have her grounded as she was.

It seemed like the most reasonable plan. Willow would understand.

She was struggling to decide if she'd rather leave at six in the morning or wait for the nine-thirty bus when her cell rang.

Dominic.

Her finger paused above the screen for just a moment before she answered. "Hello?"

"Hey, I'm so glad you picked up. I've been really worried."

"I'm sorry I didn't get hold of you sooner." Was it better to confess she didn't have the energy to even think about calling him or cut off the apology there and leave it at that?

"No, don't feel bad. I'm just glad to hear you're ok. You're all right, aren't you?"

She didn't know if he was referring to her physical well-being or not. "Yeah, I'm fine." Maybe it was the fact that he had so much training in counseling that made it awkward to talk with him. She never wanted him to think that she was using him as a free shrink if she started discussing anything too deep.

"I saw some of the videos from the flight. That must have been really scary."

"It was." Could he tell she didn't want to talk about it?

"How's your roommate?" he asked. "Is she there with you?"

"No, she's out having dinner with some new fling."

"You sound upset." Why was he always so perceptive?

She plopped her head on the pillow and put him on speaker phone so she didn't have to hold the cell up to her ear. "I'm just tired."

"Are you mad that Willow's out enjoying herself after everything that happened?"

Sometimes she hated the way he could read her thoughts. "I don't know. It did seem kind of weird, I guess."

She could almost picture his patient smile on the other end of the line. "People react to stress in different ways."

"I know that." She'd taken AP psychology back in high school. She didn't need the lecture.

"But something else is bothering you."

She let out a sigh. Maybe by this time tomorrow she could breathe regularly without feeling like every exhale was a stifled cough. "I don't know. There was a minute ..." No, she wouldn't talk about the gunman holding Willow. That didn't matter. "After the fire started. She was stuck. There was a minute on the plane I didn't think she'd make it."

He didn't say anything. She could imagine the way he would study her if they were having this conversation face to face.

"And I felt guilty for not having shared the gospel with her beforehand," she finally confessed. It sounded so stupid now. As stupid as those people who try to make bargains with God when they're faced with their own mortality.

"So now you're upset that she's out on a date when you think she should be sitting with you asking you to tell her about the God who so miraculously saved her?"

She sighed again, wondering how annoying it would be to live with someone who could sense your emotions like some kind of a sci-fi empath. "I don't know. Something like that, I guess."

Another long silence. Something else she might never get used to.

"God works in people in different ways," he finally reminded her. "Don't give up on her. This is one night. You'll have a lot of free time together in Alaska."

"If I even go."

"What do you mean?"

She didn't want to spell out all her reasons. "I'm thinking of taking the bus home. Spend Christmas with Carl and Sandy."

"Well, I'm sure they'd love to have you. Just make sure you're not pulling a Jonah."

"A what?" Suddenly she wasn't as exhausted anymore. Maybe she'd find the energy for that steaming shower after all.

"God told Jonah to preach to Nineveh, and he ran away. It took a major crisis to get him back on the right track."

Dominic didn't know what he was talking about. The way he prattled on, he made it sound as if God sent the skyjackers to kill those people and set fire to the plane as a way to punish Kennedy for not preaching the gospel to Willow earlier. Kennedy had never been to seminary and certainly didn't know as much about theology as Dominic did, but she knew God would never act like that.

"Listen, I've got to go. My throat's really sore. It hurts to talk."

"I'd love to pray for you before you hang up," he offered.

"That's ok. I'd probably fall asleep right in the middle." She forced a laugh although she found the whole situation anything but humorous. She gave Dominic a *good night* that was slightly more abrupt than he deserved, and after a few minutes of internal debate, she pulled herself out of bed and started the shower running. Usually after a long flight, she couldn't wait to get out of her travel clothes. Wash off all the germs and grime from the air. Tonight, she couldn't even bring herself to undress. For one thing, when she got out of the shower she'd have to put on the same dirty clothes she had been wearing for the past two days, but there was something more to it than that. She couldn't stand the thought of her skin contacting the hot water. Couldn't stand remembering the way the heat from the flames had come so close to her and Willow before the rescue workers arrived. She sat on the toilet lid while the shower ran, but after a few minutes the heavy vapor reminded her too much of the smoke that had blinded her on the plane, and she shut off the faucet and opened the bathroom door.

She would never tell him to his face, but Dominic was right in just about every way. She was mad at Willow. She'd figured that this brush with death would finally make her receptive to the gospel, finally eager to hear the good news. Not to spend the night drowning her terror in booze, distracting herself and numbing her fears with a one-night stand.

She hated to admit it, but Dominic was probably right about the whole Jonah thing, too. If Kennedy took a bus back to Massachusetts, she wouldn't have to feel guilty that she wasn't telling Willow about Jesus' sacrifice on the cross. If was five thousand miles and four time zones away from her roommate, nobody would expect Kennedy to share the gospel with her over Christmas break. She thought about Grandma Lucy, about her promise to pray for Willow. Kennedy had never gotten her phone number, had no way to contact her when and if that miracle ever happened. On the one hand, Kennedy was glad that Grandma Lucy had been on that flight to save Willow, but she resented the guilt that had glared down at her accusingly from the moment she met the old woman. Maybe Kennedy wasn't meant to be that outspoken of a believer. Was there any reason to make her feel so inadequate?

If God wanted Willow to be saved, if God wanted Kennedy to share the gospel with her, he would have to do all the work. He would have to direct the conversation the way it needed to go. He would have to give Kennedy the right words to say and Willow the open ears to hear. That was all there was to it. At first, Kennedy thought Willow's near-death experience would make her more receptive to spiritual matters, but if her behavior tonight was any indication, Willow planned to go on living her life as if Flight 219 never happened.

Well, God, looks like it's up to you.

Kennedy brushed her teeth with the hospital's cheap travel toothbrush and washed her face with their puny sliver of soap. It would probably be hours before Willow came back, if she returned tonight at all. Kennedy wasn't about to wait up for her. She had just made her way to bed when someone fidgeted with the lock outside. A little buzzer sounded, and the door swung open slowly.

"You asleep?" Willow's whisper flitted through the air like a mosquito.

"I'm here." Kennedy rolled over with a grumpy complaint that she stifled when she saw the soiled tears dribbling down Willow's face. "What's the matter?"

Willow shut the door behind her before letting out a suppressed sob.

Kennedy got out of bed tentatively. "Is everything ok? Did something happen with Ray?"

Willow shook her head and wiped her cheeks with the back of her hand. "It's not that." She sat down on the front of the bed, and Kennedy lowered herself beside her, feeling awkward and wondering what she should do with her hands.

"Are you upset about what happened on the flight?" she asked, recalling

Dominic's reminder that people deal with shock and trauma in various ways.

"You're gonna think this sounds so stupid." Willow sniffed and tried to laugh at the same time.

"It won't be stupid," Kennedy assured her. "You know what a mess I can turn into. I'm the last person to judge."

Willow sniffed again noisily. "You promise you won't laugh?"

Kennedy had never seen her roommate so vulnerable before. Like a little child hoping her mother wouldn't yell.

"I promise."

"Something happened on that flight," Willow began, "and I've been trying to get it out of my head since I woke up in the hospital. But even over dinner with Ray, it was all I could think about. Out of everybody I know, I figure you're the only one who might be able to explain it to me."

"What is it?" Kennedy tried to keep her voice natural. If she'd learned anything during her times out with Dominic, it was how to be a more engaged listener.

Willow sighed and stared at her hands that fidgeted in her lap. "Ok, so I'm like most people I guess. I've always believed there was some sort of afterlife, heaven or whatever you want to call it. And like most people, I just assumed that if you do enough good with what life deals you, that's where you go when you die or whatever."

Kennedy nodded, afraid that if she tried to speak now she'd scare Willow away from finishing her thoughts.

"But then with the gun ... and the fire ..." Willow scratched at her arm as if all the painful memories were an itch she could brush off if she just scraped hard enough. "I started to think, *maybe I really am going to die*, and it scared the hell out of me. Literally. It probably sounds cliché to a church kid like you, but it scared me more than anything else. Thinking that maybe I hadn't been good enough. Maybe I didn't deserve to go to heaven. And how could I ever be sure? So I just thought that this flight might be a wake-up call for me, a chance for me to focus on the things that really matter so when my time does come, I'll be ready. But then I was sitting with Ray, and I mean, we all knew how the night was supposed to end and whatever, and at first I thought that'd be a great way for me to get past my fear and start living again, enjoying life. You know, like I always do. Things were going great, we were having fun together, but I realized there was no way I could relax with him, no way I could enjoy myself with him until I talked some of this stuff out."

She let out a little laugh. "I'm sure it sounds crazy. I mean, how can anyone be positive about heaven or hell or anything, you know? I really believe there's some sort of paradise waiting for people, but it's pretty arrogant to assume that you could ever know for sure if you've earned it, right?"

"It's not arrogant," Kennedy replied.

Willow frowned. "Well, maybe not for a church girl like you, but for someone like me ..."

"That's not what I'm saying. What I'm saying is you're right. Nobody can do enough good with their life to earn a spot in heaven. That's why we have to trust Jesus to make us worthy. And that's how we can be certain where we'll go when we die."

Willow raised one of her penciled eyebrows. "You really think there's a way to know for sure?"

"I do. I mean, think about Grandma Lucy on the flight."

"Who?"

"The old woman I was talking to earlier. The one who stood between you and the general when he had his ..." She stopped herself. "Don't you remember?"

Willow scowled. "The whole flight is such a blur right now."

Kennedy ignored the uncertainty that had started to heat up her gut and nodded. "Ok, well never mind her then. What I'm saying is that if you trust that Jesus has forgiven your sins, you're trusting that he's the one who can make you worthy of heaven. So it's not what you do, the good or bad or anything like that, it's what he did when he died on the cross for you."

The corner of Willow's mouth tilted up. "You should become a preacher. You sound so convincing."

Kennedy's whole core was trembling. She hoped Willow didn't notice. She knew that if she didn't ask the next question, there was no guarantee she'd find another chance like this again. "What about you?" she began awkwardly and cleared her throat. "I mean, is that something you want to learn more about, how to have your sins forgiven and stuff?"

Willow scrunched up her lustrous hair. "You've definitely gotten me curious, but there's no rush or anything. I mean, we'll have lots of time together at home to talk about whatever we feel like, right?"

Kennedy nodded her head as a gentle peace swept over her like silk sheets on a cool spring evening. "Right."

CHAPTER 22

"I'm so glad you talked me out of taking the bus back to Massachusetts," Kennedy gushed.

Dominic chuckled on the other line. "So you've enjoyed your time in Alaska so far?"

"It's insane. A lot of people out here don't even have their own water source. Willow's parents have to drive to the city well once or twice a week, fill up this huge tank, and dump the water into their storage room in the basement."

"And it doesn't freeze in the winter?" he asked. "Just how cold is it there?"

"When I woke up this morning, it was forty-eight below. Get this. Willow's dad took a pot of hot coffee, threw it up in the air, and it formed ice crystals and then completely evaporated before it hits the ground."

"Sounds like a great way to spend Christmas Eve. I'm really happy for you."

Kennedy stared out the window of Willow's room and watched the Winters' youngest goat leaping from one giant rock to another in his pen. It was only a little after three in the afternoon, but the sun was already setting.

"What about Willow? Have the two of you had any good discussions after everything that happened?"

Kennedy paced back and forth, studying all the paintings Willow had made back in high school. "It's been incredible. We've stayed up talking 'til one or two just about every night since I've been here. She says she's still not ready to become a Christian yet, but she has some great questions. When we get home, she's going to need a long talk with Pastor Carl or something, because most of them have me totally stumped."

"Oh yeah? Like what?"

Kennedy stared at the quilt Willow's grandma had sewn for her high school graduation. It was a winter scene with dazzling stars and the aurora borealis splashing bright greens and blues and yellows across the sky. "Ok, so for example last night she said one of the biggest reasons she hasn't become a Christian yet is she's afraid it would be intellectual suicide. She's

257

really fixating on the whole evolution thing."

Dominic made a thoughtful sound. "Tell her lots of Christians believe in evolution."

"I know that, but I want her to..." What was she supposed to say next?

"You want her to believe the exact same way you do," Dominic finished softly. "It's ok. We all do that. It's just important to remember that it's Jesus who saves us, not theology."

"I know," Kennedy hurried to reply. "Oh, that reminds me of another good question she had."

"What's that?"

"So she wanted to know if she has to stop smoking weed before she gets saved."

"And you told her ...?"

"I had no idea what to tell her," Kennedy confessed. "I mean, on the one hand, the Christian life's all about making sacrifices, denying yourself, right? But God doesn't expect us to be perfect in order to be saved or nobody would make their way into heaven at all."

"Sounds like you've got a lot to think about." There was a smile in Dominic's voice.

"Really? You're the one with the master's in theology and that's all you've got to say?"

"We can talk about it more when you're here. When do you fly back?"

"The thirtieth." Kennedy couldn't understand how her vacation had already sped by so quickly.

"Good. Because my cousin's throwing a New Year's Eve party, and I wanted to ask you to be my date."

"Your date?" Kennedy felt her face heat up. Why had she repeated the word like a mindless parrot?

"Yeah. I've been thinking about it ever since I heard about your flight on the news. I didn't want to bring it up the last time we talked because you're still so shaken up and everything, but thinking about you up there, knowing I was down here and couldn't do anything to protect you, it made me realize I'd been wanting to do this for a long time. So, now that I've completely embarrassed myself, will you come with me to my cousin's? It's part of our church group, actually. A chance to worship and pray in the

New Year, ask God what areas in our lives he wants us to focus on, a real encouraging time."

Kennedy could think of better venues for a first official date, but then again, maybe this was part of God's plan for her all along. She could definitely tell her relationship with Christ was growing out here in Nowhere, Alaska. While Willow helped her mom with the barn chores, Kennedy usually hurried back inside as soon as her nose hairs froze. She'd been spending the extra time alone studying her Bible and praying. She couldn't remember another period in her life when she'd been so excited about her faith, eager to see the kind of things God was doing around her. Willow was a perfect example. The fact that they could talk for two or three hours a night about salvation and not have it turn into one giant rant about the evils of organized religion was reason enough to believe in Christmas miracles.

Footsteps sounded on the stairs before Willow came in, her cheeks flushed with cold as she took off layer after layer of clothes and tossed them onto the bed. "Dinner's almost ready," she said. "Tell lover boy merry Christmas and hang up."

"I heard that," Dominic called out, and Kennedy turned her head so Willow wouldn't see how deeply she blushed.

"I gotta go," she told him. "The Winters have been working on this Christmas Eve dinner all day."

"Well, have fun. And if I don't get a chance to call you tomorrow, merry Christmas. I can't wait to see what blessings God has in store for us this coming year."

Willow was still staring, and Kennedy was still blushing, but she couldn't help it. "Yeah, me too," she replied lamely. "Merry Christmas."

"Merry Christmas, Kennedy."

Willow raised her eyebrow and smirked. From downstairs, Willow's dad called out, "Time for dinner, girls. Hurry up, Kennedy. I can't wait for you to try your first bite of Christmas moose."

CHAPTER 23

Kennedy had never seen a Christmas spread like the one that night at the Winters' table. Willow's dad had made moose meatballs with mushroom and asparagus gravy and a separate dish of halibut in a creamy sauce served on buttery pasta. He had caught the halibut himself last summer, but the fate and demise of the moose were never mentioned at the table. The sides were as delicious as they were colorful: a green bean casserole with pine nuts, goat cheese, and stewed tomatoes; grilled cauliflower and Brussel sprouts; twice baked sweet potatoes whipped with cream and cinnamon; and a magnificent fruit salad with all kinds of produce Willow's dad had grabbed from an Anchorage fruit co-op before he picked up the girls from the airport.

"These are the best bread rolls I've ever eaten," Kennedy declared, smothering another spoonful of rosehip and fireweed jelly onto a golden-topped bun.

Mr. Winters sat up proudly in his chair. "Thanks. I mill the grains myself right before they bake."

"You should try the raspberry jam, too." Mrs. Winters passed the jar across the table. "We had a bumper crop this year."

After Kennedy was already past the point of full saturation, Mrs. Winters bent over the oven and pulled out dessert. "Here we have some strawberry rhubarb pie. Willow, did you get that whipped cream from the water room?"

Willow scooted back her chair. "No, I'll grab it now." She sprinted downstairs.

"The fridge was so full, we had to store a few things down there where it's cold," Mrs. Winters explained as she sliced through the flaky crust and heaped a generous portion on Kennedy's plate. "Now don't eat it yet. Wait for Willow. Have you ever had fresh whipped cream?"

"Not from a cow I've actually met," Kennedy answered.

Willow came up with a jar full of whipped cream and heaped two dollops on Kennedy's pie.

"Now eat it fast before it melts," Mr. Winters told her.

"No, that's the best part when it's all runny," Willow argued.

After dessert was tea, an herbal blend Mrs. Winters harvested and dried herself. "Do you like honey in yours?" she asked.

Kennedy nodded and held out her mug for a spoonful.

"Our bees did such a good job this year. Nothing like raw honey. Remind me, and I'll send some back with you to school. Great for allergies, you know."

Kennedy didn't think she had room for anything else in her stomach, but she'd been wrong. She sipped the tea slowly, enjoying the warmth and sweetness as it slid down her throat. "This is probably the most unique Christmas dinner I've ever had."

Mrs. Winters beamed at her across the table. "We're just glad you two girls are safe."

Kennedy stared at her plate. Some memories would spoil even the most abundant Christmas feast.

Willow's mom reached out and grabbed Kennedy's hand. "And we're glad our daughter's found such a good friend as you."

"That's right," her dad added. "Since her first day at Harvard last year, we've been hearing about you. How good you are with your studies, how respectful a roommate you are."

Kennedy glanced at Willow who shuffled uncomfortably in her seat. "Dad," she whined.

"What? When you have a good friend, it's important they know how you feel. It's not everybody who gets so lucky finding a best friend their first year of college."

"Dad," she repeated in the same tone.

"Ok. Ok." He raised his hands in surrender.

"But before we forget, we do have something for you." Mrs. Winters scooted her chair back. "To show you how much we appreciate your friendship with Willow." She passed Kennedy a small package wrapped in thick brown paper. "I found this at a craft bizarre I was selling at last month. The lady at the booth next to me had these beautiful handmade crosses, and I remembered Willow saying you're a Christian, and I thought you would love this."

Kennedy stared at the heavy crucifix in her hand.

"See the detail?" Mrs. Winters pointed to Jesus' brow. "See the thorns? It's so intricate. I hope you like it." She raised a questioning eyebrow.

"It's really nice," Kennedy stammered, "and very thoughtful." She'd never owned a crucifix before. Never even considered owning one, but she recognized the great amount of consideration that went into the present.

"She's not Catholic, Mom," Willow muttered.

"Well, how was I to know?" Mrs. Winters replied. "You said *Christian*. You didn't say anything else, so I just had to guess."

Mr. Winters cleared his throat. "We're a spiritual family, Kennedy," he explained, "and you probably already know this about us. We don't subscribe to one particular religion over any other, but we do consider ourselves people of faith. I was wondering if you had any Christmas traditions from your family or upbringing you'd like to share. It must be lonely with your parents doing their mission work all the way down in Africa ..."

"China," Willow corrected.

"China," her dad repeated, "so if you wanted, it would be an honor if you shared some of your family's traditions with us."

Kennedy wasn't ready to pull a Christmas Eve sermon out of her sleeve. She took another sip of tea. "Well, my dad always reads from Luke. That's the story of when Jesus was born. It starts with ..."

"Well, don't tell us," Willow's dad interrupted. "You say your dad reads it. So read it to us."

Willow stood up. "I'll go grab the Bible from upstairs. I know where it is."

Mr. and Mrs. Winters exchanged somewhat quizzical looks. While Kennedy waited for Willow to return, she stared around the Winters' dining room. A giant moose head hung on the wall, not what she expected as the décor for her vegan roommate's childhood home. Willow's grandmother had sewn several other arctic-themed quilts that were hung on the walls or draped over couches. In the far corner of the living room was a little library. On one side was a leather reclining chair next to a pile of fishing and hunting magazines and a shelf full of Greek classics. Right beside it was a rocking chair and a bookcase laden with *National Geographic*, *The New Yorker*, and literary fiction titles in pristine hardback.

Kennedy tried to picture her roommate growing up as the only child out here in the middle of nowhere.

A minute later, Willow came downstairs with the Bible already open to Luke. Kennedy hadn't realized chapter two was so long. She decided to stick to the part about the shepherds, and as she read, she had to work past a lump in her throat. This was her second Christmas away from family. As kind and open-hearted as the Winters were, Kennedy missed home.

When she finished the passage, Willow's mom leaned back in her chair with a sigh. "I just love that part about the angels, all singing together. Do you believe there are angels here on earth?" she asked.

Kennedy tried to throw together some sort of a stammered reply.

"I suppose anything's possible, isn't it?" Mrs. Winters finally concluded. Willow's dad leaned forward in his chair. "What next?" he asked.

Kennedy didn't understand what he meant.

"Is that all your family does? I mean, Jesus is the Savior of the whole world according to Christian tradition. I figured his followers would have a lot more to-do surrounding the day of his holy birth."

Kennedy glanced at Willow. Why hadn't she warned her to come to dinner prepared? "Well, we usually sing some songs."

Mrs. Winters clasped her hands together. "Beautiful! Would you like to use our piano?"

"I don't play," Kennedy hastened to explain. "I tried once, but ..."

"*A capella* it is then," Willow's dad declared with a thundering boom. "What should we start with? *Silent Night*?"

Kennedy's throat clenched shut for just a moment as she remembered her last Christmas in Yanji, as she and her parents and the refugees in their Secret Seminary sang *Silent Night* in Korean.

"Perfect." Mr. Winters breathed in deeply and started the carol for everyone.

As soon as they finished, Mrs. Winters jumped up from her chair. "Oh! What perfect timing. Take a look at this!" She scurried to the window as Willow's dad leapt from his seat, turned off the overhead lights and extinguished the candles on the table.

Kennedy was about to ask what was going on when Mrs. Winters threw back the curtains. The sky danced with streaks of green splashing from one end of the horizon to the other.

"Ooh!" Mrs. Winters pointed. "Look at that purple. I haven't seen it like that since Willow was little."

Kennedy stood mesmerized as the northern lights flickered from one end of the sky to the other. After the flashes of green came streaks of pink and violet, rippling like ribbons waved by dancers on a stage.

Kennedy felt a hymn of joy and praise rising from somewhere deep within her soul, a place that had been lying dormant until this very moment, a depth her mind had never accessed before.

She had never loved her singing voice, but she opened her mouth and let the words of praise flow from her. Willow and her family soon joined in, with her father taking a deep bass and her mother singing harmony in alto.

> *O holy night, the stars are brightly shining*
> *It is the night of our dear Savior's birth.*
> *Long lay the world in sin and error pining*
> *'Til he appeared and the soul felt its worth.*

When they reached the line about *a thrill of hope*, Kennedy glanced over at Willow, and in the light gleaming in from the glories outside, their eyes met. An understanding passed between them. The knowledge that they were now sharing Christmas not just as roommates, not just as friends, but as sisters, held together by bonds of fellowship stronger than any spiritual opposition or earthly terror.

The Winters were a little uncertain on the second verse, so Kennedy carried the melody along.

> *Chains shall he break for the slave is our brother*
> *And in his name all oppression shall cease.*

She didn't know what the future would hold. She didn't know what to expect in a week when she flew back to Boston and joined Dominic at his cousin's party. She didn't know what would happen in Willow's spirit or whether or not this new excitement in Kennedy's soul would withstand another busy semester of school.

All she knew was that right now, there was nowhere on earth she would rather be. Surrounded by a loving family, quirky as they were, and the glories of a majestic Creator who splashed his paints across the sky for everyone to see, Kennedy had never felt so thankful.

She had never felt so alive.

Infected

a novel by Alana Terry

Infected

Copyright © 2017 Alana Terry

May, 2017

Cover design by Damonza.

Scriptures quoted from THE HOLY BIBLE, NEW INTERNATIONAL VERSION®, NIV® Copyright © 1973, 1978, 1984, 2011 by Biblica, Inc.® Used by permission. All rights reserved worldwide.

www.alanaterry.com

"Praise the Lord, my soul; all my inmost being, praise his holy name. Praise the Lord, my soul, and forget not all his benefits—who forgives all your sins and heals all your diseases."
Psalm 103:1-3

CHAPTER 1

So I sing because I'm happy,
And I sing because I'm free.
His eye is on the sparrow,
And I know he watches me.

Kennedy groaned when her phone screeched at her. She knew who was calling, and she knew exactly what he'd have to say.

"Hey, Dad."

"You've been following this thing on Channel 2?" His voice was breathless. Panicked.

Just like she expected.

"Yeah, I've been keeping track." She hadn't logged onto any news outlets since breakfast that morning. Checking in with reality once a day was enough for her.

"Ok, because this isn't just something you can ignore, Kensie girl. That's what you like to do. But this is too serious."

"I know, Dad." Did he forget they'd had this exact same conversation twenty-four hours ago?

"So tell me what precautions you're taking. What will you be doing for spring break?"

She rolled her eyes, certain he could sense the gesture all the way from his printing office overseas. What time was it now in China anyway? Wasn't it the middle of the night? "I'm staying at the Lindgrens." She'd told him her plans at least a dozen times by now. For someone who knew the name and origin of every little virus that reared its head in the developing world, her dad could be ridiculously forgetful.

"So Carl and Sandy are still taking that anniversary trip, are they?"

Kennedy moved the phone slightly away from her face to try to mask her annoyed sigh. "They're just driving a few hours away. And it's only for a night."

"They've already gone?"

"No, they're getting packed right now."

Even with the guest room door shut, Carl and Sandy's good-humored bickering hummed in Kennedy's one ear while her dad's fretting echoed in her other.

"I really don't get why they decided to go."

"Because it's their anniversary." At least now that she was a college student and thousands of miles away in Massachusetts, she wouldn't get grounded for letting so much exasperation lace her voice. "Some folks do that sort of romantic stuff, you know."

"Not in the middle of an epidemic, they don't."

Kennedy glanced at her phone. They'd only been talking two minutes, and she was already sick of this conversation. What did her dad expect? For Carl and Sandy to put their entire life on hold because some people had come down with a bad infection? He might not know it from his little office in Yanji, but life was going on in spite of the fearmongering media. Passengers were still flying on planes. Children attending schools. Adults going to work, shopping for groceries, living their regular day-to-day lives. Maybe things were scarier for her dad way out there in Jilin Province, but here in the Boston area, there really wasn't anything to worry about. This was just the kind of news story that her dad loved to fixate on. Another way he tried to control her life from the other side of the world.

"Ok, so tell me what kind of safety measures you're taking. How are you going to make sure you're not exposing yourself to anyone who's possibly contaminated?"

Well, I'm not living in Bangladesh or near a herd of pigs, for one thing. Of course, that wasn't the answer her dad was looking for. He didn't need a geography lesson about the virus's origins. He'd tracked the spread of the disease for weeks before the first confirmed cases arrived in the US, before the American public ever heard the words *Nipah virus*. But he was waiting for her answer, and unless she wanted him to find some germ-proof convent to lock her away in for the rest of her life, she had to appease his paranoia.

"I'm not going to shopping malls, airports, or any other places with crowds. I'm not eating out in any restaurants. I've got my Germ-X, and I'm using it regularly." Even without her dad's constant reminding, when did Kennedy ever forget her Germ-X? She was the most germophobic premed student at Harvard, an idiosyncrasy that her roommate loved to tease her about.

"So you'll be staying inside all day then? That's good. What about Carl and Sandy's son? Is he old enough to wash his hands on his own yet?"

"Yeah, Dad. He's in the third grade."

"Well, you should probably still do it for him. Especially before you eat any meals together. And don't cuddle much. Best to keep a safe distance."

"All right." She was only halfway listening now as she unpacked her clothes into the top drawer in the Lindgrens' guest room.

"What about social get-togethers? Do you have anyone you're planning to invite over while you're babysitting?"

Kennedy suspected her dad was subtly referring to her boyfriend Dominic. The only thing more annoying than listening in while her dad's crisis training kicked into high gear was talking to him about her love life, with all his awkward half-questions and insinuations. Last January, just two weeks after she'd officially started dating him, her dad actually asked about Dominic's opinion on birth control.

"How in the world should I know?" Kennedy had shouted.

Apparently, her reaction pleased her father.

It was funny to think of her dad worrying about her and her boyfriend. Dominic had told Kennedy very early on in their relationship that he and his deceased wife hadn't kissed until their wedding day. And he'd told her time and time again since then that he planned to take the same slow and steady approach in any future relationships he entered.

That was fine with Kennedy, at least mostly. No, it was totally fine. She didn't have time to be worried about that sort of stuff anyway. She and Dominic spent time together once a week on Sundays. He'd pick her up and take her to his cousin's home church. They'd go out for lunch after that, walk around Boston Common if the weather was nice, then say good-bye. They talked every couple nights on the phone, sometimes quick check-in calls but sometimes deep conversations where Dominic would allude to the stress he was under at work or Kennedy would ask him some of the Bible questions she'd been storing up.

They didn't have a lot of time together, but it's not like she could have offered Dominic a lot more anyway. Kennedy was taking double science courses this year, organic chemistry as well as biology, each with their own lectures and weekly labs. To top it off, she'd enrolled in an MCAT prep course that met two nights a week. Part of her early acceptance into Harvard med school was contingent on her passing the entrance exam. After all the time and energy she'd put into her first two years of undergrad studies, she wasn't about to fail.

She shook her head and remembered her dad was waiting for her response. "No, nobody's coming over. At least nothing's planned." Should she mention that there was no way Dominic would come over to the Lindgrens' house, regardless of the time of day or night, without the assurance of at least two other adults present? Kennedy appreciated his commitment to purity, but sometimes she wondered what he was so afraid of. Did he think she'd turn into some sort of sex-crazed fiend and molest him the minute she found herself alone in a room with him?

"Ok, that's good. So basically, you're staying home all day then? Not going anywhere?"

"Well, I have to take Woong to school tomorrow morning and pick him up again at three. But other than that, there's nowhere else I have to be." She was glad Carl and Sandy would only be gone for one night. She still wasn't sure what she'd do to keep Woong entertained two afternoons by herself, but she'd come up with something. Woong had gotten a Wii for his birthday (a random date Carl and Sandy picked out of a calendar since the South Korean orphanage had no records of his birth), but Sandy was adamant that he couldn't play more than half an hour on school days, and then only once he'd finished his homework, his quiet reading time, and his afternoon chores.

Kennedy just hoped that when Sandy came home, she wouldn't be disappointed if she found the house a complete disaster. Kennedy had a hard time keeping her itty-bitty dorm room tidy. She had no idea how she'd keep up an entire house with a boy as rambunctious as Woong.

"So he's still going to school this week?" her dad asked, and Kennedy couldn't tell if his incredulous tone meant he wondered why all schools weren't on the same spring break schedule as Harvard's or why anyone would keep a Medford, Massachusetts elementary school open when a few unfortunate individuals across the state had found themselves fighting for their lives against some hitherto obscure Nipah virus.

"Yeah, there's still school."

Her dad whispered something under his breath. If Kennedy had to guess, it sounded most like *unbelievable*. She glanced at the time. Carl and Sandy were late.

"And what about groceries?" he asked. "Is there enough there or are you going to have to go shopping at all?"

Kennedy had only arrived at the Lindgrens' an hour earlier. How did he expect her to have the entire next thirty-six hours planned out?

"Sandy cooked a whole bunch of casseroles and stuff for us to heat up. There's enough food here to last a month," she told her dad.

He let out his breath. "Let's hope it doesn't come down to that."

CHAPTER 2

"All right, pumpkin, I showed you where the lasagna is, didn't I?" Sandy opened the fridge door absently and shut it again.

"Only about half a dozen times," Carl replied. He had two overnight bags strapped over his shoulders and kept trying to make his way to the door that led to the garage.

"Well, you know we're only going to be a few hours away. I gave you our schedule, right?"

"You printed it up and put a copy on the fridge, a copy in the bathroom, and a copy in the den. Don't you remember?" Carl tried to adjust his pants while carrying so much luggage.

"I just want to make sure I've covered it all. I'm certain I'm forgetting something."

"Like we need to check into the B&B in an hour and a half, and it's going to take us twice that long to get there?"

Sandy shook her head and frowned. "No, that's not it. I gave you the number for Woong's pediatrician, didn't I?"

Kennedy nodded, certain she'd find the number taped to the emergency contact list above the microwave if it weren't already on the three-page handwritten note Sandy had penned in her flowing cursive that sat folded in Kennedy's pocket.

"And I showed you where the car keys are hanging up by the garage door. Oh, that's something I should have mentioned. Nick might stop by to borrow the Honda. Since we're taking the van, I told him he could use the car whenever he needs."

"Yeah, no problem." Kennedy was just glad she wouldn't be the one driving the church's clunky, painted, hipster bus all over Massachusetts.

"Oh, that's another thing," Sandy went on. "Woong went to a birthday party last weekend, and he watched *Princess Bride*. It's put all kinds of fancy ideas in his head, but the rules are no sword fighting in the house. And you've got to watch him because I think he learned a bad word. I'm not entirely sure. So you listen out for that and tell me if you run into any problems."

Kennedy wondered how long ago it was that her own parents had worried about her picking up a bad word or two from a movie.

Sandy stared around the room. "So you know we won't be home until late tomorrow night, right, love? Carl's taking me out to a fancy dinner on the Isabella. It's going to be so romantic."

"If we ever make it there," Carl grumbled.

"We're almost ready, honey, just you wait." She offered Kennedy an apologetic smile. "He's upset because I'm taking him to see the opera tonight. It was the deal we made. Tonight the opera, tomorrow the new action movie with that famous guy playing in it. You know the one I mean. He's in the movie with the lady, you know. The blonde one."

Carl rolled his eyes. "Can we go now?" He nudged their bags a little closer to the door. "Otherwise I'll have to stop and use the bathroom again."

"Already? I'm serious, honey, you really need to stop drinking so much water. It can't be good for your kidneys."

"Actually ..." Carl began, but Sandy cut him off.

"Hold on, let me remember. There's something I've got to tell Kennedy. Now what was it? You know Woong starts getting ready for bed at eight, right? It takes him quite a long time to settle down."

"I'm sure we'll be fine," Kennedy said, not feeling nearly as certain as she tried to sound.

Sandy took a step toward the door then spun around on her heel. "Oh! That's what it was." She bustled past and pulled a piece of paper off the top of the microwave. "This is a letter from Woong's school. I forgot to send it with him today. It's already signed. It needs to go back with his things tomorrow. They just want to make sure we're all going to be careful about not sending our kids to school sick. You know how it is with that virus scare." She turned to her husband. "What's it called again? Napa? Something like that?"

"Napa's wine country." Carl opened the door to the garage. "You're talking about Nipah. The Nipah virus."

"No, you're thinking about where the Dalai Lama lives, aren't you?"

"Not Nepal, woman! Nipah. It's the Nipah virus." Beads of sweat coalesced on Carl's forehead.

"Oh, that's right. Well, that's why the school needs the letter, hon. Be sure Woong takes that form to school tomorrow or they might send him home."

Carl shook his head. "Government overreach," he mumbled.

"It's an epidemic, darling. People have been dying." Sandy's voice was patient, her southern drawl even more pronounced than normal.

"People die all the time," Carl inserted. "The way I see it, when it's my time to go, nothing here's gonna dare hold me back, and that's true whether it's old age or a freak accident or Nipah virus that shoots me off to glory. Now, I'm all for basic precautions. What I'm not for is fear and paranoia. The way the media's slanting this, I guarantee you there'll be riots before the week's out. And then they'll start rounding up carriers, enforcing quarantines, it'll be 1984. It begins when the government steps in and denies parents their basic rights. Just like that little boy whose family refused chemo, remember him? Courts get a whiff of it and ..."

"I don't think Kennedy needs to worry about chemotherapy today. She just needs to remember to get Woong's form to school." She turned to Carl with a smile. "Ok, babe. You ready?"

Carl sighed, dejected. "All right. I'm off my soap box." He looked back once at Kennedy. "You be sure to call if you have any problems, you hear? Especially if your problems start in the hour to half-hour before the curtains rise at the opera. Got that?" He winked.

"Oh, you silly thing." Sandy swatted him playfully and followed him into the garage, where the St. Margaret youth group's tie-dyed Volkswagon bus waited for them. Kennedy had to chuckle at the thought of the Lindgrens actually driving that thing to dinner at Isabella's and then the opera. Since she'd never learned how to handle a stick shift, she lucked out and would keep the much more respectable Honda to take Woong to and from school.

"Have fun," she called out after them. "And happy anniversary."

CHAPTER 3

"Hey, there. How was your day?" Kennedy asked as Woong flung his backpack onto the seat next to her. Kennedy wasn't sure which surprised her more, how quickly he had learned English or how fast he'd put on weight. Last summer when the Lindgrens brought all forty-two pounds of him home from South Korea, the pediatrician had said she'd guess he was only five or six, except the orphanage workers had pieced together enough of his personal history to know he had to be at least ten, probably even a little older.

Woong sulked, and Kennedy had to remind him three times to buckle his seatbelt before they could start driving. She had no idea what an ordeal it was to pick up a child from Medford Academy. The line of cars stretched two blocks down the road. If Kennedy had been even a minute later, she would have had to wait all the way across the street or else the tail of the Honda would stick out into the intersection.

"How did school go?" Kennedy asked when she finally found an opening where she could pull out into the congested traffic.

"Ok."

"Anything interesting happen?" she pressed, remembering how much she hated these interrogation sessions with her own mother when she was Woong's age.

"We got a sub."

"Oh, yeah?"

"Uh-huh." He opened the glove compartment and pulled out one of the granola bars his mom kept perpetually stashed there. Kennedy thought about having him use some Germ-X first, but he was halfway through with his first bite, and she had to pay attention to the road. Who would have thought carpool moms could be so aggressive?

"Where was your teacher?" she asked after turning onto a side street and finally escaping the minivan gridlock.

"Went home sick."

"Oh." Kennedy glanced at Woong, who was busy peeling his second granola bar. "Hey, why don't you grab the little bottle of lotion from my backpack, ok? It's in the front zipper. Right there. Just squirt a little on your hands and rub together. It helps."

"Helps what?"

"Helps you not get sick."

"Why?"

"It kills all the germs."

"Yeah? How's it do that?"

"It breaks down the fat layer surrounding the cell walls."

"Huh?"

"Never mind. Just clean your hands before you eat any more."

After a few minutes of silence while he finished chewing, Woong asked, "Are my parents gone already?" He reached into a compartment beneath the car stereo and pulled out a baggie of goldfish crackers.

"Yeah, they left a little bit after lunch time."

"When are they getting back?"

"Tomorrow night, but you'll probably be asleep by the time they come home."

"Does that mean I get to stay up late?"

"No, you still have school the next morning."

He sighed dramatically. "I don't like school."

"Really? Why not?"

He shrugged. "Not enough snacks." He shoved some crackers into his mouth and asked, "Hey, aren't you supposed to be in school, too? Don't you go to Hogwarts or something like that?"

She smiled. "No, not Hogwarts. It's called Harvard."

"Oh. Then what's Hogwarts?"

"Something else."

"Ok. So why aren't you there now?"

"It's my spring break. We get a whole week off."

Woong kicked the heel of his sneaker against the metal bar by his feet. "Medford Academy doesn't get spring break until next week. My dad's gonna take me to a Red Sox game next Monday. That's a week from today, right?"

"Right. You know how many days that is?"

She could smell the cheddar cheese flavoring on his breath when he opened up his stuffed mouth. "Eight."

"Close. It's seven."

"No, eight."

"Seven," she repeated and rattled off the days of the week. "See? That's seven."

He shook his head. "No, 'cause today's Monday, and the game is Monday." He held up his hands to count on his fingers. "It goes Monday, Tuesday, Thursday, Wednesday, Friday, Saturday, Sunday, then another Monday. That's eight." He shoved another handful of goldfish crackers into his mouth, and Kennedy wondered if Sandy had to vacuum out the car every single day to keep it free of crumbs.

"I guess you're right." Kennedy turned on Sandy's praise and worship CD before the discussion could digress any further. What had she gotten herself into? When Sandy first asked her to stay with Woong for the night, Kennedy hadn't thought that much about it. She didn't have any major plans for spring break. Her roommate Willow would be out with her theater friends running around New York City. If Kennedy weren't at the Lindgrens', she'd probably just be relaxing in the Harvard library. It'd been such a busy semester, she hadn't picked up a book for pleasure since Martin Luther King Day. Her entire reading list that semester was for the film as literature class she was taking. When she signed up for the course, she was expecting some Toni Morrison books, maybe a few foreign pieces, the sorts of flicks her dad didn't like ("too artsy-fartsy") and her mom didn't care for ("too many subtitles"). She didn't realize her professor was something of a Michael Crichton fanboy who apparently considered the time period between the release of *Top Gun* and the advent of *The Matrix* to be the golden age of cinematography. Oh, well. It was an easy A and a chance to get back into reading some thrillers, a genre she'd avoided when her PTSD was at its worst. The reading list, albeit unoriginal, was so extensive she found herself wishing she had time for the classics she'd grown to love. Now that the next day and a half stretched out before her, she thought of how relaxing it would be to spend the whole day reading and wondered if she was really the type who was cut out to babysit. At least Woong would be at school tomorrow. But what would they do with the rest of the day?

One hour at a time, she reminded herself.

Or maybe more like one minute.

Kennedy liked the melody of Sandy's worship song, the haunting tune, but she wasn't so sure about the lyrics. *Healed by the grace of my precious Savior.* What did that healing mean, exactly? She was still trying to figure it out. Dominic, chaplain for the Boston Police Department, said God could deliver her from her PTSD, that through the power of the Holy Spirit she could be completely free. It sounded nice. No, it sounded glorious. To be released from those talons of fear that would grip her heart at any hour of the day or night. To walk around campus without being afraid, to no longer find herself enslaved to panic, paralyzed and shaking from fear. Most of the time, she couldn't even recall what spooked her out in the first place.

As encouraging as her boyfriend tried to be, she couldn't shake the feeling this was all her fault. That if she were more spiritual, she could overcome these demons, whether they were real or figurative. Dominic had never said so, but his steadfast, unwavering faith made her feel ashamed that she still hadn't found her perfect healing. Then there were people like Sandy, people who assured her that God could heal her completely if he wanted to, but if he chose to let her PTSD remain, it was so that through her weakness, the cross of Christ would be lifted up for all to see. Kennedy was all for God getting the glory, but wouldn't he receive that much more glory and praise if he just snapped his fingers and took her trauma away?

Healed by the blood of the Lamb of God.

Woong reached out his small finger, grubby even after his liberal application of sanitizer, and punched off the music. "What're we gonna do today?"

Kennedy took a deep breath. Back on campus, she was used to waking up at six in the morning to get an early start on her fetal pig dissection before meeting her organic chemistry study group in the student union for breakfast. She could sit in a lecture hall for four hours and take practice test after practice test to prepare for the MCATs and still keep up with her Bible study and almost daily quiet time. She'd survived a kidnapping, a car chase, a skyjacking. She could handle two days with Carl and Sandy's son, couldn't she?

"Well, what do you usually do when you get home from school?"

Sandy had taken two and half hours that morning going over Woong's schedule, but Kennedy had her suspicions that he might try to cheat the system. What kid his age wouldn't? She expected he might try to convince her his mom let him play Wii until dinner or something like that, but he shrugged and grabbed another handful of goldfish. "We go home and have snack."

"Really?"

Sandy had warned her about Woong's appetite. Now Kennedy wondered if she'd been too flippant when she told her dad there was a whole month's worth of food stashed in the Lindgrens' home. The way Woong ate, they'd be lucky to make it last until tomorrow night.

She replayed her conversation with her overly harried father. She hated the way he always tried to make her even more afraid. As if her PTSD didn't give her enough anxiety already. Kennedy wasn't worried about this Nipah virus strain. Sure, some people were dying, but that was mostly in Bangladesh where the epidemic originated and other regions in Asia. It was different here in the States, with the decent sanitation systems and top-of-the-line healthcare system. Her dad was simply caught up in the media frenzy. This would be exactly like other epidemics in the past. People got sick, and then the researchers found a vaccine. That was their job.

All that made the Nipah virus so scary was there was no known cure. Not yet. But everyone was working. A few more weeks of doctors and nurses taking extra precautions, then they'd find some way to control it, and life would go on.

Just like it always did.

"Tell me about your sub today." The praise and worship song was still stuck in Kennedy's head even though the CD was off.

Healed by the grace of my precious Savior.

"Oh, she was weird. Made us all line up at the sink and wash our hands to the happy birthday song. Twice. And she had a funny mast."

"A mast? What's that?"

"You know. Like what the man in black wears in *Princess Bride*." He cupped his hand over his mouth and nose. "Except he wore it so people would think he was one of the bad guys, but at school she did it so she wouldn't sneeze on folks."

"I think you mean a *mask*."

"That's what I said. It was a funny mast too. Made her look like an alligator."

Kennedy tried to guess what Woong was talking about. "An alligator? What do you mean?" The only green masks she could think of were all the way back from the World War II era. Surely a substitute wouldn't wear a gas mask in a class full of third-graders. Anyone that paranoid about catching a virus would just stay home.

Woong rolled his eyes and sighed dramatically. He clapped his hands together like Kennedy had as a little kid in Sandy's Sunday school class doing the hand motions to *Deep and Wide*. "You know. Alligator. Big teeth. Chomp chomp. I think they're in Egypt."

"That's a crocodile."

"No, crocodiles are the ones you make those funny sandal things out of. I'm talking about the big ones that eat you up in swamps."

"And your teacher's mask looked like one of those?"

"She wasn't my teacher. She was the sub."

"Right. Sorry. That's the kind of mask she had?" Kennedy wracked her brain, trying to figure out what on earth Woong was talking about.

"No, it was just colored to look like an alligator."

"Colored? Like it was green or something?"

Alligator-green sanitation masks. Maybe the Nipah outbreak would start a whole new fashion trend. She should let her roommate Willow know.

"No, it was *drawled on.*"

"The right word is *drawed*. I mean, actually it's *drawn*. It had something colored on it? Like with crayons or something?"

Woong's sigh was forceful enough to fill the entire front seats with the aroma of goldfish cracker crumbs. "No. She used a *marker.*"

"I get it now." A substitute teacher who drew an animal face on a sanitation mask made a lot more sense than one who showed up in hazmat gear.

"She said she was wearing it because people are getting sick. They aren't being careful enough when they sneeze. Are you careful when you sneeze?"

Kennedy tried to maintain a serious expression. "Usually."

"Good. Because people are dying, you know."

She shot him a quick glance. "Oh, yeah? Where did you hear that?"

"Chuckie Mansfield told me at recess. His dad's a doctor, and Chuckie said they're working extra hard at his hospital getting rooms ready for all the sick people who are coming."

"Hospitals take care of sick people all the time. That's what they do." Kennedy tried to fight the nervous fluttering in her gut. Blame it on a conversation with her dad to make her anxious for the rest of the day.

"Yeah, but this sickness is really bad. Chuckie's dad says so."

Kennedy cleared her throat. "Well, then, let's pray we all stay healthy and safe."

"Ok. That's a good idea. 'Cause you're good at that kind of stuff."

"What kind of stuff?"

"You know, the praying sort of stuff. Hey, speaking of prayer, my leg's been hurting. My mom says it's growing pains, but what I'm wondering is if I ask God that he could make me grow taller without the hurting part. And maybe if I believe him hard enough I won't have no pains no more."

"Prayer doesn't work like that exactly."

"Well, my dad says we should pray for folks who are sick because sometimes God will make them well again. I was sick for a while back in Korea, you know. But then I got better. Think it's 'cause someone was praying for me then?"

"I don't know. Maybe." Kennedy wasn't used to Medford driving, or driving at all for that matter. That bank across the street didn't look familiar. Had she missed her turn?

"Yeah, I think maybe, too," Woong went on. "'Cause it was this homeless man, we called him Crazy Wu, who come and took care of me at first, and you know what? He believed in God even though he was insane."

"Oh, really?" Where was Sycamore Street? The Lindgrens lived five minutes away from Woong's school. How could she have gotten lost?

"Yeah, and he prayed for me when he found me with the sickness, and I'm guessing that's how come I got better. But that makes me think, what happens to them kids who don't have folks to pray for them, I wonder? Are they the ones who end up dying?"

"I'm sure God protects them no matter what," she mumbled. There was Sycamore. She turned abruptly, thankful there were no cops behind her to ticket her for forgetting to use her blinker. She flicked it on for a few seconds post-turn to assuage her guilt.

"Oh, I guess that make sense. I wondered about that. You know what my dad says? He says God answers all our prayers, it's just sometimes he won't do it 'til heaven. But that makes me think, what happens if two people're both praying different things, I wonder? Like what if I prayed for my mom to give me more Wii time, but she's sure it's gonna rot my brain or stuff and nonsense like that, so she gets to praying that she don't? And then even if I get to heaven where my dad says we all get our prayers answered (and he's a pastor so he knows all that sorta stuff), it makes me think, what happens to my Wii in heaven? Like, will God let me play it except he won't let my mom know I'm doing it? Because that sounds sorta sneaky-like, know what I mean?"

Kennedy's brain cells were spinning as fast as the F5 cyclone in *Twister*. "That's a good question." She wondered what Dominic would say. He was always the one with the theological answers. She almost wished he weren't so strict about seeing her without anyone else around, as if they were two junior highers who needed a constant chaperone. It might be nice to put Woong to bed, throw on a movie, cuddle together on the couch. It would be two long days without anybody besides Woong to talk with. Maybe she'd try calling Willow tonight once he was asleep.

Willow had accepted Christ earlier in the semester, had prayed and asked God to forgive her sins. Kennedy wasn't so sure how much of a spiritual impact her conversion had made, though. Throughout February, the two girls had studied the Bible together. Sandy had found them a beginner's course for brand-new believers that Willow was excited to start. But then life got busy, her theater friends wanted to know why they weren't seeing her around so much, and Willow started missing their Bible study dates. After a few weeks, Kennedy got sick of asking.

And now Willow was off to New York City to binge on Broadway shows with her friends. Sandy told Kennedy to be patient with her roommate, reminded her that people grow in their faith in different ways and at different speeds. Dominic was a little more concerned that Willow's conversion hadn't resulted in the sort of fruit he said even a baby believer should exhibit. Yet another reason Kennedy felt like she had let him down.

Well, Kennedy was doing what she could. She still asked Willow every so often to come to the church meetings at Dominic's cousin's, still offered to pick up that Bible study they'd started. The irony was that the two girls were more distant from each other after Willow's prayer of salvation than they'd been when she was a die-hard atheist with a hint of agnostic leanings.

"Hey, I've got a question for you."

"Yeah? What's that?" Kennedy wasn't sure how many more questions she could take in a single car ride. She sighed with relief when the Lindgrens' cul de sac came into view.

"I've been wondering, how come God makes some people with them really springy curls in their hair? Like, there's this one girl in my class named Becky Linklater, and she's got the springiest curls you ever saw on a girl. Or a boy too, for that matter, but I'm guessing you coulda figured that out already. 'Cause I'd never seen hair like that before I come here, but my mom said that's just because God doesn't give girls in Korea hair like that. But what I want to know is, how come he doesn't? And you're not Korean, but your hair doesn't do that springy thing. At least I don't think it does, but I don't know for sure 'cause you've always got it tied up like that in your horse's tail. But do you think if you prayed God would give you curls?"

"I don't know." Kennedy let out her breath as she pulled the Honda into the Lindgrens' driveway. "Let's go in and get a snack."

Woong sprang out of the car a second before Kennedy shifted into park. "Dibs on the blue Gogurts!" he shouted.

Kennedy waited for a minute, trying to catch her mental second wind, before she yelled out after him as loudly as she could, "Hey! Wash your hands before you touch the food!"

CHAPTER 4

"How come we've got so many skin colors do you think?" Woong asked as Kennedy prepared him a third helping of ants on a log.

"What do you mean?"

"Well, like my dad, he's got that brownish skin color, but my mom, she's nearly as pale as you are except not quite so much because she's always complaining about how hot it is and how her face is always red because she's sweaty all the time."

Kennedy tried to hide her smile behind the oversized jar of peanut butter. She glanced at the label and guessed Woong had downed at least seven hundred calories in a single sitting. She knew there were chores and homework assignments to take care of, but she had a feeling Woong was preparing to move right from snack time to dinner.

God bless Sandy and her made-ahead casseroles.

Woong was still going on about different people he knew and all their skin tones. Kennedy figured for someone from a homogenous region like the Korean peninsula, seeing people of all difference races would be noteworthy.

"And that Becky Linklater, the one with all them curls I was telling you about, she's got peachy skin but brown freckles." He rolled up his sleeve and stared at his forearm. "I don't know what color you'd call me. Chuckie Mansfield says my skin's yellow, but that's not right." He picked up a banana from the fruit basket and held it against his arm. "See?"

"No. That's not yellow."

"Then what would you call it?"

"Some people say it's olive."

He frowned. "No, olives are black. I know 'cause my mom used to buy me olives, but I went through too many at once, even when she told me just two cans a day, but she caught me sneaking them. So she says I can't have olives again until summer, but I remember they were black. And I don't mean black like my dad, 'cause he's more like brown even though folks always say that's black when it's on your skin, but I mean black like my hair." He tugged on a handful to show her.

Kennedy was distracted looking for another box of raisins and only replied with a simple, "Oh."

"So what I'm wanting to know is why they'd say I'm olive colored, I wonder."

"There are other kinds of olives too. Fancy kinds that are more like ..." She tilted her head to the side to study Woong. "Actually, those are usually green."

He pouted so far he could have fit at least half a dozen raisins on his lower lip. "I'm not green. But I seen folks who were green before. Back before I came here, you know how I was a flower swallow and taking care of myself on the streets? Well, some of them other flower swallows got so sick they turned green. I don't mean green like broccoli, more green like that pea soup my mom makes. Have you ever had pea soup? I think it's funny because peas are green like broccoli-green, but when you turn them into soup it's a different kind of green, like green and brown all mixed together, and what I'm wanting to know is why that is, I wonder."

"I have no idea." Kennedy set another plate in front of him with ten new celery sticks smothered in peanut butter and raisins.

"I wonder why they call these ants. 'Cause I've ate ants before, did you know that? Back during the hunger I did. And they weren't too bad, neither. But I'm glad I don't have to eat them now on account of folks here thinking it's gross. But you're a scientist, right? So you're used to things like that, so I'm guessing you don't think it's too gross, do you?"

"I suppose not if you're hungry enough."

"I liked ants, but grasshoppers were better. 'Course, that might have been on account of them being bigger, so you get fuller faster. You ever tried grasshopper?"

"No. I haven't."

He shrugged and took a noisy bite out of one of his celery sticks. "You'd like them if you tried them, I'm guessing, except they make a bad crunch, and sometimes girls don't like that part of it. But you're different, right? I mean, not really a girly kind of girl, aren't you?"

"That depends on what you mean."

Kennedy's phone beeped. Thankful for a distraction, she hopped to her feet and picked it up off the counter.

A text message from her dad.

Thirteen new confirmed cases in New York today.

It was three in the morning in Yanji. She couldn't guess if her dad was staying up late or getting up early. Either way, she knew he kept his eyes glued to his computer screen, his mouse continually ready to refresh his news page.

If a baby elephant in an Australian zoo came down with the Nipah virus, Kennedy would hear about it.

Another beep.

Nine deaths in Florida.

Well, it was a good thing she wasn't in Florida or New York, then. She washed her hands again since she was already so near the sink and then sat down by Woong. "Do you have much homework tonight?"

He shook his head. "Nah. Just a spelling test to practice. My mom says you're supposed to help me study. But what I'm wanting to know is how come we need to spell the words as long as we know how to say them, I wonder. 'Cause if you can say the word just fine, everyone knows what you're talking about."

"Sometimes we do things because our parents or teachers tell us to." It was the only answer Kennedy had the energy to offer.

Woong sighed dramatically. "Yeah. I can't wait to be big like you. 'Cause then nobody would ever tell me what to do. Like I could stay up all night long if I wanted and play video games like Mr. Nick from my dad's church does. Or watch as many movies as I wanted, even if they've got too much sword fighting in them. Or I could go weeks without cleaning my room at all. I'm pretty sure Mr. Nick does that too, by the way, 'cause I've been in his house before, and it's so messy you can't hardly even find a place to sit. That's what I can do when I'm all grown up. And if I got a little sick, my mom wouldn't go around worrying and telling me I hafta take some yucky medicine or eat up all my chicken soup when it hardly counts as soup because it's nearly all water."

Kennedy was about to explain how it's sometimes nice to be taken care of like that when you're not feeling well, but her phone beeped again.

A third text from her dad.

First confirmed fatality in Boston. Don't go anywhere that isn't absolutely necessary.

CHAPTER 5

"Hey, you know what I'm wanting to know? It's how come we've got to sleep at all, I wonder. Cause Chuckie Mansfield says he's got a pet goldfish, and goldfish never sleep. But what I wonder is how you'd know if your goldfish really was asleep or not, know what I mean? But his dad's a doctor so he knows that sorta stuff, and that's what he says. So if goldfish don't hafta sleep, how come you and me got to? And why do kids always hafta do it earlier than grown-ups? It's an abomination." He scrunched up his face in a perfect imitation of his father behind his pulpit.

Kennedy, guessing the impression wasn't intentional, masked her laugh with a cough.

"You better be careful," Woong said. "When you cough on somebody, that gives them your germs."

"You're right." She pulled Woong's Iron Man sheets up to his chin. "Now, your mom says you like to read before bed, so should we start that now?"

"Well first, what I'm wanting to know is how come people have adversaries to start with."

"Why they have what?"

"Adversaries."

"Like enemies?"

"No, I mean like what my mom and dad are doing."

Kennedy remained clueless.

"You know," Woong exclaimed, clearly exasperated. "*Adversaries*. When you go away and leave your kids with strangers."

Kennedy didn't know if she should chuckle or feel sorry for him. "Well, first of all, I'm not a stranger. I come over here all the time."

"Yeah, but ..."

"And second of all," she interrupted, "even when your parents go away for a night, they love you just as much as when they're here. That's why your mom's going to make a special point to call you tonight even when she and your dad are at the theater. And why she made so much good food for us to eat. Like that lasagna we had for dinner. Wasn't that yummy?"

"Yeah. Are there any leftovers? Sometimes Mom heats me up leftovers for breakfast once I finish my box of cereal."

"We'll check and see in the morning, ok?" Kennedy still hadn't cleaned up the kitchen. She'd been too busy quizzing Woong on his spelling words. She had no idea how an inquisitive child like him could stretch out a study session to the rate of one word per half an hour. When your teacher's given you a list of fifteen spelling words ...

"So what are you and your parents reading at night?"

"It's my mom who reads. Dad's too busy playing the Wii."

"Oh, yeah?" She tried to hide a grin at the idea of Carl engrossed in video games.

"Yeah, he likes to do that golf one. Mom says it's because he works so hard during the rest of the day he's allowed to do it at night. But she never sets the timer for him." He pouted.

"Well, sometimes adults get special privileges."

"Yeah, like Mrs. Winifred."

"Who?"

"My teacher. She got to leave early from school today because she was sick. My mom never lets me stay home from school, even when I have a sore throat. But all Mrs. Winifred had to do was tell the principal she had a fever, and she got to go home for the rest of the day. That's how come we got a substituent."

"You mean substitute?"

"Yeah. That's what I said."

"All right." Kennedy tried to remember what she and Woong were supposed to do next. He'd brushed his teeth after asking about two dozen questions about cavities, dentists, and braces. ("'Cause Chuckie Mansfield, his teeth are so crooked he says he's gonna need them metal things on them once he gets a little bigger, except he still has to wait for some of his first set of teeth to fall out first before it's ready, and that got me to thinking how come we got two different sorts of teeth to start with and why God didn't just make us with the ones we could use always.")

She glanced at the clock. Woong was already thirty minutes past his usual lights out time. Carl and Sandy would call as soon as intermission started at the opera, which could be any minute. She sighed. "Ok, are you ready to read?"

"Yup," he answered, snuggling down beneath his sheets. "I've been wondering what's going to happen to Violet now that she's sick, 'cause I know kids can take care of themselves even if they don't have a boxcar to live in. That's how I done it before I got adopted, you know, but it gets a lot harder if you have the sickness on account of you not being able to do anything for yourself, even get yourself someplace clear to barf. Have you read *The Boxcar Children*? Do you think Violet's gonna be ok, or do you think she might die on account of the sickness?"

"She'll be just fine." Kennedy figured a vague spoiler was justified when she saw how scared Woong looked.

He let out his breath. "Well, I've been wondering, you know, even though of course she's just a girl in a book and not a real kid at all, and I've never read a book where a kid actually dies, but I suppose it's possible, don't you think? And then I figure it's not really a book I'd wanna read, 'cause don't most people read so they can think about happy things, not things that really do happen like kids dying?"

Kennedy wondered how much Woong had endured as a street child before he found himself in the South Korean orphanage. Even Carl and Sandy were still piecing together the details of his hard life before he joined their family.

Kennedy opened up *The Boxcar Children* to where a piece of large, floral-patterned stationary marked off a new chapter. She read the first few sentences. "Does this sound right?" she asked. "Is this where your mom left off last?"

"Uh-huh. I think so."

She let her mind turn onto autopilot as she began to read.

"Why's it so cold in here?" Woong asked half a paragraph in.

Kennedy hadn't noticed anything wrong with the temperature. She pulled a blanket up over Woong. "Here you go." She started to read again.

"You know what I'm thinking?" he interrupted a few minutes later.

"What?"

"How come they thought their grandfather was so mean? 'Cause they didn't ever really know him, and I've never had a grandfather, least not one that I really remember, but in all the other stories the grandfathers are always nice. Like in the sword-fighting movie my mom doesn't like, there's a really nice grandpa in that one. He comes and reads to the little boy when he's sick even though at first the boy thinks it's just a kissing book or stuff and nonsense like that. Or there's that dancing story at Christmastime where the girl gets that funny toy doll thingy, right? And I think it's her grandfather who gives it to her but I'm not really sure, 'cause, you know, there's no talking in that one, so unless you already know what it's about, it's kinda hard to guess what's going on, know what I mean?"

Kennedy decided she'd make it through the first page and call it a night. How did Sandy handle these incessant questions all day long? Woong was a sweet kid, really bright. But Kennedy felt like she needed a twelve-hour nap just to recover from his chatter. She finally reached the third paragraph after just as many interruptions when the Lindgrens' home phone rang. She handed Woong the book. "Save our spot. I'll go see who that is." She had expected Carl and Sandy to call her on her cell to say good-night to Woong, but maybe they were calling the house instead.

"Lindgrens' residence," she answered.

"Hi, is this Woong's mother?"

Kennedy didn't recognize the worried voice on the other line.

"No, this is ..." She hesitated. Two years and thousands of miles away from home, and she still couldn't get over her dad's paranoia about admitting when she was in a house by herself. "This is Kennedy, a friend of the family."

"I see. Is Mrs. Lindgren there?"

"I'm afraid she's unavailable right now. Can I take a message?"

"Maybe. This is Margot Linklater. My daughter Becky goes to school with Woong?"

"Oh, right." Kennedy hoped Woong hadn't gotten into trouble in the classroom.

"I'm calling to get more details of what happened in school today?" She ended nearly all her sentences as a question.

Uh-oh. Was Kennedy about to have to step in as referee between a third-grader and an angry mother? "I'm not sure what you mean."

"Their teacher. Mrs. Winifred. My Becky tells me she nearly fainted in class."

Kennedy paused. "Woong said something to me about her leaving early, but I don't think he mentioned fainting."

Mrs. Linklater's voice lowered. "I'm just wondering if the school is giving us all the details."

"What do you mean?"

"Well, my Becky was very concerned. She said Mrs. Winifred was so sick she couldn't stand up. And it came on so suddenly. And according to another family, Mrs. Winifred had a fever ..." She left the thought unfinished.

"Are you worried about Nipah virus?" Kennedy asked, hoping she didn't sound too incredulous.

"Aren't we all?"

Apparently so.

"I'm sure we would have heard if it was something that serious." Kennedy strained her ears, trying to hear if Woong was making any noise from the other end of the hall.

"That's what I'm saying," Mrs. Linklater went on. "Worst-case scenario, if their teacher was that sick and got herself to the hospital today, it's still at least a full day or two before they'd get back any reports from the CDC, and then who knows how many kids may have been exposed, or heaven forbid actually infected?"

Kennedy wanted to say there was nothing at all to worry about, but what did she know? She lived most of her life with her head buried in her studies. If it hadn't been for her dad's constant text updates, she'd have no idea how far the Nipah virus had spread already or how many people were as worried as Mrs. Linklater.

"I don't want to overstep my place," she said, "but you might want to let Mrs. Lindgren know that several of us are going to be pulling our kids out for the next few days until we get some clearer answers of what's going on. You know, they've closed several schools in New York already."

No, she didn't know that. She was surprised her dad hadn't texted to tell her.

"Ok, I'll pass that on." She took a breath, thankful that it wasn't too choppy. A major panic attack while she was home alone with Woong was the last thing anybody needed.

"Tell Mrs. Lindgren she's welcome to call me if she has any questions, all right? She's got my number."

"Ok, thank you so much. I'll pass that on."

"I'm sorry to bother you so late. I'm sure Woong is dead to the world by now. I hope the phone ringing didn't wake him."

"No, don't worry about that." Kennedy had no idea how many other students at Medford Academy were *dead to the world* by 9:15, but Woong Lindgren certainly wasn't one of them. She thanked Mrs. Linklater for the call and hung up.

"Was that my parents?" Woong asked when Kennedy returned to his room. He was sitting up in bed, flipping ahead in *The Boxcar Children*.

"No, but they'll call as soon as intermission starts."

"What's intermission?"

"The part in the middle of the show they're at where they all take a break."

"You mean like halftime?"

"Yeah, like halftime. Want to keep reading until they call?"

He pouted in thought. "Ok. But you're sure Violet's gonna be ok?"

"I'm sure. I read that book like ten times or more when I was your age. She'll be just fine."

He let out his breath. "Good. 'Cause I seen people with the sickness, and trust me, it's not something you read about right before you go to bed. 'Least not if you don't want nightmares."

CHAPTER 6

Kennedy woke up the next morning to the sound of her cell screeching. As soon as she remembered what she was doing in the Lindgrens' guest room, she reached to turn off her alarm only to realize it was her dad calling.

"Hello?" She hated the way her voice sounded so groggy in the morning. Oh, well. What did he expect when he woke her up at such ungodly hours of the day and night? How early was it, anyway?

"What's the name of the school Carl and Sandy's son goes to?" her dad snapped. "Is it a charter school?"

Kennedy blinked at the digital clock beside her on the night table. 8:20? Had she forgotten to set her alarm? She was supposed to wake up Woong an hour ago.

"I'm running late, Dad. Can I call you back?"

"What's the name of his school?" he repeated.

She dragged herself up to a sitting position, wondering what it would be like to have a normal father who lived in a normal American town and who engaged in normal hobbies instead of being a perpetual news junkie.

"He goes to Medford Academy, and we both slept in." At least, she hoped Woong had slept in instead of waking up early and getting into trouble. After today, Sandy wouldn't even trust Kennedy to look after a pet parakeet. "I've got to get him up or he's going to be late."

"No, he's not. Neither of you are going anywhere."

Kennedy wasn't ready for her dad's dramatics. A five-minute shower, that's what she needed. No, there wasn't time for that. A two-minute shower then. Anything to clear away this mental fog.

"Medford Academy's closed," her dad said. "Something about one of the teachers possibly coming down with Nipah. What grade's Carl and Sandy's little boy in? First?" Her dad always assumed children were younger than they really were, which probably explained why he worried about Kennedy as if she were a preteen about to go away to her first ever sleep-away camp.

Kennedy put her phone on speaker while she checked out the Channel 2 News website. Her dad was right. Sheila Winifred, a 57-year-old veteran teacher at Medford Academy, admitted herself into the hospital yesterday morning with fever, disorientation, and swelling of the brain. The article was carefully phrased, with words like *suspicion* and *possibility* heavily sprinkled throughout. Even though Mrs. Winifred's case couldn't be confirmed yet as Nipah, enough symptoms matched and enough parents were worried that the superintendent closed down Medford Academy until the CDC reports came back. Other schools in the district would remain open, although parents were urged to keep children home if they showed any signs of illness.

Kennedy stared at the webpage and thought back to her brief conversation last night with that nervous mom from Woong's school. Had Kennedy's dad's irrational fears infected everyone around her? Or was this more than paranoia? Schools didn't just close their doors without good reason. Was it really possible that ...

"All right, Kensie girl, what's your plan?" Her dad asked the question as if he didn't already have an answer ready to dictate to her.

"I guess we stay home, and I'll try to figure out what to do to keep Woong entertained all day." Maybe she'd call Sandy and ask her to bend the rules a little bit so he could have extra Wii time.

"Not good enough." Her dad had an unassuming voice, but he could bark orders when it came to Kennedy's personal safety. "You've got to assume that Carl and Sandy's boy — what's his name again?"

"Woong. His name is Woong."

"Right. You've got to assume that Woong's been exposed. What makes Nipah so scary and dangerous is the incubation period. You can be a carrier for a couple days before coming down with any signs of illness. We have to be conservative and give it a full week to see if you're symptomatic. You know what to look for, right? And you've got to act quick, because they're talking about people going from feeling perfectly fine to ending up at the ER in the course of an hour, just like that teacher. It starts with fever, flu-like symptoms, headaches ..."

Kennedy was startled by noise at the doorway, and she snatched up her phone. Punching off the speaker, she interrupted her father's WebMD recitation.

"Dad, I really got to go. I can call back real soon, I promise."

"But wait a minute, we still haven't figured out ..."

Kennedy turned off the phone and stared at the tiny boy in his Hulk slippers standing in the doorway. His wide eyes didn't change when she beckoned him into the room.

"You ok, little buddy?" she asked, certain he wasn't.

"Was that your dad?"

"Yeah." She forced a smile. "He worries a lot about germs and stuff. He's kind of funny that way." She mentally rehearsed the last few minutes of their conversation. How much had Woong overheard?

"It's the sickness, isn't it? Teacher has the sickness."

Kennedy sighed. Why had she been so stupid as to put the phone on speaker? And why couldn't her dad tone down his end-of-the-world dramatics for a change?

Kennedy had made herself a promise that when she became a doctor she would always be honest with patients, although now she understood how toning down the truth could become a tempting option. "It's probably not Nipah, but they're going to close the school for a few days just to be sure."

She hoped the mention of an impromptu holiday might be enough to shatter Woong's fearful demeanor.

No such luck. "Is she gonna die?"

"No, little guy." Well, technically she wasn't qualified to make that promise, so she added a hasty, "At least, none of us really think so. Your principal's just doing what he needs to do to keep everyone safe so other people don't get sick."

"You mean *I* might get sick?"

Kennedy kicked herself. It was becoming more and more clear that she'd never be fit for a job in pediatrics.

"You just keep washing your hands and eating healthy foods, and you'll probably be fine." She forced a smile and wished Sandy were here. Of all the times for her and Carl to leave on an anniversary getaway ... "Come on." She went to take Woong's hand before figuring he was probably too old for that. She walked down the hall and turned around. "You coming?"

He frowned. "My legs hurt again."

She gave him a sympathetic smile. "We've got some extra time. Why don't you help me make a big breakfast to start off our day, ok? Keep your mind off your growing pains. What sounds good to you?"

"Teacher getting better." Woong stared at his massive Hulk slippers. "That's what sounds good to me."

You and me both, little buddy.

Kennedy left the thought unspoken.

CHAPTER 7

It was eleven before Kennedy cleared off the breakfast table and started a load of dishes. Woong had helped her make pancakes, except his version of *helping* involved asking about a dozen questions about each of the ingredients and why she was adding them in the way she was ("'Cause I've watched my mom make pancakes millions of times before, and she doesn't ever do it like that").

She finally got hold of Carl and Sandy just before noon. They hadn't heard the reports about Medford Academy closing but decided to head straight home. Kennedy felt bad that their anniversary getaway was cut short, but she was grateful she wouldn't have to stay here worrying about Woong by herself for much longer.

Woong was busy cleaning up his room. At least, that's what he was supposed to be doing, but Kennedy guessed by the crashing noises and numerous movie quotes coming from the bedroom that he was practicing his sword-fighting skills and pretending to be on the set of *Princess Bride*. As long as he was happy and content ...

Kennedy stared at the overflowing sink. She should have never let the dishes get so far behind. It would take two loads just to catch up, and she had a nagging suspicion Woong would be coming out of his room any minute, "wanting to know what time we're gonna have some lunch." Kennedy didn't feel like spending another minute in the kitchen. There was about a serving and a half of lasagna left over from last night, but that was hardly more than an appetizer the way Woong ate. She leaned over the stack of casserole dishes in the fridge. Chicken stir fry? Chili mac and cheese? She pulled out a small round container labeled *pork and bean soup*. That would work. She stared again at the messy sink, wondering if she should start washing the bigger things by hand.

She had just rolled up her sleeves when someone knocked outside.

"I'll get it!" Woong yelled, and Kennedy couldn't intercept him before he flung open the front door.

"Hey, Mr. Nick!"

"Hey, buddy!" Nick, the youth pastor at Carl and Sandy's church, raised his hand so Woong could give him a high-five. "Fist bump!" He held out his knuckles. Kennedy tried not to think of how many germs the two of them had just exchanged.

"Guess what!" Woong shouted. "There's no school today."

Kennedy was glad to hear the chipper excitement back in his tone.

Nick grinned and squatted down until he was eye level with Woong. "That's right. You guys get a vacation, don't you?"

"Yeah."

"Well, don't waste all that time on the Wii. Growing boy like you's got better things to do." Nick shut the door behind him and turned toward Kennedy, his blond dreadlocks flinging around after him. "Hey, there. How's it going?"

She glanced at his shirt. It had a stick figure kneeling by a bedside and a caption that read, *Prayer Warriors. Because real history makers do it on their knees.*

"Fine," she answered. She hadn't even been home alone with Woong for a full twenty-four hours, and she was already grateful for the chance to talk to a human being taller than four feet.

"Sorry to barge in like this. I was going to call while I was riding over here, and then I forgot until I was like two minutes away." He nodded to the window, where Kennedy could see his bicycle leaning on the Lindgrens' front porch. "I was hoping I could borrow the Honda. There's a few things I need to pick up from the store. You both could come along too if you wanted."

"Yeah!" Woong shouted.

"Probably not," Kennedy told him. "I think your parents want you to stay here where you'll be sure not to catch any other germs."

"Yeah, kind of crazy what's going on, isn't it?" Nick fidgeted with one of his dreads.

Crazy was one way of putting it.

"I think we'll stay here, but you're welcome to take the Honda. It's in the garage with the keys hanging up on the peg."

"All right." He stepped in the entryway. "What's that smell? It's delicious."

"Just some bean soup for lunch."

"Wow, I didn't know you could cook."

"I'm only reheating it. Sandy made it."

Nick nodded. "Oh, so that explains it."

"You can stay if you'd like a bite." Kennedy knew Nick was in the habit of eating over at the Lindgrens' several nights a week. It was probably the only way he sustained himself on his bachelor diet of frozen meals and Ramen noodles.

"Nah, I've got to go. My buddy just posted a picture of the canned food aisle at Rory's. Everyone's stocking up. It's gonna be an interesting couple of weeks."

While Nick was talking, Kennedy had been trying to lure him away from listening ears, but Woong wouldn't leave until Kennedy finally told him to go wash his hands in the bathroom. "And do the happy birthday song twice like you learned at school," she called after him.

Nick followed her into the kitchen and paused by the door that led to the garage. "I know Carl and Sandy usually have plenty on hand. You guys going to be all right if things get hard?"

He was laid back about most things. Kennedy didn't picture him as the type to get worked up over a potential outbreak. The fact that so many other people besides her father were taking this Nipah scare seriously was more worrisome than the news stories themselves.

"How hard do you expect it to get?" she asked.

He shrugged. "Most people are saying it's going to get worse before it gets better. A shame, really. I don't even want to know what this whole scare is going to do to worsen the refugee crisis."

Kennedy had hardly thought through the medical ramifications of the disease. She wasn't ready to jump straight to politics. "Are you going to be ok if they don't have any food at the store?" she asked. "Do you want to take one of these casseroles with you in case the shelves are already empty?"

"No, I'll be all right. If I get to Rory's and can't find anything, maybe I'll take you up on it, but I think if I hurry now I'll get there before they're completely sold out."

Woong was already out of the bathroom, so she was glad Nick didn't say anything else about the epidemic.

"So the keys are hanging up in their usual spot?"

"Yeah."

"All right, I'll bring the car back as soon as I'm done." He opened the door that led to the garage.

"No rush," Kennedy called after him. Where did she and Woong have to go, anyway?

After Nick left, Kennedy served up two large bowls of soup.

"Want to play a game of cards while we eat?" Woong asked.

"Sure. That sounds like a fun idea."

Woong jumped up and ran to the game closet, and Kennedy glanced at the text coming in from her dad.

Governor of New York declared a state of emergency.

Another beep.

Two deaths reported in New Hampshire. One a 10-year-old boy.

Kennedy put her phone on vibrate.

"You want to play Uno or Egyptian rat race?" Woong asked.

Kennedy had never heard of Egyptian rat race. "Let's do Uno." She couldn't remember how long it been since she'd last played it. Probably at least a decade.

Her phone shook again, and she turned it face down so she didn't have to see whatever depressing news her dad was sending her now.

"Bring the deck here," she told Woong, "and I'll deal while you start your lunch. Don't want to let your mom's soup get cold."

CHAPTER 8

Kennedy always assumed Uno was a game of pure chance, which was a statistic impossibility given how many games Woong won in a row. They had eaten up the entire pot of soup, and Woong had finished off the leftover lasagna, too. Carl and Sandy were due back in less than an hour. The house was disastrous, but at least the day with Woong had gone relatively smoothly.

"You got any other games you want to play instead?" she asked after Woong beat her for the sixth or seventh time at Uno.

"Hmm." Woong pouted. "Maybe Battleship?"

"Sure. Why not?" At the very least, it was a nice way to procrastinate from having to work on that next load of dishes.

Woong had just put the cards away, and the two of them were setting up their battle stations when someone knocked on the front door.

"Is that Mr. Nick?" Woong's eyes lit up.

"Might be," Kennedy answered, although she couldn't figure out why he'd go around to the front door after dropping the car off in the garage.

Woong followed her to the main entrance. Kennedy glanced through the window at the familiar face on the porch and threw open the door.

"Woah! Is that pink hair?" Woong shouted. "Inconceivable!"

Kennedy stepped aside to let her roommate into the Lindgrens' home. "What are you doing here?" she asked.

"Well, if you'd been getting my messages, you would have known," Willow answered. "Let me guess. You let your batteries die again?"

Kennedy rolled her eyes. "No, I just turned it on vibrate. My dad kept sending me his end-of-the-world texts." She gave her roommate a hug. "What's going on? I thought you'd be in New York by now."

"Yeah, the trip got cancelled." Willow flung her magenta-streaked hair behind her ear. "Nobody really wants to be in New York right now. It's not just your dad who's freaking out about this whole ..."

"Hey, Woong," Kennedy interrupted, "can you do me a big favor and clear the dishes off the table?"

He pouted but left the two girls alone in the entryway.

"So I guess it's getting pretty bad?" she asked Willow when he was out of earshot.

"I'll say. You heard about that teacher from ... Oh, shhhhh ..." Willow stopped herself. "I mean, oh rats. That kid goes to that school doesn't he? The one with the teacher. That's why he's home today. Geeze, I didn't even think about that. Are you ok? Do you think either of you got exposed?"

Kennedy glanced down the hall, hoping Woong wasn't listening. "I think we're ok. I mean, the chances of infection are really low."

"Yeah." Willow ran her fingers through her hair. Kennedy wouldn't be surprised if she came up with a quick excuse to leave, and she certainly wouldn't blame her.

"Kennedy!" Woong shouted from the kitchen, drawing out each syllable. "What're we having for a snack?"

"I swear that kid eats like an elephant," she muttered.

"I have an idea!" Woong called. "Why don't you get two cups of juice, and I'll put poison in one of them and you'll have to decide which one you want to drink?"

Willow raised her penciled eyebrows.

"He just watched *The Princess Bride* for the first time," Kennedy explained.

Willow nodded. "Got it. Well, want some help with figuring out a snack?" she asked. "I've got my mom's carrot-carob-zucchini drop recipe on my phone. Does your pastor keep any garbanzo bean flour on hand?"

"I don't think so." She glanced at the door. "Do you want to stay a while? I mean, you're welcome to, but if you're worried about getting sick ..."

"Pffft." Willow tossed her hair. "You know me. I'd go absolutely crazy in my dorm room all day. If I'm not hanging out here, I'd probably be at the mall exposing myself to every pathogen known to humankind. I've been taking zinc droplets since I was two weeks old. I've got a wicked strong immune system. Besides, it's not like either you or the kid are sick, right? I mean, this is all just precautions at this point, isn't it?"

"Kennedy!" Woong shrieked again.

"What?" Kennedy ignored Willow's bemused grin.

"Can you make some popcorn while we play Battleship?"

Kennedy glanced at her roommate. "So you want to hang out for a while?"

Willow shrugged. "Not like I've got anything better to do. You have no idea how bad it sucks. Oh wait, is *sucks* one of those words that's gonna get me in trouble? I know this is a pastor's house and all."

Kennedy wished Willow hadn't flaked out on their new-believer's Bible study. They could actually talk about things like grace versus legalism. She was pretty sure Willow pictured the entire Christian life as a big list of dos and don'ts. No wonder she hadn't kept up her original spiritual momentum.

"You're fine," she said. "Just be careful around Woong. I don't think his parents let him use that word."

"Ok, I'll be good. I promise." Willow shot her a dazzling smile, and the two girls walked into the dining room.

Woong was sitting in front of his Battleship display, shielding it from view. "What's for snack?" He scrunched up his eyes and stared at Willow. "And why's her hair that color? Were you born that way, or did you get it painted?"

"Dyed," Kennedy corrected.

"Who died?" Woong's eyes widened. "Someone died?"

"No, I was just talking about Willow's hair."

"Her hair's dead? Do you mean all the way dead or just mostly dead? 'Cause there's a difference, you know."

"I just mean when you color your hair, you say that it's *dyed*."

"Dead."

"What?"

"You can't say that something is *died*. You say something is *dead*. That's better grammar."

"Ok." Kennedy chose to drop the vocabulary lesson. "Hey, listen. Your mom and dad are coming home early, so you ..."

"They are?"

"Yeah, so you need to go get your room extra clean so it's perfect by the time they get back, ok?"

Woong cocked his head to the side. "What do I get if I do a good enough job?"

Kennedy wasn't in the habit of entering into negotiations with third-graders. "Popcorn?"

He frowned. "No. You need to ask me what I want."

"Fine. What do you want?"

He put on his most serious facial expression. "I want my father back, you ..."

"All right," she interrupted quickly. "That's enough movie quotes for today. Go clean up."

The excitement in his eyes clouded over, and he slumped away from the table with a half-hearted, "Ok."

Kennedy started to clear the table, wondering how long it would take her to get the kitchen presentable again.

"Looks like we're on the set of *Titanic* before everyone dies," Willow stated helpfully.

Kennedy didn't respond. She was busy glancing through the texts she'd missed from her dad. More casualties. More confirmed cases. More states. More cities. More lists of symptoms to look out for. Kennedy browsed through the list and figured anyone with a pulled hamstring, ear infection, or stubbed toe could find a way to convince themselves they were about to die.

She sighed.

Willow glanced up from the Battleship board she'd been looking over. "What's wrong?"

"Oh, just my dad."

"Yeah, I bet he's freaking out about this whole thing."

"He's been freaking out for the past three weeks." Kennedy remembered the day the first Nipah case was confirmed in the States. Her dad wanted her to go to the nearest drugstore and buy a case of at least a hundred face masks, fully expecting her to wear one every time she went out in public. He told her not to eat anything cooked in the cafeteria but to buy canned things and heat them up in her dorm room after washing her hands with antibacterial soap and ideally a few additional squirts of Germ-X.

Kennedy tuned him out at that point, told herself he was overreacting. Was this like the boy who cried wolf? Had her dad freaked her out so many times in the past over inconsequential nothings that now, when her life really might be in danger, she'd chosen to all but completely ignore his instructions?

"Don't let him get under your skin." Willow gave her a reassuring rub on the shoulder. "He's just trying to look out for you."

"Yeah, I know."

One more load of dishes later, Kennedy and Willow sat across from each other sharing some of Sandy's raspberry tea. Woong's battle sounds and impressively accurate impressions of Andre the Giant from the back room told Kennedy he was at least happy, even if he wasn't cleaning.

"I'm sorry you couldn't make it to New York," Kennedy said. That's all Willow had been talking about for weeks. "You must be really disappointed."

Willow let out a melodramatic sigh. "Yes and no. I mean, it totally blows ... I mean, it totally *stinks* that I'm gonna miss all those shows, you know? I was really looking forward to that. But then there's part of me that thinks I actually jinxed myself out of it. I don't know. Does the Bible say anything about jinxes, or is that too hocus-pocus for Christians to believe in?"

"What do you mean?"

"Well, I was gonna be hanging out with all my friends. I mean, it wasn't only about Broadway, of course. And I've been trying to cut back on certain things now that I'm saved. I'm not saying I'm doing a perfect job, and you probably know that better than anyone else, but I swear to ... I mean, I can *honestly say* I'm trying really hard. But that's just the thing. You made it sound like I ask Jesus into my heart, I ask him to forgive me of my sins, and then he gives me so much joy and happiness and hope it's like I never look back on all the stuff I had to leave behind. I mean, can you believe I haven't smoked a single joint in six weeks? I'm serious. I don't think I've been this clean since before I started getting periods. I'm not joking."

Kennedy glanced down the hall just to make sure Woong hadn't popped out of his room to eavesdrop.

"And at first, it was sort of like that. That joy and stuff. A little bit." She shrugged. "I mean, I felt something at least. And then that Bible study we were doing, it kept talking about all these things like those spiritual fruits and all that stuff, and I'm sure it's great, but it just made me realize how far I've got to go to be like you. I mean, the vocabulary, everything. It was as bad as if I were to jump into your organic chemistry class mid-semester and even though you offered to be my study partner, you couldn't figure out why I couldn't keep up. I mean, I don't even know the difference between an atom and a molecule without looking it up, but you'd be talking about chemical equations and *blah blabetty blah blah* stuff like that, and that's kind of how it's felt these past couple months. Like you're so far ahead I'm bound to disappoint you. I mean, I'm already disappointed in myself."

Kennedy didn't know what to say. She wanted to apologize, but Willow kept on talking.

"When I prayed with you that night and asked Jesus into my heart or whatever you want to call it, that night I told him I wanted him to forgive my sins, I really meant it. You said if I was sincere, he'd answer my prayers. And then the first few weeks passed, and the novelty sort of died down. I don't know if that's my fault or what, but it did, and then all of a sudden I realized what a hypocrite I was, and I don't know if you can understand this, being a goody-goody God's girl and all that. And I don't say that to be mean — I seriously envy you. Because it's so easy for you. You've never slept around, you're as clean as a whistle, your boyfriend's like Mr. Chastity Belt or whatever the male equivalent of that is, and it all just comes so easy to you. But here I am, I'm trying my hardest, and I keep waiting for that joy and stuff you told me was supposed to happen when I got saved, except it didn't. At least not for very long. I kept going through the motions for a little while, doing our Bible study and all that, but I knew myself. I hadn't really changed.

"So New York came up, and I really wanted to go be with my friends. I'm sure if I had asked, you would have told me it was a bad idea. Hanging out with all those old influences. But you never said I had to stop being friends with everyone from the past when I became a Christian. And I wanted to go. I felt a little guilty about it. I knew there'd be drinking and stuff going on. I didn't really want to get back involved in that, but by then it'd been so long since I'd felt anything of that happiness you promised me that I figured I may as well go to New York with my friends and just see what happened. It wasn't like I was planning to jump off the wagon there or anything, but who would have been that surprised if I did, you know?

"So when I heard today the trip got cancelled, I got even more freaked out. Like maybe God's mad at me for thinking about going in the first place. And you never said it counts as sin before you've actually done something wrong, but maybe it does. Or maybe I'm not saved at all. Because if I was, I probably shouldn't be experiencing all these temptations and things. I'm just starting to wonder if it really worked that night I prayed. Maybe I didn't believe hard enough. I tried. I swear to ... I mean, *I promise* I tried as hard as I could. But what if it wasn't enough faith? What if it didn't count? So now, I've given up my friends, my fun, and I don't even get heaven out of it. Excuse my language, but that just sucks."

"Yeah. You're right."

Willow leaned forward in her seat. "Huh?"

"I was just thinking out loud. And I mean, you're right. If you give up all the fun of the world and don't get anything out of it, that's a terrible exchange." She didn't know what else she was supposed to say. She'd been so excited last winter when Willow's finally accepted Christ. It was the first time Kennedy had shared the gospel with anybody, and a new soul had been accepted into the family of God. What could be more thrilling? And then the weeks passed, and Willow's enthusiasm for her new-found faith started to wane, and Kennedy was left wondering what went wrong.

She still wondered what went wrong. Had she given Willow false promises? Wasn't God's Spirit supposed to be enough to make up for the party-life she had left behind?

"I wish I knew what to tell you," she sighed. If Sandy were here, she'd have all kinds of encouragement to pour out into Willow's spirit. In fact, the very first weekend after Willow got saved, Sandy had the two girls over for a huge barbecue ribs feast with a side of tofu stir-fry for Willow. It was the same night she gave Kennedy and Willow that new-believer's Bible study to go through. It should have worked.

Willow frowned into her cup. "Well, they say religious fervor is genetically inherited. Maybe I'm just not one of the lucky ones."

There had to be another explanation. What could Kennedy say? She needed to talk to Dominic. He always had the right words of wisdom to offer in situations like these. Two years ago, Kennedy might have told

Willow to pray and read her Bible more. That seemed to be the catch-all solution to anybody interested in growing in their spiritual walk. But after suffering for over a year now from her PTSD, Kennedy realized that daily devotions weren't some sort of Band-Aid you could throw on whenever you wanted a spiritual pick-me-up. There was more to it than that.

She just didn't know what.

"I'm really sorry you've been struggling like this. You should have told me sooner." She tried not to make her voice sound accusatory. Willow was suffering from enough guilt as it was.

"Yeah, well, I didn't want to bother you. I mean, like I said, you've had it so easy ..."

"Maybe that's what happened," Kennedy interrupted, still thinking out loud and hoping that somehow God might show up and help her words make sense. "I mean, I really wanted you to know what it was like to be a Christian, and I didn't want to scare you away from the faith or anything, so a lot of my own struggles I kept hidden. Like that PTSD stuff. I'm still a mess. You know that. At least, I think you know that. God hasn't healed me completely yet. I pray he does. I hope he does. It doesn't make sense to me how if the Bible says *ask and you shall receive*, I could ask him to take my flashbacks away and have him tell me no, he's not going to do that. I struggle with that one a lot. So maybe we're not going through the same kind of issues, but neither one of us has it figured out. Not even close."

"So, what exactly does that mean?" Willow asked. "Like, you get a flashback and start wondering if God exists? That doesn't sound like you."

"No, but I start to doubt if he's as powerful as he says he is. I mean, of course I know he is, but then I wonder why if he's all that powerful he doesn't just make my issues disappear? I've heard of people he's done that for. I know it's possible. So if he'd do it for someone else, why not me? I don't doubt he exists, but I do wonder if maybe it's my own lack of faith that's keeping him from answering my prayers."

Willow didn't say anything.

"I don't know if I'm making any sense right now. I'm probably just confusing you even more."

Willow sighed. "No, it's ok. It's good to hear I'm not the only one with those kinds of questions."

"I wish I had more answers for you," Kennedy admitted.

Willow offered a faint smile. "Maybe that's why they call it faith, right?"

Kennedy tried to smile back, but her heart ached for her friend. It wasn't supposed to be like this. Over Christmas break when Willow first started expressing an interest in Christianity, Kennedy had pictured the two of them bonding like sisters, taking their friendship to deeper levels. Willow's conversion was supposed to give Kennedy that deep Christian fellowship she'd always hoped to find in college. They could pray together at night, study the Bible together in the morning. It'd be like having a built-in accountability partner and prayer partner all rolled into one blissful friendship.

Instead, the two girls had drifted farther apart over the past few months. Willow was so careful about everything now, so worried about offending Kennedy or saying something wrong. If it wasn't about when to turn the lights out or who would be back to their dorm room when, the girls hardly talked at all.

"So, you're probably gonna tell me it was God who started the whole epidemic, just so I wouldn't go to New York and start partying again, right?"

Kennedy stared past Willow's shoulder at all the dishes that still needed to get washed and put away. "Well, I'm sure there's got to be more to it than that. If all he wanted to do was cancel your trip to New York, he could have done it in a lot of simpler ways."

"Like infecting me with Nipah?"

Kennedy wasn't sure if Willow was being sarcastic or not. "No, he doesn't work like that. It's not a punishment." She hoped she was speaking the truth. Didn't the Bible say Christians were no longer under God's wrath? But what about the other verses that talked about his discipline?

"It doesn't seem fair that a bunch of innocent people should catch a disease and die because I was about to go to New York and get involved in stuff I wasn't supposed to."

"No, God doesn't do it that way." Kennedy tried to think up a Bible verse that would prove her point. Where was Dominic when she needed him?

"What about those freaks ... I mean those evangelists like that Hopewell guy who gets up on TV and says you've just got to have faith and everything's going to work out? Or if you're sick or something and don't get better, it's because you've sinned. Isn't that why that one family stopped giving their son chemo? I mean, I guess I always assumed faith healers were just a bunch of quacks, but now that I'm saved, am I supposed to take what they say more seriously?"

Kennedy didn't pay much attention to preachers like that. Even Dominic, who believed more fervently in the power of prayer than anyone Kennedy had met, disagreed with that sort of prosperity gospel, or at least he disagreed with the way it was presented by the big-name televangelists. "No, for the most part I think I probably agree with you."

"So sickness isn't, like, some big punishment from God. That's what you're saying? That it doesn't mean you've sinned or something if you get sick?"

"I don't think so."

Willow let out a heavy sigh. "And what do you think about the whole Nipah thing, anyway? Not spiritually, just in general. Figure it'll get a lot worse?"

"I don't know." Kennedy didn't want to admit she'd been basically ignoring the entire epidemic, thinking until recently it was just another of her dad's overreactions.

"You think the kid's gonna be ok? If he was at that school ..."

Kennedy shook her head. She was pretty sure Woong was still engrossed in his *Princess Bride* reenactment, but she didn't want to risk him overhearing. The poor boy had lived through enough torment already before coming to the States. He didn't need another scare on his hands.

Kennedy stood up when her cell phone rang. "Hold on," she told Willow. "That's probably my dad freaking out again. I better get it before he has a heart attack or something."

She headed to the counter and glanced at the phone.

"Hello?"

"Kennedy." Sandy's voice on the other line was breathless.

Kennedy's gut tightened. "Yeah?"

"We're back in town, but something happened. Carl's not doing well.

We're on our way to the ER at Providence right now."

"What is it?" Kennedy asked, trying to keep her voice from betraying her fears.

"I don't know. But please, would you find my journal, the one I keep up on the counter by the Bible and prayer box? A few pages in, you'll see the numbers for the St. Margaret's prayer chain. Could you call them, honey? I know it's a lot to ask. I think we have about fifteen names there. If you don't get a hold of them right away, just leave a message and ask them to call the people below them on the prayer chain when they get the chance."

"What should I tell them?" Kennedy pictured Carl's broad, smiling face. He was so strong. Of course, he could afford to lose some weight. All that brawn and muscle that had made him a formidable Saints linebacker in his day had softened and filled out over time, but he was in perfect health for his age. In fact, he could easily pass as a decade or two younger. Kennedy had seen a picture of him and Sandy on their wedding day, and the only difference between then and now was that he'd gained forty or fifty extra pounds and traded a full head of hair for a pair of spectacles.

"I don't know what's going on, sweetheart, but you know Carl. He'd go visiting folks in the hospital every day of his life but wouldn't voluntarily step foot in one as a patient unless it was something pretty severe."

"Is it ..." Kennedy wasn't sure how to ask the question. Wasn't sure she wanted to know the answer. "Does it have anything to do with the epidemic?" She didn't speak over a whisper. She tried not to glance at Willow, who was offering her a sympathetic look from the dining room table.

Kennedy heard a noise in the background of Sandy's call. She thought she recognized Carl's voice but couldn't tell what was going on. Was he coughing? Crying out? Her throat seized up.

"Kennedy, I've got to go. Why don't you grab Woong and meet us here at Providence."

Kennedy had never heard so much fear in Sandy's voice before. She croaked out "Ok," but Sandy had already disconnected the call. Kennedy stared at the blank screen.

"Was that your pastor's wife?" Willow asked.

"Yeah, she's taking Carl to Providence right now. He's having some ..."

Willow cleared her throat loudly. "Well, hello. Sounded like you were having fun back there. Which *Princess Bride* character are you?"

"I'm the funny white-haired guy with the chocolate pill." Woong gave out a squeaky impression of Billy Crystal. "You better leave or I'll call the brute squad."

They both giggled. Thank God Willow was here to entertain Woong while he recited movie lines. Kennedy's brain was too stunned to do anything but stare at the cluttered counter.

"Hey," Willow asked, "what other movies do you like? Have you seen *The Avengers*?"

Woong frowned. "Only the cartoon ones. My mom won't let me watch the real thing."

"Well, do you have a favorite Avenger character?"

"Iron Man!" Woong answered excitedly.

"Do you have any Iron Man action figures?"

"Action what?"

"You know. Toys to play with. Toys that look like Iron Man."

"Oh, yeah. Wanna see?"

"Sure do. Why don't you go pick out your favorite from your room and bring it out here?" Willow turned to Kennedy as Woong sped down the hall. "What can I do to help?"

Kennedy pressed her fingertips against her temples. She had to focus. "Sandy has some people she wants me to call. People from the church. She's got the numbers in that journal over there." She pointed to the notebook. "And she said ..." Her voice caught for just a moment before she seized control of herself. "She said we should bring Woong and meet them at the hospital."

Willow stood up and grabbed the journal with the phone numbers. "Then that's what we're going to do." She walked down the hall and handed Kennedy her sweater. "Come on. Let's go."

"I don't have the car," Kennedy explained. "The youth pastor's borrowing it for the afternoon." For the first time, she thought about Nick and wondered why he hadn't returned the Honda earlier. She'd expected him back hours ago.

"Don't worry about that. We'll take mine. I'll drive and you can make those calls on the way. Please tell me you've kept your phone charged up this time."

Willow was only trying to lighten the mood. Kennedy's negligence in keeping her phone batteries charged was a constant source of teasing. But until she found out just what was wrong with Carl, there was no way she could find anything amusing.

"Hello. My name is Inigo Montoya." Woong rushed down the hall, holding a large Iron Man action figure and beaming proudly at Willow. "You killed my father. Prepare to die."

"That's wicked awesome," she exclaimed. "Hey, how old are you again?"

Woong shrugged. "I dunno."

"No, seriously. How old are you?"

"He really doesn't know," Kenny whispered in her ear.

Willow raised her penciled eyebrows. "Oh. Well, you're old enough to put on your shoes by yourself, right?"

Woong stared at his feet. "I'm already wearing my shoes."

"Look at that," Willow exclaimed. "Well, why don't you come out with me to my car, and when you're buckled in, you can put them on the right feet, ok?"

"Where are we going?" he asked. "I don't think my mom wants me going anywhere with strangers on account of some of them turning into bad guys, and you can never tell who the bad guys are just by looking at them, you know."

Willow smiled. "Your mom's right, and you're a very smart boy for remembering what she said. Kennedy's coming with us too, so that makes it all right, doesn't it?"

"I dunno." He glanced at Kennedy. "She's not a stranger to you, is she?"

Kennedy slipped on her new spring sandals and gave a pitiful attempt of a smile. "No, this is my good friend Willow. She's not a stranger."

Woong seemed appeased enough. "Where are we going?"

She wondered how much she should tell him. Before she knew herself what was going on, was it worth making him more scared? "We're going to visit your mom and dad."

"Wicked awesome!" Woong shouted and followed the girls out the door.

CHAPTER 9

Kennedy was only able to get a hold of six of the church members from Sandy's prayer chain list. She called them on the way to Providence, while Willow and Woong held a loud, lengthy conversation about their favorite Marvel heroes and villains. By the time they pulled into the hospital parking lot, Kennedy's insides were quivering like a glass of water left out in a Jurassic Park cafeteria table.

"You holding up?" Willow asked quietly as everyone unbuckled.

"I think so." Kennedy thought about her dad, thought about how a crowded emergency room was the last place he'd want her to visit in the middle of the Nipah outbreak, but what choice did she have? She turned to Willow. "You want to just drop us off here? We don't all have to go in."

"Isn't this the hospital?" Woong asked. "Is my dad visiting someone from the church? Did someone from St. Margaret's get sick? Wait, it's not the nipple disease, is it?"

Kennedy bit her lip so no one could see it tremble. Willow reached out and gave her shoulder a reassuring squeeze. "I'll go in with you."

"You're not worried about catching anything?" Kennedy asked.

Willow shrugged. "How big of a hypocrite would I be if I were willing to go to New York City when there's been like twenty or thirty people who've died there, but I wouldn't step into a hospital to help a friend?"

Kennedy returned her roommate's smile and this time didn't have to fake it. "Thanks."

"Hey, that's what I'm here for."

They headed toward the emergency room entrance. Kennedy wished she'd brought more practical shoes than her little spring sandals. She also realized she'd left her backpack and Germ-X back at the Lindgrens' home. Oh, well. Providence had several sanitation stations. Maybe they'd have masks too. That way, if her dad ever found out she'd been here, she could at least tell him she'd taken every possible precaution, or at least every reasonable one.

"You have to be really careful when we get in," she told Woong as they entered through the automatic doors. "Don't put your hands on anything, and try not to touch your face, ok?"

"Why not?"

Kennedy didn't have the stamina to give him a well thought out, scientific response. "Just be careful, all right?" She felt like Forrest Gump's mother, repeating the same couple phrases over and over again.

Once they entered the ER, Woong frowned. "Hey, where's my dad? This is usually the room where he visits people and prays with them. That reminds me, my head hurts. If I ask my dad to pray about it, think it'll go away?"

"Your dad's in a different room this time," Kennedy told him. "In fact, buddy, your dad's here because ..."

"Oh, baby boy, come over here, little pumpkin." Sandy burst out of a doorway and bustled over to Woong, her long, flowered skirt rustling round her legs until she reached her son and smothered him in kisses.

Woong squirmed in her arms.

"I missed you so much, darling. Are you ok? Your daddy wants to see you. Kennedy, thank you so much for bringing him here. The doctors are doing tests right now, but they said I could bring him back. Were you a good boy for Miss Kennedy?" she asked. "You didn't give her too much of a hard time? Your daddy's been asking for you, honey. He'll be so happy to know you came to see him."

And with that, Sandy ushered Woong past the nurse who held open a door labeled *authorized personnel only*.

Kennedy and Willow looked at each other.

"So do we wait or head out?" Willow asked.

Kennedy glanced around. The ER wasn't overcrowded, but it was more sick people than she was comfortable sharing space with if she didn't have to. "Maybe I'll text Sandy real quick and ask." She pulled out her cell.

"Yeah, what's wrong with your pastor, anyway? I didn't want to ask in the car. Didn't want to worry the boy."

"Me either. But I have no idea what's going on. Sandy didn't really say anything, just that it seemed serious if it meant he's here at the ER. He's not that fond of doctors, actually."

Willow glanced around. "Can't blame him."

Kennedy stared at the text on her screen. "Well, that was easy enough.

Sandy said she'll keep Woong here for now, so I guess that means we don't have to stick around."

Willow shrugged. "All right. Hey, wanna hit L'Aroma Bakery? They've got this new eggless quiche I've been dying to try."

"I better not. My dad ..."

Willow smiled. "Say no more. Time to go sequester ourselves again?"

"I guess so." They started to walk toward the exit. Kennedy cleared her throat. "Thanks for coming with me."

"No problem."

"I really mean it. That was ... Well, it was nice not having to drive Woong by myself. I was pretty worried."

"I could tell. Hey, can I ask you a question?

"Sure."

"It's about your PTSD."

"Oh." Kennedy took a deep breath. Good. No choppiness. "Go ahead."

"I was wondering if you think you're ..."

"Kennedy!" The voice behind them made both girls stop and turn around.

"Dominic!"

"What are you both doing here?" he asked. Concern laced his words. "Everything ok?"

"We just brought Woong over to see Carl," Kennedy told him, hoping Dominic could give more details about her pastor's condition.

Dominic frowned. "Carl? Is he here visiting someone?"

Kennedy bit her lip. "No, he's here as a patient. You didn't know?"

"No." Dominic glanced behind him once. "I got called here on different business."

"Everything ok?" she asked.

"Oh." He cleared his throat awkwardly. "You know. Work stuff." Why wouldn't he meet her eyes? "So, you're taking off then?" he asked.

Kennedy tried to read his muted expression. She hated the way he couldn't talk to her about his job as a police chaplain. She understood the need for privacy, but she was his girlfriend, after all.

"Yeah, we're heading out right now." Was he trying to rush her out the door? What was going on?

He looked relieved. "Ok, well, I'm glad we bumped into each other."

Kennedy paused. "Are you ok?"

Dominic was looking over her shoulder. "Hmm."

She didn't know if that was an affirmative sound or not. She reached out and touched his arm. "What's wrong?"

Something beeped, and he grabbed his pager out of his pocket. "I'm sorry, I've got to run. I'll call you tonight." He took off at a sprint.

Willow chuckled. "Wow. When he said he had to run, I didn't think he meant it quite so literally."

Kennedy stared after him. What was that all about?

Willow planted on a chipper expression that clashed glaringly against Kennedy's current mood. "So, we've got a whole week ahead of us, no kids to watch, and nowhere to go. Sounds like the perfect recipe for a little bit of fun."

Willow was right. This was spring break, after all. Even if the stupid epidemic meant they were trapped indoors, at least they could have a good time together. Board games. Movies. They'd find ways to keep each other from getting stir-crazy. And even though they were in the midst of an epidemic, maybe they could stop by the gas station on the way home and pick up a gallon of ice cream. What her dad didn't know couldn't hurt him.

"All right, let's head out." Even though she felt bad for her roommate, she was thankful the New York trip had been cancelled. If you had to sit around hiding from a horrific virus, might as well do it with someone you enjoyed spending time with.

"Sounds like a plan." Willow rubbed Kennedy encouragingly on the back. Kennedy tried not to think of her strange run-in with Dominic. He was always serious at work, but that's because he did his job so well, felt so much compassion and empathy for the families he prayed with and assisted. She knew he'd keep his word, and they'd talk more tonight. Until then, she and Willow could afford a day of fun.

"Hold on." Kennedy stopped at the hand sanitizing station by the exit. "All right." She wiped the excess lotion on her pants legs and smiled at her roommate. "Let's go."

The automatic doors swung open as an alarm blared across the hospital PA system.

"This is a hospital-wide code 241. Repeat. Code 241, hospital wide."

Kennedy and Willow stopped and glanced at each other as a security officer came up behind them. "Excuse me. I need you both to have a seat in the lobby." He stepped in front of them, blocking their exit.

"What's going on?" Kennedy asked.

"Just have a seat." He nodded toward the chairs in the waiting area as the announcer on the PA system repeated the encrypted announcement.

Kennedy and Willow slowly made their way to two empty seats. Kennedy's open-toed sandals, cute as they were, pinched against the sides of her feet. Another security officer closed the doors that connected the ER to the main hospital then stood there, mute and expressionless. Across from her, a middle-aged man coughed into his coat sleeve. A mother held her small son against her chest and adjusted his face mask to cover his mouth and nose. A baby cried somewhere behind her, but Kennedy didn't turn around to look.

"What do you think's going on?" Willow asked.

Kennedy made a valiant attempt to control the terror swirling around in her gut. She visualized herself compressing it into a tiny, infinitesimally small singularity, burying it along with all her other fears and anxieties.

"I don't have the slightest idea."

CHAPTER 10

Kennedy tried calling Dominic's cell five different times. Either he didn't have it on or something kept him from answering.

She went up to the nurses' station and stood in line behind ten other people until the petite triage nurse finally told her that a Code 241 meant no one could enter or leave the building.

"For how long?"

"I can't say."

"What are they keeping us here for?"

"I really don't know."

Did she know anything? "I came in to check on a friend. Carl Lindgren," she explained. "Is there any way I can go back and see him?"

She shook her head. "I'm sorry. Right now I can't let you back there. Not with the hospital on lockdown."

"Is this a quarantine or something?"

"I really can't say. I'm sorry."

"Is it about the Nipah virus?"

"I'm afraid I don't know any more than you do. I'm sorry."

I'm sorry. I'm sorry. I'm sorry.

Kennedy was sick of it.

"Would you like a sanitation mask?" the nurse asked.

"Sure. Actually, can I have two? I'm here with a friend." At least they'd be waiting out this lockdown in style.

"No problem."

Kennedy plodded back to her seat and handed her roommate a mask.

"No answers?" Willow asked.

"Nothing."

And so they waited. Willow wanted to play Scrabble on their phones, but Kennedy's battery was running low.

Willow sighed dramatically. "This stinks."

"Yeah."

"What's the Bible have to say about stuff like this?"

Kennedy had grown used to Willow insulting religion for so long at first she thought she was joking. Her eyes alone proved Willow's question was earnest.

"I don't know. I guess there's Romans." She shifted in her seat. It was uncomfortable the way the mask made her talk so much louder than normal to keep her words from getting muffled. "It says all things work together for good for those who love God."

"Yeah? Like we're here on a hospital lockdown, and while we're stuck here, I'm gonna end up meeting the love of my life? That sort of good?"

Kennedy smiled. "No, it could just mean he's teaching us patience." Wasn't there a verse like that in James? Or maybe it was one of the Peters. A verse about being thankful for your trials because they mature your faith. Why couldn't she have done a better job memorizing Scripture and keeping track of all those references?

Willow crossed her arms. "I could think of less painful ways to learn patience if you asked me."

Kennedy glanced around. At least hospitals were interesting places to people-watch if you found yourself stuck in one. Across from her, a toddler in an adult-sized mask was sleeping on his mother's lap. His legs were curled up until he was no bigger than a beach ball, and his hands were tucked down by his knees. He looked almost cherubic. A middle-aged man was talking to the security guard in front of the ER entrance. Kennedy couldn't tell if he was animated because he was angry or worried.

She looked behind her. Nipah was one of those diseases that made people contagious a few days before they developed symptoms. How many people weren't sick now but would be by the end of the week? Would Kennedy be among them? How long was this lockdown going to take?

"So what else does God have to say about this sort of stuff?" Willow asked.

Kennedy had to get used to her roommate taking spiritual matters seriously for a change. "Well, I guess he tells us not to be anxious. Have you read the verse about the birds? He says that not even a sparrow falls to the ground apart from God's will and that we're worth a lot more in God's sight than they are."

"So if we die of some horrific disease, it's only because God wanted us to?"

Kennedy sighed. "I guess that just about sums it up."

They were silent for a few minutes before Willow took off her mask. "Can they really keep us here like this?" she asked in a whisper. "I mean, legally and stuff?"

Kennedy shrugged. "I guess if they have a good enough reason."

Willow shook her head. "This country is so messed up. You know, this whole Nipah virus probably already has some homeopathic cure, but they're not telling us about it because it doesn't profit the big corporations. It all comes down to money in the end. Like that couple who nearly got sent to jail because they refused chemo for their son." She shook her head. "Wicked insane. What do you think?"

The question caught Kennedy off guard. "About chemotherapy?" Her mind was still reeling after her brief encounter with Dominic and the mysterious lockdown. She couldn't even remember when they started talking about cancer.

"No, about sickness in general. And medicine. I mean, aren't there a lot of religious folks who deny medical care because they just assume God's going to heal them and that's that? Is that in the Bible or something?"

"No, I mean, it's just ..." Why couldn't she give a straight answer?

"But what about how Jesus healed so many people in ancient times? Is that something he still can do today? Or does he just leave it up to the doctors and nurses now?"

Kennedy knew Dominic would have a better answer for her. They'd talked about the power of prayer and healing before. Dominic knew a little girl who'd been hit by a drunk driver. The doctors thought she was completely brain-dead, but Dominic and the parents prayed over her, and within a few hours she woke up from her coma and eventually made a full recovery that left the medical community baffled. Of course God could still heal people in miraculous ways, but that still didn't explain how it worked or how he picked which Christians got divine intervention and which didn't.

"Well, it's definitely possible for God to heal someone," she began, but Willow's questions compounded too fast before she could answer any of them thoroughly.

"And what about those Christians who say God will cure anyone who has enough faith? Like Cameron Hopewell or whatever his name is, strutting around on TV shouting at people to be healed. Makes it out like if you go to a doctor or something you're not trusting God enough. Tells diabetics to go off their meds, that sort of thing. Is there something to that?"

"No, I mean, there's nothing wrong with seeking medical treatment. It's just ..." Why was she always fumbling her words like this?

"So it's not wrong to go to a doctor and take medicine."

"Not at all."

"But what about the dangerous drugs with all their horrible side effects and things like that? What's the Bible got to say about those?"

Kennedy didn't have a ready answer and would be surprised if any of the theologians in her contacts list would fare better on that one. "I guess it's up to each person to make the choice that seems best to them." It was a cop-out, but it was all she had to offer.

They were silent for a while longer. Kennedy hadn't stopped worrying about Carl. She wished she knew what was going on.

Willow had pulled the mask back over her face. She leaned back in her seat and asked, "So what are we supposed to do now?"

"Do?"

"Yeah. You know. Do. It's a verb. Means take action."

What did Willow expect? That Kennedy could snap her fingers and bring an end to the lockdown? That she could call up Dominic and tell him she and Willow wanted to go home? "I don't know."

"Well, what would your pastor or his wife do if they were out here? What do you think they're doing right now?"

"I'm sure they're back there praying together." Kennedy took a small slice of comfort at the thought of the Lindgrens' strong faith, but her emotions were clouded by her fears for Carl's health. Why hadn't Sandy given her more information? Kennedy should call, but her battery was nearly dead after all those messages she'd delivered to the prayer chain on the way to Providence. She'd seen enough hospital dramas with her mom to know a real quarantine could last several days. How long did it take for Nipah symptoms to develop? Where was her dad's WebMD recital when she needed it?

"So what is it they're praying for exactly? Do you just pray you won't get sick and then everything works out? I feel like a lot more Christians would be healthy if it were that simple."

Kennedy shook her head. "No, it's not that simple." She knew all too well there were some sicknesses you just couldn't pray away. How it all worked was a mystery to her and would probably remain so until the day she died.

Willow nudged her softly in the ribs. "Ok, so your pastor and his wife are praying. Doesn't that mean we should be doing it too?"

"Praying for what?"

"You're the one with all those years of Sunday-school-girl living under your belt. Why don't you tell me?"

Kennedy glanced around the crowded waiting room. "You want to pray right here? Like just drop our heads and start talking to God?"

She shrugged. "Unless you've got a better idea."

"No. Not really."

"Then let's have at it." Willow folded her hands and bowed her head like she did the night she prayed to be saved.

Kennedy shot one more nervous glance around and then decided if her brand-new baby Christian of a roommate could pray out in public, she could too. She pulled down her mask so she wouldn't have to feel like she was yelling and took in a deep breath, wondering how to start. How did you pray in a situation like this? What was there to say other than *your will be done*? Isn't that what was going to happen anyway? So why pray for anything else? When it came right down to it, why bother to pray at all?

To Kennedy's surprise, Willow started first. "Dear Jesus, hey thanks so much that we got Woong here in time to see his dad before they locked the doors. We hope that Carl's just fine. And please tell the hospital folks to let us leave. If people here are sick, we hope that you make them well. I guess that's all. Amen."

She looked up and raised an eyebrow at Kennedy. "You gonna pray, too?"

Kennedy unfolded her hands. "No, I think you covered everything."

Willow frowned. "Felt pretty short."

"I'm sure it was fine." She couldn't explain why her throat had chosen now of all times to threaten to close in on her and cut off her breath. Or why her heart decided to start racing as fast as the police officer had to drive that bus in *Speed*.

She stood up, thankful that her muscles could still support her weight. She was dizzy, but she could make it to the bathroom. She grabbed her phone. "Excuse me. I'll be back in just a sec."

Willow acted like she was about to stand up. "Where are you going? Something wrong?"

Kennedy held out her hand. "Yeah. Don't worry. I've just ... I have to pee. I'll be back soon."

"Sheesh, woman. You'd think you had a bladder the size of a ping-pong ball."

Kennedy didn't reply. She just hoped she'd make it to the bathroom before panic took complete control over her body.

Panting, choking, half-sobbing, she floundered almost blindly into the restroom. She sank onto one of the toilets, too paralyzed to even worry about germs. She fumbled with her phone, praying she wouldn't drop it into the bowl.

Please be there. Please be there.

She didn't bother to think about what time it might be right now in Yanji. There was only one voice she needed to hear.

"Kennedy? Everything all right?"

She sniffed loudly, thankful there wasn't anyone else in the bathroom with her.

"Daddy?" Her voice cracked, but she didn't care.

"What is it, princess? What's wrong?"

She bit her lip, praying for her cell phone to hold its charge for at least a few more minutes.

"What's wrong?" her dad repeated.

"You watching the news?" she asked in a shaky whisper.

"I've got Channel 2 up right here. Looks like there's something happening over at one of the hospitals. Providence? Is that near you?"

Snot dribbled down her nose. Tears raced down her cheeks. Her breath caught twice before she could hiccup out the next words.

"I'm here, Dad. I'm at the hospital right now. I'm in the middle of a lockdown."

CHAPTER 11

"Kennedy. Princess." Her father's voice was authoritative. Not a trace of panic. Not a trace of impatience as Kennedy wheezed and choked and tried desperately to keep from suffocating in the cramped bathroom stall. "Where are you right now? Where exactly?"

"In the bathroom," she managed to reply.

"Not good enough. What part of the hospital are you in?"

"The ER."

"What are you doing there?" Her dad spoke to her as if she were a preschooler practicing her animal sounds. *And what does the cow say?*

She sniffed. Something about her dad's authoritative tone grounded her. She tried to cling to whatever strength he was offering her from the other side of the planet. "Carl ... Something was wrong with Carl. Sandy called and said I should bring Woong here to see him."

"And what are Carl's symptoms? Does he have a fever? Swelling in the brain? Aches?"

"I don't know." Kennedy wiped her nose on a wad of scratchy toilet paper.

"Ok. So where's Woong? Is he there with you?"

"No. He's with his parents. We were just about to leave when they shut the doors." Her lungs spasmed as she tried to take in a pained breath. "We were just a foot away from the exit."

"Who's we?" her dad demanded. "Who are you there with?"

"Willow. I came here with Willow."

"She's not sick, is she?"

"No, we're both fine. But we're stuck here. And they're not giving us any answers or telling us when we'll be able to go."

"That's all right." How could her dad lie to her like that? This was the guy who was freaking out when some unnamed 72-year-old pig farmer in Bangladesh came down with the Nipah virus. He'd freaked out way back then, and now here she was, stuck in a hospital in the middle of an outbreak about to reach the level of global pandemic, and he was telling her she was fine.

"I don't know what's going on. They haven't told us anything."

"Is it the Nipah?" he asked. "Have you been exposed?"

"I don't know. I just came here so Woong could be with his dad." Tears slipped down her cheeks. She couldn't erase her brain's projected images of Carl, weak and sick in a faded hospital gown, faintly holding his son's hand. What was wrong with him? Would he be ok? She could almost endure the thought of being locked here if she knew he was all right.

"What about the other patients in the ER? What kind of symptoms have you seen there?"

"I don't know. I don't know anything." That's what made this entire scenario so unbearable. The uncertainty. When would they get released? What if they weren't sick yet but would catch the disease while they were all shut up in here like the prisoners in *Shawshank Redemption*?

"Ok. Well, hospitals get locked down for all kinds of reasons. Is it just the ER or the whole thing that's closed?"

"I think it's the whole thing."

"You think?"

She felt the edge of annoyance creep through her veins. Being angry at her dad was preferable to feeling so panicked and terrified. "How should I know? Nobody's telling us anything."

"Just calm down. Don't get so worked up if you can help it."

Don't get so worked up. He was the perfect person to tell her that. Mr. The-World-is-Ending. *Thanks, Dad. That's really helpful.*

"Take a deep breath," he instructed.

As if Kennedy weren't trying.

"Ok, listen to me. If this lockdown has something to do with the Nipah virus, if they're worried about infection, they're going to set up triage stations. Figure out who needs to be quarantined, who needs to be isolated, who may or may not have been exposed. That's what's going to happen if they think there's been some sort of outbreak. Understand?"

"Yeah."

"And you know how fast people end up getting sick, right? Perfectly fine and then bam, they're too sick to walk in half an hour's time. So you got to stay alert. Keep your eye on all the other patients there. Avoid getting close to anyone."

"I know." She wished she'd listened to her dad sooner, wished she hadn't ignored all his earlier advice.

"And I know Nipah's scary stuff, but remember it might not be that. There are plenty of other reasons hospitals go into lockdown."

"Like what?"

"Could be anything. Terrorist attack. Security breach. Armed gunman."

Did her dad honestly expect any of this information to be helpful?

"What you want to do is stay close to the people you think are in charge. Look around. Position yourself near the ones who are most likely to have the answers. And then just wait it out. Nearly all of these situations get resolved in less than twenty-four hours."

It was confirmed. Her dad would never be invited to give a motivational speech anywhere.

"Ok." At least she could breathe a little easier now. At least she knew what to look for. If this was some sort of quarantine, they'd separate them into groups. Isolate the sickest. Keep the healthy from getting exposed.

"Listen. Who do you know that you could call? Someone who might know what's going on? What about that journalist friend you've got? Do you have his number?"

"I don't remember." She didn't want to admit her phone was just a quarter of a bar away from dying. It had already beeped at her once.

"Think of people you know who might be able to tell you what's going on. Keep your phone right next to you. Don't waste your charge on games or anything like that. You never know how long this sort of thing will take to get resolved."

"All right." She was only listening to his words with half her mental energy. With the rest, she was begging God to keep the phone working until they were through with their conversation.

"I'm going to let you go now, princess. I'll call my lawyer friend. See if Jefferson knows anything about what's going on."

Kennedy couldn't figure out what information a Worcester attorney would have about a hospital lockdown, but she didn't ask. Maybe her dad just needed to feel useful. Feel like he was taking some sort of proactive measures.

Maybe she was more like him than she cared to admit.

"I love you, baby girl. You know that, right?"

"I love you too, Daddy."

"You take care now. And save your phone battery. I'll text you if I find out anything."

"Ok."

"Stay safe. Be smart."

"I will."

"Ok. Love you."

"You, too."

She sniffed and stared at the phone, thankful her battery had lasted through the entire conversation. She should write down her dad's number before it completely died. That way she could call him on Willow's phone if she needed to.

God, I just want to get out of here.

At least her breathing had calmed down. She wasn't hyperventilating anymore. She could do this. Walk back out to Willow. Give a smile. Pretend like everything was ok.

But was that what she should do? If Willow was open with her own struggles and doubts, shouldn't Kennedy try to be at least somewhat transparent? Then again, it's not like she was keeping her PTSD a secret. They'd talked about it just a few seconds before the lockdown.

No, Kennedy was doing what she needed to do. Get through the day without turning into a complete mess, a psychological puddle too pathetic to do anything. She just had to keep on functioning. That's all the victory she could expect at a time like this.

One minute at a time.

She went to the sink and washed her face, studying herself in the mirror to see if her eyes would betray her recent tears.

She jumped when her phone rang.

"Hello?"

"Kennedy, it's Dominic."

He cut her off when she started to ask about a dozen different questions at once.

"Listen to me. Listen very carefully. You might be in danger. You and

Willow need to get out of the ER and meet me at the ..."

She pressed the phone harder against her ear as if that would make her to hear better. "What? Where'd you go? What did you just say?"

Silence.

"Dominic?"

She stared at her phone.

Completely dead.

Kennedy bit her lip and hurried out of the bathroom.

It didn't matter anymore who could tell that she'd been crying.

CHAPTER 12

"Ok, just calm down," Willow whispered, "and tell me exactly what he said."

Kennedy tried to keep her voice low so the other people in the waiting room couldn't overhear. "He said we might not be safe in the ER, and we should go meet him somewhere."

"Where?"

"I don't know. I lost the call before he could tell me."

"So call him back."

"My phone's dead."

Willow pulled her cell out of her purse. "Then use mine."

"I don't know his number."

Willow sighed. "Ok, well, let's think through it then. If he said the ER wasn't safe, then maybe there's somewhere else we could go."

"Yeah, but what about the security guards? They're not letting anyone get anywhere."

"So maybe we just ask."

"You can't just walk up to a guard in the middle of a lockdown and say, 'Hey, I need to find my boyfriend. He's in another part of the hospital and I don't know where, but can you let me get past so I can try to find him?' It doesn't work like that."

Kennedy was sulking, but she didn't care. If God wanted her to be a good example of spiritual maturity for her roommate, he needed to stop throwing her into these situations where her life was constantly in danger.

Willow didn't respond. At first, Kennedy thought she was just being moody too, but then she noticed her staring somewhere past Kennedy's shoulder.

"What are you looking at?"

"Holy cr ... I mean, *holy cow*. Don't turn around right now, but some guy with gorgeous hair just walked into the waiting room."

Kennedy rolled her eyes, but something about seeing her roommate fawning over a man made her feel a little better. Some things didn't change. Even in the midst of a hospital lockdown, life went on.

It always would.

"Man, you should see him. No, don't turn yet, he's looking here. Oh my L ... I mean, *oh man*. He's walking this way. He's looking right at me. He's coming straight over here." Willow ran her hands frantically over her magenta highlights.

"Hey, Kennedy. What are you doing here?"

"You mean you actually know him?" Willow hissed.

Kennedy turned around. "Oh, hi, Nick." She glanced at the large bandage on his head and momentarily forgot how big a fool her roommate was making of herself. "What happened to you? Are you ok?"

He let out a jocular laugh that carried through the entire waiting room and pointed at his bandage. "Oh, yeah. Got this defending some little old lady at the grocery store."

He sat down and stretched out his hand to Willow. "Hi, I'm Nick."

Willow stared for several seconds until Kennedy wondered if she'd forgotten her own name. "This is Willow," she answered for her. "She's my roommate."

"Hi, Willow."

Her hand was still in Nick's. "Oh. My. Goodness. That *hair*."

Nick laughed and pulled his hand away. "Oh, that. Yeah. I get that a lot."

"It's so long." Willow reached out her hand but stopped. "Can I? I mean, may I ..."

Nick shrugged. "Sure. Go ahead."

Willow picked up one of his dreads and ran her fingers all the way down to the tip. "That is the most wicked awesome thing I've seen in my entire life."

"What are you doing here?" Kennedy asked.

Willow still had his hair in her hand. "Yeah, what was that you said about a little old lady? Was that just a joke?"

"No. I'm dead serious." Nick unzipped his coat.

"Good grief." Willow stared. "Does that shirt make you a Christian?"

Nick chuckled. "No, I'm pretty sure only God can do that."

"Then does it mean you're a Christian?" Willow stared at the praying stick figure on Nick's chest.

"Nick's the youth pastor at Carl and Sandy's church," Kennedy told her.

"Oh. My. Goodness."

Kennedy was certain that beneath that sanitation mask, Willow's mouth was hanging wide open. "So what happened to you?" Kennedy asked again.

"Well, I went to go get groceries at Rory's, and like I told you earlier, nearly everything was gone. But they had a few things left, and I got my basket filled, but there was this little old lady. I mean, she probably wasn't even five foot tall. She had gotten the last few cans of chili beans. And these two thugs, I kid you not, they knocked her over just to get at her shopping basket. So I jumped in and ..." He shrugged and pointed to his bandaged forehead. "Ten stitches and a possible minor concussion later, here I am. Sorry I didn't get the car back to you on time."

"That's ok," Kennedy assured him.

"You were so heroic," Willow breathed.

Nick shrugged again. "Yeah, well, you should see the other guys."

"Really?" Willow asked. "Are they that bad off?"

"Who? The other guys? No, they walked away without a scratch." He grinned broadly. "But at least the little old lady got her chili beans."

Kennedy hadn't realized until now how nearly everyone in the waiting room was staring at them. Had they been talking that loudly? She'd been so amused watching her roommate's reaction to meeting Nick that she'd almost forgotten for a moment that they were in the middle of a lockdown.

Apparently, Nick was even more oblivious and kept chatting away. "What about you two? Everything ok here?" He pointed to his face. "What's up with the masks?"

Kennedy didn't even know where to begin explaining everything. "We were just bringing Woong here to see Carl."

"Carl? Isn't he still away with Sandy?"

"Not anymore. They cut their trip short when school got cancelled, then on the way home Sandy called and said she was bringing him here."

Nick's face dropped. "Why? What's wrong?"

Kennedy shrugged. "Wish I knew."

"Is it serious?"

"I don't know any more than that."

"So you two are just staying here until he gets out?"

"No," Kennedy answered. "We were on our way out when the lockdown started."

"Lockdown?" Nick glanced around the waiting room, apparently taking in the security guards near all the doors for the first time.

"You didn't hear?" Kennedy asked.

He chuckled nervously. "Truth be told, I don't handle needles all that well. I didn't really exactly pass out, but I'm not sure how with it I was while they were stitching me up."

Willow reached out and rubbed the top of his knee. "You poor thing. That's terrible."

Nick sighed melodramatically. "So what's going on then? What's this lockdown thing all about?"

"Nobody knows for sure," Willow piped up. She seemed eager to be the one leading the discussion for a change. "We think it might have something to do with ..."

Kennedy had been distracted watching Willow and Nick's interactions and hadn't noticed the security officer coming up behind her. She had no idea he was there until he cleared his throat and tapped her on the shoulder.

"Excuse me, Miss."

"Yes?" She turned around. What was wrong? Were they in trouble for talking about the lockdown?

"Are you Kennedy Stern?"

Her stomach dropped as if she were in freefall on a rollercoaster. How did he know her?

"Yes," she answered tentatively. Her face heated up with the certainty that everyone in the waiting room was staring at her.

The security officer kept his voice low. "I need you to come with me, please."

"Is something wrong?" She stood up. "What's this all about?"

"Follow me," he repeated.

Kennedy didn't look back but knew that if she did, she'd see the worried glances of Willow and Nick following her as she shuffled behind the man in uniform and headed out of the ER.

CHAPTER 13

"Where are we going?" Kennedy's voice was timid. Afraid. At least she could breathe. Everything would be just fine as long as she kept on breathing.

Please, Jesus ...

"Just come with me." The security guard walked several paces ahead. Kennedy had to scurry to keep up. Why had she worn her little heeled sandals and not something more practical? Then again, when she left the Lindgrens', she'd only been thinking about making it to Providence fast. She hadn't stopped to worry about shoes fit for racing down empty hospital corridors.

"Is everything ok?" What kind of a stupid question was that? Nothing was ok. That's what happens when you're stuck in a hospital lockdown in the middle of a horrific epidemic. Why hadn't she taken her dad more seriously? Why had she breezed through the past few weeks taking her health for granted, refusing to think of all those people getting infected?

Folks were dying. Not just in far-off reaches of the globe. In New York. Florida. Right in her backyard in Boston itself. The Nipah virus didn't care if you were young or old, strong or weak. It didn't pay any attention to your medical history, your immunization record.

Kennedy was the queen of germophobes. Did her little bottle of Germ-X delude her into thinking she'd march through this whole epidemic unscathed?

She thought about different outbreaks she'd studied in history class. The black plague. More than decimated the world's population. Typhoid Mary. Infecting scores of individuals before doctors forced her into quarantine. Lived completely alone for decades before she finally died of pneumonia. More recently there'd been SARS, swine flu ... Kennedy had heard about all of those but never knew anyone who actually got sick from any of them.

Maybe that's where her little bubble of perceived invincibility came from. She'd never been seriously ill. Of course, there were all the typical childhood conditions. Colds. Stomach viruses. An ear infection or two.

She'd had chicken pox, though she'd been so young she had no memories of it. Is that why she assumed she could blitz through this whole Nipah scare without having to worry herself about it?

She glanced at the hallways lined with closed doors, wondering how far she'd have to go before she'd learn what she was doing here. Was she infected? Did they suspect she was a carrier? Had Woong's teacher tested positive for Nipah? Were they quarantining everyone who was possibly exposed? How long would they keep her here? And what about Willow? Had she put her roommate in danger?

She hated hospitals. Hated the bleached, antiseptic smells that only vaguely masked the odor of vomit and blood and bodily fluids. She hated the way hospital air made her skin crawl, as if every single germ in a ten-foot radius swarmed her like a mob of hungry mosquitoes. It was ironic, really. Before starting college, she'd pictured herself in that white gown, stethoscope hanging from her neck like a mantle, walking stately from one needy patient to another. Now she just hoped she could make it down a single hallway without turning into a hyperventilating mess.

Her counselor said that maybe Kennedy's academic drive was related to her trauma experiences. That maybe she threw herself into her studies to combat how helpless she'd felt watching a young girl nearly hemorrhage to death on a grimy bathroom floor at the start of her freshman year. It sounded logical, but he hadn't met Kennedy before the PTSD. She'd been like this for as long as she could remember. Always been a control freak. An overachiever. With or without the panic attacks, she'd always pushed herself past her breaking point. Anything for the grade. For the sense of accomplishment. That's how she'd gotten into Harvard's early acceptance medical program to begin with.

She was destined to become one of the nation's top physicians. Except she couldn't stand five minutes in a hospital.

Who ever said God didn't have a sense of humor?

If anything, her disdain for hospitals started over a decade ago, at her grandmother's bedside as she lay dying from lung cancer. Kennedy had been so young. So naïve. So certain that what the Bible and her Sunday school teachers always told her was true. If she prayed, God would answer.

And so she'd prayed. So fervently. With that impossible to imitate faith of a child. A child who foolishly believed that if she trusted hard enough, God would always give her what she asked for. It's not like she was praying for a pony to ride or a castle to live in. She just wanted her grandma to be healed. To be able to go back to her own home. Enjoy her evenings with *Wheel of Fortune* and *Jeopardy* and her cans of plain black beans she heated up for dinner. To be there every Christmas and every summer break in that beautifully quaint little cottage in upstate New York. Far from the city, from traffic. Kennedy's perfect little refuge. Where she'd catch dragonflies in the summer and race her dad down giant sledding hills in the winter.

All she'd wanted was for Grandma to stay alive. It wasn't fair she'd gotten lung cancer in the first place. She'd never smoked a day in her life. Hated cigarettes. But still came down with the dreaded disease after spending forty years married to a chain-smoking addict.

In the end, it's what killed her. Killed her in spite of Kennedy's prayers. In spite of Kennedy's perfect, childlike faith. In spite of all the Bible promises Kennedy read and claimed and called her own.

Grandma still died, but not until after six months of torment. Six months of torture. With her hair falling out in clumps, her entire body hooked up to tubes and machines that reminded Kennedy of some scene from *Star Trek: First Contact*. No wonder there were those parents who refused chemo for their kids. Six months while the medicine ravaged her grandma's body. Poisoned her blood. It shrunk one of the tumors for a few months. Enough time for Kennedy to assume her prayers really had worked.

Until a routine checkup showed the tumor had grown. And spread. And by then, there was nothing to do but make hospice arrangements.

And still Kennedy held onto faith that God would heal her grandma. Held onto that faith until the morning her grandma died, surrounded by family, covered in tubes, her body shrunken to nearly half her pre-diagnosis weight.

Is it any wonder Kennedy hated hospitals?

She let out her breath. This line of thinking wasn't going to get her anywhere. *Come on.* She gave herself the best pep talk she could muster. *Think about something else and snap yourself out of this.* The last thing the guard needed was a hysterical basket case on his hands.

She bit her lip, focusing on the pain it caused. She glanced around her, desperately hoping her eyes would land on something to ground her. Something to snap her brain back to the present. Her counselor had given her clear instructions when she felt a panic attack rising up in her chest. Name four things you can see. Four things you can hear. Focus on her senses, not on her irrational fear.

It made perfect sense on paper. Harder to do when your lungs have already decided to seize shut on you. Harder to do when your breath is so short and choppy your brain's overcome with dizziness until you're certain you're about to suffocate. When your heart's racing so fast you wonder if you're about to become the first sophomore in the history of Harvard University to die from cardiac arrest.

She bit her lip even harder when the officer unlocked a small room at the farthest end of the impossibly long hallway. Her thoughts flashed back once more to Typhoid Mary, locked up for decades to keep from infecting anyone around her.

That couldn't be what was happening to her. She was a citizen. She had rights. Her dad knew lawyers ...

"Kennedy? Thank God they found you."

At the sound of the welcomed voice, she rushed toward Dominic who held out his arms to her.

"It's ok," he whispered. "You're safe here."

CHAPTER 14

"What's going on?" Kennedy had lost track of how many times by now Dominic had seen her cry. He'd seen when her panic was at its worst. She was too relieved to find him here to feel embarrassed. It was one of Dominic's greatest strengths, what made him such an effective chaplain. He had such a calming presence. Even when he wasn't whispering his powerful prayers over her, Kennedy got the sense he was interceding for her anyway. The impression that when she was with him, her spirit and body were surrounded by an extra layer of heavenly protection.

"It's ok." He stroked her hair and then led her to a small couch. She glanced around and realized they were in the same small conference room where she'd met him a full year ago.

"What's going on?" she asked again.

"Shh." He patted her hand and sat down beside her. "I can't stay long. I just wanted to make sure you got out of the ER."

Kennedy glanced at the door and discovered the security guard who led her here was already gone. "What about everyone else? Willow's still there."

"It's going to be ok." He was sitting next to her. So close. She leaned her forehead on his shoulder, wishing she could stay like this forever. Or at least until the lockdown ended and everyone was able to go home safely.

"What about my friends? Are they going to get exposed?"

"Exposed?" He furrowed his brow. "To what?"

"The Nipah." She paused, studying his features. "Isn't that what this is about? Lockdown? The epidemic?" Her stomach sank like oil droplets falling in her roommate's lava lamp. "It's something else?"

Dominic glanced at his watch. "No, the lockdown has nothing to do with Nipah. At least not directly."

"Then what is it?" She tried to keep her body from trembling, praying to God he wouldn't answer back with his usual rhetoric about confidentiality.

Another furtive glance at his watch. "Have you followed the case of the Robertson boy? The ones whose parents wanted to deny chemotherapy treatments?"

She nodded. "Yeah, I've heard a little about it."

"Well, Timothy Robertson is a patient here. His mom brought him in two days ago. Agreed to submit to the court order. But his dad's not too happy about that. About an hour ago, he attacked the nurses who were transporting his son to radiology. Grabbed the boy and made a run for it. Got him within thirty feet of the exit to the parking garage before security stopped them. The boy's back in his room safe and sound with his mother now, but the father is still somewhere in the hospital. Apparently, he's got a history of mental instability and could be quite dangerous."

"You mean like he's armed or something?"

"I wish it were that simple." Dominic shook his head slowly.

"Then what kind of danger do you mean?"

"I mean that as we speak, the bomb squad members of the SWAT team are sweeping the ER for explosives."

"What?"

"They found evidence in Brian Robertson's house that he's been making bombs. They also found detailed blueprints of the ER."

Kennedy hadn't realized until now how small the room felt. Small and suffocating. Where did all the oxygen go? "So why don't they just evacuate?"

"This information doesn't leave the room, but one of the patients brought into the ER today has what's almost definitely a case of Nipah. Once we get this bomb thing under control, we need to know exactly who got exposed and for how long so we can keep a finger on it all."

"Wait, have you seen Carl? Is that what he's doing here?"

Dominic shook his head sadly. He looked so tired. "I don't know. I didn't have time to check on him before everything else exploded. I mean ..." He cleared his throat. "Well, you know what I mean." His pager beeped, and he frowned at the screen. "I hate to do this to you, but I need to hit the ground running again. There's going to be some very scared people in the ER, and I've got to be there for them. I just couldn't stand the thought of you being in harm's way."

"What about my friends?"

He frowned. "I told them to find you and Willow and bring you both back here, but the message must have gotten garbled. We're going to do everything we can. Right now, we don't know if there's a genuine threat or not. I just want you to stay here and wait to hear from me, all right?"

Kennedy nodded. "My phone's dead."

Dominic's eyes softened but he didn't smile. "If you had a dollar for every time you let your battery die ..."

Kennedy was in no mood for teasing, no matter how well intentioned. "Be safe, ok?"

"I will." He stood up and then stopped. "You be careful too." He leaned down and let his lips brush against her forehead. It was the first time he'd ever kissed her. Kennedy just wished they weren't in the middle of a hospital lockdown with a bomb scare and Nipah outbreak so that she could enjoy the moment.

"I'll be back soon, Lord-willing."

Kennedy didn't like the ominous heaviness behind his words. She forced a smile.

"Be careful," she called after him, but he was already out the door.

CHAPTER 15

Kennedy sank back in the couch, breathless and light-headed. At least she wasn't hyperventilating. Not yet.

Here she was, far enough removed from the ER so Dominic wasn't worried about a bomb blast reaching her, but how was that supposed to bring her any comfort? Everyone she cared about, every single one of her friends, was in that emergency room. The Lindgrens. Willow and Nick. And now Dominic. She squeezed her eyes shut. What she wouldn't give for a phone charger. Call her dad. Let him know what was happening.

Timothy Robertson. Kennedy hadn't followed the boy's case very thoroughly. Mostly, she'd heard details from others. Carl decrying the government overreach in depriving a couple of their parental rights. Willow was sympathetic from her homeopathic, anti-vaxxer philosophy on medicine, but the media was talking about the family as if they were negligent idiots at best and mentally unsound nutcases at worst. What was the truth? And how in the world could Kennedy expect to get to the bottom of any of it?

She couldn't. That wasn't her job anyway. Her job was to wait here for Dominic. Pray that her friends would be ok, that they wouldn't die in some explosion or contract the Nipah virus while sitting it out in a waiting room full of potential carriers.

Her mind raced over what Dominic told her about a patient brought in earlier that day with Nipah symptoms. What if that was Carl? He couldn't die. He was so healthy. So vigorous. He had children. Grandchildren. A God-ordained ministry. He couldn't just catch some stupid disease and leave all that behind. What about his family? What would they do without him? Even worse, what if Sandy and Woong were exposed now too? What if they all ...

No. She couldn't let her mind dwell on all those horrific possibilities. Seize her thoughts. Take them captive. That's what she had to do.

Her conversation with Willow earlier about God watching over the birds got an old hymn stuck in her head. *His eye is on the sparrow.* She couldn't remember the last time she'd heard it sung in church. In fact, the only reason she knew the words was because it was on the soundtrack of one of the *Sister Act* movies. She tried to let the lyrics lead her into a spirit of worship.

She'd been working on her prayer life all semester, practicing the mental focus that was so hard to maintain in the midst of a busy, chaotic college schedule. She and Sandy talked about it quite a bit, and Sandy had been sharing some prayer tips with her, ways to keep her mind from getting distracted while she prayed. Keeping a journal was probably the most helpful thing Kennedy started. She didn't always write out her prayers verbatim. Sometimes she just jotted down short lists, but even then she found the act of putting pen to paper kept her mind far more focused than it was whenever she sat down without any plan and simply tried to talk to God.

Unfortunately, she didn't have her journal here. And her brain was far too scattered, far too anxious to allow for that quiet communion with the Lord that she'd been trying to achieve in her regular prayer times.

She stood up, hoping that pacing might help channel her focus just a little bit. Sandy sometimes prayed out loud, but even though Kennedy figured it might help keep her thoughts from wandering, she couldn't get over her crippling self-consciousness to try it. Instead, she made a compromise and started mouthing the words to what she hoped would be an effective prayer for her friends in the emergency room.

The difficult part was knowing what to pray for. Most of her energy was spent begging God to get them all out of there alive. Kennedy couldn't wait to leave the hospital. Hopefully, she wouldn't be coming back for a very long time. Maybe not until she was ready to start her residency. She'd had enough drama for the immediate future. She sighed, wondering if hospitals would always bring this sense of heaviness or if she'd get used to it once she started working in one. There were other places for doctors to put their skills to use after graduating med school. She sometimes thought about medical missions, about all the developing countries and the physicians who traveled the world serving others. Of course, she'd have to pay off her med school bills somehow, and volunteering her time while she trotted across the globe probably wasn't the best way to work off student debt. She had time to figure out all those details later, but ...

Kennedy stopped herself. Wasn't she supposed to be praying? No wonder she was such a failure in her spiritual life. She couldn't even hold a five-minute conversation with the Lord.

She sighed, remembering Sandy's admonition to be gentle with herself. *Sometimes those distractions are what God's telling us to pray about most.* But Kennedy couldn't believe that God would expect her to pray about student loans she hadn't even started to accumulate while her best friend, her boyfriend, and her pastor's family were all in danger of getting blown to pieces.

She'd just have to try again.

"Dear God." She whispered the words this time, hoping that hearing her words spoken would keep her from getting off track again. "I pray that you watch over ..."

She stopped. Was that someone coughing? Her eyes shot around the room and landed on a skinny closet. It didn't look large enough to hold more than a broom. Was she just making things up?

"Dear God," she tried again, but this time her voice was so quiet she couldn't even hear herself. "I pray that you'd watch over me while ..."

Another cough. Kennedy froze halfway between the closet and the exit, her mind too stunned to react. Her body stood frozen, ready to protect herself or ready to run away but unable to decide which she would need to do first.

She braced herself in the ready stance she'd learned in her self-defense class as the closet door swung open. Her eyes focused on the barrel of a gun before they made out the features of the man holding it.

"Hands up," he ordered. His voice was nearly as quiet as hers had been while she was trying to pray. He waved the gun in her direction. "Step away from that door. Slow and easy."

Kennedy had no choice but to obey.

CHAPTER 16

"I don't want to hurt you. Got that? The last thing I want to do is hurt you." He took a step closer to Kennedy.

She hurried behind the couch. Anywhere to put more distance, more obstacles between herself and her intruder.

He locked the deadbolt of the conference room. "Listen, you don't have to be afraid." He slid a small loveseat in front of the door as a barricade. "I'm not planning to hurt anyone."

He sounded so earnest. Like he was scared of himself. So why did he have a gun?

"What's your name?" He nodded at the couch. "You can sit down. We're going to be here a while, I'm guessing. May as well get comfortable."

Finding a cozy seat was the last thing on Kennedy's mind.

"Who are you?" he asked. "What are you doing here?"

She ran through all of her dad's stupid crisis training lectures. Had any of them prepared her for this?

"My name's Kennedy Stern. I'm a college student at Harvard." There. Give him details to prove that she was a flesh-and-blood human. Not some sacrifice or human shield he could hide behind.

"Harvard, eh?" He raised his eyebrows. "Impressive. What're you studying?"

"Biology." She couldn't raise her eyes to his. Hated the thought of that gun in his hand. Couldn't find anywhere to focus her gaze. Wasn't she supposed to be praying?

"Oh, yeah? Premed?" She nodded, and he let out a little scoff. "Be a doctor, save the world? Is that the goal?"

She didn't reply.

"Let me guess. You're really smart, but you've got something of a bleeding-heart complex, so you're going into medicine to improve the lives of your patients. Did I get that about right?"

She glanced at the locked door. Someone would find her. Dominic would come to check on her. All she had to do was stay calm. Stay focused.

His eye is on the sparrow, and I know he watches me ...

The man shrugged. "I guess you're young enough not to know any better." He sat down on the opposite side of the couch, keeping a full cushion length between them. "Doctors. Thinking you can play God. Thinking you alone possess the power to choose who's going to be healed and who isn't."

He lifted his eyes to hers and held her gaze. "Do you know who I am?"

She had a good suspicion but still hadn't found her voice.

"I'm Brian Robertson. My son Timothy, you've heard about him in the news maybe."

She nodded slightly.

"I don't want to hurt anybody." His voice sounded reassuring, but he still hadn't let go of his weapon. "I swear, I don't want to hurt you." There was something earnest in his voice. Something that made Kennedy feel like he needed to convince her. He shook his head. "I'm so sorry. You must be terrified." He slid his gun into the holster and reached for a bottle of water from the coffee table. "Need a drink? Go on. Take it. It's perfectly safe. I haven't even opened it."

Kennedy reached out. Hoped he didn't see the way her whole body trembled.

"Drink it," he ordered again. "You'll feel better. Man, I must have really terrified you. I hope you'll forgive me."

Kennedy took a few small sips from the bottle, felt the cool water slip down her throat.

"That better?" he asked.

"A little."

"Good. See? I'm trying to help. Just like you becoming a doctor. You and me both, we're just trying to heal people. Know what I mean? It's just that only one of us is doing it God's way."

Kennedy stared. Wondered how long it would take before Dominic realized she was trapped in here. He was a man of prayer. A man full of the Holy Spirit. Couldn't God tell him she was in trouble? Tell him to come back to the conference room and check on her? Dominic was the kind of believer who would listen to that sort of thing. Follow those promptings, those Holy Spirit urges.

Please, God. Tell him to come back.

"So you know why I'm here?" Brian leaned back in his seat and stretched his arm across the back of the couch.

"I'm guessing it has something to do with your son."

He nodded. "My wife and me, we love that kid to death. Didn't get pregnant until I was forty-one. Shannon, she was thirty-eight. We'd tried everything by then. Almost given up. Turns out all we needed to do was stop doubting and believe. Believe that God would give us the child he promised. And he did. When our little Timmy came to us — you've never met a better baby. I swear, you've never met a better little boy." He stared past Kennedy's shoulder. "Do you remember your first day of grade school?"

"Not that well."

"Know what our Timmy was doing the first day of school? Having his third MRI. Know where he lost his first tooth? Right here at Providence. Peds floor. Know where he spent his sixth birthday? The hospital cafeteria. His aunt and cousin came and we ate plain rice with raisins before wheeling him back up to the oncology ward of the Children's Hospital. Think that's the kind of life any little boy deserves?"

Kennedy shook her head. If she kept on agreeing with Brian, if she kept him from getting upset, this whole scenario might end peacefully.

He frowned. "Not the kind of life he deserves at all. Which is why last summer, Shannon and I took him to a Cameron Hopewell crusade. You know him? Gift of healing. He's the one who told us God would cure our son, but he wanted to do it without the aid of Western medicine. That's the only way God would get all the glory. So we told the oncologist we were done. Done with the tests, done with the chemo, done with the poison they were drip-feeding him through those IVs. We believed God was going to heal our son, and he was going to do it through natural remedies and the power of prayer." He let out a mirthless laugh. "Three hundred thousand dollars in lawyer fees later, and you know what? Here we are. Right back where we started."

"That's got to be really hard."

"Know what Timmy told Shannon he wished for last Christmas? He told her he wished God would come down and carry him off to heaven so he wouldn't have to hurt anymore."

Kennedy bit her lip.

"What kind of monsters do this to a family? Do this to a child? Bishop Hopewell didn't say alternative medicine was out. He just said no more radiation. No more chemotherapy. It's not like we've been negligent. We took Timmy to several clinics, plunked down fifty grand for one consultation with the country's most renowned naturopath. We had another virtual consult set up with an herbal oncology expert in Switzerland. He's cured over a dozen cases just like Timmy's. I don't see all those other parents getting lined up and fined. I don't see judges threatening to remove their children from their homes, land them in state custody." He let out a heavy sigh. "You ever know anyone with cancer?"

"Yeah, my grandma."

"She die of it?"

"Uh-huh." She stared at a painting behind Brian's shoulder. The portrait was of some stuffy-looking businessman, maybe one of the hospital's founders or patrons.

"Did your grandma get chemo? Radiation?"

Kennedy nodded.

"And still died, huh?"

Another nod.

Brian lowered his head. "I'm sorry to hear that."

"I'm sorry for your son, too," Kennedy whispered.

"You must think I'm a horrible person."

She searched his face, hunting for clues that he was trying to trap her. She only saw pained earnestness. "No, I don't think that." She knew what was happening. Brian was trying to prey on her feelings of helplessness. Trying to convince her that he was doing the right thing. It was a classic case of Stockholm syndrome. Cognitive dissonance morphing into misplaced sympathies.

"Well, you have kids one day, maybe you'll understand. Heaven forbid they have to go through what my little Timmy has."

Kennedy didn't know how to respond.

"It just doesn't make sense. You've got heroin addicts, prostitutes, abusive drunks — they all get to keep their kids. Abused children falling through the cracks in the system because someone passes one drug screen or takes one two-hour anger management seminar. But we're the negligent ones. We're the ones who would lose custody of our kid unless we bring him here, strap him to a gurney, listen to him scream his little heart out while nurses poke and prod his veins. It's a test. I kept telling my wife God was going to test us, but she couldn't stand the thought of Timmy being taken away from us, no matter what Bishop Hopewell said. In the court's mind, we're the bad parents. We're the ones who don't know what's best for our child. We're the religious nutcases who would rather see our son cured by the Holy Spirit, who heals completely and fully and doesn't leave horrific side effects. But we're told that we have to accept their poison, that if we don't consent to chemo and radiation, not only will our son die, but he'll die in the custody of foster parents while we rot in jail for neglect."

Kennedy's plan of placating Brian wasn't working. She had to calm him down. "I remember my grandma wondering if it was worth going through another round of treatments." Her voice was shaky, but she ignored the fear in her gut. "By that point, the doctors said it wouldn't do much other than buy her a few more months. But she was so uncomfortable the whole time. I think she did it for her kids though. They wanted her to hold on a little longer."

Brian nodded. "That's pretty common. That's because doctors can't heal. No offense to you, but you may as well accept it right now. Doctors don't cure. They treat a few symptoms, rack up the big bucks, and that's it. You believe in God?" he asked.

She nodded, thankful to see his shoulders relax slightly even though she wasn't equipped to jump into the middle of a theological debate. That was a calling for someone like Dominic, someone who'd studied up on the issues and had all the right answers to offer. She was ready to change the subject when Brian asked, "What religion are you?"

"Oh." She felt her face heat up and hated herself for it. Didn't the Bible tell her to be ready at any moment to explain her faith to those who asked? Of course, she'd never expected to be asked by someone who'd been pointing a gun at her face just a few minutes earlier. "I'm a Christian." She tried to slow down her breathing. Why did that make her so nervous to admit?

He nodded. "Born again, Bible believing, all that stuff?"

She nodded. "I guess so."

"So you know exactly what I'm talking about. How our Savior healed people by faith. How faith — believing the Holy Spirit dwells inside you — can cure even the most fatal diseases. That's what we've been trying to teach Timmy. He's young, of course, but sometimes it's that childlike faith that makes the difference. You know what I mean? Jesus talks about it all the time. The faith of a child, it's strong enough to move mountains."

Kennedy wasn't sure he was quoting the passage right, but she didn't have it memorized and wouldn't have had the guts to correct him even if she did.

Brian's voice was animated. "The Bible talks about it all over the place. *Call on the elders, and the prayers offered up in faith will raise the sick to life.*"

Another reference Kennedy wasn't sure if he was botching or not. It sounded slightly familiar, but she wouldn't have even known where to look it up in the Bible if she had one with her.

"That's what it is my wife and I were trying to get that judge to understand. It's not only the fact that these treatments are harmful to our son. It's that it undermines whatever faith we're hoping to instill in him. We took him to meet Cameron Hopewell at two different crusades. The bishop told us Timmy would be cured, but we couldn't go back to the oncologists. That's what he said. God wanted to cure our son, but he wanted to be the one who got the glory for it. And by bringing him back here, by accepting the drugs and radiation and all that, it's like spitting in God's face after the healing he promised us."

Kennedy was lost on a theological level, but at least Brian sounded sincere. Or was that the cognitive dissonance playing tricks with her head? The Stockholm syndrome. Making her believe he was sympathetic since being trapped with a loving, wise father who just wanted what was best for his child was easier to accept than being trapped with a desperate, armed father who was also a raving lunatic.

In the end, it didn't matter what Kennedy thought of Brian or his son Timothy or the family court's order to submit to chemotherapy or relinquish parental rights.

It didn't matter because in the end, it was still Brian who had that gun, and Kennedy was sitting beside him, praying to God and hoping to heaven that he wouldn't decide to use it.

CHAPTER 17

"You ever watch faith healers on TV?" Brian asked after a few moments.

The question startled her. "Faith healers?"

"You know, Bishop Hopewell, others like him. Praying for the sick, curing them right there in front of thousands of witnesses."

"No. I've never watched them do that."

"They get a bad rap because they charge money for their events. As if any other Christian minister doesn't have the right to earn their living by their work. I don't see them complaining about Christian authors charging a fair price for their books, do you? Or pastors asking their congregations for a monthly paycheck. But Cameron Hopewell charges a hundred dollars for one of his healing handkerchiefs that he's personally prayed over, and people throw a fit. Say he's a charlatan. You know why he charges that much money, don't you?"

Kennedy figured greed and gullibility had quite a bit to do with it, but Brian was ready with an answer of his own.

"Faith. Just like Jesus turned out the crowds who didn't have enough faith to see Jairus's daughter raised up to life. The only people he wanted around were the people he knew actually expected the miracle to happen. So you ask someone to believe that God will use a healing handkerchief to cure their disease, and if they're willing to pay that hundred dollars, it shows they have enough faith for that healing to work. You go around sending free handkerchiefs to everybody, you get all the folks who don't have enough faith, so of course they aren't going to get the same results. Not to mention you go bankrupt and can't continue on in your work for the Lord.

"It's scientific fact. You can appreciate that. That's why patients receiving a placebo still show signs of improvement. Because they believe the medicine's going to help them, and that faith is what brings them healing. They've done experiments on it, you know. If the patient has to pay for a placebo, or even if they're simply told that the drug is expensive, there's a higher chance of recovery. Just from a sugar pill. It's not wacky science. It's faith, pure and simple. You have faith, you find your healing. Just like Jesus talks about in the New Testament."

Kennedy didn't know what to say. She'd read some of those same studies about placebos, but she'd never thought about it in the context of Christian faith or miraculous healings.

"You think I'm crazy, don't you?" Brian asked.

Kennedy forced herself to shake her head. Reminded herself that in this situation it was perfectly acceptable to lie to keep herself out of danger. "You're not crazy. You're just a father trying to look out for his son."

He sighed. "I never expected it to come to this. Look at me. A year ago, I was bringing in three hundred grand a year. Three hundred stinking grand. Does that sound like the kind of father who would lose his son to state custody? Does that sound like the kind of father who would bring a gun into a crowded hospital, who would risk ..." His voice caught.

Kennedy tried to steer the conversation away from his schemes. She tried to think of something to say. Anything that would get Brian's mind off of his gun or any other plans he'd made. "How is your son doing right now? I mean, how is his health?"

Brian let out his breath in a controlled hiss. "They started the chemo yesterday. He's been puking all morning and is too sick to eat. Doctors are talking about surgery to put in a feeding tube right into his intestine. Bypass the stomach entirely."

"I'm sorry. What's your wife think of all this?"

"Shannon? She tried to be strong, but the devil knew where she was weakest and attacked her the hardest. She idolizes that child. Couldn't think of the state taking him away, even when I told her this was all just a test from God. A test I just hope I'm strong enough to pass ..."

Kennedy realized the conversation was still veering too close to Brian and whatever plans he'd conceived to rescue his child. But what else could she talk about? It's not like she could strike up a conversation about the weather.

Brian scowled at the floor for several seconds. Kennedy glanced surreptitiously at his wristwatch, but she didn't know what time it had been when Dominic left her here. Didn't know how long they'd already been waiting.

"You got Internet on your phone?" he asked. "I wonder if the news has already picked up the story."

"No, my batteries are dead."

"Just as well. Otherwise, you'd probably have found a way to call the cops on me by now, right?"

Kennedy still wanted to keep him placated. "I wouldn't do that."

"Oh, yes you would. Don't be afraid to admit it. I'm not saying I'm doing the right thing here. But what choice do I have? God told me through the bishop that the only way my son would be cured was if we deny the chemotherapy. It's a hard road, but it's the one he's called me to walk. And my son's worth it."

Kennedy didn't want to hear any more excuses. She glanced at the screen on the wall. "There's a TV over there. Maybe you could watch the news on that." She tried to keep her voice steady while she planned how fast she'd have to act to move the loveseat, unlock the door, and escape while he fiddled with the television controls. She was pretty sure after talking to him that he wouldn't shoot her in the back while she ran.

But what if she was wrong?

Brian tilted his head toward the small shelf. "Go over there and hand me that remote."

So much for attempting to flee. For a second, Kennedy thought about simply asking him to let her leave. Promising she wouldn't tell the guards where he was if he just unlocked that door. Instead, she walked slowly over to the far wall, keenly aware of his eyes on her. She handed him the remote.

"Thank you." So polite. So gallant.

"You're welcome." She couldn't make herself speak in anything more than a whisper.

"Please don't think I'm a monster." His voice was so earnest. Kennedy forced herself to look straight at him.

"No," she lied. "I don't think that at all."

CHAPTER 18

Providence Hospital was the first image that popped onto the television screen. A news anchor stood out front of the entrance, and the camera panned wide to get a shot of all the police cars stationed outside.

"I'm here in front of Providence Hospital, where the general director has issued a hospital-wide lockdown. At this point, it's only speculation what the problem is or whether or not it has anything to do with the Nipah scare that's now blown to full pandemic proportions. With New York in a state of emergency and Florida expected to follow suit, it's anyone's guess right now whether Massachusetts will be the next state to shut its borders in hopes of stopping the spread of the disease. Meanwhile, in Medford ..."

Brian shut off the volume and swore.

"Not what you wanted to hear?" Kennedy asked.

"It just makes me so sick. Here we are in the middle of a pandemic, and my son's dragged out of his home where we could have kept him isolated, free from exposure, and instead he's brought here. I swear, if he doesn't die from the chemo, it'll be the Nipah next, and his precious soul is going to be on the consciences of all the lawyers and all the attorneys and all the stinking politicians in this whole mess of a country. God will hold them accountable, I tell you that much."

"It's not going to come to that." Kennedy forced conviction into her voice even though all she could focus on was escape. Out of all the rooms Dominic could have led her to, he picked the hiding spot of a murderous father.

No, not murderous. He hadn't hurt anybody yet. And hadn't he promised her several times, assured her he didn't want to harm her? Was that the truth or was that just what he told Kennedy to keep her in line?

Brian shook his head. "I just wish ..."

Kennedy's breath caught in her throat. "Wait," she interrupted. "Wait. Turn the volume back up." She stared at the familiar face on the television screen while Diane Fiddlestein, one of Channel 2's studio reporters, talked into the camera. "Turn it up," she told him again and reached out for the remote.

"I got it," he said and unmuted the TV.

"... admitted to the ER with a fever and swelling of the brain."

Kennedy's lungs were paralyzed. Brian could have pulled out his gun and held it to her temple right then and she couldn't have been more surprised.

"The patient's symptoms came on suddenly this afternoon, and he is currently being treated in an isolation room at Providence."

"Do you know him?" Brian asked.

"Shh."

"The patient's family has included this photograph so that anyone who's come into contact can take necessary precautions."

Kennedy leaned forward as if that would keep her from missing any of the words. "Turn it up."

"Doctors have sent lab samples to the CDC. They can't confirm Nipah at this stage, however they are recommending that anyone who's had exposure to the patient in the past two days monitor their temperature every hour, avoid crowded areas, and seek medical attention immediately if symptoms appear."

Kennedy probably hadn't blinked during the entire segment. They still hadn't taken the picture off the screen. It couldn't be. It wasn't possible. He'd been perfectly healthy ...

"Who is that?"

Kennedy couldn't answer. She shook her head, disbelief coursing through her system. He'd said something about a headache, but that didn't mean ...

"Who is that kid?" Brian asked again.

The news anchor continued her report, even though Kennedy's brain did its best to shut out every word.

She lowered her head. "His name is Woong."

CHAPTER 19

Breathe. She couldn't breathe. Her counselor had given her an assignment. There was something she was supposed to do when she felt the start of a panic attack. She was supposed to look around. Find... Find what? What was there to find while she was stuck in a cramped conference room with a deranged father who was ready to blow the brains out of anyone who got between him and his son? What was there to listen for when all she could hear was the droning on of Diane Fiddlestein's nasally voice as she talked about Woong Lindgren as if he was some nameless patient and not the spunky, mischievous little boy Kennedy had been watching for the past two days?

Woong. Too curious for his own good, asking more questions than Tom Cruise in *A Few Good Men*, but sweet enough to work his way into the hardest of hearts.

Woong. He couldn't be sick. Kennedy tried to remember what time it'd been when they first arrived at the hospital. He'd been fine. Complained a little bit about his legs aching in the morning, and that was all. That and a little headache. Otherwise, he was totally normal. He wasn't sick. He couldn't be sick.

Brian swore and turned off the TV. "Nothing. Not a single word about my son."

Kennedy wasn't sure what he'd expected.

"If it weren't for that outbreak ..."

Someone knocked on the door. "Kennedy?"

Air rushed back into her lungs. She glutted herself on the influx of oxygen.

"Kennedy?"

"Who's that?" Brian stared at the barricaded door and then at her. "You know that guy? Who is he?"

"It's the chaplain," she told him.

"The one you were talking to earlier?"

She nodded.

"Kennedy! It's me. You can unlock the door. Kennedy?"

Brian grabbed her by the upper arm, his fingers pinching into her flesh. "Not a word," he snarled in her ear. "Got that? Not a cough, not a hiccup, don't even think of breathing loud."

"Kennedy!"

Brian jerked her by the arm off the couch. "Come on."

She didn't ask where he was taking her. Didn't dare make a noise. She tripped over one of her stupid sandals as he yanked her toward the broom closet. Dumb heels. She kicked them off. She had to be ready to run when she got the chance.

"Kennedy!" Dominic's voice was strained. Tense. Did he have any idea what was happening? Had he put enough of the pieces together to figure out what was going on?

Brian shoved Kennedy into the closet while Dominic jostled the doorknob. Brian pulled out his gun. *No!* She had to warn Dominic about the weapon. But how can you scream when you don't have any breath? How can you warn your boyfriend away from imminent danger when you can't even control your own lungs?

Brian hefted her up. She was in his arms now, her bare feet dangling a foot off the ground. "Get up there," he grumbled. Kennedy reached up into an open air vent. Did he expect her to crawl through? "Get up," he repeated and pushed her higher, his hands on the back pockets of her pants as he tried to force her through the narrow opening.

Now she wished she'd kept her sandals on. "No!" she screamed and kicked. She'd been aiming for his nose but ended up with her heel smashing into his eye socket instead. She gave him one more sturdy kick to knock him off his balance and jumped down. Pain raced up both ankles when she landed.

He grabbed her by the wrist as she tried to run past him. She kicked his shin without causing any harm. Why hadn't she thought to bring better shoes? She'd trade in her GPA for a pair of spiked cleats right about now.

He had both arms wrapped around her, and she felt something hard across his chest. A bullet-proof vest, maybe? She'd have to warn Dominic and the security officers when they got into the room.

"Stop struggling, will you?" His breath was hot against her ear. She flailed in his grip, fighting to be set free but causing about as much damage as Simba the lion cub wrestling with his dad.

She snapped her head back. Controlled, forceful, like she'd practiced so many times in her self-defense class. She heard the snap of cartilage, Brian's angry curse as he bent over. It was the chance she needed. With a grunt of exertion, she freed herself from his hold and ran to the door. She flung back the deadbolt as she strained to push the barricade aside. "Dominic!" she shouted. "He's got a gun! Be careful!"

The door opened a few inches before hitting the loveseat. Kennedy was stuck between the couch and the wall.

"Kennedy!" Dominic's voice flooded her senses with relief. It was ok. Everything was going to be ok.

Brian grabbed Kennedy by the collar of her shirt. The cold metal of his pistol pressed hard against her temple. "Don't move," he told Dominic. "I've got a gun to her head. You step inside, I shoot."

"It's ok." Dominic's voice was reassuring. Calm.

The door was open, but only slightly. Kennedy couldn't see Dominic on the other side. She was afraid the second he poked his head around the corner, Brian would turn the gun on him and shoot. Her body was too terrified to even tremble.

"Listen, Brian. My name's Dominic. Dominic Martinez. I'm a chaplain. I'm not here to arrest you. I'm not here to get you into any sort of trouble. I just want to talk, maybe pray with you. You're a man of prayer, aren't you?"

Kennedy held her breath. If anyone could talk down a psycho with a loaded gun aimed at her occipital lobe, Dominic was the man for the job.

Brian didn't respond.

After a minute, Dominic continued. "Listen, we know about the explosives. We know you had hospital blueprints in your home. If you help me out, you can keep a lot of people from getting hurt. Good people, Brian. Can you help me?"

"Why would I do that?" he snarled.

Kennedy didn't know if it was wishful thinking or not, but she thought she sensed him lessen his grip. If the stupid loveseat wasn't in the way, she could run. As it was, she was pinned between the partially-opened door and the wall. Was this how she was going to die, with Dominic there on the other side, so close, so helpless?

"You're a good man, Brian. Lots of people know that. A man of faith. Everything you're doing, you're doing because you think it's best for your son. And now I'm asking you to think about the other people, too. There's a lot of scared folks in the ER, Brian. Some of them are kids. Same age as your little guy. I know you want them to be able to go home and spend a safe, peaceful night with their families, right? So I need you to tell me where the bomb is. If you help me, then all these innocent people don't have to get hurt."

"You think the bomb's in the ER?" he asked. His voice had lost its hardened edge. Were Dominic's calm presence and softly spoken words actually working?

"We found the blueprints of yours. But our teams have looked everywhere and we haven't found it yet. So we're hoping you can go ahead and tell us. It'd mean a lot to those scared boys and girls who just want to be safe."

"There's no bomb in the ER."

Kennedy couldn't be sure, but it sounded like a boast.

"We know you were building something, Brian. Can you tell us what you were planning? I want to help you and your family. I really do. I'm not saying what that judge did was right. But if you go on like this, if you injure a bunch of innocent people, there's no chance the legal system's going to change its mind. You know that, right?"

"Maybe."

It wasn't happening. It couldn't be happening. Kennedy didn't dare raise her hopes too high. Was Dominic actually about to convince Brian to give up the location of the explosive?

"So where's the bomb, Brian? We really want to take care of this so all these scared people can go home and be safe."

"It's not in the ER," he repeated.

"Then where?"

Brian loosened his hold. This time, Kennedy was sure of it.

"Brian?" Dominic's voice revealed a strain of tension. "Talk to me, buddy. What's going on behind that door?"

"Why don't you come in here and find out?" The words themselves might have sounded ominous, but Brian's tone was polite and subdued.

Kennedy mentally begged Dominic not to listen. The minute he exposed himself, Brian could shoot.

"Ok, I'm stepping into the conference room right now, all right?"

Kennedy squinted, preparing to close her eyes so she wouldn't have to watch her boyfriend getting murdered.

"I'm keeping my hands up. I don't have a gun or anything, ok? I'm nothing but the chaplain. Just here to talk. That's all I want to do."

Kennedy's legs nearly collapsed when Dominic walked slowly into the room and stood in front of them. His eyes flickered once to her then settled back on Brian.

"Now listen to me. I've already said I don't want to hurt you. I'm just here to get a little information, ok?"

Brian didn't answer.

"I want us to trust each other, Brian. And right now, it's hard for us to trust each other when you have that gun to an innocent girl's head. See what I'm saying? What if you set it down for a minute? I don't mean to take it from you. That's not what I'm suggesting. I just think we all might be a little more comfortable if you put it back in its holster. What do you say about that?"

"I think I'll wait and see for myself and make sure you don't have an army of SWAT team members behind you for backup."

"That's ok with me. I can understand a smart guy like you wanting to be as cautious as possible. But tell me something. My friend you've got there, her name's Kennedy. And I know you and I both would hate to see anything bad accidentally happen to her. So maybe what you can do is let her go, and then you and I can keep up our conversation."

Brian didn't say anything, and he didn't let go either. Kennedy stared at the clock. She had never experienced such long seconds in her life.

Brian let out his breath. Kennedy thought she felt his body tremble just a little.

Come on, Dominic. Keep him calm. No matter what it takes, you've got to keep him calm.

"By the way, I've got a message from your wife," Dominic said. "From Shannon. She wants you to know Timmy's doing well. She said the side effects haven't been too bad this round. There's a chance I could ask and see if we could get you to talk to her on the phone. Would you like that? To talk to your wife?"

"What do you want from me?" Brian shifted his weight from one foot to the other.

"What I want is to know what you've done with the explosives you made. Is that something you think we can talk about now?"

Kennedy felt Brian nod. The motion was so slight she was afraid at first she imagined it, but Dominic must have seen it too.

"Good. Because the sooner you tell us about the explosives, the sooner this whole thing is over for all of us. What did you do with the bomb, Brian? Where did you put it?"

Now Kennedy was sure Brian was trembling.

"I'll tell you, but first the girl gets behind me."

"Listen," Dominic said, glancing once again at Kennedy. She couldn't read his expression. "I'm really grateful you're ready to talk about that bomb. Really grateful. But I want you to think about Kennedy for a minute. She's been through a lot. She's scared ..."

"I'll do it," Kennedy interrupted. She was surprised at the forcefulness of her own voice. "I'll do it," she repeated. As long as Brian holstered that gun. As long as he remained calm. As long as he told Dominic where the bomb was, she didn't care where she stood. Without waiting to hear any arguments, she stepped several paces back. She didn't know why Brian wanted her behind him, but she was thankful to be free from his hold. She backed up until she was standing near the closet with the air vent.

"Ok," Dominic said. "I'm listening."

Kennedy was dizzy. Dizzy and weak. Her legs could hardly support her weight.

Brian started to unbutton his shirt.

"What are you doing?" Was that fear now in Dominic's voice? That voice that had remained so calm and composed for so long? "Brian?" he asked again. His words were shaky.

Brian took one arm out of his shirt sleeve and then the other. Kennedy could see it now, too. Could understand the tension in Dominic's tone.

"Here it is." Brian pointed to the heavy vest strapped to his chest, covered in wires. "This is the bomb you've been looking for."

CHAPTER 20

"Kennedy, I want you to get behind me." It was the first time Dominic had spoken directly to her since he entered the room.

Brian shook his head. "No. She shouldn't do that."

"Kennedy, do it." Dominic's voice was authoritative, no longer soothing and calm but laden with emotion. "Get behind me. Right now."

Brian aimed the gun at Dominic. "I said she shouldn't do that."

"Now listen." Dominic held out one hand in a conciliatory gesture. "She doesn't have anything to do with any of this. She's just a girl who was at the wrong place at the wrong time ..."

His words echoed mirthlessly in Kennedy's terrified mind. *Wrong place at the wrong time.* Yeah, story of her life.

Dominic was staring at her again. Addressing her directly. "He's not gonna shoot me, Kennedy. Now you come this way and get behind me."

Even from where she stood several feet away, Kennedy could feel the heat of Brian's growing anger. Dominic was wrong. He wasn't thinking clearly. All he was doing was making a crazy man strapped with explosives even more agitated.

Shut up, Dominic. She wished telepathy really worked.

"The girl stays where she is." Brian's voice trembled. Shakier than it had been throughout this entire engagement. Dominic didn't know who he was dealing with. Didn't know what this man was capable of.

"Kennedy," he barked again. "Come here and get behind me."

The hand that held Brian's gun shook violently.

Kennedy's limbs refused to move. Her ears rushed with the sound of her pounding pulse.

Dominic took a step forward. "Listen, Brian, I know you love your son. That's what makes you such a good father for him."

Kennedy wondered how he could get the words out without wincing.

"So what I want you to do right now is think about Timothy. Think about how much he needs you. This isn't about his treatment anymore. This isn't about what medicine he is or isn't going to take. This is about your son needing to know his dad is one of the good guys. How is Timothy going to feel if he grows up and learns you killed yourself and a whole bunch of innocent people? How will that make Timothy feel?"

"He won't have a chance to grow up if I don't do what I've got to do." Brian's voice trembled just as much as the gun in his hand, which was still aimed at Dominic's chest.

"Listen." Dominic's tone grew more authoritative as he spoke. "What you're about to do, it's not going to help your son at all. It's just going to take away his father. What if Timothy learns how many other people you killed, too? What will he think about you then?"

"He'll think he had a father who did what he had to do when he was faced with an impossible test."

Kennedy's lungs took in oxygen a few puny milliliters at a time.

"You and I both know that's not how he's going to see it." Dominic took a step forward. "So why don't you put that gun down ..."

"Not gonna happen."

"I really think you might want to ..." Dominic began.

"I really think you might want to shut up." Brian poised his finger on the trigger.

Kennedy braced herself, her only hope that Brian was so distraught it would throw off his aim.

"You don't want to do this." Dominic's voice betrayed no fear. Kennedy wished he could lend her some of his confidence. He hadn't looked at her in several minutes. It was as if he were in some sort of mental zone and was deliberately ignoring her. Maybe that made it easier for him. Pretend he was in a room with a nameless victim, an anonymous bystander, not his own girlfriend.

Kennedy tried to control her breath. *Please, God, don't let him die.*

With his free hand, Brian pulled a cell phone out of his pocket. "I press one button, we all get blown to bits, got it?"

Dominic nodded. "Ok. I hear you. I understand. Don't you think you'll feel better once you give that phone to me?" He reached his hand out and took a step forward.

No! Kennedy wanted to yell the word, but she was afraid any sudden sound would startle Brian into detonating his explosive vest. She cringed. Tried to look away. Tried to brace herself for the fatal blast she knew was coming.

"Get back." Brian's voice rose in pitch. Didn't Dominic see how worked-up he was getting? How desperate?

"Ok." Dominic held up both hands. "All right. I'm sorry. I'll stand here by the door. Will that make you feel better?"

Kennedy imagined her body turning into a small ball. Like an armadillo that could wrap itself up in its own personal, bomb-proof armor. She thought about the closet behind her. If she could get to it, somehow get up to that crawl space ...

But she couldn't leave Dominic here. Not alone. Any sudden move would spell death for them both. She still wasn't sure if Dominic was the man she was meant to spend the rest of her life with. Up until now, she'd figured she could take months or even years to figure that out. She certainly never expected them both to die together a few short months into their relationship at the hand of a deranged explosives engineer.

Brian still held the cell phone in his hand. At least while he was focused on it, he wasn't aiming the gun at Dominic's chest, but that was only a small comfort considering the fact that if he detonated that bomb, Kennedy, Dominic, and anyone unfortunate enough to be in the proximity of the explosion would die.

I didn't even get to say good-bye to my parents. Kennedy's body had stopped trembling. She leaned against the wall, unable to stand on her own. Unable to take in the horror that surrounded her. Her mind had wrapped itself up into some sort of emotional cocoon. She wasn't scared. She couldn't describe what it was she felt. Like her brain was filtering out the raw horror of the situation, only allowing tiny bits and pieces of realization to settle into her being a few seconds at a time. Even though she appreciated the mental numbness compared to the paralyzing weight of panic, she felt her body was too sluggish to know what to do if the chance came to react. Her body was maxed out on adrenaline. The fight or flight response wouldn't work. Not right now. She'd sooner pass out from weakness than find a way to save herself.

She had to get her mind more alert, but to do that, she had to admit the terror. Welcome the devastating horror that would crash through her psyche like the tsunami in *Deep Impact* if she let even the slightest trace of fear slip past her emotional barriers.

Brian's cell phone trembled in his hand. "You're both my witnesses that I'm doing this for my son."

"There are other ways, you know." Dominic took a step forward.

Brian was so concentrated on his phone he didn't seem to notice.

"Your son can have a comfortable life. You'll have other chances to show him how much you love him."

Brian shook his head. "This is my test. I can't fail."

Dominic took another step. "I know you feel helpless. I know you feel desperate and lost. I would too. But blowing yourself up, that's only going to create a lot more problems for your family, don't you think?"

"I don't care." He holstered his gun. Five minutes ago, the gesture would have brought a flood of relief crashing through Kennedy's system. Now she realized how tame a single pistol looked compared to a homemade explosive vest.

How far would the blast radius extend? How many people would die? How many more would be injured?

How would the authorities tell her parents about Kennedy's death?

She'd never gotten the chance to introduce them to her boyfriend.

A hollow chasm radiated out from the pit of her gut, ripping that emotional armor she'd erected into tiny shreds. She didn't want to die. Didn't want her last vision on earth to be Dominic's calm face right before the two of them were blown apart by the force of a violent explosion.

How did a detonation kill you exactly? Was it all the shrapnel slicing through your body's vital organs? Or was it the energy itself? Would it be hot? Would she feel it at all? Would she even know she was about to die? Or would she simply blink and find herself in heaven? It was too late to wonder now. She'd find out soon enough. She'd expected so much more out of her life. Out of her relationship with Dominic.

He'd never kissed her yet, at least not for real.

She wasn't ready to go.

What about Willow? Her roommate was so new to the faith. Had so much growing to do. Kennedy wanted to be there for that. To witness God finish what he'd started in her.

Dominic's voice was tense but it didn't quiver. "Listen to me, Brian.

You're going to feel a whole lot better when you give me that phone, all right?"

"You want the phone, do you?" Brian's tone was deathly calm.

No! Kennedy's whole spirit screamed out as Brian's fingers tensed around his cell.

"Kennedy, get down!"

Dominic's panicked cry was drowned out by the horrific eruption that burst in her ears and the terror that exploded all around her.

CHAPTER 21

Beep. Beep. Beep.

Was she dead?

"Vitals stabilizing."

"Pressure starting to rise."

Beep. Beep. Beep.

Where was she?

"Let's get her transferred."

"Careful."

Her body swinging. Pain in her arm. She tried to speak but couldn't.

Beep. Beep. Beep.

"Kennedy? Is your name Kennedy Stern? Can you hear me?"

Why couldn't she form any words?

"You're going to be ok. We're taking good care of you."

Thank you, she tried to mouth. She was heavy. Her whole body was heavy. Her ears echoed with the screeches of terror. Was she even conscious?

She couldn't remember where she was. All she knew was she didn't want to be here.

God, I want to go home.

A desperate prayer. Did he hear her? Did he see her?

Was she all alone?

Beep.

Beep.

Beep.

CHAPTER 22

Kennedy blinked herself awake. How long had she been knocked out? Her eyes were dry, as if her contacts had crusted onto her corneas.

Thirsty. She was thirsty.

"Easy, now." The voice was garbled somehow, like someone talking at her through a wall of water. An enormous hand covered with a yellow glove held her down.

She tried to ask for a drink, but all that came out was, *Wifter.*

"Calm down. You were injured, but you're going to be just fine."

Kennedy's eyes traveled up from the hands to the giant rubber suit. The hazmat helmet.

"Where am I?" This time, the words came out more clearly.

"You're in an isolation unit."

She blinked as memories coursed and flooded through her brain.

The explosion. The lockdown. The epidemic.

"Am I sick?"

She didn't know if the healthcare worker was avoiding her gaze or if the helmet just distorted the view.

"Am I sick?" she repeated, assessing her beaten, battered body. Her arm throbbed. She couldn't turn her head without experiencing a horrific muscle spasm throughout her entire neck. The entire right half of her body felt so heavy she was sure it must be swollen to twice its usual size. A piercing headache. Her heart fluttering slightly and her lungs still stinging from the aftershocks of terror and smoke. Bruises on her hip. An excruciating pain radiating outward from her tailbone. At least she didn't feel feverish. That must be a good sign.

"No, you're not sick. This is just a precaution. You were potentially exposed before the accident," the nurse explained. "We're treating your injuries in isolation just to be safe."

It took Kennedy a few seconds to piece everything together, to remember why she'd ended up at the hospital in the first place. The epidemic. The man with the gun. The news reports. "Is Woong ok?"

"The little boy you were babysitting? We're keeping him under quarantine until we get the lab results back. He's got the right symptoms for Nipah, but it will be another day until we know for sure. The good news is if you remain symptom-free, you can be released from isolation tomorrow evening."

Tomorrow? Kennedy didn't even know what day it was. The bomb, the lockdown — how much time had passed? Had she slept a whole day through? Maybe more? Heavy plastic curtains were drawn on all sides of her bed. There were no windows, no clocks. It could just as easily be suppertime Monday night or first thing Wednesday morning or the middle of the night a week later.

Pain pulsed through her temples, behind her eyes, pounding on her optical nerves. She just wanted to sleep. Forget. Wake up in the morning in the Lindgrens' guest room to find this entire ordeal had been a terrible dream.

The nurse fidgeted with Kennedy's throbbing arm, adjusting some sort of a bandage. "You just rest up now and try not to worry."

Try not to worry? After everything she had gone through? The epidemic. The lockdown. The explosion...

"Where's Dominic?"

The nurse's face was completely shielded through the thick visor of her hazmat suit.

"The chaplain," Kennedy pressed. "He was there, too. When can I see him?" Her lungs clenched off, and she coughed trying to force a breath.

"Just calm down now, ok? There's a detective waiting to talk to you. He'll fill you in on everything that happened, and I know he's got some questions for you too. There's no rush, though. He said he'd wait as long as he needed until you felt like talking."

"I'm ready now."

Kennedy felt rather than saw the nurse frown at her. "You just woke up. It might be a good idea to save your strength."

"I'll talk to the detective. Answer any questions he's got."

"You've got some shrapnel in your arm. Cuts on your shoulder. Bruises and burns."

"I said I'll talk to him now."

"Ok." The nurse's voice was uncertain, but she pulled back one of the curtains and pointed to the tall man standing on the other side of a thick window. "This is Detective Drisklay. Says you already know him."

"Yeah." Kennedy's voice was flat. The nurse was probably right. She should have slept some more before voluntarily hopping into the witness chair with someone like Drisklay. He held up a Styrofoam coffee cup in silent greeting.

"There's a phone by your bedside you can use to talk to him through the glass. You sure you're up for this?" the nurse asked one last time.

Kennedy swallowed. She had to find out what happened to Dominic.

"I'm ready."

CHAPTER 23

"I hear they expect you to recover from your injuries." Drisklay stared through Kennedy's window.

She rested the hospital phone against her ear so she wouldn't have to hold it in place. "Yeah, it's nothing too serious, I guess. How's Dominic?"

"What can you tell me about Brian Robertson?" Drisklay went on as if he hadn't heard Kennedy's question. Was the mouthpiece of her phone working?

She tried to remember what details she could give the detective. "He had a son. He was upset about the court order." Kennedy squeezed her eyes shut, trying not to think about the young cancer patient. About how much sorrow the poor boy had already endured in his short life. About how horrific it must be for him to learn about what his father had done.

"We know about the son." Drisklay took a sip out of his Styrofoam cup so noisily Kennedy could hear it through her phone. "We want to piece together what happened in the conference room. My coffee is just now kicking in, so you may as well start at the beginning."

Kennedy's thoughts were too disorganized, her brain too stunned for her to put her words into any coherent order.

"He had a vest. A bomb. With his phone."

"When did you meet him?" Drisklay interrupted. "How long had you been in that room with him before he decided to blow himself to bits?"

"I don't know."

"Was he holding you hostage?"

"No. I mean, I'm not sure. He locked the door so I couldn't get out."

"So he was holding you hostage."

"He didn't want to hurt me."

"Which is why he lit himself off like a firework? You're one lucky young woman. You know that, don't you?"

Lucky? She doubted her definition of the word would match the detective's very closely.

"Did he say anything about any other explosives? Did he make any other threats?" Drisklay spoke in his regular monotone, but Kennedy could tell by the way he clenched his coffee cup that he was tense.

"No, the one he was wearing, that was the only bomb he mentioned."

"And not a very strong one," Drisklay added as an afterthought. His words gave Kennedy a small boost of hope.

"What about Dominic?"

The detective frowned. "Who?"

"The chaplain." Her abs quivered. Even though she was reclining in the hospital bed, every single muscle in her body engaged at the same time.

"Martinez?" He shrugged. "You're lucky he was there. Lucky he put his training to good use. Puny as the explosive was, you still would have been obliterated if Martinez hadn't tackled Mr. Robertson. Absorbed eighty percent of the blast or more." Drisklay nodded appreciatively. "Smart thinking."

Kennedy wished the curtains on either side of her were open. She was suffocating in this cramped enclosure. She had to breathe. Had to find room for her lungs to expand. She tried to sit up, but the pain in her arm and shoulder was too intense. "What happened to him, then?" She stared at Drisklay's expressionless face, searching, pleading, begging for any trace of softness or sympathy.

He took another noisy gulp of coffee. "Who, Martinez? Let's just say the chaplain's legacy and sacrifice will go down in history. It's because of him that you and everyone else in the west corridor are alive and not in gallon-sized biohazardous waste baggies."

Legacy? Sacrifice? Did that mean ...

Drisklay shrugged. "Just be thankful it was one of our men and not someone you knew personally. Be thankful you're safe and forget what anyone tells you about survivor's guilt or myths like that."

Was Drisklay really saying what she thought he was? She had to be imagining it. No creature could be that callous.

"Just how bad was it?" She had to know.

Drisklay took another sip from his cup. "Let's just say the chaplain will be getting a hero's funeral, but it won't be open-casket."

CHAPTER 24

Tears. Somewhere behind Kennedy's dry eyes were tears. Someplace beneath her shocked psyche was a grief that would threaten to carry her down to the pit of despair. Angry. Demanding God tell her why he took Dominic away. Devastated. Wondering how she could find healing after a loss like this.

But right now, there was nothing. The numbness was so tangible, so fierce even her limbs felt cold. Unmoving. Had her circulatory system shut down entirely?

Beep. Beep.

The hospital monitor mocked her, reminding her seventy-two times a minute that she was alive. That she still had a pulse. That there was nowhere for her to go but forward. Forward without him. Without what could have been.

He'd died for her. Wasn't that supposed to make her feel something? Guilty? Thankful? Wretched?

Beep. Beep.

She would never see him again. No more Sunday morning walks through Boston Commons. No more late-night phone calls asking him her most recent theological musings.

No more Dominic.

Beep. Beep.

And yet Kennedy lived on.

Beep.

Her heart pumped blood. Her lungs took in oxygen, albeit in short, shallow bursts.

Beep.

And she felt nothing at all.

CHAPTER 25

She didn't know how long it had been since Detective Drisklay left when the phone by her bedside rang. There was nobody in the window in front of her room. Who was calling?

She reached her uninjured arm across her body and winced as she tried to pick up the receiver. "Hello?"

"Kennedy, sweetheart, thank God I got hold of you." Sandy's voice was breathless. Constantly bustling, just like her. "The nurses told me you were awake now. Has the detective come by, hon? I really want to talk to you before he gets ..."

"Yeah. We already talked."

"Oh." Her chipper voice fell flat. "So, he told you then?"

"Yeah. He told me."

"Baby, I'm so, so sorry. I wish I could come over there and give you a big hug. You know that, don't you? You know I would if it weren't for the isolation rules, right?"

"Yeah."

"Talk to me, precious. Tell me what you're thinking. You don't need to keep things bottled up, you know. Tell me everything. You know I'm always here for you."

Kennedy's throat seized up. She loved Sandy, but talking to her pastor's wife on a hospital phone was no substitute for burying herself in her mother's arms and crying. Releasing all that fear. That tension. That sorrow that hadn't yet even crept up into her spirit. It was there, buried somewhere beneath the surface. She couldn't access it now even if she wanted to. She felt as callous as Detective Drisklay himself. So unfeeling.

So homesick.

"What are you thinking, baby?"

Kennedy bit her lip. If Sandy kept on talking to her with so much compassion, so much concern, she'd start crying. And once she started ...

"I'm ok. I'm just glad more people weren't hurt, you know?"

"Well, yes. We're all praising God for that, I'm sure. But honey, you know what I'm asking about. I'm talking about Dominic. You do know that he ..."

"Yeah. The detective told me."

"Honey, I'm so sorry. I begged the nurses to let me talk to you first. I thought maybe ..." Sandy's voice caught. "I thought maybe it'd be easier for you coming from me. I'd come right in that room and hold you if they'd let me. You know that, right?"

"Uh-huh."

"How you feeling, babe? Your injuries, are they pretty bad?"

God bless Sandy. It was infinitely easier to talk about her physical wounds. "My arm hurts a lot. And my shoulder. But it's nothing too serious."

Thanks to Dominic, she added silently. What was that verse in John? *Greater love has no one that this ...*

She couldn't think about it. Not right now.

"Are you ok?" Kennedy hated herself for not asking sooner. "How's Woong? And what about Carl? Is he all right?"

"Carl and I are fine, precious. In fact, he's right here." Sandy lowered her voice. "Here, babe. Say hi to Kennedy for a minute. It's been a rough day for her."

"It's been a rough day for all of us," came the pleasant-sounding grumble.

"Carl?" Kennedy wasn't sure he'd picked up the phone yet or if he was still bantering with his wife.

"Kennedy." His voice boomed. She was grateful to hear the strength in his tone. "Hey, next time we ask you to babysit our son, I promise not to do it in the middle of an epidemic, all right?"

She smiled. "Sounds good."

"Let's plan to avoid any more hospital lockdowns while we're at it, ok?"

Good old Carl. Ready to remind Kennedy that joy still existed in spite of terror and heartache. Reminding her that one day she too would find courage to laugh again.

"Are you all right?" she asked. "We were really worried about you. All I heard was Sandy was driving you to the ER."

"Pshaw. I'm fine. You know me. God's not about to call me home yet. Not with all the work he's still got left for me to do."

"What was wrong?" Was it rude for her to ask? Should she have worded the question more delicately?

Carl chuckled. "Well, turns out that being fifty pounds overweight and snacking on my lovely wife's cookies and muffins for decades was enough to kill my pancreas, that's all."

"What?"

"He's got diabetes, hon," Sandy's voice rang out in the background.

"Oh. Is it serious?"

"Not very," Carl answered.

"His blood sugar levels were 485 when we admitted him."

"I'll be fine," Carl thundered. "Like I said, God's not even close to finished with me yet, and when it's my time to go, there isn't a soul in a hundred miles who could stop me. But until then, the devil can try to take me all he wants, but God's not through with me, and I'm just gonna keep on giving him glory."

"Except now you'll be giving him glory with diet and exercise," Sandy added.

"Woman, we got more important things to worry about right now than my insulin levels. Listen, first we get Woong over this infection, we get ourselves home as a family again, and then we'll talk about my diet. Promise. Here. You take the phone again. I'm about to die of thirst. These hospital meals ..." His voice trailed off, and Sandy came back on the line.

"You still there, pumpkin? Sorry about that." She lowered her voice. "He's an ornery patient. Just ask his nurses."

"I heard that." There was laughter in Carl's tone. Laughter that squeezed Kennedy's heart between her ribs and sent pangs piercing through her spirit with the intensity of the nuclear explosion at the end of *Armageddon*.

"Did they say when they're going to let you out of isolation?" Sandy asked.

"Tomorrow night if I don't show any symptoms."

"That's good. It's the same with me and Carl."

"You're in isolation, too?"

"Oh, yeah. It's horrible, isn't it? When I should be there taking care of Woong. But they've got us two rooms right next to each other, and speakers so you don't even have to use phones to talk. And the nurses, they're letting him play XBox when he's got the energy for it, so he's the happiest little patient in the history of Providence Hospital. When he's awake," she added quietly.

"How is he? Is he really sick?"

"We're still waiting on his test results, hon." Sandy's voice betrayed her heaviness for the first time since they started talking. "Waiting and trusting in the good Lord to do what's right. His teacher turns out to have a bad case of meningitis, but at least it's not related to Nipah, so there's hope there. It just breaks my mother's heart thinking about all the things it could be, so I'm trying to focus on the fact that right now, right at this minute, Carl and me are together, and our son's right next to us. He's sleeping now, but when he wakes up, he'll want nothing more than to play his silly racing games, big grin on his face. His fever's down just a tad. So until the doctors tell me it's time to worry, I'm sitting here counting my blessings."

"That's nice that you and Carl get to be by him." Kennedy would give just about anything to have her parents with her right now, even if she could only see them through the glass.

"Oh, we wouldn't have it any other way. At first, they wanted to split us all up. When the bomb scare went off, they would have just evacuated, you know. Sent everyone home except for the patients and workers who couldn't leave. But by then, Woong had come down with this fever all of a sudden. We told them he was one of the students in Mrs. Winifred's class, and that was before they got her test results in, so they realized they couldn't just send everyone away. You should have seen the flurry over here. Running and racing and figuring out who'd been in contact with Woong. Once they got it sorted, they let most folks out, but a few of us they had to put in isolation. Problem was they wanted to keep us as far away from the ER as possible, back when they still thought the bomb was in there, and there weren't enough isolation rooms for everyone. So me and Carl, we just told them to put us together. We said if our son's sick, well, we'd rather all be sick together, come what may, than stand back and watch each other suffer from a distance. I just wish they'd found a way to put all three of us together, but that has as much to do with Carl still needing a hospital bed as anything else. He won't tell you this himself, but he's still hooked up to

IVs. Still working to get his blood sugar under control."

Kennedy was glad Carl and Sandy were together. But she couldn't figure out how Sandy could be so happy with her son so ill. Well, maybe she wasn't exactly happy, but if Kennedy had been in her place, she would have been freaking out. Screaming, pleading with God to save her son's life. Begging every doctor and nurse in the entire country to do what they could to help him.

Of course, she'd never go so far as murder, but she thought she understood a little more clearly what must have been running through Brian Robertson's head when he strapped himself with explosives and walked into Providence Hospital.

"Well, I'm sure I've yacked your ear off by now, but you can call whenever you want to chat. I mean it, I don't care what time it is. You call, and I'll be here for you." She let out a pleasant, ringing chuckle. "It's not like I'll be going anywhere any time soon."

"Thank you." Kennedy wished her weary spirit could feel the gratitude she knew Sandy deserved. She winced again when she reached over to hang up the phone. She still didn't know what time it was. Still didn't know how many more hours she had to go to find out if she'd caught Woong's disease or not. She didn't know if grief would overtake her now or if it'd take weeks before her soul could fully realize everything she'd lost in the past twenty-four hours.

All she knew was that she was tired. And that she wanted to sleep for a very long time.

CHAPTER 26

"Well, you'll be glad to hear you're in picture-perfect shape." The nurse pulled the thermometer out of Kennedy's mouth and took off her hazmat mask. "I'll get that bandage changed for you one last time and bring you some gauze so you can take care of it at home. After that, you're free as a sparrow."

Kennedy let out her breath. She hadn't caught Nipah. No fever. No aches besides the ones that could be explained from the explosion. The explosion and the gnawing, gaping wound in her spirit.

"Well look at that," the nurse prattled pleasantly. "Looks like you already have your first visitor." She took off her enormous gloves and held the door open. "Come in. Come in. You're right on time, and she's just gotten her clean bill of health."

Kennedy looked at Willow standing in the open doorway and offering a smile, somewhat less certain than her usual brilliant grin.

"Hey."

"Hey."

The girls stared at each other before Willow finally asked, "Can I come in?"

"Yeah. I'm not sick or anything."

"Me either."

"They kept you in isolation?"

"Only for the first night. I would have been wicked bored, too, except I had someone to talk to."

Kennedy could tell she was trying hard to hide a grin. "Oh, yeah? Who was that?"

"Just your friend Nick. Man, if I'd have known the youth pastor had such gorgeous hair and an even hotter personality, I would have been begging you to take me to church for the past two years. Oh, and did you know his uncle's in a band? It's wicked awesome. You should listen to their album. But enough about that." Willow sat down on the foot of Kennedy's bed. "How are you doing? I heard about everything. You must feel terrible."

"Yeah, something like that."

"I'm not trying to make you feel worse. I mean, I don't even know what Christians are supposed to say at times like this. Do you?"

Kennedy shook her head.

"Well, I started thinking about your pastor and his family and how you said when the lockdown started they were probably all in their room together praying. I figured that even if I was completely clueless when it came to finding the right things to say, I could at least offer to do that with you, right? I mean, you don't have to say anything unless you really want to. And you know me. I'm still learning all the stuff, so I probably won't even do that good of a job with it, but I'll be happy to pray with you if that's what you want."

Kennedy swallowed past the painful lump in her throat and nodded slightly.

Willow scooted closer to her on the bed. "So, like, are we supposed to hold hands or something? Does that make it better, or do we just sit here or what, because I really don't want to mess up after all you've been through."

"It doesn't matter." Kennedy squeezed her eyes shut. Felt the first trickle of a tear starting to form.

"Ok. So if it doesn't make a difference how we do it, maybe you can just sit here, and I'll like rub your back or something, unless it feels strange to you. It's ok for me to do that, right? Doesn't weird you out?"

Kennedy didn't trust her voice, so she shook her head.

"All right. I'm gonna pray for you now. So, God, or Father, whichever you prefer, we're here, and Kennedy's heartbroken, I'm sure, and she's gone through more than anybody should have to endure in an entire lifetime. And even though she probably thinks she's just one big mess, you and I both know how strong she is. How brave of a person she is. How much faith and courage it takes to go through everything she's gone through and still have the confidence to say, 'I believe in a good and loving God who knows how to take care of his children.' So that's what I'm asking right now, Lord. Or Jesus. I'm asking you to show Kennedy that she's stronger than she thinks, and she's braver than she feels right now, and even when she feels like she's nothing but a big screw-up, or I mean... Well, Lord, you know exactly what it is I mean. And even though what happened to her boyfriend sucks royally — or stinks, I guess that's a better way of putting it

— I'm asking you to please just teach my friend here what she taught me earlier, that you won't even let a sparrow get hurt without knowing about it in advance and saying it's going to be ok. So please help Kennedy remember right now that you've got her whole life planned out, and I know you have so many good things in store for her even if she can't feel or believe in them now."

Willow continued to rub Kennedy's back. "There, was that ok? Do I say *amen* next, or does God just know when I'm done, or do you have to do the whole *in Jesus name* thing, or can you do whatever? I spent a lot of time thinking about what I was going to pray, so I want to make sure it gets through."

Kennedy wanted to assure Willow that her prayer was perfectly acceptable, but she couldn't find her voice through her trembling and her silent, crippling sobs.

CHAPTER 27

"Want me to buckle you in?" Willow asked.

Kennedy lowered herself carefully into the passenger seat of her roommate's car. "No, I can get it." She grimaced as she twisted around to grab the seatbelt.

"You've got to learn to accept a little help sometimes, you know." Willow plopped into the driver's seat and started up the engine.

Kennedy smiled. "Maybe next semester."

Willow rolled her eyes. "Maybe after the apocalypse, you mean. Wait, is that a real thing? Is that like actually in the Bible? Do I need to do anything to get ready for it?"

"It's in the Bible, but maybe we can save that topic for later." Kennedy held her breath as Willow bounced the car over a speed bump and pulled out of the hospital parking lot. The sun was just starting to set, glorious hues of pink and orange highlighting the oversized cumulus clouds.

It felt so good to finally be out of Providence.

"I talked to your pastor's wife," Willow said. "She made me promise to find you something nutritious for dinner on campus and make sure you get some good rest and actually go to sleep. I don't remember entirely. I think there might have been something about tucking you in and kissing you goodnight too."

Kennedy smiled through her pain. "Thanks for being with me."

"Hey, what are friends for? Besides, if it hadn't been for you, I would have never met Nick."

"I thought you were going to say without me you would have never met Jesus."

"Oh, well, there's that too. But Nick ... Man. Why didn't you tell me about him years ago?"

Kennedy let out an awkward chuckle. Would she ever remember what it felt like to laugh naturally? She took in a deep breath, thankful for the fresh air whipping across her face.

Willow turned up the radio so they could hear the music over the breeze roaring in through the open windows as they sped toward campus.

"Please don't tell me I have to give up my classic rock station now that I'm a Christian."

Kennedy wasn't sure if she was serious or not.

They listened in silence. *Here I Go Again on my Own.* Ironic song choice now that Dominic was gone. Except Kennedy wasn't alone. She had Willow, her best friend and sister in the Lord. She had Carl and Sandy, who had thankfully both been released from isolation and cleared of any Nipah scare. She had her mom and dad, even though they were on the other side of the world. From the time she woke up in Providence, not an hour had gone by where at least one of her parents hadn't called to check in on her. Smother her with love and care. It didn't bother Kennedy at all. She didn't even mind when her dad told her she should check her temperature a few times during the night just to make sure she really hadn't caught whatever Woong had.

Poor Woong. Kennedy and Willow had stopped to check on him before they headed back to campus. Whatever energy he'd found to play Xbox earlier was clearly expended. When Kennedy went over to visit, he was lying half-awake in bed while Sandy read him the last chapter of *The Boxcar Children* through the window of his room. Even though Carl and Sandy had been cleared, the doctors were still holding Woong in quarantine until his test results came back.

There were so many things Kennedy had to worry about, had to process. She was glad she wouldn't be spending the night alone. She would have been infinitely more comfortable at the Lindgrens' than at her dorm, but with Woong being so sick, nobody was allowed into their house until they found out if he really had Nipah or not.

"What do you want to have for dinner?" Willow asked. "You know you have to eat more than your usual craisins and Cheerios."

Kennedy didn't want to think about anything. "We'll figure something out when we get to campus."

"What do you want to do after that? It's not that late. We could watch a movie or play some cards or take a little walk. It's a nice evening."

It felt so wrong to be here. Sitting next to her friend, the wind whipping through their hair. The sunset so soul-hauntingly glorious. So intense. The kind of scene you'd expect to see on a postcard or movie trailer. Not in real life.

The world was so stinking beautiful. But ever since she'd learned about Dominic's death, Kennedy's soul had been longing for those things to come. That glorious rapture, that heavenly melody that would one day beckon to her as it had to her boyfriend.

When Jesus is my portion; my constant friend is he.

His eye is on the sparrow, and I know he watches me.

She'd heard her whole life that heaven was her true home, but she never fully realized what that meant until now.

"Well? What sounds good?" Willow interrupted her thoughts, her voice full of forced cheer. "We could even call Nick and invite him over if you feel up for some company. I bet he'd be willing to pick us up a pizza from Angelo's or something."

Kennedy knew exactly what Willow was doing. Trying to distract her. Trying to keep her mind off the pain. Off the loss.

Reminding her that life on earth was here for the living. Heaven was the prize for those who had already passed.

CHAPTER 28

Kennedy woke up the next morning to the sound of rain pounding on her dorm room window.

Her roommate was reclining in her beanbag chair reading a screenplay. "Morning, sleeping beauty."

Kennedy glanced at the clock. Already past ten.

"How're you doing today?" Willow set down her book.

How was she doing? Kennedy wasn't sure yet.

"Your dad called. Twice." Willow smiled. "I told him you were perfectly fine. He wants you to check your temperature and text him."

"Ok." Her dad annoyed her ninety percent of the time, but today, she was glad to know someone was worried for her. Someone was still there to fret and fawn over her every move.

"Sandy called too. She said that Woong's been asking for you. Wants you to read to him if you've got the energy. I told her you might not want to go back to the hospital just yet, and she said she understood." Willow frowned. "Is that ok? I wasn't sure what to say."

"I don't know." Kennedy glanced around. She was still more thirsty than usual. Her arm ached, but it was nothing compared to yesterday. She would heal. She would recover. She hadn't looked beneath the bandage yet. Didn't know if she'd end up scarred or not from the shrapnel.

Did it matter?

She tugged at her sleeve. "If Woong wants me there, I don't mind." It was nice feeling needed. Surrounding herself with people who loved her. Who wanted her around.

Willow shrugged. "I can give you a ride."

"That'd be nice."

"Hey, you want some tea? I just heated some up."

"Thanks." Kennedy reached out and took the oversized *Alaska Chicks Rock* mug. The steam heated her face. She sensed Willow staring at her. Kennedy hated the sad, almost embarrassed expression in her eyes. She just wanted to move on. How long until she could forget this week? How long until she could look at her roommate without seeing that pained, guilty expression?

Life would go on. Kennedy knew it would. She just wished she had some idea how.

Half an hour later, after a quick bite from L'Aroma Bakery, Kennedy and Willow made their way back to Providence.

"All I can say is Woong must be a very special little boy if you're willing to go back to the hospital to see him."

Kennedy couldn't explain. It wasn't just Woong. She loved him. Prayed that God would heal him of whatever sickness he had. But it was more than that. She wanted to be with the Lindgrens. To support and encourage each other. Carl and Sandy needed her, and she needed them. The Lindgrens were the closet thing Kennedy had to a family in the States, and during her own time of sadness and mourning, she wanted to be with family most of all.

Besides, this was the morning they would get Woong's lab results back from the CDC. If it really was the Nipah virus, Kennedy wanted to be with Sandy. Help shoulder some of that burden like Sandy had done for her countless times over the past two years. She thought about her first week on US soil when she arrived for the start of her freshman year at Harvard. How much she'd seen since then. How much she'd grown.

How much she'd changed.

She wasn't sure all the changes were positive, either. Kennedy lived now with a constant heaviness, a sense of fear even when she knew she was perfectly safe. That little bubble, that sense she'd had as a child that she was completely invincible, popped within her first few weeks of college. She'd never be able to recreate that same sense of security.

But still, God had sustained her. Carried her through every trial she'd had to endure. He'd given her strength when she was so weak she was sure she'd collapse. He'd sent heavenly protection to shield her when she was sure she was about to die. He'd shown her love, the kind of love you couldn't read about in a book. Sacrificial love. Christ-like love.

And he'd shown her comfort. Kennedy couldn't feel it right now, but she had in the past and knew that it would come to her again. She'd have to learn to be patient, that was all. The comfort would come, that sweet heavenly balm that would smooth over her scars. It would never erase them completely. She'd given up praying for perfect healing, but she knew that in time, the pain would lessen. Joy would find her once more. Teach her to smile again. Hope again.

Love again.

It would happen. She just had to be patient. That was the hardest part, but God would give her the grace even for that.

"What are you thinking about?" Willow turned down the radio. Rain pelted onto the windshield and splashed up from the car tires in front of them.

"Everything."

"Yeah." Willow sighed. "Me, too." She reached out and shut off the music. "Hey, can I ask you something?"

"What?" Kennedy was thankful for the chance she'd had this week to connect with Willow on a deeper level. To discuss the spiritual matters they should have been talking about from the moment of Willow's conversion. But she was so tired. She didn't know if she could focus on a heavy conversation right now.

"I'm still wondering about sickness and prayer and all that stuff. I mean, I'm thinking about Woong, I guess. And I know you said even a bird won't get hurt outside of God's plans, but ... I don't even know how to ask my question. I guess what I'm wanting to know ... It doesn't make sense to me ..."

"How God chooses to heal some people and not others?" Kennedy finished for her.

"Right. How exactly does that work?"

Kennedy sighed. "I wish I could tell you." She knew Willow was hoping for a deeper answer than that, so she tried to snap her mind into a more alert state. "I think it's kind of like ... Ok, so let's say that ..." She wasn't going to be able to get out one coherent sentence without the Holy Spirit's intervention. "It's like this," she tried again. "At least, I think it is, because I'm definitely not an expert. But let's say someone you love is sick. Use Woong as an example, right?"

"Right." Willow sped up her windshield wipers.

"Ok, so we're all praying for Woong to get better. I mean, who wouldn't be?"

"Right."

"So we all want him to get better." Kennedy had to pause for a moment. She couldn't imagine the grief that would flood the Lindgren household if Woong didn't recover. "We want him to get well, and so we pray for him, and that's the right thing to do. But there's more to it than just that. Like when Jesus was in the Garden of Gethsemane. Do you know that story?"

"Gethsemane? Sounds like the name of a big music festival."

"I guess. Well, that's where Jesus went to pray the night before he was crucified. I mean killed. He's praying there, and he says, *God, please don't let me have to die, but it's not what I will, but what you will.* So he was praying to God for his own desires, but then he also started to pray that if God wanted something different, that should be what happens instead. Does that make sense?"

"No. Because if Jesus is God, why would he pray to himself?"

Kennedy sighed. She couldn't think through everything logically right now. "Ok, that's a whole other question we can talk about a different time." She was just about to make a mental note to ask Dominic how he would answer that when she remembered. She wondered how long it would take before she fully realized he was gone. It was like losing a limb but for weeks, even months, you keep trying to use it. Keep surprising yourself when you rediscovered it isn't there. Mourn its loss all over again.

She tried to remember Willow's original question. "Well, with God, we should pray like Jesus did. We can tell him what's on our hearts, what we want out of the situation, but there should also be the submission to recognize that he might know better — he *does* know better — and that even if he doesn't answer our prayers the way we expect him too, we still have to have faith that he's good."

"So basically, you're saying that if Woong's gonna die, Woong's gonna die, and that God has some sort of good reason for making that happen. So then why do we pray for his healing at all?"

She didn't have an answer. Where was Dominic when she needed him? Why couldn't he be here to tackle these questions for her? Why did God take him the way he did? Did Kennedy even believe everything she was telling Willow? Did God actually *want* Dominic to die, or did he just choose not to intervene when some lunatic took his life? She let out her breath. "I really don't know. Prayer's important. I just don't know ..." She let her voice trail off before apologizing. "I wish I had more to tell you."

Willow slowed down to turn into the Providence parking garage. "That's ok. I guess I probably picked a bad time to come up with heavy questions like that. I'm sorry. I know you have other things on your mind right now."

"Don't feel bad. I love that you're asking these things. It's just that ..." Her voice caught. "He was always so much better at theology than me."

Willow reached out and rubbed Kennedy's leg. "I know."

Kennedy swallowed and reminded herself it wouldn't always be so painful. Right now, she had other things to think about. Like Woong and his parents.

Willow parked, and the girls walked into the hospital without talking. Kennedy was thankful Willow didn't try to fill the silence with empty words or platitudes. She was thankful her friend knew her well enough to leave her to her own thoughts for a while. When Kennedy was ready to talk, when she was ready to laugh and play and live again, Willow would be there for her. And she was with her now, right beside her on the way to Woong's hospital room. Right next to her as Kennedy fought through the trembling in her gut.

Sandy was in the hall, leaning against the window and talking into the phone outside the quarantine chamber. She smiled tiredly when she saw Kennedy and Willow. "Good morning, girls." She wrapped Kennedy up in a sturdy hug. "I love you, sweetie. I've been praying for you all morning. You and Woong. That's about all God's heard from me today, I'm afraid."

Willow held back when her phone beeped.

"How's Carl?" Kennedy glanced around looking for him.

"He's doing a lot better. Got himself discharged last night. And good thing, too. He was about to drive those nurses crazy."

Kennedy smiled. "How's his health?"

"Got his sugar levels under two-hundred. Praise the Lord for that. He'll be on meds for it. Have to change the way he eats, which means less sweets. I either need to find some new recipes or come up with a new hobby." She twirled a strand of gray hair that had fallen out of her braid. "But listen to me prattle. Are you all right, hon? Did you sleep ok?"

Kennedy nodded.

"And your roommate? She's taking good care of you?"

Kennedy glanced over at Willow, who was laughing at an incoming text. "Yeah. She's been great."

"I'm so glad you two have each other."

Kennedy had to agree. Leave it to Sandy to help her focus on her blessings even in the midst of such turmoil.

"How's Woong today?"

Sandy sighed. "I don't know, pumpkin. I just don't know. One minute he's fine. Playing Xbox, wanting me to read to him. Next thing, his fever spikes, and he can't even hold his head up. It's a sad business, darling, to see your own child that sick." She shook her head. "I feel so bad, dear. You're going through your own storms all by yourself, and I've been too worried to do you any good, I'm afraid."

"No, you've been great." Kennedy wanted to give Sandy another hug but felt self-conscious about it. Usually, Sandy was the one hugging her. "And I hope you know we're praying hard for Woong. Willow and me both."

"Well, I appreciate it, love. That boy needs all the prayer covering he can get."

Kennedy wanted to ask Sandy the same question Willow had asked her on the way to Providence, but it wasn't the right time.

A nurse stepped up behind Sandy and tapped her on the shoulder. "Excuse me, Mrs. Lindgren. The doctor told me they have your son's test results back. They're waiting for you in the conference room."

Sandy smoothed out the fabric of her flowery skirt. "Oh, that soon? Oh, dear. Let me just tell Woong I need to step out for a minute ..."

"He's asleep." The nurse pointed through the window.

"Ok, that's good. Poor little angel hardly slept a wink last night. Now, I just need to wait for my husband. He stepped into the men's room down the hall. I doubt he'll be ..."

"My supervisor already found him. He's at the conference room. They're just waiting for you."

Sandy gave Kennedy a nervous smile. "Oh, then I guess I better go. You don't mind waiting here in case he wakes up, do you, sweetie? I hate the thought of him all alone in there, finding everyone gone, all by himself in that big room ..."

"I'll stay here," Kennedy assured her.

Sandy gave her a weak half-hug. "Then I guess I'll be back."

Kennedy thought she felt Sandy's body quiver just a little.

"I'll see you then."

Sandy offered a brave smile then turned around, her long skirt rustling around her as she followed the nurse down the hall to hear her son's prognosis.

CHAPTER 29

Kennedy had never spent a longer fifteen minutes. Once Willow finished texting, Kennedy filled her in on what was going on, and they both decided it was time to join together in prayer. A few minutes later, after praying through every possible outcome and every possible contingency they could collectively imagine, there was nothing to do but wait.

"Nick wants to know if you want to swing over to his house tonight. He's making spaghetti and says we can play some cards afterwards. I told him I'd only go if you feel up to it."

Kennedy could hardly focus on her words. How long would those doctors take?

"Sure, that sounds fun."

"You don't have to decide right now. We can always play it by ear."

"Yeah, ok."

"You don't have a clue what I'm talking about, do you?"

"I'm listening."

"What did I just say?"

"Something about tonight. You want to play cards."

Willow gave Kennedy's uninjured shoulder a reassuring squeeze. "It's going to be ok. You'll see." She smiled. "I've got a good feeling about this."

Kennedy doubted that Willow's positive outlook made any real difference, but she was thankful at least one of them was optimistic. Kennedy wished she could bottle up and borrow some of that hope.

"I'm serious. I don't know how to explain it. But a few minutes ago, back when we were praying for Woong, I got this really settled feeling in my heart. Like someone was reaching out and letting me know it's going to be just fine. Do you think that was God? I mean, does he work that way? Or do I have my signals crossed?"

Kennedy tried to smile. "I really don't know. I guess it might have been the Lord."

"Yeah, your pastor, he was saying something like that in his sermon last Sunday."

Kennedy studied her quizzically. "Saying something like what?"

"That God can talk to you through the Holy Spirit. What'd he call it? A still, small voice. Something like that."

"You went to Saint Margaret's?"

Willow stared at her neon-green fingernails. "No, but I listened to the sermon online while I was doing my yoga the other day. What are you looking at me like that for?"

"I didn't know you were listening to any sermons."

Willow shrugged. "Gotta learn somewhere, right? He's a pretty good preacher, you know."

"Yeah," Kennedy sighed. "He really is."

"So anyway," Willow went on, "what do you think about what I was saying? Think that really was God talking to me? Telling me everything was going to be fine?"

Kennedy didn't want to discourage her friend, but she didn't want Willow to get her hopes up too high only to be disappointed, either. "I don't know. It could have been anything. Could have been God, could have been wishful thinking ..."

"No, this was different. There was something ... I don't know. Something special about this. I'm new to all this Christian stuff, you know, but I really don't think it was me making it all up. Does that make any sense?"

"I guess so. Who knows? Maybe it really was God talking to you, telling you Woong would be ok."

"I hope so. But like you said, who knows, right? I mean, God probably lets lots of things happen to you all the time without giving you warning, right?"

Kennedy stared blankly into Woong's quarantine room, the deafening thunder of Brian Robertson's explosives still echoing in her mind.

"No, you don't often get a warning."

CHAPTER 30

"Good news, girls!"

Kennedy had been so lost in thought that Sandy's chipper voice startled her.

Good news? Kennedy was ready for a heavy dose of that.

Willow elbowed her gently in the side. "See? What did I tell you?"

Sandy bustled up to Kennedy and Willow and gave them both giant hugs. "Oh, the Lord is good. The Lord is so good!"

"What'd you find out?" Kennedy asked.

Sandy let out a melodic chuckle. "Our son has typhus."

Kennedy stared, certain she'd heard wrong.

Willow paused with her fingers halfway through her hair. "I thought you just said ..."

"It's not Nipah," Sandy interrupted joyously. "It's just plain old, regular typhus. Serious, of course, and it's a good thing they've had him in quarantine, but it's definitely treatable."

"How'd he catch it?" Kennedy asked.

"That's the funny thing. Well, not really funny. But the thing is, the doctors think he's already had typhus once. You know, he talked about falling real sick before he made his way to the orphanage. Back when he was still living on the streets. And we never knew what it was he had, but now the doctors think what happened was he caught typhus while he was still in Korea, recovered from it by the grace of God alone, and the infection he has now is basically a repeat of the same one. Something about the disease never completely leaving his system, and then it coming back up ... Oh, you'd have to ask the doctor for all the medical details. But what it means is it's perfectly treatable. I mean, poor thing'll have to stay in the hospital for a couple more days, but he'll be out of isolation soon. Won't have to sit in there all alone. I can be there with him, long as I wash up real good every time I leave and come back in. Have to wear a gown and whatnot, but at least we'll be together."

Kennedy didn't have to force her smile. Sandy's joy was wonderfully catching. "I'm so glad to hear that. You must be so relieved."

"Oh, you have no idea. I told God, I said to him, *Lord, I'm doing my hardest surrendering this boy to you, but God, I just can't give him up yet. I just can't.* And the whole time, there was something in me that knew. Knew I wasn't supposed to just roll over and accept this terrible illness. Knew I was supposed to pray for his healing and pray boldly. But I wasn't sure if that was coming from me or not. But I started out doing my best to surrender, surrender my child to the Lord just like Abraham on that mountain, and the more I prayed, the more I determined that God wanted me to pray that my little boy would be healed in Jesus' name. That I needed to go to battle for him and rebuke that sickness he had. I was so scared to believe it, but praise God, what really matters is Woong's going to be just fine. I'd invite you girls in to celebrate with us, but they still want to limit his contact with others. You'll excuse me if I'm rude and say good-bye for now, won't you? I just have to get in there and give my little boy a hug."

Kennedy glanced through the window, where Carl was already putting on the hospital's protective gear.

"You go in there," she told Sandy. "We'll talk to you soon."

Sandy blew a quick kiss and bustled through the door to the scrub station.

A few minutes later, Kennedy stood at the window and watched while Sandy scooped both arms beneath Woong and wrapped him up in a protective hug. Carl stood over them both, sobbing softly as he held his family close.

Kennedy blinked, surprised to find Willow's arm slipping around her.

"We should go," Willow whispered.

"Yeah," Kennedy agreed. She glanced once more at the emotional reunion, wondering if even heaven itself could contain that much joy, and then pried her eyes away. "Yeah, let's get out of here."

CHAPTER 31

"Well, this has been a great night so far. Anybody want some more spaghetti?" Nick held out the pot, which was almost completely empty.

"I'm stuffed," Kennedy admitted.

Willow hadn't stopped smiling at Nick. "Me, too."

They were seated around Nick's living room, which was surprisingly tidy compared to the other times Kennedy had been here.

Nick grabbed a deck of cards from his coffee table. "Who's up for a game?"

Willow glanced at Kennedy. "You tired, or should we stay for a little while?"

All Kennedy wanted to do was get to sleep, but she knew Willow would be disappointed if she didn't get a little more time with Nick. Kennedy had never seen two people connect as fast as they had. She didn't have a clue what happened while she was being held hostage in the conference room, but Nick and her roommate had already jumped past the awkward new-crush stage and were comfortably holding hands and making ridiculously goofy ga-ga faces at each other every chance they got. The picture was bittersweet. Kennedy was so happy her roommate had found someone, but still ...

"Ok, you guys wanna play some rummy or hearts or Egyptian rat race?"

"What exactly is Egyptian rat race?" Kennedy asked.

"You mean you've never played?" Willow raised her penciled eyebrows incredulously.

"No. And I'm starting to think I'm the only person in Massachusetts who hasn't."

"You probably are." Nick explained the basic premise of the game. There was no way she could remember all the rules, but she was willing to give it a try. She glanced around his messy bachelor pad. At Willow's sappy smile. At Nick's shining eyes each time his hand brushed Willow's while he dealt out the cards.

So many good things had happened in the past few days. Woong's optimistic prognosis, at least compared to what it might have been if he'd really contracted the Nipah virus. Willow and Nick — apparently soulmates — finding each other in the chaos of a hospital lockdown. Willow's renewed interest in maturing her faith.

There was so much to be thankful for. So much joy around her. Kennedy wasn't about to burst into a belly laugh or forget the sorrows she'd experienced, but she could at least recognize and quietly rejoice in the happiness surrounding her.

She had no idea what the next few days and weeks would hold, but there was a peace in her spirit she couldn't deny. There would be tears. There would be grief. The heaviness of mourning. The weariness of sorrow. But through it all, the Lord would be with her. And so would her friends.

The comfort she felt wouldn't bring Dominic back to her, but somehow, she knew that it would be enough.

CHAPTER 32

Why should I feel discouraged,
Why should the shadows come,
Why should my heart be lonely,
And long for heaven and home,
When Jesus is my portion;
my constant friend is he.
His eye is on the sparrow,
and I know he watches me.

"That was wicked insane how many people showed up," Willow said as she and Kennedy followed the crowd out of the church.

"Yeah." If you included the photographers and members of the press eager to cover the funeral of Massachusetts' most recent hero, Kennedy guessed nearly a thousand people had shown up to pay their respects to the fallen chaplain.

"How are you doing?" Willow put her arm around Kennedy as the spring breeze whipped through their hair.

"A little better than I thought I would be. The service was really nice."

Willow nodded. "Yeah, it was. I like that last song they sang. What's that one called?"

"*His Eye is on the Sparrow.*"

"Yeah, that's a good one. It was fitting for today, too. Some of the others were so upbeat, it was like we were at some big fiesta instead of a funeral."

Kennedy didn't reply. As they crossed the street into Boston Commons, the spring sunshine warmed Kennedy's shoulders, soft and gentle heat streaming down on her from above.

"Hey, beautiful. Where are you speeding off to so fast?" Nick jogged up and pecked Willow on her cheek.

Kennedy glanced away when their fingers intertwined.

"Hey." Willow turned to look at Nick and kept her voice hardly above a whisper. "I think maybe we could use a few minutes. You know. Alone."

Nick nodded his head, his dreadlocks pumping up and down vigorously. "Yeah, I get it. Sure thing. Just don't forget I'm treating you both

402

to Angelo's Pizza later on, right? We still up for that?"

"Yeah, I think so." Willow gave him a kiss. "I'll text you when we're ready."

Nick dashed off like a puppy who'd just been thrown a stick.

"You didn't have to send him away," Kennedy said. "I really don't mind. You two are adorable. It's like you were made for each other."

"Oh, I know. Just last night, we were talking about how we both ... Oh, never mind. You don't want to hear about that. Not on a day like this."

Kennedy didn't respond. Willow was right about one thing. Dominic's funeral had been lively and full of joy. Joy and pain at the same time. As she listened to the eulogies, she realized how much about him she'd never had the chance to learn. How much closer they could have grown. How much more they could have shared with each other if only God had given them more time. She couldn't explain how her heart could be so heavy but full of peace in the same instant. She thought about the first night she met Dominic, how his prayers for her had stopped her panic attack mid-sob. How heavenly healing had flowed from his intercession. If there was a common theme to any of the speeches made about Dominic today, it was his prayer life. Kennedy felt she could read a thousand books or listen to a thousand sermons on the subject and never come close to maturing into the kind of prayer warrior Dominic had been.

Had he known? That was Kennedy's biggest question, the one that kept her awake so many nights long after her tears and pillow both dried up. Had he known they would only be together for such a short time? Had he prayed for her? Had he prayed before the explosion that God would take care of her? Give her that sense of peace that had wrapped her up for the past week and a half?

Sure, there were tears. Not only at night, and sometimes at the most inappropriate times. Like when Willow made Nick laugh until Coke sprayed out his nose, and then Willow thought it was so funny she lost control and fell out of her chair. Kennedy pictured Dominic's expression if he had been there, that bemused, patient kindness softening his features even if he didn't join in the hilarity.

And she missed him.

She missed him when she went to St. Margaret's last Sunday instead of his cousin's home church and when the Christian radio station played his favorite hymn.

She missed him when Willow asked her difficult theological questions, like if God only has one person in mind that he wants you to marry or if there are several different options that would be good fits and it's up to you to make a wise decision.

She missed him when she looked out at the crowded Boston Common, at the children trying to fly their kites around or chasing after soccer balls and Frisbees.

She missed him when she was awake.

And she missed him when she was asleep.

She missed him when she realized that now he was in heaven, reunited with his wife, worshiping in the presence of his Savior. Even if he had the ability to think about her down here at all, he'd have no real reason to.

"Hey! Hey, Kennedy!"

She slowed down at the sound of small tennis shoes plodding on the pavement behind her. She smiled down. "Hi, little buddy."

Woong was panting from running so hard. He still hadn't regained all his energy back after his illness, but he'd been symptom-free now for over a week. "I finally caught you," he said breathless. The warm sunshine lit up his cheeks, making him look strong and healthy.

"Did you enjoy the service?" she asked him.

"Uh-huh." Woong started walking alongside Kennedy.

She glanced back and spotted his parents to make sure they knew where he was. "What did you like about it?"

"When it was over. It got kinda long. Hey, you know that big box they had him in? It looked heavy, huh?"

"Yeah. It did."

"So that got me wondering, why do you think they make the box out of wood, I wonder? 'Cause back when people got the sickness in Korea, it weren't like they all got buried in wood like that. Sometimes it was just holes, know what I mean? And it got me thinking that maybe it wasn't so heavy when you do it that way, but it might get people upset, especially the ladies and little girls and ..."

"Ok," Willow interrupted, "maybe you should go find your parents so you guys don't get separated."

"Oh, I don't have to worry about that," Woong assured her. "Ever since I got out of the hospital, my mom won't leave me alone. One night, I even woke up, and guess who I saw sitting in a chair just staring at me? And I asked what she was doing there, and she said she was praying for me, and that got me wondering, why do you think she had to be in my room to pray for me? 'Cause I haven't read any of the Bible yet for myself, but my dad, he reads it tons, and he says you can pray to God anywhere. And you know he's gotta be telling the truth, him being a pastor and all."

Kennedy smiled. She'd take Woong's theological questions over discussions about caskets any day.

"So what I'm trying to figure out," he went on, "is why she had to be in my room to pray if God coulda heard her just as well in her own room. But I was still pretty sleepy-like on account of being so sick earlier, and that's why I hafta have an earlier bedtime now, at least until I get some of my energy back. And I lost a lot of weight in the hospital too, which is kinda funny if you think about it in a certain way. 'Cause my dad, you know he had to go to the hospital from having too much fat and calories and sugar and stuff and nonsense like that, so they put him in the hospital for those things. But me, they put me in the hospital, and now everyone's talking about how they want me to gain weight, not lose it like my dad has to. I told mom that means I should be able to get double desserts, ones for me like normal and then the ones my dad can't eat no more on account of him having the ... oh, what's it called? Anchovies? No, that's not the right name. It's that thing with the sugar problem. You know what I'm talking about."

"Diabetes."

"Yeah, that. I don't know why, it always sounds like anchovies to me, but my mom says those are something else. She says there are some folks crazy enough to put fish on their pizza if you can believe that, but that's different from what my dad's got. But that reminds me. Mr. Nick, you know, he works with my dad. And he says that he really likes diabetes on his pizza because they're so salty." He turned to Willow. "But I bet you already know that, you being his new girlfriend and all. I think it's kinda funny if you ask me, 'cause two weeks ago the two of you didn't even know each other, and now you're kissing every minute or two. Once I seen you do it right on the lips when I bet you thought no one was looking."

"I'll make sure we're more careful next time." Willow scratched her cheek, and Kennedy thought she detected a hint of a blush.

"You better," Woong continued, "'cause that kissing, it's serious. Like my sister Blessing, she's got this son a little smaller than me and she's got an even tinier baby too, and so actually I'm their uncle which is pretty funny if you think about it, right? But she didn't get married until after Jayden started growing in her tummy, so I asked her how that worked when my mom and dad say you gotta be married before the babies come along and all, but she said she wasn't careful about who she kissed and that's how she ended up with my nephew. So all I'm saying is you and Mr. Nick better know what you're doing, 'cause you look a little too skinny for a baby to even fit in your belly, right?"

Willow couldn't control her laughter. "You run back to your parents now, ok?"

"All right. But before I go, there's something I wanted to give Kennedy." He reached into his pocket and pulled out a piece of paper folded up into a small rectangle. "Mom said you're probably gonna be sad for a while, with Mr. Dominic who's dead being your old boyfriend and all, so I asked her what she thought might cheer you up and she said this would probably do it. It's a picture I drawed. It's got a sunset, because I asked her and Mom said you always liked pictures of pretty sunsets. And then I told Mom I wanted a Bible verse on it, since whenever you come over and talk to her, she's always saying verses from the Bible and stuff and nonsense like that. So I told her to pick a Bible verse, but she wanted me to do it, so what we ended up doing was she gave me a few choices, and I picked from there. I wrote it myself too. Mom helped a little with the spelling is all."

Kennedy unfolded the page. "It's just perfect."

"Good, 'cause I was a little worried when Mom said I spelled *fatter* instead of *Father*. See? But I guess it's all right because you know what it's supposed to mean, don't you?"

Kennedy stared at the drawing. The sunset itself was crude at best, but she had to give Woong credit for his imaginative use of color. It was the first time she'd seen either purple or pea-green streaking across the sky, but there was enough orange and red to balance it out.

In the middle of the picture was a cloud with a verse scribbled on the inside. Kennedy might not have recognized all the words if she didn't already know the passage by heart. In fact, it had been quoted several times at Dominic's service.

Not even a sparrow falls to the ground apart from the will of your Father.

Woong reached out a finger and pointed to a few black M shapes by the clouds. "Them are the birds. You know, the sparrows it talks about."

"It's beautiful." She gave him a quick hug, and then he squirmed free and ran to his parents.

Willow glanced at the picture over her shoulder. "That's really sweet."

Kennedy had lost her voice and could only nod.

"You know, most girls just dream about being loved so much someone would be willing to die for them. You actually had it happen to you."

"He would have done it for anyone." Kennedy knew that with absolute certainty.

Willow shrugged. "Maybe. But that doesn't change the fact that he did it for you."

"Yeah." She glanced once more at the picture and sniffed.

Willow hugged her from the side. "You know he wouldn't want you to stay sad forever."

"I won't."

Kennedy glanced around her, and her ears soaked in the sounds of spring. The chatter of the young kids chasing after the ducklings near the ponds. The birds warbling in the trees, chirping exultantly in the glorious sunshine. Willow's phone beeping every few seconds with more texts from Nick.

She'd never known you could feel so full and so heartbroken all at the same time.

She wondered what else about life she hadn't yet discovered.

She was ready to find out.